C000098280

Sex, Lies

& Spinnakers

Also by Steve Van Slyke

KAVENGA'S WAKE

Sex, Lies

& Spinnakers

Steve Van Slyke

© 2010 by Steve Van Slyke

All rights reserved. No part of this book may be reproduced or transmitted in any form by any means electronic or mechanical including photocopy, recording, or by any information retrieval system without the prior written consent of the publisher, except where permitted by law.

First Printing

This is a work of fiction. Names, characters, incidents and organizations are products of the author's imagination. Any resemblance to actual events, organizations or persons, living or dead, is entirely coincidental.

Threadfin Publications
411 Walnut St. #2792
Green Cove Springs, FL 32043
threadfin_books@att.net

ISBN: 978-0-9825549-0-6

Published in the United States

Threadfin logo source image courtesy of National Oceanic and Atmospheric Administration/Department of Commerce.

Cover photo and design, © 2010 Threadfin Publications.

To Kay, the facilitator of my dreams.

In Memory

Mirjam Crago, for her encouragement

John Madell, LAPD, for his sound advice

Mirjam and John lived far apart and did not know each other. In a tragic twist of fate both of them died the day I finished the draft incorporating their suggestions. They will always live for me within the pages of this book.

SEX, LIES & SPINNAKERS

PART ONE

BAJA

199 miles south of San Diego

The morning wind blew hard from the northwest. *Houdini* sailed dead downwind under a reefed mainsail to starboard and small jib poled to port. The forty-foot sloop skidded down the face of a steepening swell, momentarily surfing at twelve knots. Robotic chirps and whirrs emanated from the electronic autopilot as it anxiously went about returning the yacht to its programmed course.

From his vantage point beside the helm, Mitch Sanford raised a pair of binoculars and focused on the reddish brown triangle two miles ahead. The tanbark sails of another yacht stood out against a background of white-capped seas and gray overcast sky. The sails appeared to have grown smaller since he'd last looked ten minutes earlier. Clearly, *Walden* was continuing to pull away, slowly but steadily leaving *Houdini* behind. *Walden's* skipper, Mitch's friend and mentor Henry Fullerton, had yet to reef. "He's nuts," Mitch muttered.

Across the cockpit a few feet away, cocooned in long johns and her foul-weather suit, Vivian Sanford stirred only slightly from her huddled position in the sheltered nook beneath the cockpit spray dodger. "Why, what's he doing?"

"It's what he's not doing. He still hasn't reefed. And it looks to me like he's taking *Walden* awfully close to the shoals off Punta San Antonio."

"*Houdini, Houdini, this is Walden, on seven-one.*" The VHF radio's cockpit speaker added a static lisp to Henry's gravelly voice.

"He probably heard me." Mitch handed the binoculars to Vivian, descended the companionway steps to the cabin and keyed the mike. "*Walden, Houdini.* Go ahead Henry."

"*Yeah, hey Mitch, just took a couple of bearings on you. You look a little far offshore.*"

"I was just telling Viv you look awfully far *in*shore."

"*Naw, we're passing San Antonio with room to spare. You don't want to get too far out. You'll be running close to Sacramento Reef.*"

Mitch paused. Henry's tone of voice concerned him. "We have been steering about ten degrees to the right of our original course for the last hour. It felt like the wind and current were setting us toward shore."

"Don't trust your eyes. Did you check your distance off with the radar?"

"Hadn't thought of that." Mitch felt a sudden urge to return to the cockpit.

"I'd do that if I were you."

"Roger." Mitch punched the radar's power button as he spoke. "Call you back in a few minutes."

Vivian called down from the cockpit. "Mitch, I'm seeing something ahead. I think it's kelp."

Mitch took the companionway steps two at a time. Vivian stood looking forward over the spray dodger. "See? Right there." She pointed beyond the bow and a few degrees to starboard. Long, thin coppery streaks momentarily blemished the blue-gray back of an advancing wave.

Mitch's face had grown warm talking to Henry. It turned suddenly cold. He left the cockpit and moved forward as fast as the rolling deck allowed. More kelp appeared. "Vivian, take the helm!" He turned and saw she had already disengaged the autopilot and was standing behind the wheel.

Houdini charged into the shallow waters of Sacramento Reef. The scattered collection of partially submerged rocks lay like a mine field, camouflaged by the profusion of white-capped seas. With both sails held in place by guys and preventers, a quick reversal of course was out of the question. If Vivian turned more than twenty degrees or so in either direction, one sail or the other would backwind. The wind and seas would quickly push *Houdini* onto the rocks.

"HARD LEFT!" Mitch shouted. A pinnacle of rock sliced past to starboard. Another emerged dead ahead. "HARD RIGHT!" *Houdini* swerved. The mainsail's boom slammed against the rigging sending a shudder through the hull.

Patches of kelp and rocks bloomed everywhere. Brown shards splotched with white barnacles flashed by in glassy troughs. Mitch shouted a staccato series of rudder commands. *Houdini's* sinuous course avoided one rock after another, taking her farther into the encircling reef.

The water turned dark. Mitch strained his eyes, scanning forward. For a moment he saw nothing. He started to breathe.

Geysers of spume suddenly erupted from the crest of the swell immediately ahead. The deepening trough behind the advancing wave uncovered a line of rocks like crocodile teeth set across *Houdini*'s path. Avoiding them would be impossible. Mitch envisioned the agonizing moment of *Houdini*'s keel being sheared from her hull. He couldn't allow himself to drive her straight onto the rocks at full speed. He'd put the helm over, backwind the main, drift onto them broadside and hope for the best. "HARD RIGHT!"

His words still hung in the air when he saw a small gap off the port bow. It looked barely four feet deep. *Houdini* drew six. Still, it was a shot. Mitch countermanded his order. "NO! COME LEFT! COME LEFT!" When the bow pointed at the gap, he shouted, "STEADY AS SHE GOES!"

He knelt on the foredeck and braced himself. Fifty feet from the rocks, the next swell lifted *Houdini* and flung her toward the gap. The sound of a giant fingernail raking a blackboard screeched from below.

The crisis had lasted less than a minute. As quickly as it started, it ended. Scarred but not wounded, *Houdini* sailed free, into deep water and clear of the reef.

PART TWO

PUERTO VALLARTA

Mitch let go of the headstay, leaned forward, and propped his six-foot frame against *Houdini*'s bow pulpit. The stainless steel rails felt warm and greasy in his sweaty grip. Although he had made his decision, the internal debate had yet to completely subside, sending a dull pain throbbing through his eyes. His gaze followed the anchor chain down into the murky harbor water and continued slowly upward until he stared across the channel. Through palms on the sand spit Banderas Bay and the Pacific Ocean shimmered in the morning sunlight that warmed his back.

The Pacific. What a name. The pitiless body of water was out there, waiting like a giant roulette wheel, daring him to enter and try his luck. He imagined *Houdini*'s beige hull whirling around the steepening slopes of a blue vortex. If he lacked the skill to sail her safely to French Polynesia, if he made another error like Sacramento Reef, he could accept paying the tab with his own life, but the thought of surviving Vivian in some disaster at sea, even if only for a few seconds, was the cruelest fate he could imagine.

Puerto Vallarta's April was a valid excuse. The last four months, harbor-hopping from Cabo San Lucas to PV, had been great. Once *Houdini* and *Walden* left the cool and blustery coast of Baja, the seas had been relatively benign, the anchorages calm, and the weather gorgeous. Why sail three thousand miles to French Polynesia when the ambiance right where you are is perfect? Hell, you could fly there in a few hours. Why spend three to four weeks rolling your guts out at sea?

Nothing Henry could say—or even Vivian for that matter—could convince him the rewards justified the risks. The adventure, the sense of accomplishment, the freedom of seeing remote tropical islands from the deck of one's own sailboat might be worth risking his own life, but not Vivian's. It gave him some relief to finally see the roots of his indecision. Vague feelings of apprehension had grown steadily as the date of their planned departure for the Marquesas drew nearer. He'd avoided examining those feelings too closely, fearing he'd have to face a simple lack of courage. Perhaps that was still an issue, but his responsibility for Vivian's well-being took precedence.

Telling his friends Henry and Jill Fullerton at nearly the last minute wasn't going to be easy. He and Henry were more than friends, in some ways, closer than brothers. They'd known each other as long as either one could remember. Henry and Jill would be disappointed, but they'd accept the sudden change of plans—and Mitch's reasons—with a minimum of embarrassing debate. However, they'd most likely view any statements of concern for Vivian's welfare to be a face-saving shield, designed to hide his doubts and fears. And maybe they'd be right. Puerto Vallarta's exceptionally fine weather was, in reality, a lame excuse for staying in Mexico, but at least it wouldn't sound so melodramatic.

"Mitch, I'm ready."

He turned to see Vivian emerge from behind the tan canvas spray dodger. She tilted her head sideways, scooped long flowing brunette hair in one hand and pulled it through a frilly red scrunchy. As she raised both hands to figure-eight the elastic, it became obvious she wasn't wearing a bra. This new indulgence of hers was routine among other women in the close-knit community of cruising sailors. In Vivian's case, however, the effect was slightly more arresting. Mitch found her claims to be unaware of causing any undue notice to be at least naïve, if not disingenuous. Unrestrained or not, her shapely figure still mesmerized him after fifteen years of marriage. He made his way aft, meeting her at the lifeline gate.

"What's up?" she asked. Her hazel eyes seemed to detect his unsettled mood. "You're usually waiting in the dinghy with the outboard running."

"I've changed my mind."

She brushed a wisp of sun-bleached hair from his eyes. "About what?"

"I think we should stay in Mexico."

Her dark lashes blinked in slow motion. "*What?*"

"Yeah. We could hang around here another couple of weeks, then head north with the others and spend hurricane season in the Sea of Cortez." He waited for a response. Nothing came but Vivian's continuing expression of disbelief. "We never got north of La Paz, Viv. I'd kinda like to see the rest of the Sea."

Vivian glanced at the boats anchored on either side of *Houdini*. "Isn't it kind of late to drop this on Henry and Jill?"

Mitch nodded.

"When did you make this decision?"

"At the *Hard Rock,* last night, while we were dancing."

"Why didn't you say something then?"

"Too noisy."

"Your lips were right next to my ear. I heard everything else you said."

"I mean it was too noisy to tell Henry and Jill. I wanted to talk it over with you first, then tell them without the others around."

"Then why not in the taxi back to the marina? We were alone with them then."

"After what happened with Bill and Marjorie, I didn't want to unload this on Henry, too. He wasn't in a great mood, if you'll recall."

"He wasn't that upset."

"You don't know him like I do. Besides, I hadn't talked it over with you, and I really hadn't made a decision. That's just when the feeling hit me, that we should stay in Mexico."

Vivian looked down and shaded her eyes from his view. "We're all provisioned for the passage except for fresh fruit and vegetables. Jill's under the impression she and I are going shopping for those this morning. Henry thinks you're going with him to Customs and Immigration this afternoon."

Mitch paused to make sure she was through. "You're saying we should go."

Vivian dropped her hand and looked him in the eye. "I've said from the very beginning, you're the captain. I'll salute and go along with whatever you decide. I just think it's pretty darn late to be laying this on our best friends."

"It is. However, when we first agreed to this, I warned Henry we might only go as far as Mexico."

"Mitch, that was two years ago. For the last few months we've led him and Jill to believe we'd buddy-boat with them at least as far as Bora Bora before heading home."

Mitch briefly considered telling her the true reason behind his change of mind. He turned and backed down the swim ladder into the red inflatable tethered alongside. "They're probably at the yacht club by now. Let's not keep them waiting."

More than a dozen assorted tenders crowded an empty slip near the A-dock ramp below the yacht club. Mitch eased the outboard's throttle and headed toward a narrow gap between two other inflatables. From the bow, Vivian pushed their sterns apart, allowing Mitch to barge his way to the dock.

Ordinarily, there wouldn't have been so many dinghies at the yacht club before noon, but with the onset of hurricane season less than a month away, the crews of transient yachts that had tarried in Puerto Vallarta were finally snapping out of their languor and moving on. Morning coffee at the yacht club had become a ritual. Friends going in opposite directions met for last good-byes. Others, headed in the same direction, discussed routes and weather. The majority were returning north to the Sea of Cortez. Another contingent prepared to continue south, to Costa Rica and the Panama Canal. The adventurous remainder were westbound, on trade wind runs to Hawaii or the South Pacific.

Through the yacht club's iron gate entrance, Mitch spotted Henry and Jill seated at a table in the far left corner of the open-air dining area. Another couple, a woman with long blonde hair and man with wavy silver hair, sat opposite them.

Mitch stopped outside. "Damn."

"Now what?"

"Look who's sitting with Henry and Jill."

"Victor and Sharon. So?"

They'd first met the Canadian couple six months earlier in San Francisco. Sharon and Victor had invited him and Vivian, and Jill and Henry aboard their luxurious fifty-four-foot cutter, *Dream Lover,* for cocktails and hors d'oeuvres. Since getting to know him, Mitch had often kidded the refined and good-natured Victor about *Dream Lover*'s multitude of labor-saving gadgets and creature comforts. But like Henry and Jill, Victor and Sharon were bound for the Marquesas Islands of French Polynesia. Victor would find it amusing to hear that Mitch had decided against making the arduous passage.

"Earth-to-Mitch. *Hel-lo.*"

"I was hoping to tell Henry and Jill in private."

"That's what you get for waiting until the last minute." Vivian waved at Jill. "They've spotted us. Come on."

Henry and Victor stood as they approached. Mitch shook Victor's extended hand and took the empty chair between him and Henry. Vivian sat opposite, between Jill and Sharon. A young Mexican waiter arrived with a carafe of hot coffee.

One glance at Sharon told Mitch he needn't be too concerned about Vivian's animated T-shirt attracting all the attention. Sharon wore a white silk shirt, with the sleeves rolled up and the tails knotted over a bare midriff. The unbuttoned blouse revealed an aqua blue, floral bikini top that matched the color of her eyes and displayed her tanned bosom to perfection.

"Eager to get underway, Mitch?" Victor asked.

"Uh, yeah, you bet," Mitch replied.

Jill leaned in front of Henry and touched Mitch's arm. Her straight raven hair fell along side a high-cheeked Italian face. She whispered, "Mitch, do me a favor. Convince my husband that it's not a good idea for him to go over and apologize to Bill and Marjorie."

"They're *here*?" said Vivian.

"Behind us, far corner," Jill said.

"The way Bill acted last night," Vivian turned to look over her shoulder, "I'm surprised he's letting Marjorie off the boat."

Mitch spotted the middle-aged couple at a table overlooking the channel. Bill leaned on his forearms, saying something to his wife. Marjorie sat with her head propped between two hands like blinders on a carriage horse.

"I don't believe it," Mitch said. "He's *still* giving her a hard time. Jill's right, Henry. Talking to him won't help."

Sharon said, "Mitch, will you please tell us what this is all about? Henry and Jill are being annoyingly discreet."

Henry slouched in his chair. "Go ahead, Mitch, you tell 'em."

Mitch suppressed a smile and leaned toward Victor and Sharon. "Last night, a bunch of us went to the *Hard Rock Cafe*."

Sharon nodded. "Victor and I had reservations at *Bogart's* or we'd have been there as well."

"With the exception of Bill and Marjorie, all of us danced at least one or two songs." Mitch tilted his head toward Henry. "Fred Astaire here was reliving his misspent youth, dancing with all the ladies in our party."

"Ooh," said Sharon, "now I'm truly sorry we didn't go along."

"We were about ready to call it a night," Mitch continued, "when Jim bets Henry he can't get Marjorie to dance."

"Jim?" asked Victor.

"Jim and Litea, on *Phoenix*."

"Don't believe we've met them." Victor turned to Sharon. She shook her head.

"You'd remember them," said Mitch. "Anyway, Henry rises to the challenge. You know how shy Marjorie is."

Victor nodded. "Not sure I've ever heard her utter a complete sentence."

"How can she," Sharon said, "around that blowhard husband of hers."

"Amen," added Vivian.

"Henry'd already asked her to dance once before. But he goes to the end of the table and asks her again. She shakes her head. Bill shrugs like, 'okay by me.' Henry holds out his hand says 'come *on*.' Marjorie refuses, but now she's starting to blush because all of us are watching. Henry takes her gently by the wrists and slowly pulls her out of her chair."

The scene returned to life in Mitch's mind as he described it. Henry, the six-foot-four-inch blonde bear, egged on by the group, skidded petite Marjorie onto the dance floor. She shook her head and pleaded to be released. The band launched into a fast oldie, *At the Hop*, by Danny & the Juniors.

Henry began to dance. Marjorie just stood there, trying to cover her crimson face with her one free hand. Henry wasn't about to give up. Slowly, Marjorie began to dance. It was less embarrassing than being jerked around like a rag doll handcuffed to a gorilla.

It soon dawned on everyone that Marjorie could dance. She wasn't just *capable* of dancing, she could *really dance*. Once she relaxed, Henry wrapped her up in his twisted arms and unleashed her like a spinning top. They went through one pretzel-like move after another. It was as though they'd time-warped back to high school. The other dancers got out of their way.

When the song ended, Marjorie covered her face and headed off the floor. The group cheered for more. Henry caught her by the arm. The young Mexican combo started playing *The Latin Hustle*. Marjorie shrugged, gesturing that she didn't know it. Henry soon had her gliding around the floor to the silky, rhythmic beat. Marjorie was a natural.

Henry finished the number by spinning Marjorie backward and catching her in a Valentino dip just above the floor. Everyone applauded. Marjorie didn't rush to escape this time. She seemed finally to be enjoying herself. The brassy band segued into a steamy instrumental Lambada. Marjorie took one look at what the couples around her were doing, hunched her shoulders, and tried to sneak away. Henry snagged her again. Within a few seconds, they looked like cast members of *Dirty Dancing*. "They were like an oak tree and ivy," Mitch said.

"You can't be serious," said Sharon. "I'd have thought our little Marjorie was raised in a convent."

"You wouldn't," said Mitch, "if you seen the way—"

Henry slapped a hand on Mitch's arm. "They get the idea."

Victor raised his eyebrows, shifting his receded hairline forward. "This is what you owe Bill an apology for, dancing with his wife?" Victor turned to Jill. "Did it bother you?"

"Me? Not at all. It was good to see Marjorie having some fun for a change."

"Yeah, but I went a little too far," said Henry. "Bill's obviously still pissed."

"I take it there was some unpleasantness?" Victor said.

"After the Lambada," said Mitch, "Henry and Marjorie headed for their seats. Before she could sit down, Bill grabbed her and steered her out of the club, chewing on her ear all the way."

"I agree with Victor," Sharon said. "You did nothing wrong, Henry."

"Maybe."

"I'm telling you, pard'," said Mitch, "it's better to let him cool off. You know how Bill is. In a couple of days he'll be his good-ol'-boy self again."

Henry glanced left toward Bill and Marjorie across the crowded room. "I'm not so sure. And in a couple of days we'll be far out to sea."

Vivian's gaze locked on Mitch's eyes as she spoke. "Speaking of which, can we change the subject?"

Mitch hesitated. Before he could act on Vivian's cue, Jill ended the awkward silence. "By all means," she said. "When you two arrived we were talking about skiing. Victor had just started to tell—" Jill looked past Vivian and Sharon. "Here come Jim and Litea."

A stocky, muscular white man and a slender black woman came through the yacht club door. Victor turned to Mitch. "I see why you said we'd remember them." He held out his hand as Jim slid a chair between him and Mitch. "Don't believe we've met. Victor Westridge. That's my wife, Sharon. We're on *Dream Lover,* over on K-dock."

Jim nodded at Sharon as he shook Victor's hand. "I've seen her over there. She's beautiful."

Victor arched an eyebrow. "My wife or my boat?"

Jim blushed. "Your boat...that is...well, *both.*"

"Why thank you," Sharon said smoothly, as though accustomed to such compliments. "And you are?"

"Jim D'Autremont, on *Phoenix.* We're anchored out in The Pond beside Mitch and Vivian."

When Jim neglected to introduce Litea, Sharon turned to her. "I didn't quite catch how Jill pronounced your name."

Litea smiled, revealing a mouthful of perfect white teeth. "Li-TAY-uh. Litea Jackson."

Even though the community of foreign yachts cruising the west coast of Mexico was a highly social one, it came as little surprise to Mitch that these two couples had never met. They were at opposite ends of the fleet's economic spectrum. *Phoenix* had about as much in common with *Dream Lover* as an aging VW hippie-bus had with a white stretch limo.

According to Vivian, Litea had worked as a teller where Jim banked in Oakland. She'd gotten to know him during the painful time when his excavating business failed and his wife divorced him. Jim used what money remained after liquidation to purchase a neglected old 41-foot Formosa ketch. Litea helped him restore her. When Jim invited her to 'cut the mooring lines' and sail to the South Pacific, Litea said it was difficult to say which of them was more surprised when she said yes. After sailing *Phoenix* only two or three times on San Francisco Bay, they'd headed out the Golden Gate and turned south.

Until meeting Jim, Mitch believed there wasn't a skipper in the cruising fleet less prepared for blue-water sailing than himself. *Houdini* had at least come with a SatNav that provided a fix of latitude and longitude once every few hours. Jim's *Phoenix* had neither a SatNav, nor one of the newer GPS units like Henry's, which provided a continuous fix of position. And while Henry had taught Mitch the basics of celestial navigation on the way down the coast, Jim's stated plan was to learn how to use his sextant en route to the Marquesas. When Mitch compared his own attitude toward ocean voyaging to Jim's, he wasn't sure if the difference was due to intelligence, economics or guts.

"Is that an African name?" Sharon asked.

"Fijian," said Litea. "My mom's from Fiji."

"Really? Are you and Jim planning to sail there?"

"Yes. My father's American and I've only been to Fiji once, as a baby. I've got dozens of relatives there I've never met."

"I just love your hair," Sharon said. "Is it natural?" Litea's lustrous black hair spiraled outward to her shoulders in tight curls, framing her small attractive face like a pharaoh's headdress.

Litea nodded. "Wash and wear."

"How unfair. Do you mind if I touch it?"

"No, of course not." Litea turned her head slightly. Sharon's fingers brushed Litea's caramel cheek as she combed down through the springy spirals.

"Marvelous. You weren't a model by any chance?"

Litea laughed. "Be serious."

"I am. With your angelic face, svelte figure and that hair, Victor and I might have helped you make a lot of money if we'd met a few years ago."

"That's quite a compliment coming from someone as gorgeous as you. I'll bet *you* were a model."

Sharon smiled and nodded. "For a few short years."

Sharon's age had never been revealed. Mitch knew Victor was fifty-five, and Vivian had guessed Sharon to be fifteen years younger than him, although she and Jill had speculated that the miracle of medical science had made it appear more like twenty. On that basis, Mitch guessed Sharon to be about his age, possibly a year or two older. Prior to becoming a senior partner in his Vancouver advertising agency, Victor had been an account exec and had met Sharon when he selected her to pose for an ad for one of his firm's key clients.

"Jim," said Mitch, "you've seen those billboards with the blonde in a slinky black dress, lying beside a bottle of Black Velvet."

"You mean—" Jim's gaze shifted between Mitch and Sharon, finally resting on Sharon. "*You're* the one in those billboards?"

Sharon paused before answering, as if basking in the glow of Jim's obvious admiration. "They're not all me. They've used several different models and celebrities."

"There was a time, though," said Victor, "when my lovely wife's face and figure graced the byways of every major city in the world."

"When was that?" asked Jim.

Sharon placed a restraining hand on her husband's forearm. "Let's just say it's been a few years since they used my shots."

Late sixties, early seventies Mitch guessed. Nevertheless, Sharon still turned heads wherever she went.

Jim removed a small cloth bag of tobacco and cigarette papers from his shirt pocket. "Henry, I see Marjorie over in the corner. Want to go double-or-nothing?"

"Very funny," Henry said.

Mitch followed Henry's glance toward the corner. Marjorie's hands still hid her face. Bill now leaned back. He seemed to be staring at her in silence.

Jill shook a finger at Jim. "You're becoming a bad influence on my husband. You be good, or I won't let him play with you anymore."

Jim sprinkled tobacco into a trough of paper. "Just kidding. Litea and I are heading *Phoenix* out to sea tomorrow. When's everybody else leaving?"

Henry answered without hesitation. "Oh-seven-hundred tomorrow. Right, Mitch?"

"Yeah, right." Mitch glanced at Vivian. Her eyes rolled slightly and she gave a barely perceptible shake of her head.

"You're all provisioned and checked out?" Victor asked, looking first to Mitch, then Henry.

"Soon will be," Henry answered. "Jill, Mitch and Vivian are making one last provisioning run to the *Commercial*, while I change the diesel's oil and filters on *Walden*. Then Mitch and I are headed for Customs and Immigration to get our clearances. How about you two?"

Victor glanced at Sharon. "I dare say we'll be another two or three days, eh love?"

"Heavens, yes," Sharon replied. "I've tons of shopping to do, and there are one or two restaurants we simply *must* try before I face three weeks of my own cooking."

"Speaking of restaurants," Jill said, "are you and Victor coming to *Los Arbolitos* tonight?"

"Something happening?" Sharon asked.

"Several crews thought it would be nice to have one last dinner together before we all go our separate ways."

"Marvelous idea," said Sharon, turning to her husband.

"By all means, count us in," said Victor. "Are you sailing directly to Fiji, Jim?"

"No, we're headed for the Marquesas, taking the Milk Run, like *Houdini* and *Walden*.

"Splendid! Say, we must have the entire Puerto-Vallarta-to-Marquesas fleet sitting at this table."

Mitch heard Vivian clear her throat as he began to speak. "Uh yeah, with one exception."

"And who might that be?" Sharon asked.

"Bill and Marjorie."

"Oh, yes," said Victor, "I'd forgotten they were headed that way, too."

Henry twisted in his seat, glancing briefly toward Bill and Marjorie, then back to Jim. "Did you buy that used SatNav from the guy up at Nuevo?"

"Naw, he wanted to much for it, especially since it'll be obsolete in a year or two."

"Going to spring for a GPS then?"

"There aren't any for sale in PV, and it's too late to have one shipped down. Besides, my wallet can't take that kind of hit.

Hey, I got an idea. You're Prince Henry, the celestial whiz-kid. Why don't you loan me *your* GPS. Just till we get to Hiva Oa. Maybe by then I'll have learned which end of the sextant I'm supposed to look through."

Henry chuckled. "Much as I enjoy shooting an occasional round of stars, I don't miss being a slave to the daily routine. Besides, you'll figure it out long before you reach the Marquesas. Even Mitch is getting the hang—" Henry's head snapped left. Everyone at the table heard the cause of his halted sentence. From across the room, had come the words 'two-bit whore' in Bill's unmistakable twangy drawl. "That does it," said Henry, sliding his chair back from the table. "I'll be back in a minute."

Jill watched him thread his way through the tables then quickly turned around. "I can't watch this. Victor, finish the ski trip story you started when Mitch and Vivian arrived."

"Right, well, let's see...my college roommate and I were driving from UBC in Vancouver to Salt Lake City in his beat up Karmann Ghia."

"Darling," Sharon interrupted, "do you really think you should tell this...ribald tale? If not for the sake of your own reputation, what about those of others, not here to defend themselves?"

"Don't worry, love, I'll not mention any names."

Mitch only half-listened as Victor continued. He was more interested in seeing Bill's reaction to Henry's arrival. Neither Bill or Marjorie saw Henry coming until he stood at their table. Bill's head jerked, as if alarmed. Then he seemed to relax, smiling up at Henry, leaning back in his chair, listening to whatever Henry was saying.

"You know," said Jill, "this story sounds vaguely familiar, Victor, like I've heard it before."

"Really?"

"Yes. One of my former clients in San Francisco—"

"Oh shit," Mitch blurted. Everyone turned on Mitch's comment to see Bill rising from his chair. Henry backed away from the shorter, older man. Bill rubbed the flats of his palms together in front of his chest as he stopped listening and started talking. The plastic smile was gone, replaced by a squinting mask of hate. Mitch recalled witnessing similar scenes involving Henry in high school. In every case, the other party had received bruises and humiliation for his trouble. Yet Mitch couldn't ever remember Henry picking a fight. It seemed that being popular made him a target for every delinquent who wanted to make a name for himself.

Suddenly, Bill poked his right index finger in Henry's chest. Bill's salt-and-pepper flat-top and his speech mannerisms reminded Mitch of his Army drill sergeant. Bill raised his voice loud enough for everyone to hear "you son-of-a-bitch," as he poked Henry a second time. Henry backed away another step, holding his open-palmed hands out away from his sides.

"Mitch," said Vivian, "you'd better get over there."

Mitch slid his chair back, hesitating briefly before standing up.

"I'll go," said Jim, rising to his feet. "It's partially my fault."

By now, everyone in the club had stopped talking and turned to see what all the swearing was about.

Jim was still en route when Bill pointed at Henry's face and shouted, "You want her, hot shot? Then fuck her, she's all yours!" Without warning, he punctuated his sentence with a vicious right jab, catching Henry on the mouth; his head snapped backwards. Henry raised his arms to defend himself. Bill cocked for another swing. Before he could unleash it, Jim leaped in from the side and bear-hugged the wiry man's arms to his sides. With the physique of a wrestler, Jim had Bill completely under control by the time Mitch arrived. He found Henry dabbing a split lower lip with his fingertips.

"You okay?" Mitch asked.

"Yeah," said Henry, looking down at the spreading streaks of blood on his yellow T-shirt. Jill and Vivian arrived simultaneously.

"Turn me loose!" Bill growled, struggling in Jim's grasp.

Jill looked at her husband, then stepped directly in front of Bill and in a low voice said, "If they gave merit badges for being an asshole, you'd be an Eagle Scout."

Bill wriggled futilely, his face now firecracker red. "Damn it, Jim, let go of me. I ain't finished with that gigolo son-of-a-bitch."

"Oh yes you are," Jim replied. He lifted Bill and carried him toward the door like a rolled-up carpet.

Mitch stepped aside giving Jill room to inspect Henry's lip.
She stood on tiptoe. "You'll live. I hope you're satisfied."

Henry lifted the hem of his T-shirt and wiped the blood
from his chin and mouth. "Something is definitely wrong with
that guy."

"Oh really?" said Jill. "What was your first clue?"

"Seriously. It was like he didn't hear a word I said."

"Henry, Mitch and I both told you it wouldn't do any good.
All you've succeeded in doing is humiliating Marjorie even
more."

Henry looked down at Marjorie being comforted by Vivian.
"Sorry Marjorie."

"My husband doesn't care how I feel. Why should you?"

Jill shot Henry a see-what-I-mean look. "You'd better get
back to *Walden,* put something on that lip and change shirts."

"I might as well change the oil first." As he turned to leave,
Jill grabbed him by the arm and kissed him on the cheek. "You
big dope."

Jim returned a couple of minutes later. "Where's Henry?"

"Went back out to The Pond," Mitch replied. "What about
Bill?"

"Escorted him down to the corner and let him go. Called me
a couple of names, then stormed off, muttering something
about heading for the golf course."

Jill looked up from the table beside Vivian. "Golf course?"

Jim shrugged. "I don't know, maybe he's going to take his
hormones out on a bucket of balls."

Vivian looked at Mitch. "What about Marjorie?"

Now it was he who shrugged. Vivian's cold expression said
'wrong answer.' She turned to Marjorie. "Would you like to go
back to *Silver Cloud?*"

"Yes, I suppose. But—"

"Mitch would be happy to run you out to The Pond,
wouldn't you, Mitch?"

"Sure, right, no problem."

"But that will spoil your plans," said Marjorie.

"No it won't," replied Vivian. "Jill and I are headed over to
the Plaza. Mitch will catch up long before we're finished
shopping."

"If everything's cool," Jim said, "Litea and I need to be on our way to Customs and Immigration."

"We're fine," said Jill. "Will we see you at *Los Arbolitos* tonight?"

Jim paused, rubbing the back of his neck. "I don't think so. We've got other plans."

"In that case, we'll either see you out on the ocean tomorrow, or in Hiva Oa in three or four weeks."

"Right," said Jim. "We'll be monitoring the radio for your position reports."

Marjorie slid her chair back. "Well, I don't want to keep you all waiting."

Vivian put a reassuring hand on Marjorie's shoulder. "Talk to Jill for a second. I need to speak to Mitch before you go." Vivian took Mitch by the arm and guided him to the empty bar. "Okay, fine. I'll take care of telling Jill we're not going, but you be sure and stop by *Walden* and tell Henry before you come pick us up. Right?"

Mitch nodded. "Yeah, no problem."

"And try to show a little compassion when you take Marjorie out to *Silver Cloud*. You do know what compassion is?"

"Yes."

"I wonder sometimes."

———————

Outside the yacht club, Vivian watched Mitch follow Marjorie down the A-dock ramp to the dinghy. "Take your time," she called after them, "we'll be at least an hour, probably more." She turned to Jill. "Once in awhile, Mitch can be so insensitive I could strangle him. He should have offered Marjorie a ride without me having to volunteer him."

Jill pursed her lips to one side. "Hmm, I never thought of Mitch as insensitive. Compared to Bill, he's a prince."

"That's not saying much." Vivian took one last look at her husband before turning to start the mile-long walk to the Plaza Marina mall. "Mitch is pretty good about the big things, but it's like he has this *blind* spot for the little things that mean a lot. I think he actually believes Hallmark invented Valentine's Day. And although he usually gets me something nice for our anniversary, I'm lucky if his card has anything more sentimental scribbled on it than 'Love, Mitch.' "

"I remember that time he forgot your anniversary a couple of years ago."

Vivian nearly froze in mid-step. "Don't get me started."

"Really?" said Jill. "I recall being amazed at how well you took it."

"I...cut him some slack because of everything else that was going on."

"Oh, that sexual harassment mess happened about the same time, didn't it?"

Vivian nodded. "Mitch almost resigned that week. That was the same week you and Henry hit us with the news that you were selling your house and your businesses and sailing off to the South Pacific."

"I guess Mitch did have a lot of things on his mind."

"So did I."

"Wait a minute. That night we had you two over for dinner, when we told you about our plans, that's when you told me about Mitch forgetting your anniversary. I remember thinking the Vivian that *I* knew ought to be boiling mad. But you seemed so subdued—I guess I assumed the sexual harassment business had you worried. Neither of you said much about it so..."

"That wasn't it. Mitch wasn't the accused, and I knew Kathy Hale, the woman involved. The stuff about her and Mitch having an affair was a fabrication intended to keep them from pressing charges against Mitch's rival."

Jill's eyes opened wide. "Oh my God, you were going to tell me something else that night and I cut you off, didn't I?"

"I suppose it's ancient history now." Vivian sighed. "I did something stupid."

"How stupid?"

"*Really* stupid. I was so mad at Mitch I almost had an affair."

"*You*? With who?"

They reached the highway and turned left. Vivian ignored the leering line of taxi drivers leaning against their cabs. "He was one of my patients, a bachelor."

"A man propositioned you while you were cleaning his teeth?"

"After I'd finished. He always flirted, every time he came in. Complimenting me on my looks, asking me to have lunch with him."

"This time you said 'yes'?"

"It was the day after our anniversary—I still hadn't said anything to Mitch. I was feeling really low. I don't think we'd made love in a month. Earlier that morning, when I got out of bed I remember looking at myself in the mirror and thinking, 'So this is it, you're not sexy any more, the days of wine and roses are over, kaput.' "

"Oh, for God's sake, Vivian, every woman I know hates your figure, and there's still not a single line on your pretty face. But anyway, you're feeling like a discarded housecoat and this guy hits on you, then what?"

"I thought, 'what's the harm in having lunch?' Hah! Brother, was I naïve."

"Weren't you afraid someone would see you?"

"No, that was the *whole idea*. I was hoping someone *would* see us—just having lunch—and tell Mitch. I thought it'd give him something to think about. I was feeling so sorry for myself, it just felt good to know that a handsome man, and *younger* I might add, found me attractive."

"So...what happened? More than lunch, I gather."

"Jill, you realize if you ever breathe a word of this, *especially* to Henry, no one will recognize your corpse, provided they ever find it."

Jill pantomimed zipping her lips, locking them and throwing away the key.

"He drove to a new restaurant he said he wanted to try. It just *happened* to be part of that new motor inn on I-5, south of Tacoma. The first inkling I had that I'd made a mistake came when he parked his car in a remote section of the parking lot behind the building. He turned off the ignition, looked deep into my eyes and said, 'Do you know you're the most seductive woman alive? I can't get you out of my mind.' Can you believe that? Of course, *I* believed him. Before I could stop him—or myself—I let him kiss me. God, what a kiss. I could taste the fluoride treatment I'd just given him."

Jill laughed. "Then what?"

"He gave me this serious, Jack-Nicholson-hold-that-thought kind of look and said he'd be right back. I knew he was going to get a room. Part of my head was screaming 'girl, get out of the car and run for your life.' But some weird, psychotic part of me was entranced by the effect I thought I was having on him. I wanted to see just how desperate he was to have me and hear what he would say next. It was like not being able to quit watching a bad movie on TV, even when you know you're going to hate how it ends. And the danger of it all affected me like being on a roller coaster while breathing nitrous oxide. I was dizzy, euphoric and scared to death all at the same time."

"But you said you *almost* had an affair, so I take it you didn't go to a room with him."

"If I hadn't gone to the room, Jill, I'd have told you about it a long time ago. But I did go, and I think I would have let him have what he wanted if something embarrassing hadn't happened."

"Don't tell me he handed you a whip and put an eight-by-ten of his mother beside the bed?"

"Not quite that weird. He was sort of kneeling over me on the bed, kissing me and unbuttoning the top of my uniform. When he started fondling my bra, the strangest feeling came over me. I had this vision of Mitch touching another woman the same way, at the same time. It was so real, I freaked. My knee came up by itself and hit him square in the groin. I think I smashed his balls like ripe grapes."

Jill's hand came to her mouth. "Vivian!"

"Shit, he almost passed out. I waited a few minutes until I was sure he was okay, apologized and left. I caught a bus downtown and all the way back I kept thanking my lucky stars I hadn't gone through with it. But Jill—I think if I hadn't unintentionally kneed him, I'd have let him make love to me. I'm almost sure of it. I felt just as guilty as if I had."

"That's nonsense. Your conscience just kicked in—pardon the pun."

Vivian felt a burden being lifted. "Thanks. I wanted to tell you about it that night at your place, but later I was glad I didn't."

"Why—because of what Mitch was going through at work?"

"Partly, but mostly because of what happened the following week."

"What was that?"

"It seemed like all the political back-stabbing at work finally woke Mitch up to what was important in life and made him realize what a rut he was in. The following Monday he came home at a normal hour and announced that he wanted to take Henry up on his proposal that we buy a boat and follow the two of you to the South Pacific."

"Was that the night he called and asked for Henry's help finding a boat?"

"Right. After Mitch got off the phone, he proceeded to apologize to me for everything from not paying enough attention to me, to forgetting to take out the garbage. We had a romantic evening, and things have been getting better ever since. My only wish is that I'd had the courage to confess to him that night. The longer I've let it go, the harder it's become to bring it up, and the easier it's getting to simply forget it ever happened."

"That's what you *should* do. If you tell Mitch at this late stage, it might make you feel better, but it certainly won't do him any good."

"That's what I've told myself countless times."

"I take it you never saw Mr. Smashed Grapes again?"

"Absolutely not! That cured me once and for all. Besides, he never came back to the clinic. Can you blame him?"

Jill smiled and shook her head. As her smile slowly faded, she began to speak, then glanced away.

"What?" said Vivian. "You were going to say something."

Jill drew a long breath. "Henry has always told me they don't come any straighter or more honest than Mitch, but don't you think there's a slight possibility he changed so suddenly because he *was* feeling guilty—about more than just forgetting your anniversary?"

"You mean, like maybe there really was something going on between him and Kathy Hale?"

Jill winced and nodded.

"Jill, Henry's right about Mitch. And he has such a guilty conscience he even confessed to me once when he and a couple of his buddies at work went to a topless bar with table dancers.

He was afraid I'd find out and get angry with him. In matters
like that, I can read him like a book."

Marjorie followed Mitch down the yacht club dock. "I really
appreciate this, Mitch. I'm sorry to be such a bother."
"Don't mention it. Really, it's no trouble."
Mitch boarded the inflatable and held it to the dock while
Marjorie stepped in and took a seat in the bow. As he idled
away, she stared blankly toward the Isla Iguana luxury villas
across the channel. When he sped up she held the dinghy's
grab line with one hand and brushed windblown strands of ash
blonde hair from her eyes.

Mitch recalled his first encounter with her and Bill six
months earlier. Just prior to their departure for Mexico, they
had briefly moored *Houdini* at San Diego's Kona Kai Yacht
Club in a slip adjacent to Bill and Marjorie's *Silver Cloud*. Bill
had struck him as a bit pompous, but friendly and occasionally
humorous. The hypercritical, chauvinist facets of his nature
had either been held in check or gone by unnoticed. Marjorie
seemed typical of the many cruising wives being swept along in
the current of their husband's dreams: she was apprehensive,
but at the same time, excited and looking forward to the
adventure of sailing south of the border.

Since entering Mexican waters, *Houdini* and *Walden* had
shared several anchorages with *Silver Cloud* on both sides of
the Baja peninsula. The abusive side of Bill's personality had
become increasingly apparent as Mitch spent more time
around him. In contrast, Mitch couldn't remember any
behavior on Marjorie's part that would justify the way Bill
constantly belittled her. Marjorie always seemed shy and soft-
spoken in public, with hardly anything to say, let alone a word
tipped with venom. The few times Mitch had seen her apart
from Bill, she seemed quick to laugh at the slightest joke.
Maybe it was because she had so few opportunities.

Bill certainly couldn't harbor any complaints that Marjorie
neglected her appearance, or had given in to middle age. On
New Year's Day in Cabo San Lucas, Mitch recollected how the
crews of several boats had dinghied out to Lover's Beach for a
day of sun bathing, snorkeling and a potluck lunch. Marjorie

surprised everyone when she arrived wearing a very small navy blue bikini. Mitch and her other friends were not so much taken aback by the dark suit's contrast with her fair skin as with her demure personality. She had been in an uncommonly relaxed mood that day and hadn't seemed to take any notice when the entire gathering of cruising couples stopped what they were doing to watch her jump into the surf and help Bill beach their dinghy. She had walked up the sandy beach and greeted the other women with no more concern than if she were dressed for an informal dinner. Not many women in their mid-fifties could have worn such a revealing costume and appeared as unconcerned as Marjorie.

Mitch eased the outboard's throttle as they approached the small craft anchorage. By anchoring bow-and-stern, the crews of a dozen sailboats managed to squeeze their vessels into a tight but ragged line abreast, filling the cramped anchorage to capacity. Over the years, the narrow refuge along the channel leading from the cruise ship harbor to the marina became known among transient sailors as The Pond.

The majority of cruising couples stopping in Puerto Vallarta preferred the luxury of dockside fresh water and electricity, and were more than happy to pay for the privilege of a berth in Marina Vallarta. Although Henry and Jill could easily afford the marina's moorage rates, they favored The Pond's relative quiet and its small-town feel over the marina's wall-to-wall condos and restaurants. Mitch's preference was to stick close to Henry, so that had made The Pond his and Vivian's choice as well.

Jill and Henry's *Walden* held innermost position in the line. Mitch glanced at the blue and yellow inflatable tied at *Walden*'s boarding ladder. He hoped Henry would be in a decent mood when he stopped by on his way back.

The rust-streaked hulk of an abandoned charter boat close on *Walden*'s port side separated her from the other yachts in the anchorage. The large rusty links of the derelict's anchor chain stretched toward mid-channel in a low flat curve. A one-legged pelican favored the heavy chain for its daytime perch. The bird eyed Mitch and Marjorie closely, nervously adjusting its wings as they passed. On numerous occasions, while sitting in *Walden*'s cockpit with Henry and Jill, Mitch had watched

the crippled bird plop head-first into the water, coming up
with an unwary fish in its fleshy bill pouch. It then began the
laborious process of hopping one-footed up the links to begin
the cycle again.

Beyond the derelict, the Rio Salado, a small mangrove
estuary, flowed into the channel, creating a shallow bar at its
mouth. The remaining yachts in The Pond formed a crooked
line from the bar's edge to the gray patrol boat moored in front
of the Mexican navy base.

Mitch and Vivian's *Houdini*, Jim and Litea's *Phoenix*, and
Bill and Marjorie's *Silver Cloud*, were the seventh, eighth and
ninth boats in the line beyond the derelict. Mitch idled past
Silver Cloud's high clipper bow and turned down the narrow
slot between her and the next yacht in the line. Marjorie
reached to catch the boarding ladder as he killed the engine
and coasted alongside.

She held the ladder and hesitated before stepping out.
"Thanks again, Mitch, for being so kind."

Mitch stood and grabbed *Silver Cloud's* caprail to steady the
dinghy for her. "My pleasure, Marjorie."

Once on *Silver Cloud's* deck Marjorie paused, her back to
him. She turned and looked down. In her face, Mitch saw a
sadness so heavy he half expected her to collapse under the
weight of it. He wished he could conjure up the appropriate
words to comfort and cheer her, but such words seemed to
always escape him.

"I don't know what to do, Mitch," she said. "I honestly don't
know how much longer I can take it." She began to sob. She
knelt beside the boarding ladder and covered her eyes.

He placed a hand on her shoulder. All he could think to do
was stand by, try to share the pain and thereby reduce the
severity of its impact.

"I'm sorry to do this to you," said Marjorie without
removing her hands from her eyes. "You go ahead, I'll be all
right."

He remembered Vivian's admonition. "There's no rush, I've
got plenty of time."

"I have to stop doing this. I'm getting so I can't *stand*
myself."

"I wish I...there was..."

"Would you like to come aboard for a minute?" she sniffed, sliding her hands down just enough to expose her tear-filled eyes.

"Sure." Mitch quickly looped the tender's painter around *Silver Cloud*'s amidships mooring cleat.

"How about a glass of lemonade?" she said, wiping away the wetness from her reddened cheeks.

"That'd be great, but why don't you let me get it," he said, stepping aboard. "You just sit in the cockpit and relax, okay?"

"Well...if you insist?"

"I insist."

Marjorie took a seat in the shade of *Silver Cloud*'s bimini-style cockpit awning. Mitch kicked his running shoes off before going below. In *Silver Cloud*'s galley he found a Tupperware pitcher of lemonade in the ice box and emptied it into a plastic tumbler. "Marjorie," he called out to the cockpit, "there's only a little bit left, barely enough for one glass."

"There should be some Crystal Lite in the cabinet over the ice box."

Mitch opened and scanned the cabinet. "I'm afraid I don't see it."

Marjorie quickly descended the companionway steps. Mitch stepped aside, giving her room in her galley.

"Maybe we're out. No, here they are." She snatched a white cylindric container from the shelf and jerked the lid off, causing three tiny plastic tubs to fly out and roll across the counter. Grabbing one, she ripped off its foil lid and dumped the powder into the pitcher. She looked up at Mitch as she filled it with tap water. "I think we have some ice. I'm sorry to be keeping you. Are you sure you have time?"

"Honest, Marjorie, I'm in absolutely no hurry."

She dropped two cubes of ice into the glass Mitch filled, causing lemonade to splash onto the counter. She placed two cubes in the empty glass and filled it. She handed the colder one to Mitch.

"Cheers," Mitch said.

"Cheers."

Mitch leaned against the galley counter near the foot of the companionway steps. Marjorie stood at the entrance to the tunnel-like passageway that led under the cockpit to the aft cabin. She looked at the galley floor between them.

"When Bill first announced he was going to sell the meat-packing business and buy a seagoing sailboat, I thought it was just more of his big talk. I soon discovered he was serious. At first, this crazy dream of his of sailing around the world was a godsend. The time while we shopped for a boat and then learned how to sail her was the best we've had since our youngest son left home. When it came to sailing, he and I were both novices, almost equals, at least for awhile. I even began thinking this cruise could be the salvation of our marriage.

"Then gradually, over the course of the sail down the West Coast, the old Bill came creeping back. Now that he's gained confidence with the boat, it's worse than ever. He's the Captain, I'm the bungling galley slave, and we're cooped up together in this 42-foot prison he refers to as his 'ship.' At least at the house in Wichita I could get away from him when he got into one of his foul moods."

Mitch again searched for the words. The silence became awkward. He took a sip of lemonade.

Marjorie's moistened eyes reflected a beam of sunlight streaming through the galley port. "I'm sorry if I'm embarrassing you."

"No, it's not that, I only wish I knew what to say."

"I've noticed that about you; you listen more than you talk."

Mitch smiled. "It's a trait of the Sanford men. We take it to an extreme, never talking, never knowing how to express our emotions. Drives Vivian bonkers."

"My problem is the opposite of hers. It helps to have someone who listens. You just happen to be around at the wrong time."

"I can't understand why Bill treats you the way he does. I still wouldn't condone it, but maybe I could at least understand it if you were the bitchy, whiny type, but from what I've seen, you're not like that."

"I don't know, Mitch. I've asked myself the same question a thousand times. I *am* always forgetting things and I get confused sometimes about what I'm supposed to be doing when we're changing sails or setting the anchor. I know he doesn't find me attractive anymore."

"I can't believe that. You're a good-looking woman, Marjorie, especially when you smile."

Marjorie set her drink down on the counter and shaded her eyes from his view. Her shoulders trembled. "I don't think I can go on like this. I wish I could just go to sleep and not wake up."

Oh, good. Way to go, asshole. Mitch stepped over to her, taking her small shoulders in his hands. At his touch she fell against his chest, sobbing freely, her head resting underneath his chin. "Come on, Marjorie, don't talk like that."

A minute passed before she stopped shaking. He remained quiet, only moving his hands from her shoulders to her shoulder blades. He felt the wetness of her tears through his T-shirt where her cheek lay against him. Her hands settled lightly on his hips. He remained still. Marjorie's breathing slowed, her sobs reduced to sniffling. Her breasts rose and fell against his stomach. He moved his feet to improve his balance. Marjorie's hands slid around him, meeting each other at the crease in his back. He gently pressed his hands against her back to reassure her he hadn't intended to pull away.

The wake of a passing boat rocked *Silver Cloud* but Mitch's stance was secure and Marjorie continued to hold him close in silence. He smelled the fragrance of a floral scented shampoo in her hair. The rocking of the boat, and the childlike way she held him, reminded him of his first slow dance, the way it felt when the young girl had pressed herself against him.

Marjorie spoke without moving her head from his chest. "Thanks for taking pity on me, Mitch."

"Hey, it's not pity." He gave her a reassuring hug. "I'm sorry I made you cry."

"Don't be sorry. Half of these are tears of gratitude. That's the first time in years a man has said something nice about the way I looked, even if it was a lie."

"It wasn't a lie."

Marjorie's fingers fanned out against his back. It was at that moment Mitch realized he had an erection-in-progress.

Oh shit.

He concentrated, trying to make his body behave. Concentrating made it worse. His awakened penis seemed to have a will of its own, pressing painfully outward against his confining briefs.

Maybe she doesn't feel it.

He tried inching his lower back slowly away. He'd gained a fraction of an inch separation and started breathing again when Marjorie's arms slid around him until they overlapped. She pulled herself firmly against the object he was trying to conceal. The pain increased. Immediately, he realized his problem had escalated.

"Marjorie," he whispered into her hair, "maybe we should go back out—"

She threw her arms around his neck, pulled his face down, and covered his lips with her own. He stood paralyzed, lips frozen, arms out like a scarecrow. Marjorie's left hand went to the top of his head. She pulled up tight rows of his fine brown hair and locked them between curling fingers. Her mouth opened; a tongue slipped between his lips and flicked against his clenched teeth. Electric shock radiated through him. *Holy shit.*

He lowered his outstretched hands to her hips. He had to push her away, gently but fast. He'd lost control of his body. If he didn't act immediately, his willpower might follow. He'd explain; she'd understand. She pressed harder against him and he heard a dissenting voice from within; a primitive but persuasive biological whisper.

As if hanging from the lip of a rocky ledge, he feared letting go but suffered from the agony of hanging on. Marjorie's embrace, the desperate way she held him, was like a person dying of thirst. He relaxed his lips, momentarily accepting her kisses. His hands slid up to encircle her small waist. She held him close, so close he felt her heartbeat pounding against his uncomfortable erection.

"Marjorie, Marjorie," he said, pulling away and shaking his head, "this is...this is nuts! Let's stop and think—let's talk for a minute."

She half groaned, half whispered, "Please, Mitch." Her eyes pleaded with him. Like two-way mirrors, he saw behind them the pain of many loveless years. When he hesitated to push her away she writhed against him and resumed her kisses.

She inched backwards, pulling him. He tripped over her feet. Awkwardly, they stumbled toward the low narrow passageway.

"Marjorie...no-no, Marjorie. No...No...NO!"

He resisted but she fought back, pulling at him, kissing, twisting, keeping him off balance and moving, almost daring him to hit her or throw her down. He would have to tear her away and shake her to her senses. *Stop this...you have to stop this.*

Three portholes in the transom and a large overhead hatch brightly lit the queen-sized berth set athwart the large stateroom. Once she maneuvered him into the cabin, he stood upright and regained his balance. She continued kissing him, maintaining a tight and painful grip on his hair. Her hands suddenly slid down to his waist and the top of his faded blue-jean cut-offs. Her fingers nimbly unbuttoned the top button before he could react.

"Whoa, whoa, Marjorie, wait!"

She had become a different person. Ignoring his protest, she slid the zipper to its stop, yanked the ragged hem and sent his cut-offs falling to the deck.

Mitch moved his hands to her shoulders to push her away. When he hesitated once more, Marjorie's hands came to the front of his underwear and molded the outline of his aching penis. He flinched. His red bikini briefs held it captive, bent to one side. He froze. The dissenting voice spoke again: *What's the problem? You're male. Perform your function.*

Her fingertips went inside the confining garment's elastic, pulling out and down. He heard her sudden intake of breath as his cock sprang from its confinement. Shame washed over him the same moment he felt the physical relief of being unbound. Marjorie pushed the briefs down, took him with both hands, and began to kneel at his feet.

Mitch grabbed her arms and lifted her up. "No!" He shook her by the shoulders. Their eyes met and locked. Hers were dreamy, almost trance-like, and yet they sent an unmistakable message.

Marjorie quickly pushed her shorts and panties past her hips and wriggled out of them. With one determined effort she pulled him off balance toward her until they fell backward on the bed.

At that point Mitch lost the battle, not only with Marjorie, but with himself. His hand went to her.

Marjorie thrust herself against his touch, moaning as if pleading for relief. Her hands found him, pulled toward her, guiding him in. She let go and Mitch entered.

She gasped.

Once in unison, their bodies collided rhythmically in a rough mutual assault. Her arms curled under his; her nails digging into his shoulder blades. Her hips stepped up the pace and he matched it. Mitch had no intention of prolonging it. Her breaths came louder, more labored. She cried out. Her knees came up. Mitch eased his weight. Her hips rose slightly from the bed. He paused, holding her in motionless suspension.

Marjorie collapsed, her body limp. Gently, he settled with her, taking the burden of his weight with his forearms and then rolled onto his back beside her.

Two minutes passed in silence. Mitch struggled to keep his mind totally blank, hoping the experience could somehow be erased.

Marjorie shifted her dreamy gaze from the cabin overhead to Mitch. "Wow, I had no idea. I needed to know. I don't know what else to say, Mitch."

"Believe me, Marjorie, neither do I." *Except that I'm completely fucked in more ways than one.*

"I had to know if it was me. I don't think I could have gone on. It's been so long. Can you understand what I'm trying to say?"

Mitch looked through the open hatch at cloudless blue sky. "The way Bill talks you wouldn't think it'd been long at all."

"That's all it is though, talk. It's been years, Mitch; many, many years. I swear it."

Mitch paused, letting the significance of the remark sink in. "It's sad. I suppose it's that way in a lot of marriages. Over the years people come to know each other so well the mystery and excitement disappears."

"It wasn't that way for us. It was more sudden; why, I'll never know. As wonderful as this was, Mitch, I could go without it the rest of my life if Bill would simply show me a little kindness and respect. Something has to change, or *else*."

Mitch rolled his head toward her. "*Marjorie*."

"I didn't mean that. I'm not sure what I mean. But I do know I'm going to start standing up for myself, regardless of the consequences."

Mitch sat up. "Holy cow, we really trashed your bed. We have to change the sheets."

"I'll take care of it. You'd better hurry to The Plaza and pick up Jill and Vivian." Marjorie's left hand moved to cover her eyes. "Oh dear God—Vivian."

Mitch shook his head slowly. "You got that right." The mention of Vivian's name out loud sent a shiver snaking down the muscles of his back. He dressed quickly while Marjorie lay on the bed watching him. Her face was devoid of expression, registering neither pain nor pleasure, as if she had found a moment of peace. He didn't quite know how to say good-bye. "Well, I...I guess—"

"Come here, Mitch." Marjorie spoke to him as an adult comforting a nervous child.

He leaned across the bed and she kissed him on the forehead. "You're a dear man, thank you."

Still no words came. He forced a smile and started through the passageway, then stopped and turned. "It smells like an aerobics class was held in here."

Marjorie rolled onto her side, striking a sexy pose. "One was."

I am in deep, deep shit.

Mitch slowed the inflatable as he crossed *Walden's* bow and shot a look for Henry's dinghy. It was still at the boarding ladder, but another small boat was now there as well. Two Mexican men stood in a small wooden rowboat behind Henry's dinghy, holding on to *Walden's* caprail for support. They seemed to be looking into the cockpit. The closer of the two heard Mitch's outboard, turned, and waved. It was Manuel. Mitch waved back. Henry was out of sight.

Mitch glanced at his watch. Vivian and Jill would be waiting, wondering. *Shit.* He'd have to tell Henry about the change in plans later. Suddenly he sensed a strong odor. He smelled like...like sex.

He twisted the throttle. Instead of speeding straight for the marina, he carved a sharp right turn into a canal leading to the Puerto Iguana villas behind Isla Iguana. Each villa in the development came with its own private moorage berth on the man-made lagoon. With many of the new units unsold and very few owners in residence, most of the slips were empty.

He motored to the T intersection at the end of the canal and coasted straight ahead into a vacant slip. In bare feet, he walked up the finger pier's ramp and turned left down the concrete walkway fronting the townhouse-style villas. He tried to appear casual, glancing around to see if anyone had noticed his arrival.

Cutting across the grass he reached his destination: an I-shaped swimming pool with a small arched bridge spanning the narrow center section. He removed his T-shirt and cut-offs, tossing them at the foot of a young coconut palm near the edge of the pool. Wearing only his red briefs, he dove into the cool water, pulling himself to the bottom. As he drifted slowly to the surface, he pulled the briefs down and quickly cleaned himself.

Should he tell Vivian? On the one hand, it would be deceitful to maintain a intimate bond of secrecy with another woman. That sin seemed worse in some ways than the physical transgression itself. On the other hand, why hurt Vivian unnecessarily?

Given the scene she had just witnessed between Bill and Marjorie at the yacht club, a chance existed Vivian might understand and forgive. Mitch considered the odds as he hopped out of the pool. Yes, the chance existed, and the odds were about as good as those of the Pope going on a date with a Las Vegas showgirl. Vivian wouldn't see it as falling within her definition of compassion. She would see it as an unpardonable violation of their marriage vows.

I can't believe I did this.

He'd never been able to understand how men—or women, for that matter—cheated on their spouses. He'd always despised such traitorous and self-centered behavior in others. A feeling of intense self-loathing came over him for allowing himself to be seduced. Yet, when he considered Marjorie's situation, it seemed unfair to condemn her for accomplishing it.

The long walk beneath the hot sun dried his hair before he reached the Plaza Marina mall. Having been gone more than an hour, he headed straight across the parking lot to the *Comercial mexicana* supermarket rather than walk through the air-conditioned building. He found Vivian at the *Comercial's* exit, helping Jill with several plastic bags loaded with fresh produce and groceries.

He tried to remember how it felt to speak and smile normally. "Hi. Looks like I'm just in time."

Vivian looked up. "Oh, hi. Yeah, we just finished and were about to get a taxi. What took you so long? I told Jill. Did you stop and talk to Henry?"

Mitch looked at Jill. Her expression registered both disappointment and understanding. "Ah, no."

"*Mitch.*"

"Well, when Marjorie and I got to *Silver Cloud*, she started crying. She sounded a little desperate so I thought...maybe I should...you know, hang around for awhile, make sure she was okay." The closer he stayed to the truth, the better.

Vivian regarded him coolly. "I don't believe it."

"Well, I—"

"You actually stayed there and gave her comfort?"

"Well, yeah. I wasn't sure I should leave...she seemed pretty depressed."

Vivian turned to Jill. "Henry was right, Jill. He said cruising would change us all for the better." Turning back to Mitch she took his hand, kissed him on the cheek. "Honey, I'm proud of you. And I'll bet Marjorie appreciated it too, didn't she?"

Mitch rubbed the back of his neck. "Uh, yeah, she seemed to."

Mitch peered through his reflection in the dusty window of the northbound bus. Henry sat beside him studying the clearance certificate he'd obtained at the port captain's office. Considering how easily Henry had accepted the news that *Houdini* wouldn't be following *Walden* to the Marquesas, Mitch wasn't sure if he cared to have his friend's advice on handling the situation with Marjorie. He hadn't expected a big emotional scene from Henry, but he'd assumed there'd be some show of disappointment. Frankly, he was feeling a bit hurt by Henry's rapid adjustment to the new order of things. Maybe when Jill told him about the change of plans, she made him promise not to badger Mitch. Or perhaps Henry was still distracted by his confrontation with Bill. Clearly, Henry was not being Henry.

Mitch looked over his friend's shoulder at the document he held in his hands. The impressive blue and white certificate stated that *Walden* and her master had legally cleared out of Mexico and were required to depart Mexican waters for Atuona, Hiva Oa within twenty-four hours.

The nearly suspension-less bus accelerated as it left the cobblestones of downtown Puerto Vallarta and merged onto the relative smoothness of Highway 200, leaving billowing dust clouds in its wake. Mitch glanced forward to see a thin young girl rise from her seat and stand in the aisle. She caught him looking at her, smiled shyly and looked away. A clean, white-frilled, indigo dress clashed with her surroundings. The reason for the traditional costume, and her standing in a half-empty bus became clear when the weathered, white-haired man in the seat beside her picked up a battered guitar and strummed a three-chord introduction. She sang softly at first, increasing volume as she gained confidence. Mitch marveled at how she sustained a beautiful vibrato on the long full notes of an old Spanish love song. She walked slowly toward the rear of the bus as she sang.

When she'd passed them, Henry turned to him and said, "Sounds like the next Linda Ronstadt."

"No kidding," Mitch replied. "So you're sure you're not pissed off?"

Henry shook his head as he slipped the clearance certificate back into a leather-bound notepad. "Disappointed...surprised maybe. I have this feeling there's something you're not telling me."

Mitch stopped breathing. The whole time he'd been with Vivian aboard *Houdini* until it was time to leave to pick up Henry, he'd felt like a flashing, blue-light special: *Attention shoppers, adulterer on display in Automotive.* He wasn't yet prepared to tell her the truth about Marjorie. Was Henry picking up guilt vibrations? "What do you mean?"

"Like there's probably more to your decision than just wanting to see more of the Sea of Cortez."

"Well, yeah, I suppose there is."

"Like what?"

"Three thousand miles is a lot of ocean, Henry."

"It's Sacramento Reef isn't it? You're still spooked by what happened there."

"Maybe."

"Mitch, that was *one* mistake. You learned from it, and you never made it again. Besides, there are no reefs between here and the Marquesas."

"Yeah, but something else could go wrong and you won't always be in sight, telling me what to do before I screw up. You've got enough to worry about. I don't want you and Jill feeling like you have to constantly watch out for us."

"No one *needs* to watch out for you. You and Vivian are entirely capable of making this passage with or without us. And if you *were* to have some mechanical or navigation problem at sea, I'd be there on the radio to help you dope it out."

"If it were just me, Henry..."

Henry paused; a light of recognition seemed to flash through his eyes. "Jill and I've had a great time having you and Vivian along for the last eight months. I'm thankful for that. We knew from the start you guys couldn't follow us forever. In fact, it still amazes me that you both quit your jobs, sold your house and came this far. For a guy who'd never invested a cent in anything riskier than money market funds, that in itself was quite a bold step."

"I still leave the stock market to gamblers like you and Vivian's hare-brained brother-in-law. As for quitting my job, you know how easy that was."

"You should thank the SOB that shafted you. If he hadn't, you'd be the division vice president instead of him, working on a good case of ulcers or a heart attack."

"He's not the vice president anymore."

Henry's brow furrowed. "Just a couple weeks ago, you said you got a letter saying he'd got the job."

"Turned out to be the shortest tenure of any VP in company history. Another letter arrived yesterday."

"From the woman he accused you of having an affair with?"

"Right, Kathy Hale. The lawyer she and I hired located two other women within the company that he'd pressured into having sex with him. They were willing to testify in a joint sexual harassment suit with Kathy. The company agreed to an out-of-court settlement and fired the guy."

"I guess it's true, time wounds all heels."

"In this case it did. His wife is divorcing him and going after everything they own."

"I still say you owe him a debt of gratitude. If it hadn't been for him, you wouldn't have given any serious thought to quitting and coming with us."

"Don't give the jerk credit he doesn't deserve. What he did played a very small part in my half of the decision."

"Really? When you changed your mind so suddenly about coming with us, I assumed it was because of him. In fact, you told me it was."

"I lied."

Henry raised his eyebrows in mock surprise. "So what did change your mind?"

"Ask me again in twenty years."

"What? You're holding out on *me*? First, you wait until the last minute to tell me you're not sailing to the Marquesas. Now, you're keeping secrets from me?"

"It's not exactly my secret. And hey, I'm really sorry I didn't tell you about the change of plans sooner, but I honestly didn't make up my mind for sure until this morning. I was going to stop by and tell you on my way back...from running Marjorie out to *Silver Cloud*, but I saw you had company."

"Company?"

"Carlos and Manuel."

"Oh, yeah. They came by to show me all the pámpano they caught with one throw of their net. Must of had twenty or thirty flopping around the bottom of that little tub of theirs. Sort of a sales demo, I guess. By the way, how was Marjorie doing after I left? I take it Bill left her stranded."

"She's doing okay. Did you buy the net this time?"

"Naw, Carlos is still asking eight-hundred-thousand pesos. I offered him three hundred. Think it offended him. If he comes by again before we head in for the restaurant this evening I'll probably buy it. He seems like a nice enough guy, and looks like he could use the money. I'll have to give him dollars though. Trying to get rid of all our pesos before we leave."

"I doubt Carlos will object to greenbacks. They stopped by *Houdini* yesterday afternoon while Vivian was hanging out laundry. Manuel had some nice sea shells for her. Picture this: Vivian is standing on deck leaning over *Houdini*'s lifelines, which she'd just decorated with her freshly laundered underwear. Manuel's directly in front of her, standing in their little boat beside Carlos who's talking to me. Vivian's totally oblivious to the fact that Manuel's eyes are about to pop out and bounce off her forehead because he's got a Cinerama view all the way to her belly button."

"Poor guy. Must have been in a lot of pain."

"Speaking of pain, how's your lip?"

Henry touched a fingertip to his fat lip. "Already forgot about it."

The young singer passed them again on her way forward.

Henry reached into his pocket and pulled out a handful of coins and a stainless steel money clip. "Does *Los Arbolitos* take Visa?"

"Yeah, I think so."

"Good." He unfolded the bills and peeled off the two remaining ten thousand peso notes worth about three dollars each from a wad of US twenties. "Think Vivian would mind if we took the bus tonight instead of a cab?"

"I doubt it. Why...oh, I gotcha." Mitch pulled out his wallet.

The girl finished her second number as she arrived back at the seat occupied by the old man with the guitar. He handed her a worn cigar box. Starting at the front of the bus, she made her way down the aisle, meekly holding the box out to each passenger. Most dropped in a few coins. Arriving at Mitch and Henry's seat, the young beauty regarded the two gringos nervously. She held out the box tentatively and was about to pull it back and move on when Henry tossed in his two ten-thousand peso notes. Mitch followed suit. He reckoned the stunned look on the girl's pretty face was easily worth the price.

Her sparkling dark brown eyes panned slowly upward from the money. "*Gracias, Señor!, Gracias Señor!*" curtsying awkwardly to each of them as she spoke.

"*De nada*," they chorused as she turned and rushed back to show her *abuelo*.

Henry watched her for a few seconds before turning to Mitch. "Jill said to ask what the plan is for this evening?"

"Since not everyone's been to *Los Arbolitos* before, we're rendezvousing with the other couples at the dolphin statues on the Malecón at six. We'll all walk to the restaurant together from there." Mitch sensed a flatness in Henry's tone. "You two are going, aren't you?"

"Yeah, we're going. We'll meet you and Viv at *Dream Lover's* slip around five-thirty. How's that?"

"Sure. Is something bugging you, Henry?"

"Nothing's bugging me."

"You're sure you're not mad at me?"

"Positive."

"Still thinking about your run-in with Bill?"

"I don't give a rat's ass about Bill. You think they'll come tonight?"

Mitch doubly regretted having been the one who originally informed Bill and Marjorie about the bon voyage dinner. "After everything that happened this morning, I'd be very surprised if they showed up." He considered telling Henry what had transpired aboard *Silver Cloud* with Marjorie. He could use some advice as to whether he should tell Vivian, and, if so, how. On the other hand, Henry and Jill would be heading out into the Pacific tomorrow. Henry had enough on his mind without having Mitch's dirty laundry dumped on him.

Henry banged a fist on the roof of the bus, informing the driver they wanted off at the next stop.

———————

Mitch shifted the outboard to neutral and coasted toward *Dream Lover's* K-dock slip. Henry and Jill's inflatable lay alongside the big cutter, tied to a dock cleat, but neither they nor Victor and Sharon were anywhere to be seen. True to form, he and Vivian were fifteen minutes late.

"Think they got tired of waiting and went to catch the bus?" Vivian asked.

Mitch brought the dinghy along the dock. "No, I see them. Over there, sitting in front of the Italian restaurant." Jill and Henry sat on a wrought iron bench, arms propped on knees, heads together, apparently in the midst of an intimate tête-à-tête.

"Sorry we're late," said Vivian, as she and Mitch hurried up to them.

"No problem," Henry said. "We'll make it on time. Anybody else coming from The Pond?"

"Don't think so," Vivian answered. "Jim said he and Litea had other plans. And I didn't see either Marjorie or Bill stirring on *Silver Cloud*. What about Victor and Sharon? There didn't seem to be any signs of life on *Dream Lover* either."

"They're below in the cabin," answered Henry. "We talked to them for few minutes. Sharon's not feeling well, so they've decided to pass."

"You look a little pale yourself, Jill," said Vivian. "Are you okay?"

"Me? I'm fine. Let's go."

Hotel housekeepers, clerks and gardeners filled the rush-hour bus to capacity. The foursome of *Norteamericano* sailors held onto the overhead grab rails and swayed from side-to-side in unison with the other standing passengers. Mitch looked behind Vivian's back to see a well-dressed Mexican man in tight white slacks standing butt-to-butt with her. The thought crossed his mind that he should have sprung for a taxi and that his sense of spousal possessiveness had not diminished as a result of his own misstep.

Upon reaching Paseo Diaz Ordaz, Mitch pounded the roof. The crowded bus slowed to a rolling stop, allowing them to make a hasty exit from the rear door. A short distance up the palm-lined sea wall, a half dozen couples, the crews of other cruising sailboats, sat on the edge of a circular pool surrounding a bronze statue of three leaping dolphins.

Temporary street galleries of painters, silversmiths and other artisans spread out along the Malecón were doing a brisk business as tourists ventured forth from their pool-side and air-conditioned oases to enjoy the perfect atmosphere of Puerto Vallarta at sunset.

The assembled group of sailors left the beach-front promenade and walked in a column of twos up narrow streets lined with white stucco buildings, trimmed in reddish brown. Terraces loaded with terra-cotta pots full of green flowering plants overhung the sidewalks. Ornate wrought iron gates protected intricately carved doors of mid-town residences.

Mitch liked the old downtown section of Puerto Vallarta. Its rough cobblestone streets had more character than the smooth paved streets of Ensenada and La Paz. And despite its quarter million inhabitants, Puerto Vallarta's pace was slower, more rural than Mazatlan's big-city bustle. In the few irregular blocks clustered along the banks of the Río Cuale, he could imagine the tiny, inaccessible fishing village that had existed there only fifty years earlier.

They followed Avenida Lázaro Cárdenas to its terminus at the bend in the Río Cuale near the back edge of town. The narrow, three-story *Los Arbolitos* restaurant enjoyed a view of the swift flowing river and the Sierra Madre mountains rising in the distance. Undiscovered by most two-week tourists, *Los Arbolitos* was well known in the cruising fleet and highly regarded by Puerto Vallarta's more prosperous residents.

The mustachioed owner, dressed in white slacks and shirt, enthusiastically greeted the large group of familiar guests. They followed him upstairs to the third floor where several tables had been pushed together, forming a long banquet table. The far end of the table extended onto a private terrace projecting out from underneath the restaurant's red tile roof.

Henry and Mitch seated Jill and Vivian in the next to last chairs, taking the end seats themselves. Two waiters in white uniforms and red aprons took orders for two *cervezas,* a Margarita and a Piña Colada.

"Isn't this wonderful, Jill?" said Vivian.

"What do you mean?" answered Jill.

"A table under the stars, the river, the mountains."

"It's very pretty."

"Are you okay? You're unusually quiet tonight."

"She's just a little nervous about heading out tomorrow," said Henry.

"I'd be more than just a little nervous if we were going," said Mitch.

The drinks arrived and Mitch was taking a pull from a bottle of Carta Blanca when he saw the owner coming up the stairs with more guests. He choked, then winced as cold beer shot up his nose. "Oh, shit."

"What?" said Henry.

Mitch took a deep breath. "Don't look now, but Bill and Marjorie are here."

Before he could finish the sentence, everyone was looking. Bill's deeply tanned face looked darker than usual. Marjorie's expression seemed uncharacteristically serene. Her page-boy ash blonde hair looked freshly shampooed and set. The host seated them in the two remaining chairs at the far end of the long table.

"Marjorie looks great," Vivian whispered. "She seems in much better spirits than this morning. Maybe she finally let Bill have it after his stunt at the yacht club."

Mitch couldn't help noticing the sullen expression on Bill's face.

"Bill, on the other hand," Vivian continued, "looks as though someone borrowed his favorite toy and broke it."

Mitch chugged half the remainder of his beer.

Vivian stole another glance. "I think he's still mad at you, Henry. You should have seen the look he just shot your way."

"He can give me all the dirty looks he wants," Henry replied.

"He looks calmer than when he came by this afternoon," said Jill.

"He stopped by *Walden*?" said Vivian.

Jill nodded. "Henry was in town with Mitch. I'd finished stowing provisions and was catching up my journal in the cockpit when he motored up in his dinghy. Said he wanted to talk to Henry. He was acting really weird."

"How so?" Vivian asked.

"I don't know. Like he was trying to conceal his emotions. When I told him Henry was in town, he muttered some ambiguous nonsense and left."

"*That's* why you've been so quiet," Vivian whispered. "Under the circumstances, it would have unnerved me, too, if he'd come by *Houdini* looking for Mitch."

Mitch rose from the table. "Excuse me, I'm going to see if I can find the men's room."

"Shall I order for us, honey?" asked Vivian.

"Yeah, go ahead."

"What would you like?"

"Uh, the *chile rellenos*."

"Can we split a bowl of *pozole* too?" she asked.

"Sure, whatever you want."

Mitch passed quickly behind Bill, glancing at Marjorie for a split second. She seemed to sense he was there but did not look up. He found the clean, ceramic-tiled rest rooms around a corner at the rear of the floor. Inside the men's room, he rest his head on a forearm braced against the cool wall. "Come on, Sanford, get a grip." Adultery was definitely overrated.

After a few minutes, his breathing returned to normal and the lightheadedness faded. He stepped outside to the opposing men's and women's wash basin counters which were screened from the dining area by a low brick wall festooned with pots of large green plants. He filled cupped hands with water from the tap and splashed it in his face. Drops trickled from the end of his nose. He grabbed paper towels from a stack on the counter and patted his face dry while mentally composing himself.

"Hi, Mitch."

He recognized the tentative voice coming from behind him immediately.

"Bill didn't want to come," said Marjorie. "I told him he could stay on the boat if he wanted, but I was coming to see our friends one more time before we sailed."

Mitch wiped the towels from his face and turned. Marjorie's small face registered concern but not fear. "So why *did* he come? What changed his mind?"

"He wasn't about to let me off the boat alone."

"Jesus, Marjorie, did you tell him?"

Marjorie lowered her voice to a barely audible whisper. "I didn't have to. He figured it out. I mean, it was...pretty obvious."

"Marjorie, you *said* you'd straighten up. You did—you changed the sheets—right?"

"I'm afraid not. As a matter of fact, I didn't even get dressed." She smiled as if she'd just told him her apple pie had won a blue ribbon at the fair. "Except for my reading glasses and a paperback, he found me the way you left me."

Holy shit! Mitch peered through the plants to see if anyone was coming. "Marjorie, what's got into you—don't answer that." His face grew suddenly warm again. "Don't you think it's pushing your—our—luck just a tad, being over here talking with me?"

Marjorie shook her head. "Oh, Bill doesn't think it was *you*."

Mitch's shoulders slumped, his brow furrowed. "He doesn't?"

Marjorie whispered: "He thinks it was Henry."

"Holy shit!"

"I said it was none of his damned business who it was, not after what he said and did at the yacht club this morning."

Henry's going to love this. Mitch would have to tell him after all. It was no longer a simple case of needing marriage counseling. "Marjorie, you are playing with fire. You can't let Bill go on thinking it was Henry."

"I know. That's the real reason I had to come tonight, to warn you. If I'd flatly denied it was Henry, I was sure Bill would figure it had to be you. By refusing to discuss it, I bought time to warn you. He strongly suspects Henry, but he's got no proof and he's not absolutely sure."

"Didn't he ask how you got back to *Silver Cloud*?"

"I told him you *and* Vivian took me back. As long as he doesn't talk to her..."

Mitch brought his palms together as if in prayer. "Damn it, Marjorie, did you have to throw it in his face?"

"I didn't think it through. I guess I just couldn't resist letting him know that not every man finds me as unappealing as he does. You didn't do it solely out of pity, did you Mitch?" Marjorie's face compressed, betraying a fear of his response.

Mitch looked into her desperate blue eyes. He had to be honest. "Compassion had something to do with it, but I wasn't faking anything, if that's what you mean."

Marjorie's eyes relaxed to dreamy crescents. "Thanks. I've no right to ask for more. It was foolish. I realize that now." She glanced briefly at the floor. "But if I'd known that's what it takes to get Bill's attention, I'd have done it a long, long time ago. After what I've put up with, I've decided I'm not going to swallow his crap anymore. Instead, he can start eating some of mine, and he's chewing on his first installment right now."

Mitch scanned Marjorie's face and arms. "He didn't hit you or anything?"

"Oh no, his abuse is never physical. I guess I should be thankful for that. He ranted and raved, slammed books across the cabin, but never touched me. Mostly, he just sulked and swore. For once it's *his* feelings that are hurt."

Mitch peered through the plants again. "I'd better get back."

"Will you warn Henry?"

"First chance I get. But Marjorie, one of us needs to tell Bill the truth."

"Are you sure? You know he'll try to get even. He'll tell Vivian."

Krakatoa and Mt. St. Helens, together. "I was probably going to have to tell her at some point anyway."

Marjorie's gaze fell; her hand came up to shade her eyes from his view. "I've created a mess, haven't I?"

"It's as much my fault as yours."

He moved to leave but she caught his arm. "Part of me is sorry, Mitch, part of me isn't. Can you understand that?"

Mitch nodded. "Let's just try to limit the damage."

As he approached the table, Mitch couldn't resist a surreptitious glance at Bill. Bill appeared to be listening intently to the skipper of a yacht bound for Costa Rica sitting across from him. Was Bill actually smiling? Mitch slid into his chair beside Vivian.

"We were just about to send out a search party," she said.

"I was talking to Marjorie."

"How's she doing?"

"She's fine."

"Jill's not feeling well," Vivian said.

"We're going to skip dinner and head on back," said Henry.

Mitch dropped his napkin on the table and slid his chair back. "Let's go."

Henry raised his hand. "No, we discussed that with Vivian. She's already ordered. You two stay, have your dinner. We'll see you tomorrow morning before we leave."

"If Jill's not feeling well," said Vivian, "maybe you two ought to delay your departure. You don't want to set off across the Pacific if she's sick."

"I think a little open ocean sailing may be just what I need," said Jill.

"We'll see how she is in the morning." Henry rose from his chair and helped Jill out.

Mitch rose at the same time. "Henry, I need to talk—"

"Give us a shout on the radio around oh-seven-hundred. We'll let you know then if we're getting underway as planned."

Mitch glanced at the far end of the table and saw Marjorie looking his way out the corner of one eye. "Believe it or not Henry, I think I'm actually envious of you heading out to sea."

"It's not too late to change your mind."

Wednesday, April 17

Mitch grabbed his wristwatch, silencing its high-pitched double-beep. Vivian rolled toward him and placed an arm and a leg across his body.

"What time is it?" she asked.

Mitch yawned. "Six forty-five."

Vivian snuggled close. "I think I overdid it last night."

Mitch tried to roll out. Vivian entwined her limbs around him tighter. "Viv."

"Mmm, just a minute."

Mitch relented and remained still. Although they slept with neither blanket or sheet, their cozy double berth felt as warm as an incubator. Finally, he stirred. "Come on, Viv, I have to call Henry."

"You're no fun." Vivian pretended to pout and turned away.

Mitch levered himself out of the Pullman-style berth. *Houdini*'s teak and holly cabin sole felt pleasurably cool on his bare feet. He walked to the galley, filled a copper-bottomed stainless teakettle with water, and placed it on the propane stove. From a utensil drawer he took out a piezoelectric stove lighter. He reached for a red switch mounted on the bulkhead but stopped short of flipping it on. The switch controlled a solenoid valve at the propane tank near the stern of the boat. The valve prevented gas from reaching the stove when it was not in use.

"Viv." He raised his voice so she could hear him. "Somebody left a burner on again."

"Wasn't me," she said.

"Wasn't me either."

"That's what you said last time, remember?"

That was just one time. "We're going to blow ourselves to smithereens one of these days." He held the lighter's long probe close to the burner and flipped the solenoid switch. A red indicator light came on and a barely audible hiss emanated from the burner. He pressed the lighter's plunger. A tiny spark ignited a blue halo. As he set the teakettle on the burner, a change in the pattern of light coming through the port hole above the stove caught his attention. He leaned forward and looked both ways to make sure his eyes weren't playing tricks on him. "Guess what. *Phoenix* is gone."

A few seconds paused before Vivian answered. "She *can't* be. She was there last night when we came back from the restaurant."

"I kid you not; she's gone. Jim and Litea must have been extremely quiet about getting up their anchors." Mitch looked straight across the gap previously filled by *Phoenix* to Bill and Marjorie's ketch-rigged *Silver Cloud.* "They must have left before sunrise."

Vivian appeared from the forward cabin, fluffing her long hair. She stifled a yawn. "That was considerate. The way I slept, I'm not sure it mattered."

Her sleep-wear consisted of an extra-large LA Raiders T-shirt. She leaned across the starboard settee and peered through a screened porthole. "They *are* gone. How did they get away without us hearing their engine?"

"Probably picked up their stern anchor and pulled themselves out into the channel with their bow anchor before they started it."

"Wonder why they left so early?"

"I'll see if I can raise them on the radio after I talk to Henry." Mitch crossed to *Houdini's* chart table and punched the power button on the VHF. A luminous green 16 appeared on the small LED screen. He spun the channel selector until the display read 71. Clearing his throat, he grabbed the hand mike. "*Walden, Walden,* this is *Houdini,* channel seven-one." He paused several seconds then repeated the call.

"Must not have it on yet. I'll try *Phoenix.*" He switched back to 16, the hailing channel. He waited until two Mexican boats finished conversing in Spanish. "*Phoenix, Phoenix,* this is *Houdini.*" He hesitated, then tried them again.

"Maybe they're out of range," said Vivian.

"Unless they left in the middle of the night, they shouldn't be more than fifteen miles out."

"Should you try Henry on 16? Maybe he forgot to switch to 71."

Mitch keyed the mike and called *Walden* on channel 16, again with no response. "Perhaps the problem is our radio." He keyed the mike again. "Any station, any station, this is

Houdini. Radio check, please." No response. "I give up. I'll run over in the dinghy."

"Shall I throw some clothes on and come along?" asked Vivian.

Maybe this would be his one last chance to speak to Henry in private. "Take your time. I'll just find out if they're leaving. If they are, I'll come back and get you."

In deference to sleeping neighbors, Mitch tilted up the dinghy's outboard and unshipped its oars. He rowed quietly along a fence row of anchor chains. Sparsely scattered puffs of cumulus to the west decorated the otherwise clear, rose-blue morning sky. A soft breeze trickled in from the northwest. Conditions for *Walden's* departure looked perfect.

The one-legged pelican was already at his post. Mitch maintained a respectful distance from the bird's anchor chain. The pelican nevertheless eyed him suspiciously until he was well past.

Upon crossing *Walden's* bow, Mitch feathered his left oar and made the turn for the boarding ladder. The wake of a departing sportfisher rocked him as he reached it, causing his port oar to strike *Walden's* hull. *Don't get excited, Henry, it was an accident.* Standing up in the inflatable, he knocked on the cutter's teak-planked deck. "Ahoy, *Walden!*"

Walden's rigging rattled and creaked as she gently rolled in the sportfisher's wake. Her blue inflatable tender trailed astern by its yellow bow line.

"Reveille, reveille, all hands on deck!" *Come on guys, you're supposed to be leaving today.* Mitch slid the dinghy aft along *Walden's* caprail to where he could see the companionway.

The companionway doors and the main hatch were closed. That was odd. Normally, Henry closed the doors only when they locked up and went ashore. At night, he slid the hatch closed but left the doors open to increase ventilation. The bug screen that fit in a slot behind the doors lay on the cabin roof beside the hatch.

Mitch was about to rap the deck again when he noticed the padlock. When in use, it secured the main hatch to the companionway doors, preventing all three from being opened. It was locked, but instead of holding the bronze hasp up, as it should, the lock hung down from the end of the hasp. The hasp's small U-shaped pad-eye had been wrenched from the hatch. Two of the pad-eye's four wood screws lay on the bridge deck below the lock. The other two hung from their holes in the padeye.

Mitch rapped on the deck. "Henry! God damn it, if this is a joke..."

His hands automatically tied the dinghy to the gate stanchion. *Aren't they here?* He stepped aboard. Where the heck did they go last night? There had to be a logical explanation. He placed his hands on the main hatch. His heart pounded. He pushed the hatch forward, sliding it open.

A fetid cloud of humid air rose from the cabin, filling his mouth and nose with the stench of human waste. He peered below. His eyes instinctively slammed shut. Jesus, no! He forced them to reopen.

Jill Fullerton lay sprawled face up on the starboard settee, naked from the waist down. Her right leg hung over the settee's edge, her bare heel resting on the teak sole.

Mitch tried not to breathe, to block out the fog of odors. He opened the companionway doors. His eyes shifted from Jill's motionless form to points around the cabin as he felt his way down the steps. Her right arm hung in midair, reaching out across the fore-and-aft passageway. Her delicate fingers curled like talons. The embroidered Mexican blouse she'd worn last night was ripped open from its hem to the collar. A white bra had been pushed up, exposing the undersides of her breasts. A bloodstained white skirt and pair of panties lay on the cabin sole near her foot. Her left leg was covered with a jumbled mass of papers, manuals and books.

Jill, no, Jesus no. Mitch swallowed hard, repeatedly. "Henry?" he said softly. *Henry, where the hell are you?*

Reaching the bottom step, Mitch prayed to himself. He's not here. He's not here.

He stepped down to the cabin sole and moved rigidly towards Jill. Those dark hypnotic eyes that had once sparkled at the slightest hint of light, now dull and gray, stared lifelessly at the cabin ceiling. The right half of her neck below the jaw was deeply cut. The arterial spray of blood from her throat had reached across the passageway to the port settee. A dark red arc curved across the backrest like an ugly rainbow.

Mitch took a step down the passageway and stopped. A foot protruded from behind the mast's rosewood compression post. Mitch grabbed the galley counter and braced his arm against the bulkhead. His face tingled. He forced another step and looked below the dining table. Henry lay crumpled underneath the table, curled around its pedestal. His head twisted sharply to one side, held up by the wooden base of the settee against his cheek. His eyes were closed.

Mitch sank to his knees on the cabin sole. "God, no! Please, God, not these people."

On the deck below Henry's head and in front of his chest, spread a dark burgundy, almost black, pool of congealing blood.

Mitch put the knuckles of his fists on the deck, letting his head hang limp between his shoulders. *Why, why?* Images from the past and future flooded in: two boys playing with a dog; the winning smile of a high school athlete; the happy face of a bride in white; a funeral; Vivian. He slumped between his two dead friends, sobbing quietly.

Walden's brass ship's clock chimed. He wiped his eyes and nose on his T-shirt. He willed his head to rise and forced himself to look around the cabin. Port and starboard locker doors were all open. Books were pulled from their shelves. The radio locker next to the chart table was empty. The stereo, the VHF radio, and the ham radio; all gone.

He staggered, losing his balance as he stood up, pitching forward then catching himself on the starboard settee. His hand landed on Jill's ankle. She was cold. He recoiled from her. *Sorry—I'm sorry.* Fresh air. He needed fresh air or he would lose it.

He clambered drunkenly up the companionway, across the cockpit and jumped into the inflatable. He forced the outboard down into the water and whipped the starter cord. It sputtered and died. He twisted the choke and lashed it again. This time it screamed to life and he flipped the shift lever forward and twisted the throttle to its limits. He ignored a neighbor's wave as he streaked down the line toward *Houdini*.

"That was quick." Vivian said, as he vaulted down the companionway. Her expression changed from interest to concern as she read the frozen look on his face. "Is Jill all right?"

Ignoring her question, he went straight to the radio.

"Mitch, what is it? What's wrong?"

The radio was still set on channel 16. Mitch began calling, "*Capitania de Puerto, Capitania de Puerto,* this is *Houdini.*"

"Mitch, for God's sake, tell me what's happening!"

"*Capitania de Puerto, Capitania de Puerto,* this is *Houdini.*" *Come on, damn it, answer.* He looked at Vivian for the first time. He ran a hand below one eye. "Henry and Jill—"

"*Vessel calling, this is Capitania de Puerto, channel one-six,*" The heavily Spanish accented voice sounded annoyed.

Mitch continued looking at Vivian as he keyed the mike. "*Capitania de Puerto,* this is the sailing vessel *Houdini.*"

"*Houdini, Capitania de Puerto, how may we assist you, Señor?*"

Mitch hesitated, not sure if he could say the words. "There's been...a murder...on an American sailboat anchored near the Navy base. Could you please call the police?"

Vivian slumped against the stove. The radio was silent for several seconds. Mitch's eyes remained locked on her uncomprehending gaze.

A different voice, less accented and more formal came from the radio. "*Houdini, Capitania de Puerto, may I have your name, Señor?*"

"My name...my name is Mitchell Sanford."

"*Where is your boat, Capitan?*"

"We're anchored just beyond the Navy base, the fourth boat in the line."

"*Señor Sanford, we will bring the policia out in our launch. Please do not leave your vessel.*"

A throaty rumble signaled the arrival of the port captain's launch. Mitch hugged Vivian close once more before separating from her. She followed him topside to meet the launch.

A thirty-foot, light-blue and white powerboat came in along *Houdini*'s port side. A young deckhand knelt on the bow, ready to pass a mooring line. An unusually tall, heavy-set Mexican man, wearing aviator-style sunglasses, stood on the port side, amidships. As the launch came alongside, he called to Mitch.

"*Señor*, you are, Mr. Sanford, the gentleman who has called the *Capitania de Puerto*?" The moderately accented English words came wrapped in an enigmatic bass voice.

"Yes, I am."

"I am Gilberto Martinez Carillo, a detective with the *Policia Judicial Federal*. Do you speak Spanish Señor?"

"*Lo siento*, only a few words."

"It is no problem I think, if you pardon my poor English."

"Your English is very good."

"Señor Sanford, will you please guide us to the other vessel?" Martinez gestured for Mitch to come aboard. The inflection of the detective's voice made it clear his statement was not a request.

Mitch stepped aboard the boat, leaving Vivian standing in *Houdini*'s cockpit. He turned and watched her as the launch backed into the channel. Her eyes looked back at him over a hand that veiled her mouth and nose.

The launch skipper soon had them situated alongside *Walden*'s starboard rail. Mitch's insides began churning at the prospect of reentering *Walden*'s cabin.

"Please wait here, Señor," Martinez said.

Mitch released the breath he was holding as the detective stepped off the launch and onto *Walden*. Martinez pulled a handkerchief from a back pocket, covered his mouth and nose and descended the companionway steps.

Less than a minute passed before he reappeared, rejoining Mitch aboard the launch. "These people were your friends, Señor Sanford?"

"Yes."

"It must have been very hard for you. I am truly sorry. I must ask some questions."

Martinez started with Mitch's relationship to Henry and Jill and the names of their next of kin. He then guided Mitch through a series of probing questions causing him to recount Henry and Jill's movements over the last twenty-four hours, concluding with how and why he had boarded *Walden* and discovered their bodies.

Even though still dazed and recovering from shock, Mitch had enough presence of mind to be impressed by the Mexican investigator. He sensed the progressive order and logic behind the detective's seemingly routine questions.

He guessed he and Martinez were about the same age. Definitely a plainclothes detective: bright blue and red floral-patterned sport shirt, casual navy blue slacks, and a pair of clean white running shoes. His straight-parted wavy black hair looked as if each strand knew its place and never moved. Maybe a little overweight, but certainly not fat. Mitch couldn't recall having met a taller or more physically imposing Mexican. No sidearm. Probably didn't need one.

"What were the occupations of the deceased, Señor?"

"They each owned a business. Henry ran Fullerton Construction. They did commercial construction, like shopping centers and small-to-medium-sized office buildings. Jill headed a five-person consulting firm that specialized in writing user manuals for software products."

"They owned these businesses at the time of their deaths?"

"No. They both sold out before leaving on this trip. They planned to be on a circumnavigation for five to seven years and didn't want the complications."

Martinez made detailed notes in a small spiral bound notepad as Mitch answered each question. He asked for the names of everyone who Mitch could remember having been recently in contact with Henry and Jill. When Martinez stopped writing and folded the notebook, Mitch braced himself; time for them to enter the cabin.

Martinez spoke to the launch skipper in Spanish, then to Mitch in English. "They will take you back to your boat now." The detective stepped aboard *Walden* and turned. "I will have more questions later, Señor Sanford. I will send the boat for you this afternoon. Is that a problem?"

"No. Not at all."

On board *Houdini* he found Vivian curled up in a fetal ball on the dinette settee, sniffling into a handful of tissues. "How're you doing?" he asked.

She stretched out. "Not too good. How about you?"

Mitch's chest heaved; he shook his head. "I don't know. I don't feel like it's completely hit me yet."

"What happens now?"

"This detective—Martinez—wants me to go back to *Walden* sometime later today."

"You'd better lie down for awhile."

He leaned against the chart table and stared at his feet. He felt empty. He moved to the settee across from Vivian and lay down. He shielded his eyes with the back of his hand. Even when his long term prospects had been hazy, the immediate future had always been clear. He always had a plan in the short run, always knew what would happen next. Suddenly it was a white-out, a blizzard, an empty canvas. The clock of life had stopped. It would have been easier for him to accept the idea that Africa no longer existed than to believe that Henry was gone.

At three in the afternoon Mitch awoke from a fitful nap to the sound and jolt of the port captain's launch coming alongside. Instead of Martinez, Mitch found a younger man carrying a small holstered automatic on his hip waiting for him on the powerboat's rear deck. He was slim, wore black denim jeans, harness boots and a dark blue, long-sleeve double-knit shirt. His only resemblance to Martinez was a pair of gold-rimmed sunglasses. He shook Mitch's hand and introduced himself simply as Ortega.

When the launch crossed the derelict's bow, Mitch spotted Martinez on *Walden* conversing across the narrow gap with three men in a flashy twenty-foot speedboat tied to the abandoned vessel. Two of the men were scuba divers, still wet and wearing their tanks. Martinez pointed astern of *Walden* and swung his arm around to the bow. The divers nodded.

Martinez crossed over and met the launch as it arrived at *Walden*'s starboard lifeline gate, motioning for Mitch and Ortega to come aboard. Mitch took a slow, deep breath and stepped from the launch to *Walden's* deck.

Martinez' eyes caught Mitch's. He spoke softly, hardly loud enough for Ortega to have heard. "The bodies have been taken away, Señor." He suggested they sit in the cockpit.

The white cockpit awning shielded them from the hot afternoon sun, yet permitted them the benefit of the fresh breeze coming in from the ocean. Nevertheless, the sickening odors of violent death reached Mitch's nostrils on brief occasions when the wind died and then resumed.

Martinez removed a pack of Marlboros from his shirt pocket, shook it and offered one to Mitch.

"No thanks."

The detective took one and prepared to strike a match. "With your permission, Señor?"

"Please, go ahead."

Mitch caught Ortega eyeing the cigarettes. Martinez ignored the junior detective and put the pack away as he shook out his match and tossed it over the side. He started to speak to Mitch, then hesitated, as if interrupted by something remembered. Twisting in his seat, he shouted two bursts of Spanish at the speedboat driver. The man acknowledged and quickly began to climb aboard the derelict.

Martinez exhaled a stream of blue-gray smoke and turned to Mitch. "I know this is difficult, Señor Sanford, but your assistance is critical to my investigation." Martinez leaned back against the cockpit coaming, his elbows resting on its varnished cap. His mildly accented English came in wave-like clusters interspersed with short pauses. His calm manner helped Mitch compose himself.

"Yes, I understand," Mitch said. "I'll try to help any way I can."

Martinez asked him to start from the beginning and recount in as much detail as he could remember, all of Jill and Henry's movements for the last several days leading up to the last time he saw them alive. Martinez left the chore of taking notes to Ortega. Mitch felt the senior detective intently studying his face as he answered. His gaze was so unwavering Mitch found it necessary to occasionally avert his eyes. His answers rambled into alleys of irrelevant detail.

More questions came after the chronology. With which of the other transient cruisers were Jill and Henry acquainted? Had Mitch seen Jill or Henry talking to any strangers?

"Señor Sanford, did the Fullertons quarrel or argue with anyone recently?"

An image appeared, yesterday morning at the yacht club, Bill's face. But the way he'd found Jill...the missing radios...Bill and Marjorie at *Los Arbolitos*. It didn't fit. It couldn't fit.

"Señor Sanford?"

"Yes, there was one incident." He told Martinez of Henry's confrontation with Bill at the yacht club. Martinez waited, as if expecting more. "That's it," said Mitch.

"Very well, Señor. We must go inside now." Martinez rose and moved to the companionway. Mitch gathered control of his emotions. The investigator led the way down. The main hatch and doors had been open for several hours. The strong smell still lingered. Ortega followed close behind Mitch. The young detective made a sound universally translated as revulsion.

Martinez walked forward, turned and stood in front of the doorway leading to the forward berth. Mitch stopped at the galley. He focused on Martinez' face, restricting his peripheral vision from the spattered settees and cabin sole.

"Señor Sanford," Martinez began, "you have already told us about the radios. I would like you to describe them in as much detail as you can remember. Then, please inspect the boat carefully and tell us of anything else you see. Anything missing...or unusual. Do you understand?"

"Yes," Mitch said. He described the radios slowly for Ortega, spelling the brand names as he went. Slowly, he scanned the cabin. He hesitated to touch anything.

"Fingerprints have already been taken, Señor. Be very thorough."

Mitch moved around the cabin opening and closing lockers. Henry's Magellan GPS was gone from its bracket above the chart table.

"G-P-S?" said Ortega, halting his pen.

"Global Positioning System," said Mitch. "It uses satellites to tell you where you are at sea." Ortega nodded and resumed writing.

The combined TV-VCR should have been on the bookshelf above the port settee. Mitch opened the locker where Henry kept his expensive Japanese sextant in its black foam-lined case. It had not been taken.

Mitch paused, making a mental checklist of things Jill and Henry had had aboard that a thief would want. He searched further and determined a pair of binoculars, a 35mm camera, a Sony camcorder, and a laptop computer were also missing. His search of *Walden*'s compartments took nearly an hour. He searched the port quarter-berth last. He told Martinez he could find nothing else missing that should have been on board. "Oh, wait. Did you find a money clip in Henry's pocket?"

Martinez shook his head. "Money clip?"

Mitch described it for him. "I think it had at least two or three hundred dollars in it."

Martinez paused, letting Ortega catch up with his notes. "What about Señora Fullerton's jewelry?" Martinez asked.

"She and my wife both left their good jewelry at home."

"A wise decision," Martinez said. "If you can think of nothing else, Señor Sanford, we will return you to your vessel." The two detectives followed Mitch up to the lifeline gate.

"If I do think of something, how can I contact you?" Mitch asked.

"Ah, yes." Martinez removed a card from his wallet.

Mitch took the card and stepped aboard the launch. Martinez nodded at the skipper and the deckhand began taking in his mooring lines. "Señor Sanford, we would prefer that you remain in Puerto Vallarta until further notice."

"No problem. We'll stay as long as you need us."

"In fact, I must ask you to report to the *Capitania de Puerto,* and return your clearance papers."

"But I haven't cleared out."

Martinez' eyes narrowed. "You said that you and Señor Fullerton visited the offices of the *Capitania de Puerto* and *Immigración,* yesterday."

"That's correct, but only Henry cleared out, not me."

"You were not continuing your travels together?"

"No. No we weren't."

"I see. You may inform other yacht captains that we have asked the *Capitania de Puerto* to suspend granting outward clearance to foreign yachts until further notice. I will talk with you again soon, Señor. We will do all that is possible to catch whoever is responsible for the death of your friends."

"*Gracias*, Señor Martinez."

Martinez motioned to the skipper and the deckhand whipped his line off *Walden's* cleat. As the launch turned and crossed *Walden*'s bow, Mitch looked for the divers in the gap, but they were gone.

Thursday, April 18

Mitch's eyelids fluttered between closed and half-opened. Something far away seemed to urge him not to wake, as if warning him the visions in his mind's eye were more than a bad dream. He raised his arm. It was late, almost eight-thirty.

Vivian lay on her side facing him. He studied her sleeping face. Long, slow exhalations from her nostrils ruffled a thin curtain of dark brown hair falling over her small straight nose and mouth. Carefully, he lifted the strands from her face and swept them behind her ear. She unconsciously wet her full lips but didn't wake. The sudden loss of Henry and Jill made him realize how much he depended on her companionship and love. He'd become accustomed to it, assumed it would last forever. He mustn't lose her. Nothing else really mattered.

He slipped out of the berth and padded quietly to the galley, put the teakettle on to boil, and glanced through the porthole toward *Silver Cloud*. No sign of Bill or Marjorie. Probably not up yet.

The sound of an approaching outboard motor attracted his attention to the opposite porthole. It was Victor and Sharon in *Dream Lover*'s tender, a large white inflatable. Mitch looked around the cabin. Where'd he leave his cut-offs? He found them under the dining table and stumbled aft, stepping into them as he went, zipping his fly as he emerged from the companionway. Sharon stood in *Dream Lover*'s tender, holding onto *Houdini's* caprail. "Good morning," he said, making an effort to sound happy to see them.

"Good morning, Mitch," Sharon said, "Sorry to get you out of bed."

"No, I was up, just hadn't dressed yet."

"We heard the terrible news and wondered how you and Vivian are doing." Victor shut off the outboard and rose to stand beside his wife.

"Better," said Mitch, managing a tight-lipped smile.

"We can't believe it's true," said Sharon.

"If there's anything we can do," said Victor, "anything at all. We're completely at your disposal."

Mitch sat on deck in front of them. "Thanks Vic, that's very thoughtful. When did you hear?"

"A detective was waiting for us at the marina yesterday evening when we returned from a day trip to Yelapa. He asked us about the business at the yacht club the other morning, and whether or not we'd seen Jill or Henry talking to any strangers."

"I guess you have me to thank for that."

"Why's that?"

"They asked me for the names of everyone who'd recently—"

"Naturally," said Victor. "You needn't apologize. Of course, we were quite shocked by the news, but well understood their need to speak with us—and we're quite anxious to help find the guilty parties. He didn't appear to have any theories or suspects when he spoke to us."

"No, he hasn't shared anything with me either. But it looked obvious."

"Really? Why?" asked Sharon.

"Henry and Jill left *Los Arbolitos* early that night. Jill wasn't feeling well. It looked as though they returned to *Walden* and stumbled upon burglars who weren't expecting them back so soon."

"Oh my God," said Victor. "Was it you that found them?"

Mitch nodded.

Sharon gasped, her flawlessly smooth face transformed into harsh lines of anguished compassion. "How dreadful, you poor dear." She placed a hand on Mitch's wrist. "And if they'd stayed at the restaurant they might still be alive?"

"There's a good chance," answered Mitch. "At least, all four of us would have been coming back at the same time.

"What a tragic twist of fate," said Victor.

"You didn't happen to see or talk to them when they returned from the restaurant, did you?" asked Mitch.

"Unfortunately, no. Sharon and I had left the boat for a drink at *El Faro*. But let's hope the bastards who did it are stupid enough to get themselves caught. The police and local businessmen are desperate for a quick resolution."

"How do you know that?" Mitch asked.

"You probably haven't been ashore, have you? It's the headlines in the local papers, but that's not what's got them in a lather. It was on CNN International last night. CNN used the story to contrast the recent murders of foreign tourists in Florida."

"CNN?" said Mitch.

"Amazing, isn't it?" Victor replied. "You can bet the mayor of Puerto Vallarta and the tourist businesses are sharing their anxiety with the police."

"Victor," said Sharon, "I suppose we should be getting back."

"I'm sorry," said Mitch. "Excuse my manners. Would you like to come aboard? I'm making coffee."

"No, no, Mitch, that's quite all right," Victor answered. "We simply wanted you to know you have our full support and our deepest sympathy."

"Perhaps we'll swing by and look in on you again this evening," said Sharon. "Or next time you're in the marina, please stop and see us." Victor started the outboard. "And tell Vivian we're thinking of her."

"Will do, thanks for stopping by."

Sharon sat down in the bow of the inflatable and pushed clear of *Houdini*. Once in the channel, Victor opened the throttle and in seconds they were gone.

He found Vivian awake but still lying in their bed.

"Sorry for being such a lump. Was that Victor and Sharon?"

"Yeah, they stopped by to see how we were bearing up."

"How are we bearing up?"

"Okay, I guess."

She reached out and took his hand. "You feel like breakfast?"

"I could eat. But first, I should make a run to the port captain's office."

"What for?"

"To call Henry and Jill's parents."

———

Above and beyond the palm trees lining the shore, humid bands of haze wreathed the jungled foothills of the Sierra Madres. Black, fork-tailed frigate birds soared hundreds of feet overhead and a squadron of six pelicans made a low-level strafing run down the center of the channel. Mitch twisted the outboard's throttle and sped past the gray patrol vessel moored in front of the naval base. The small harbor was strangely quiet and deserted. The fishing and sightseeing charters had left hours ago. The cruise ship wharf was empty. He idled the dinghy in alongside the stub of an old concrete pier inland of the cruise ship wharf and tied its bow line to a rusted hook of re-bar.

"Mitch! How're you doin'?" came a shout from directly overhead.

"Jesus!" Mitch started, lost his balance and narrowly avoided falling out of the dinghy. Upon gaining his footing again, he glanced up to see Bill looking down at him eight feet above his head. "Bill, hi, you startled the shit out of me."

"Sorry, didn't mean to."

"Where's your dinghy? I didn't see it."

"Over there," he said, pointing behind him. "No cruise ships in so I parked at the passenger launch dock. I was coming back from the port captain's office when I saw you zipping this way."

Mitch stepped from the inflatable to the boulders along the bank. Bill waited for him as he climbed the steep incline to where the pier met the bank. Mitch tensed as he reached the top, not knowing what to expect. Instead of crowding him, Bill moved back and gave him room.

"Mitch, I'm...well, I'm real sorry about Henry and Jill." Bill paused and gazed momentarily at his feet. "You know how it was, but I never wished this on him—or Jill."

Mitch could see Bill was truly shaken. His own tensed muscles relaxed. Marjorie must not have told him. "Where's Marjorie?" Maybe it was time to get it out in the open.

"Marj? She's out on *Silver Cloud*."

But then, what's the point of telling him now? "How's she taking it?"

"Not too well. I think it happenin' so close by and all, you know." Bill tilted his head and winced. "And she was fond of Jill...well, both of 'em, I suppose."

"Yeah, sure." Mitch looked away toward the port captain's office. "You on a mail run?"

"No. Came over to talk to the bureaucrats about this clearance restriction business. Wanted to know just how long they think they can keep us cooped up here."

"What'd they say?"

"They ain't clearin' nobody out till the police give 'em the go-ahead. Damn it to hell, I'm ready to blow this bean town. We all need to be moving on within the next week or two or we'll be stuck here for hurricane season. Right?"

"We were planning to stay anyway."

"I thought you were headin' for the Marquesas, too."

"Changed our minds at the last minute."

"Hadn't heard. Well, Jim and Litea were sure smart, lightin' out when they did."

"Say, did you or Marjorie hear or see anything funny around *Walden* when you came back from the restaurant?"

"No, no I didn't. Police asked me the same question. Marj and I left 'bout a half hour or so after you and Vivian. Time we got back to The Pond, *Walden* was quiet and dark. I'd heard they were headin' out the next day, so I just figured they'd gone to bed early."

"That's what Vivian and I thought."

"Well, s'pect I better be getting back to *Silver Cloud*. I have to collect Marj and catch a taxi. This arrogant Mex detective, Martinez, came by yesterday evenin' and says we both have to show up at the police station, answer some more questions and get fingerprinted. *Fingerprinted*, can you believe that horseshit?"

"You ask him why?"

"Hell yes, I asked. He says they have to fingerprint everybody who's been aboard *Walden* recently so's to eliminate their prints from those that might belong to whoever did it. Makes sense I guess, but it's a pain in the butt and a waste of time if you ask me."

"You want to help the police, don't you?" Mitch's harsh tone surprised even himself.

"Sorry, Mitch, didn't mean it to sound the way it did." Bill glanced away and gestured toward the port captain's office. "It's just—these people don't think nothin' of havin' you sit on your butt all day, waitin' till they're good and ready to take care of your business."

"Martinez didn't strike me as that type."

"Well, I hope you're right. Don't mean to rush off, but he told us to show up before ten." Bill turned and headed toward the cruise ship wharf.

Mitch walked toward the doughnut shaped *Terminal Maritima*. A long line of passenger vans and taxis stretched from the turnaround in front of the circular building to the highway. Drivers stood in small groups, talking and smoking cigarettes. It didn't take an IQ above room temperature to read the signs that a cruise ship was due in.

He went to a blue international pay phone and looked at his watch. It would be early, but he doubted they'd still be in bed. Frank and Dinah Fullerton were an indelible part of his earliest childhood memories. They, and Henry's two older brothers, had been an extended family for him. He stared at the phone but saw instead the Fullertons laughing with his parents around a bonfire during a camping trip. After Mitch's parents died, the Fullertons were all the family he had left besides Vivian.

He lifted the phone's receiver, punched the US access code and followed it with the Fullertons' number. A gravelly voice answered on the third ring.

"Frank?"

"Yes, who's this?"

Mitch could already hear the fatigue and strain in Frank's voice. The normal good cheer was missing. "It's Mitch, Frank."

"Mitch, hi, I'm sorry I didn't recognize your voice. I should have expected your call. How are you and Vivian?"

"We're okay, how are you and Dinah doing?"

"Not very well. Neither of us slept last night. Chuck and Fred and their wives are here. That's helping Dinah a great deal. We're just trying to cope with it, Mitch. At first we thought it had to be a mistake. Then friends called, said they'd heard it on CNN."

"I couldn't believe it either."

"What the hell happened, Mitch? A Mexican police detective called—Martinez, I think. He would only say they'd been murdered."

"It looks like they stumbled into a burglary in progress. Martinez isn't saying much, just asking lots of questions. I trust him though, Frank, I think he's a good man."

"Weren't there any witnesses?"

"Apparently not. *Walden's* anchored by herself, out of sight from us and the other boats in the anchorage."

"*Who found them?*"

Mitch paused, the visions returned. "I did."

Several seconds of silence passed before Frank spoke. "*I wish you'd been spared that. It...it must have been tough, Mitch. Did they suffer?*"

Mitch tilted his head and looked up to keep the moisture in his eyes from forming into tears. What was so great about the truth? What was the truth? "No, I don't think so, Frank."

"*This Martinez fellow said they'd send them home on a flight tomorrow. We'll be going to SeaTac to...to meet them...damn it, Mitch, Henry was special.*"

"I know, Frank. He was. When's the funeral going to be?"

"*We're not sure. Don't worry, Mitch, we'll take care of things here. You stay there and help the police find whoever did this.*" Frank's voice grew louder and he spoke as though giving an order to a surviving son.

"We will, Frank. What about *Walden?*"

"*Hadn't even thought about that. I'll talk it over with Chuck and Fred. I suppose when the police say it's okay one of them could go down and make arrangements to have her shipped back. Is that possible?*"

"It should be. Vivian and I will keep an eye on her. Should I call Jill's parents? I don't really know them."

"*They're on their way here. I'll tell them you called. If they do want to talk to you, how can we reach you?*"

Mitch gave him the number for the office of the port captain. "If there's anything Vivian and I can do for you and Dinah at this end, Frank, just name it."

"*Just keep on top of what the police are doing and call me if you learn anything new, okay?*"

"Yes, sir. Please give Dinah our love."

"*Houdini, this is Capitania de Puerto. Please respond, channel one-six.*

Vivian picked up the VHF mike. "Capitania de Puerto, this is *Houdini.*"

"*Señora Sanford?*"

"Yes."

"We have a message from Señor Martinez. He requests you and your husband go to his office at Policia Judicial Federal at one o'clock this afternoon. Is that possible?"

"Yes, it is."

As Mitch motored the dinghy toward the marina, Vivian noticed a change in The Pond's makeup. *Walden* was gone. The cutter's mast no longer protruded from behind the hulk that previously hid her from view of the other anchored boats. She pointed out the discrepancy to Mitch. Neither of them spoke as they approached and passed the boat's former location. The one-legged pelican was missing as well.

Their anxiety was short-lived. *Walden's* gold mast came into view as they approached the marina. She rested quietly in a 70-foot slip just off the main channel. A blue-uniformed police officer leaned against her caprail, smoking a cigarette.

Mitch showed Martinez' card to a taxi driver waiting in the tree-shaded cul-de-sac beside the Marina Del Rey condos. Ten minutes later he delivered them to a small, white stucco, tile-roofed building up a side street off of busy Libramiento. Large block letters in blue read *Policia Judicial Federal*. Mitch paid the driver and was closing the taxi's door when he heard a familiar voice yell "Wait!". Mitch and Vivian both turned to see Victor and Sharon hurrying toward them.

"Damned decent of you to fetch us a cab, Mitch," said Victor.

"I try to be helpful," Mitch replied, reopening the door for Sharon. "How long have you two been here?"

"About forty-five minutes," Sharon answered.

"Asked a few new questions and took our fingerprints," said Victor, holding up his still gray-smudged fingertips for inspection. "Rather exciting. Stop by for a visit on your way back if you have the time."

Victor slid into the cab's back seat and waved as the driver pulled away. When Mitch turned around he found Ortega standing behind them.

"*Buenos dias*, Señor, Señora," he said. "Señor Martinez will see you now."

Ortega led them through an exterior door directly into a medium-sized office illuminated only by its one large glass window. The dark paneled walls were bare except for three large photocopied posters of the faces and profiles of three wanted men. The office furniture consisted of one metal desk and three chairs. The surface of the desk was similarly uncluttered, a telephone on one side and an ashtray holding one freshly lit cigarette on the other. Beside the phone lay a sheet of official-looking letterhead stationery with one short, typed paragraph and an ornate signature below it that consumed a third of the page.

Martinez rose from the swivel chair behind the desk to greet them. His eyes looked tired as though from lack of sleep, but then Mitch hadn't seen him without sunglasses. Maybe his eyes always looked that way.

"Please, sit down. Thank you for coming."

Martinez picked up the cigarette. He was about to take a drag, but stopped, glanced at Vivian and stubbed it out. "I know this must be a painful and difficult time for you, Mr. and Mrs. Sanford, however, I need to ask you a few more questions."

"We appreciate your concern," said Mitch, "but we want to help in any way we can. Have you learned anything new?"

"I'm afraid I am not at liberty to say."

"We've heard the case has gained international media attention," Vivian said.

Martinez picked up the sheet of paper lying on the desk in front of him and glanced at it. "This is a letter from our *Presidente* Salinas, addressed to my commander expressing his concern over this tragedy. He also expresses his confidence that we will rapidly bring the responsible parties to justice."

Mitch looked at Vivian and then at Martinez. "It's good to know he's taken a personal interest."

"Si, Señor Sanford, he is very interested. He is extremely concerned about what happened to Mr. and Mrs. Fullerton. It happens that he also has a substantial interest in the company that owns Marina Vallarta and many of the properties around it." Martinez shot a quick look at Ortega leaning against the wall. Neither man smiled.

"What about the divers," Mitch said. "Did they find anything?"

"Mr. Sanford, I cannot discuss that either. Now, if you—"

The phone rang. Martinez' attention shifted. He hesitated, letting it ring again, as if contemplating whether or not he should answer. "Please, excuse me one moment." On the third ring, he picked up the receiver, putting it to his ear. "*habla Martinez.*" His voice carried an edge that implied annoyance. "*Si...Si...Para qué? Increíble!...No...No!...Ahora mismo...Si, si, bueno.*" Martinez replaced the handset in its cradle, staring at it for three full seconds before returning his attention to Mitch and Vivian. "Mr. and Mrs. Sanford, I am afraid I must excuse myself. My questions will have to wait until another time. But since you are here, Ortega will take your fingerprints. This is necessary because—"

"Yes, we know," said Mitch. "Bill explained it to us."

"Bill? Ah, Señor Schneider, from the vessel *Silver Cloud*, correct?"

"Right."

Martinez stood and felt for his pack of cigarettes. "I will contact you again shortly." Mitch and Vivian began to stand. "Please, wait here." Motioning for Ortega to follow him, Martinez walked outside to a red Dodge Ramcharger parked directly in front of his office window. He opened the vehicle's door and spoke quietly to Ortega. A minute later he reentered his office. "Señor Sanford, I am in need of a favor?"

"Sure," said Mitch.

Martinez pulled a spiral-bound pocket notepad from his hip pocket, flipped it open and studied it briefly. "Could you relay a message to Señor and Señora Schneider of the yacht *Silver Cloud* and also Señor and Señora Westridge of the yacht *Dream Lover* when you return to Marina Vallarta?"

"We'd be glad to. What's the message?"

"I would like to meet with all of you at Marina Vallarta this evening, say around 6 o'clock."

"Where?"

Martinez thought for a moment. "*El Faro.* I will look for you at the bottom of the lighthouse. You know it?"

"Of course," replied Mitch. "Can I tell them the purpose of the meeting?"

"No, I'm afraid—" Martinez paused and looked away toward the street. "You may tell them there has been a new development in the case that we wish to discuss with each of them."

Victor and Sharon's initial reaction to Martinez' message was one of surprise, followed immediately by expressions of hope that perhaps the killers had been caught. Bill asked Mitch to repeat everything Martinez had said.

"You're sure he wanted Marj to come too, not just me?" asked Bill.

"He said 'Señor and Señora Schneider," Mitch replied.

The white, stucco-covered six-story tower at the head of the channel leading into Marina Vallarta could be easily mistaken for a genuine lighthouse if not for the saucer-shaped *El Faro* bar at its top and the ice cream parlor situated beneath its open base. Mitch and Vivian arrived shortly before six. The crews of *Dream Lover* and *Silver Cloud* were not in sight.

"Over here, Mitch!" Victor stood beside Sharon who waved from her seat at an outdoor table in front of *Captain Morgan's,* the restaurant across the alley from the lighthouse. The alley led to Avenida Paseo de la Marina, the main loop around the marina and the nearby hotels and condominiums.

Victor pulled out a chair for Vivian. "We thought as long as we were waiting, we might as well be comfortable."

While Mitch and Vivian ordered drinks, Victor spotted and hailed Bill and Marjorie. With borrowed chairs they managed to squeeze around the one small table. Neither Mitch nor Vivian had seen Marjorie since the night at *Los Arbolitos.* Marjorie placed a hand on Vivian's shoulder after sitting down beside her. "It's so sad," she said. "How are you two doing?"

"Still in a state of shock," answered Vivian, "but we're coming out of it, slowly."

"I can't believe it either," said Marjorie. She gazed briefly at Mitch, then to her lap.

The new confidence and determination Mitch had seen in Marjorie's face and heard in her voice at *Los Arbolitos* had disappeared, replaced by grief and sadness, and something else he couldn't quite discern.

"It's after six," said Bill. "Where the hell is he?"

"Bill," Victor said soothingly, "You've been in Mexico now, what, four, five months?"

"I know, *Mañana*-time. I don't care. I don't like being jerked around. Say, what the hell does a person have to do to get a drink around here?"

He hadn't finished the sentence when the waiter appeared with Mitch's beer and Vivian's Piña Colada. Bill ordered a tall Scotch on-the-rocks for himself and a diet cola for Marjorie.

"I think the *Federales* have arrived," said Sharon.

The rest of the group turned to look across the alleyway. The burly Mexican detective exited the passenger side of the Ramcharger. Ortega emerged from the driver's side.

Two uniformed police officers exited from the rear seat. The three junior policemen huddled around Martinez who gestured as though giving them instructions. Upon finishing, he and Ortega walked toward the lighthouse.

Victor stood. "I suppose someone should inform them we're over here."

Victor caught the two detectives as they reached the base of the lighthouse. After exchanging a few words, he returned.

"Sharon, you and I have the honor of being first on stage in this little drama." Victor took the back of his wife's chair, helping her away from the table.

Bill watched them depart and approach the detectives. "What are those Frito-banditos up to?"

"We'll find out soon enough," said Mitch.

"I don't trust 'em. The police down here don't care who they arrest just so long as they arrest somebody. They use methods that'd squeeze a murder confession out of Mother Teresa."

"Come on, Bill," Vivian said, "you've seen too many old movies."

"You think so? Hell, I read in *Newsweek* just a few months ago where they put a guy's head in a plastic bag filled with ammonia fumes until he confessed. And that's what they do if you're a foreigner, or if they like you. If you're some poor local yokel with no pull, they're not so gentle."

The waiter returned with Bill's Scotch and a Diet Coke for Marjorie. Two minutes passed without conversation as they watched Victor and Sharon talking to the detectives on the far side of the red truck. They seemed to be looking at something

Martinez was showing them but with their backs to the restaurant and the car between, it was impossible to see.

Another few minutes passed when Vivian said: "Looks as if Victor and Sharon are finished."

Victor and Sharon walked away, leaving the two detectives talking to each other. Ortega nodded several times and started toward the restaurant.

Ortega looked at Mitch. "Señor and Señora Sanford, will you come with me, please?" Then turning to Marjorie, "And you, Señora Schneider?"

Bill shifted in his chair and started to rise.

Ortega held up his hand. "Please wait, Señor Schneider. We will come for you in a minute." Ortega led Marjorie, Mitch and Vivian to the Ramcharger where Martinez and the two uniformed men were talking. As with Victor and Sharon, Ortega took them to the far side of the vehicle. In one hand, Martinez held a small stack of Polaroid photos by their edges.

"I would like each of you to look at these photographs carefully, but say nothing until I ask. Understood?"

When they all nodded, Martinez handed the first of the photos to Marjorie. She studied it for several seconds and passed it on to Vivian who did the same and passed it on to Mitch.

The first photo was of a man in his late thirties or early forties wearing a blue work shirt, dark trousers and a black baseball cap standing beside Martinez against a white building. The next photo was of a younger man, a muscular type with a short haircut, wearing a tank top shirt and shorts, also standing next to Martinez. The third photo was of a man in his mid-to-late forties, wearing a smudged orange T-shirt and brown shorts. He wore a baseball cap similar to one worn by the man in the first picture. The top of his head barely reached Martinez' shoulders. Mitch studied this picture longer. He then looked back at the second photo.

The fourth photo Vivian handed him was of an athletic looking type in a rugby shirt, with neatly combed hair and nearly as tall as Martinez. In the fifth picture, the man standing next to the detective was fat, with a mustache and acne scarred complexion. Mitch scanned through the stack a second time before handing them to Martinez.

Martinez fanned the photos apart like a poker hand, looked at them briefly and turned to Marjorie. "Señora Schneider, other than myself, have you seen any of the men in these pictures before?"

"I don't think so," said Marjorie, "none of them look familiar to me."

"Thank you, Señora, please wait for your husband on the other side of the lighthouse."

Martinez turned to Vivian as Marjorie departed. "Señora Sanford?"

Vivian glanced at Mitch before answering. "Yes, I've seen two of them."

"Which two?" said Martinez, fanning out the photos. She pointed at the second and third photos. "These?" said Martinez, taking the two photos out of the group and holding them so Vivian could clearly see both faces.

"Yes." She looked at Mitch.

Martinez merged the two photos with the rest and shuffled them. He moved in front of Mitch. "And you, Señor Sanford?"

"Yes, this one and this one," he said, touching the tops of the same two photos Vivian had indicated.

Martinez removed the two pictures from the group of five and studied them for a moment. "How do you know these two men?"

Mitch exchanged glances with Vivian. It was clear that she was no more anxious to speak than him. "They're the fishermen I told you about," he said, finally. "The ones who visited us and the Fullertons in their small boat."

"The ones you referred to as 'Carlos and Manuel'?"

"Yes," said Mitch, pointing to the picture of the older man in the grimy orange T-shirt, "this is Carlos," and then pointing to the younger one, "this one is Manuel."

"Describe their boat, please." Martinez said.

"A small wooden row boat," Mitch answered. "Very old and beat up."

"No motor?"

"No."

"What were they doing around the anchored yachts?"

"Catching fish with a net, mostly."

Martinez nodded his head in comprehension. "Yesterday, you said these men talked to Señor Fullerton on more than one occasion about buying one of their nets, a *tarraya*, correct?" Martinez made a motion like a matador throwing his cape.

"Yes, one of those."

"And the most recent of these conversations took place at the Fullertons' vessel two days ago?"

"Yes."

"You saw them there?"

"Yes."

"Were they on board?"

"No, they were standing in their boat holding on to the side of the sailboat."

"Did you ever see them go aboard the Fullertons' yacht?"

"No."

"Did Señor Fullerton buy the net?"

"No, he said they wanted too much for it."

"Did he perhaps buy fish from them?"

"He said they showed him a bunch of pámpano they'd just caught. But he didn't say anything about buying any, and I doubt that he would, since he was heading out to sea the next day."

"Why would that make a difference?"

"Henry liked dorado and tuna. He'd have caught one or the other within a day or two."

Martinez turned to Ortega who leaned over the Ramcharger, using its hood as a writing surface. When Ortega stopped writing, Martinez took his notepad and flipped back, scanning several pages. After inspecting the notes he spoke to Ortega in Spanish and gestured toward the uniformed officers with a tilt of his chin. Ortega walked to the rear of the vehicle and led the two men a short distance away.

Martinez turned back to Mitch and Vivian. "You have been most helpful. I may have more questions later. For now, you are free to enjoy the rest of the evening. My apologies for the inconvenience."

As they were leaving, Mitch saw Ortega and the two uniformed men entering the restaurant. Bill rose to his feet as the three police officers walked toward him across the covered patio.

On the other side of the lighthouse tower, beside the ice cream parlor housed in its open base, they found Marjorie sitting at a picnic table with Victor and Sharon.

"So, how about you two?" Sharon asked. "Did you recognize any of the men in the photos?"

Vivian glanced at Mitch. "I guess we can talk about it now. Yes, we recognized two of them."

"Two?" said Victor. "We recognized only the short one in the dirty orange shirt and baseball cap."

"Where did you see him?" asked Mitch.

"We've seen him in the marina on one or two occasions, usually after dark or in the early morning hours."

"Why did they split us up the way they did?" asked Marjorie.

"I suppose they didn't want us to influence each other," answered Victor.

"But why did they have me come with Mitch and Vivian— and leave Bill by himself?"

"Yes," agreed Vivian, "that was odd."

"How is it that you recognized the two men?" Victor asked

Mitch explained how he and Vivian, and Henry and Jill, had come to know the two men.

"So it's possible," said Victor, "the fishermen became unhappy with Henry for not buying their net and decided to rob him when they observed him and Jill leaving their boat that evening?"

Mitch nodded. "I'm afraid that's how it's looking. However—"

Bill cut him off as he came huffing through the ice cream parlor and plopped down on the bench next to Vivian. "That high and mighty son-of-a-bitch," Bill's face was flushed and beads of perspiration dotted the edges of his receding hairline.

"Did you find out why they kept you alone?" asked Marjorie.

Bill shook his head and looked across the marina. "I have no idea, other than it's the international pastime of police everywhere to get their jollies messing with people's minds, especially foreigners. If he wanted us to look at some pictures, why the hell didn't he just tell Mitch that this afternoon?"

"Did you recognize any of them?" asked Mitch.

"Did *I*?, didn't you? I've seen two of 'em in the marina once or twice, and I thought for sure they're the same ones I saw in a beat-up excuse for a rowboat talking to you and Vivian alongside *Houdini* about a week ago. Didn't you recognize them?"

"Yes, we did," answered Mitch.

"Well, good. Now that they've caught the guilty bastards maybe we can get the hell out of here."

Monday, April 22

Friday and Saturday, Detectives Martinez and Ortega returned to Marina Vallarta. They visited the crews of all other transient vessels not previously questioned, showing them the photos of Carlos and Manuel. Crew members who had seen either of the two men in the marina or in the vicinity of *Walden* were asked to come to the offices of the *Policia Judicial Federal* on Monday to give official statements, along with the crews of *Dream Lover*, *Silver Cloud*, and *Houdini*.

Mitch and Vivian arrived for their appointment at 5:00 PM. According to the cruisers' grapevine, they had the distinction of being last on the schedule of seven.

Ortega met them outside Martinez' office. A large metal ring containing a single key twirled around his right index finger. He explained that Martinez hadn't quite finished interviewing another couple. Bypassing Mitch and taking Vivian by the elbow, the young detective showed them to a low brick wall in the shade of a large Strangler fig where they could sit and wait more comfortably.

When Martinez crossed the small courtyard to greet them twenty minutes later, his friendly smile and quick step seemed to indicate he was under less stress than on their previous visit. "*Buenas tardes, Señores.* My apologies for making you wait. Before we take your statements, we need to have you make a positive identification."

With Ortega following, Martinez led them into the main building and down a narrow flight of stairs to a basement. A metal door with a small, shatterproof glass window stood at the end of a long, dimly lit hallway. Ortega inserted the key in the lock and followed the door inward as it opened. Standing back against the wall, he made room for the others to enter a small anteroom outside a large holding cell. As Mitch followed Vivian into the room, he wished she'd thought to wear a skirt. Her snug shorts made her long legs look extremely naked in these surroundings.

The reality of a Mexican jail failed to live up to the horror stories. The faint but unmistakable odor of urine tinged with another acidic smell was not overpowering. And although not well lighted, the large lock-up looked relatively clean. Five men, all of them Mexican, sat on benches lining the perimeter of the cell. An exposed urinal and toilet without a seat sat in the far right corner.

Most of the men were asleep sitting down, their heads tilted to one side, resting against the concrete wall. A thin man with no shirt or shoes sat on the end of the bench closest to the front of the barred cell. His hollow eyes scanned Vivian from head to toe like a copy machine making several copies. Another man stared at the ground between his feet, supporting his head between his hands. A sixth man at the rear of the cell stood below a barred window well, his back to the visitors. His hands hung loose at his sides. He looked up toward the opening that admitted light and a small amount of precious ventilation from outside.

When everyone was inside the anteroom and the door closed behind them, Martinez signaled Ortega with the tilt of his chin.

"*Formense!*" barked Ortega. The skinny man rose to his feet, followed by the man with his head in his hands.

"*Formense!*" Ortega shouted again, causing the sleeping men to begin to stir and rise. As if rehearsed, they formed a line six feet behind the bars. "*De frente!*"

The man standing below the window turned and moved to the far end of the line. Mitch recognized him immediately. It was Carlos, the fisherman he'd shared a beer with on a hot afternoon, hardly more than a week ago. He no longer had his baseball hat but still wore the same soiled T-shirt he wore in the picture taken with Martinez. His legs below his brown shorts were a mass of scrapes and scratches as were his forearms. As he assumed his place in the line-up, he glanced to his right and saw Mitch looking at him. He immediately looked away, staring straight ahead. His face slowly contorted into a frozen mask of deep furrows and protruding lips.

Vivian stood partially behind Mitch, holding on to his left arm as they viewed the line of pathetic figures. Mitch looked at the man who had been sitting with his head cradled in his hands. His eyes met Mitch's for an instant, then quickly averted. It was Manuel.

Martinez waited until Mitch and Vivian shifted their attention from the line-up to him. "Do you see the men here you saw last Tuesday, speaking with Mr. Fullerton at his yacht?"

"Yes," said Mitch, "the man on the end is Carlos and this one is Manuel."

"Señora Sanford?"

"Yes, it's them," Vivian whispered.

Martinez reached for his Marlboros while exchanging a long glance with Ortega. Mitch couldn't tell if their nearly blank expressions indicated resignation or satisfaction. Martinez lit his cigarette and blew a cloud of smoke toward the cell. "We are finished here."

Ortega dismissed the prisoners and they slowly moved toward their places on the bench, except Carlos, who remained standing, staring straight ahead through the bars.

Back in his office, Martinez picked up a cardboard box from behind his chair and set it on the desk. He opened the flaps and began placing objects in front of Mitch: a yellow sports model Sony video camera, a Nikon 35mm camera and a laptop computer.

"Do you recognize any of these items?" he asked them.

Considering the expression on Vivian's face, it surprised Mitch that Martinez had to ask the question. They had been the target of Henry's camcorder dozens of times during the last nine months.

"Yes," said Mitch, "those all belonged to Henry and Jill."

Martinez motioned for Ortega to take the items of evidence away while he punched four numbers on his phone. When the party at the other end answered, he said a word or two in rapid Spanish and hung up without waiting for a reply.

Within seconds an attractive young woman appeared at the office door holding a pen and yellow legal pad attached to a clipboard across her chest. She wore a beige dress suit, cream colored long-sleeved blouse and dark-rimmed glasses. Her raven hair was pulled back severely and tied in a neat bun. She paused in the doorway until receiving a nod from Martinez then entered.

Ortega moved quickly behind a fourth chair that had been brought in and placed on Martinez' left. The young detective adjusted the chair's position slightly, as if to make sure it was in the most convenient location for her to do her work. She regarded him coolly, took the seat, crossed her legs and balanced the clipboard on her right knee.

"Señor Sanford," began Martinez, "I am going to restate what you have previously told me and my trusted associate, Señor Ortega, *who will now return to his work*." Ortega tore his eyes away from the young woman, glanced at Martinez, and left.

"Señorita Torres will record what I say as if it were your own words. If at any time I am incorrect or if you wish to change your statement, please stop me. Is that understood?"

Mitch and Vivian answered "yes" in unison.

Referring to his and Ortega's notes, Martinez recounted how Mitch had boarded *Walden* and discovered the bodies. Item-by-item, he went through the things Mitch had said were missing. It amazed Mitch, even with notes, at how accurately Martinez could recite nearly his exact words. The detective paused occasionally to ask him if he had related his statements correctly. It was almost an hour before Martinez concluded with a short statement from Vivian, indicating that the two men she had just identified were the same men she had seen on at least one occasion visiting the victims' sailboat a few days before the night of the murders.

"Very well, if you have no further additions or changes, Señorita Torres will prepare...wait, there is one more question I should have asked. Can either of you tell me if the suspects were acquainted with the people on the vessel, *Phoenix*?"

"Yes," Mitch replied, "they knew them well. They gave Jim fresh fish almost every day. I think he gave them fishhooks and beer in return."

"I see. As I was saying before, Señorita Torres will prepare two typed copies for you to sign, one in English and one in Spanish. She will certify that the Spanish translation matches your statements in English. I will then need you to come to our office once again to review and sign them in her presence. Is that clear?"

"Yes," answered Mitch.

"I will detain you no longer then. Thank you for coming."

Vivian started to rise but hesitated when Mitch failed to move.

"Yes, Mr. Sanford, there is something else?"

"I was wondering if you could now share with us how you came to arrest those two men?"

Martinez leaned back in his chair rolling a pencil between the thumbs and index fingers of each hand. "I suppose you have a right to know." The stenographer rose from her chair. "*Gracias, Maria, hasta pronto.*" She said good day to Mitch and Vivian and disappeared out the door.

"When you were here last Thursday you will recall our meeting was interrupted. We received a call from a storekeeper who buys and sells used merchandise. Ordinarily, this man is not overly concerned where the items he buys come from. But in this instance he became nervous when he realized the video camera he had purchased that very morning matched the description given him by a city police officer an hour later. As you know, it is an unusual, distinctive model. If it were not for the seriousness of the crime and the publicity, I doubt we would ever have heard from him. Fortunately, he panicked and called us."

"He identified Carlos and Manuel as the men who sold him the video camera?" Mitch asked.

"Yes. We had been searching for the two men for questioning, based on your original statement and description, but had been unable to locate them. The information received from the storekeeper told me he had dealt with the same individuals. When we arrived at these men's homes to question them, we found they had been warned we were coming and had fled into the hills. It was relatively simple to apprehend them with dogs and horses."

"That's what all their scratches and bruises are from?" asked Vivian.

"Yes, Señora. We have not tortured them, if that it is what you thought."

Vivian glanced at Mitch, then back to Martinez. "Have they confessed?"

"Not yet. They claim they found these items in a trash receptacle at Marina Vallarta."

"I suppose that's possible," said Mitch.

"But not likely. The preponderance of evidence suggests otherwise. Aside from having possession of items belonging to the victims, these men's fingerprints match those found on the victims' yacht. We also discovered a small number of fish scales on the steps leading down into the cabin and on the cabin floor which match the type of scales in the bottom of the suspect's rowboat."

Martinez paused to open a drawer in his desk and remove a manila envelope. "And finally, we have this." He opened the envelope and let a wooden handled knife slide on to the desk in the beam of sunlight that passed between Mitch and Vivian. Its thin eight-inch, slightly rusted blade swept up in a shallow curve to a fine point. The area where the metal of the blade entered the wooden handle was speckled with fish scales glinting like sequins in the late afternoon sunlight.

"It looks like a filleting knife," said Mitch.

"Yes," said Martinez, "it is a common knife, the kind used by many local fishermen." Martinez leaned forward and rolled the knife over. Crudely carved in the handle were the letters C-A-R-L-O-S.

Vivian's hand came up to cover her mouth.

"One of our divers retrieved it from the bottom of the canal between the Fullertons' yacht and the old tourist boat. The knife's blade is consistent with the configuration of the victims' wounds."

"I see what you mean about preponderance of evidence," said Mitch.

"In their haste to load the stolen goods into their boat and leave, it is likely that one of them dropped the knife in the water. Good for me, bad for them."

"I take it they have no alibis for that night?"

"The marina harbormaster ordered them out of the marina just before dark, about 7 o'clock. They claim they rowed out to where they hide their boat in the mangroves near the mouth of the Rio Salado. They say they sat around talking and drinking for awhile, and then walked home, arriving sometime before 10 o'clock."

"What do you think they really did?" Mitch wasn't sure he wanted an answer.

Martinez ran the fingers of one hand through the hair at the nape of his neck. "I'll tell you what the evidence suggests. Señora, do you mind if I smoke?"

"No. Please, go ahead," Vivian answered.

Martinez withdrew a cigarette and tamped the filter end on the corner of his desk. "The harbormaster observed the suspects rowing their boat out of the marina and down the main canal toward the harbor. But instead of heading up the side canal behind Isla Iguana, they saw your friends' vessel dark and still. The fishermen had been at the marina when the two of you met the Fullertons. It is likely they observed the four of you dressed for an evening out and on your way into town."

Martinez paused to light his cigarette. "The victims' sailboat is isolated, shielded from view of other boats in the anchorage by the old charter boat. Rowing between it and the Fullerton's sailboat, the fishermen are mostly hidden from vessels transiting the channel as well. What little moon there was that night had yet to rise. It is very dark.

"They realize they have what you call a golden opportunity. And perhaps they are angry with the harbormaster or Señor Fullerton. They climb quietly aboard, pry the lock open, and begin removing items from the cabin. While they are searching for valuables, they hear the sound of an outboard motor coming alongside.

"They panic. They do not expect the Fullertons back so soon. One man hides in the toilet compartment, the other in the sleeping room beside the steps coming down. The Fullertons board their vessel but do not see the small boat tied to the opposite side. Even in daylight it could go unnoticed there.

"But they find the lock broken. They know there has been an intruder." Martinez shook his head. "Here they make a fatal mistake. Hearing nothing and seeing nothing, they go below. They think the thieves have gone. Perhaps Señora Fullerton remains in the cockpit or at the bottom of the steps. When Señor Fullerton opens the door to the toilet compartment, he is stabbed through the heart and killed instantly. Before Señora Fullerton realizes what has happened, she is either grabbed from behind or pulled down into the cabin. She may have screamed but no one heard."

"Was she...raped?" Mitch asked.

"No, Señor, we do not believe so. From the blood stains on her clothes, it appears as though they were removed after her throat was cut, and then—" Martinez halted as Vivian dropped her face into her hands. "I beg your pardon, Señora, I should not have—"

"It's not your fault, I'll be okay." Mitch put an arm around her shoulders.

"As I said," continued Martinez, "it is possible Señora Fullerton screamed. In any case, the murderers took what they had and fled." Martinez leaned back into his swivel chair and inhaled a long drag from his cigarette. "Except for one or two details and a confession, that is what the evidence suggests."

"Do you think they will confess?" asked Vivian, regaining her composure.

"I do not believe they yet comprehend the degree of evidence against them, Señora. Once that reality is absorbed, there is a good chance they will confess."

Mitch stood and extended his hand. "Thanks, Señor Martinez, it helps to know what happened. When do you want us to return and sign our statements?"

Martinez stood and accepted Mitch's handshake. "Señorita Torres has volunteered to work late. She hopes to have all the statements ready for signatures tomorrow afternoon. But if you could wait until Wednesday it would make her job easier."

"That's fine. We're in no rush."

"Then you are the only ones who aren't, Señor. All the others wished to know how soon they would be free to leave Puerto Vallarta."

"Is the *Capitania de Puerto* going to begin clearing yachts again?" asked Vivian.

Martinez stubbed out his cigarette, grinding it into the ashtray. "It is my understanding, Señora, that he will recommence granting clearances on Wednesday, barring any new developments in the case."

"You don't sound too pleased," Vivian replied.

"I would prefer the restrictions be maintained until we have a confession. However, my commander is satisfied, and many of the yacht owners have expressed concerns about the approach of hurricane season. Also, our mayor and several businessmen have suggested it would be in everyone's best interest to let foreign yachts leave Puerto Vallarta."

Thursday, April 25

By Tuesday morning, news that the port captain would soon resume granting clearances to leave Puerto Vallarta had become common knowledge. The ship-to-ship radio channels once again crackled with the chatter of friends trading departure plans and last good-byes. Crews hoisted their dinghies on deck and scrubbed them clean. Sail covers came off and the exodus began.

With their own plans in limbo, Mitch had fallen into the habit of escaping into a novel immediately after breakfast. Two loud blasts of an air horn levitated him off the settee.

"Shit-oh-dear!, that sounded close." He followed Vivian as she bolted up the companionway.

"It's *Dream Lover*. She's on her way out," said Vivian, watching as the large white yacht crossed in front of them.

Mitch followed Vivian to *Houdini*'s bow for a closer look. "Damn, that's a big boat for two people."

Sharon stood waving from the vast expanse of foredeck as they passed. "We'll miss you two!" she called. "Wish you were coming with us."

Victor stepped away from the wheel in the big cutter's pilot house long enough for a quick wave. "Send a post card to Atuona and let us know what happens."

"Will do," shouted Mitch, managing a smile. "Write and tell us about the Marquesas."

Vivian cupped her hands around her mouth. "You two take care and have a safe passage."

Sharon gave them one last wave, then turned her attention to the next boat in the line. Marjorie stood in *Silver Cloud*'s bow waving back to her. Bill walked forward from *Silver Cloud*'s cockpit in time to give Victor a parting salute.

Mitch called over to Bill. "What about you two? When are you leaving?"

"Right now," Bill answered.

"Need any help with your stern anchor?"

"Be much obliged, Mitch."

Five pulls on the dinghy's oars brought Mitch to *Silver Cloud*'s transom. Standing in the inflatable, he pulled himself hand-over-hand toward the shallows along the slackened anchor rode. When the short chain lead came up vertical, three successive upward jerks broke the wedge-shaped anchor free of the muddy sand. Bill pulled the anchor line in, towing Mitch and the inflatable back to *Silver Cloud*'s stern. Mitch repeatedly dunked the anchor near the surface, splashing the mud loose from its flukes then handed it up to Bill.

"Thanks, Mitch. You two made up your minds on what you're going to do?"

"Not yet. We may head up to the Sea of Cortez, or we may stay here and follow the trial."

"I wouldn't mind seein' those two Mexican cutthroats get a taste of their own justice myself." Bill stood and looked toward the bow. "Okay Marj, start takin' up on the chain."

Marjorie used the heel of her right foot to press a large, rubber-covered button on *Silver Cloud*'s foredeck. Immediately, the electric windlass commenced hauling in the heavy chain.

Mitch watched from astern as the windlass pulled the ketch toward mid-channel. From the corner of his eye he caught a movement in *Tango*, the sailboat on *Silver Cloud*'s port side. *Tango* edged slowly toward *Silver Cloud* though no one was on deck.

"Bill," Marjorie shouted, "the chain's not coming in as fast as it normally does."

"I think you've snagged *Tango*'s chain," Mitch yelled.

Bill looked over as the other boat's bow converged with *Silver Cloud*'s. "Stop, Marj!"

Mitch rowed quickly between the two boats. "Have you got a boat hook handy?"

"Marj! Give Mitch the boat hook!"

Mitch reached *Silver Cloud*'s bow and Marjorie handed him the long aluminum pole with a small knobbed hook at one end. "Marjorie, bring your anchor up slowly to where I can get the boat hook under *Tango*'s chain. Then lower the anchor until it's clear and pull it up."

Bill remained at *Silver Cloud*'s wheel alternating forward and reverse gear to keep from hitting the other boat, not much more than six feet away.

"There, that's good, Marjorie, I see it." Mitch reached down with the boat hook, snagged the other boat's chain and braced himself to take its load. "Okay, lower your anchor!"

Mitch hadn't fully considered the amount of tension on the other vessel's heavy chain. He managed to hold it up for the brief moment it took Marjorie to lower *Silver Cloud*'s anchor and clear it. The boat hook then snatched Mitch out of the dinghy before he could take a breath.

From her vantage point on *Houdini*'s bow, Vivian had been concentrating on Marjorie's efforts. She heard the splash, and saw the ripples and watched the inflatable drift out of sight behind *Silver Cloud*. "Marjorie! What happened? Where'd Mitch go?"

"I don't know! He was there a second ago."

Mitch refused to let go of the pole and spiraled down into the murky water. When it felt like his eardrums were about to implode, the chain's tension eased and his descent stopped. He pushed the pole toward the bottom to free it, but the knob at the end of the pole's hook had become wedged between the links.

"Marjorie!" Vivian shouted. "Where is he?"

Mitch gave the pole a vicious thrust, popping the hook free, stabbing it into the muddy bottom. Pulling himself down, he placed his feet in the mud and lunged upward toward the light. He broke the surface, gasping for breath and flailing for the dinghy.

After putting the boat hook in the dinghy, he looked up at Marjorie. "Guess we need more practice on that one."

Bill eased *Silver Cloud* forward into the channel. Mitch clambered aboard his dinghy and caught hold of a midships lifeline stanchion as the 42-foot ketch moved slowly past him. "Here's your boat hook, Marjorie."

Marjorie knelt, took the pole and spoke barely above a whisper. "Good-bye, Mitch." She tried to smile but managed only a crinkling of her eyes.

"So long, Marjorie. You take care."

"You too. And take care of Vivian." She glanced at Bill, then held out her hand to Mitch. "You haven't told her, have you?"

Mitch took her hand and gave it a gentle squeeze. "Not yet. I take it you haven't said anything to Bill."

"He stopped asking after...what happened," Marjorie whispered.

Mitch nodded, let go of the stanchion and drifted aft.

"What a hell of a way to get started," Bill shouted, as Mitch slid past him.

"This was the hard part, Bill. It'll all be downhill to the Marquesas from here."

"I hope you're right. Thanks, Mitch; sorry you're not headin' our way." The parting remark sounded more perfunctory than sincere.

"So long, Bill." Mitch watched them motor away as he rowed back to *Houdini*. He wished better times for Marjorie, but didn't share any regrets Bill might truly hold over their parting.

Once back aboard *Houdini*, Mitch walked forward to where Vivian continued watching *Silver Cloud's* departure. Standing close behind her, he put his arms around her waist.

"You're all wet. Are you okay?" she asked.

"I'm fine."

Silver Cloud turned west toward the harbor entrance. Her bow began to rise and fall on the small swells coming in from Banderas Bay.

"Are you sorry we're not going?" Vivian asked.

"Yes, but only for one reason. I know it's what Henry would have wanted."

Monday, April 29

Vivian glanced at her watch. She'd stood bent at the waist, gazing out the port hole over the chart table for several minutes and hadn't yet come up with a satisfactory way to open the conversation she wanted to have. A short distance up-channel from *Houdini,* a young couple emerged from the cabin of their light-displacement sloop and began checking the tension of its rigging. Vivian turned partly sideways, leaned on one arm and crossed her tanned legs. When she spoke, she refrained from looking down at Mitch lying on the settee. "Looks like the couple on *Mar* are getting ready to leave."

Mitch didn't stir from behind his paperback. She'd be damned if she'd ask him again. It was clear he hadn't given any thought to their own next move. Or, if he had, he hadn't been in a mood to share them.

In the four days since *Silver Cloud* and *Dream Lover*'s departures, a steady stream of yachts had sailed out of Puerto Vallarta. *Houdini*'s cabin was beginning to feel like a prison cell. Even a short move into the marina, or six miles up the coast to Nuevo Vallarta, would feel like progress. Watching the crews of the other vessels resume their travels—and their lives—reminded Vivian how suspended and indefinite her own had become.

She cleared her throat. "There'll be only two of us left in The Pond after *Mar* leaves." This time she glanced down at him. His book tilted half an inch then raised back up.

It wasn't as if she didn't know or sense what he was going through. Henry and Jill had been his friends originally, but in the seventeen years since she and Mitch first met, she had become very close to both of them. Jill had been her closest friend outside her cronies at the clinic.

Mitch dealt with his grief differently than she did. He gave in to it, submerged in it, let it enfold him like a cocoon. Between spontaneous bouts of crying Vivian had gone through her own periods of silent grieving. But with the slow acceptance of their friends' deaths, came the need to go forward, to resume living, now that the storm of tragedy had passed.

"Mitch, we can't sit here forever." She sensed the book had dropped but resisted the urge to look at him or to soften her accusatory tone.

After a long pause, he said, "Another day won't make a big difference. Tomorrow I'll go check with the marina harbor master about renting a slip."

"So, have *we* decided that we are staying in Puerto Vallarta?"

"That would be the easiest thing to do."

He still wasn't tuned in. "So now we're doing whatever's easiest?" Finally, she turned. He looked utterly defenseless but she let the edged words hang between them.

"Vivian, what? What is it? What do you want?"

"I would like to know what we're doing. I would like to discuss our plans."

"I *said*, I'll go see the harbor master tomorrow."

"Thanks for involving me in the decision." She grabbed her running shoes and sat down at the chart table. She felt his eyes on her flushing cheeks as she jerked the laces into tight bows. "In case you're interested, I'm taking the dinghy to the port captain's office to check for mail. I may go for a walk after that, so I'm not sure when I'll be back." She half-expected him to attempt to calm her down. She slowed at the top of the steps, but he said nothing.

She boarded the dinghy, choked the engine and whipped it to life with one determined jerk of its starter cord. She scooted across the rippled harbor, controlling the tiller with her left hand and trapping a large straw hat on top of her head with the other. Although she still lacked confidence at *Houdini*'s helm, the ten-foot inflatable had become as familiar to her as the family car.

The short walk from the old cruise ship pier to the port captain's office helped her think. Mitch sometimes made minor decisions himself and then innocently asked her opinion as if the question were still open to discussion. She knew that game. She got a kick out of maneuvering him into admitting those little deceits. He would get embarrassed and apologize. It was one of the things she loved about him.

But this was not a minor decision. It determined where they would shelter for the hurricane season, and it was the first step in the continuation of their disrupted lives. Mitch wasn't playing by the rules. He was supposed to talk to her.

He probably wasn't yet thinking about the future, hadn't really made a decision—until she pushed him. Maybe she'd been too harsh. It was only a couple of days ago that she herself had started to think seriously about their options. One unpleasant thought kept pestering her. Her license to practice still had two months to go before it expired. If she returned now, took a few hours of continuing education classes, and resumed her practice, she could avoid major re-licensing hassles. But after ten months of sailing, hiking, swimming and spending hours of carefree time with Mitch, the thought of sitting bent over a dental chair with her rubber-gloved hands in people's mouths all day sounded like a reasonable description of the outskirts of Hell.

Inside the front door of the port captain's office, she knelt beside a large white plastic tub filled with mail for yachts in transit. She flipped through unsorted letters and thick manila envelopes. She was neither surprised nor disappointed when her search came up empty. Her last call to the mail forwarding service in Seattle had instructed them to hold all mail until further notice, on the assumption they would be en route to the Marquesas. She stood and turned to leave.

"*Señora* Sanford?"

Vivian looked to see a Mexican woman in a gray suit standing behind the counter. "Yes?"

"I wasn't sure it was you, *Señora*. We have been trying to reach you by radio since yesterday afternoon."

Vivian walked to the counter. "I'm sorry. I guess we haven't been turning it on the last day or two. Is there something wrong?"

"No, *Señora*, no problem. We received a telephone call for your husband late yesterday morning. I took the message." She handed Vivian a slip of pink paper.

Vivian read the note: *Mitch Sanford, call Frank Fullerton, not urgent.* She let go of the deep breath she was holding. She hated receiving cryptic messages to phone home. She always feared it was bad news about her mother.

"*Gracias,*" said Vivian, "I'll see that my husband gets this."

Vivian's sudden angry departure cracked the shell Mitch had let form around him. He couldn't blame her for her reaction. She had a right to be upset—for more reasons than she knew.

She was right. They had to move forward. It was time he stopped absorbing himself in past events, events he could not alter. When he heard the outboard, he went up to the cockpit to meet her.

"That was quick," he said, taking the bow line for her.

She met his eyes briefly. "I decided I could do without the walk."

He quickly tied the line and helped her up the boarding ladder, pulling her to him as she stepped to the deck. "Hey Babe, I know I've been kind of a putz the past few days. It's just..."

"Henry and Jill were my friends too, Mitch," she said, nestling her chin on his shoulder.

"I sort of forgot that. You want to talk about whether we should rent a slip here or start heading north?"

Vivian reached into the front pocket of her shorts and pulled out the small square of pink paper. "Yes, but first, maybe you should take care of this."

He continued holding her with one arm while he read the note.

"The port captain's been trying to reach us since yesterday morning. Frank's probably wondering why you haven't called."

"Guess I'd better go call him."

Vivian tightened her arms around him, giving him her first smile in days. "Not without a kiss first."

Mitch stuffed the note in his pocket and pulled her close again. He kissed her softly, a romantic, first-date kiss. He massaged the small of her back. "You want to come with me?"

"No, you go ahead. I'll stay and listen to the news and decide what to make for dinner."

———————

Frank answered after ten rings.

"Hi Frank. It's Mitch. How are you doing?"

"It's tough, Mitch. The news of the arrests helped, but it's been a week since the funeral and we still can't believe it. If it weren't for Fred and Chuck..."

"I know, it's been the same here.

"Mitch, it was about Fred and Chuck that I called. They're planning a trip down to make arrangements to have Walden shipped back, that is, unless they can make a quick sale down there."

"How soon are they coming?"

"They can't both get away until a week from tomorrow."

"No need to worry, Frank. Marina Vallarta is providing a slip for *Walden* and the police have posted a guard. She's safe and sound for the moment."

"That's good to hear. Say, if there's anything you and Vivian need off her—food, supplies, equipment, whatever—it's yours."

Mitch paused, his eyes began to mist over. "Thanks, Frank, that's very thoughtful. We were all provisioned and ready to go ourselves when—when this happened. But I'll mention it to Vivian and see what she thinks."

"One other thing. Jill's parents called last night. They asked if you'd do them a favor."

"I'll try. What is it?"

"They say Jill always kept a journal. They have a copy of one she kept when she backpacked through Europe. It would mean a lot to them to have the one she started on this trip. You think you could find it and mail it to them?"

Mitch remembered the dark brown, gold-trimmed book. "Yes, Frank, I've seen it several times. I may need permission from the police to board *Walden*."

"I have an appointment to call Detective Martinez tomorrow morning. I'll tell him about Jill's parents' request and that you have our permission to retrieve the journal and take anything else off you or Vivian want."

"That would speed things up."

"Consider it done. Will you still be in Puerto Vallarta when Fred and Chuck get down there?"

Mitch looked across the harbor toward *Houdini*. "That's a distinct possibility, Frank. It's beginning to look as though we may spend the hurricane season here in Puerto Vallarta."

"I know Fred and Chuck would appreciate any help or advice you can give them. Say, maybe Vivian and I could set up a schedule on the ham radio. She could let us know when they have arrived and maybe help us keep tabs on them, that is if you don't think she'd mind."

"I think she'd love to help. We can even have Chuck and Fred aboard *Houdini* so they can talk with you directly. I'll have her call you to set up a time and frequency."

"No need to make another long distance phone call. Just tell her to leave a message for me with the Mañana Net. I'll check in with the net every day until we make contact."

Tuesday, April 30

Mitch waited until after lunch to call Martinez.

"Yes, Mr. Sanford," said Martinez, *"I received a call from Mr. Fullerton."*

"He told you about his daughter-in-law's journal?"

"Yes, he did. And you have my permission to retrieve it and send it to her parents—with one condition."

"Which is?"

"Before you mail it, I would like you to bring it to my office so I may inspect it."

Mitch wondered if he wasn't overdoing it a bit. "Sure, no problem."

"When do you think you might have it?"

"If your guard will let me go aboard, I'll head over there right now."

"I have already notified him," said Martinez. *"He is expecting you."*

"How would it be if I bring the journal to your office tomorrow morning?"

"I would prefer you bring it to me this afternoon, Señor Sanford, if that is not too much trouble."

The young guard sitting on *Walden*'s caprail moved quickly to his feet and flipped a cigarette butt into the water as Mitch steered the red inflatable into slip number three on O-dock. He stepped out of the dinghy and faced the young man, who appeared grateful for a break in his monotonous duty.

"*Señor* Sanford?"

"*Si.*" Mitch pointed to *Walden*'s cockpit. "Okay?, *con su permiso?*"

"*Si, si,* okay, okay." The stocky, short-haired officer gestured with both hands for Mitch to go aboard. "*No hay problema, Señor.*"

Mitch stepped over the gunnel to the deck and into the cockpit. All three of the cutter's deck hatches were tilted open at 45-degree angles. The companionway doors and main hatch were open as well. The police had allowed the boat to ventilate. That lessened one of his concerns.

Contrary to plan, he hesitated at the dodger rather than proceed directly down the companionway. The images returned. He'd managed to repress them all the way from *Houdini* to the marina. Now his heartbeat raced and he was hyperventilating. His attempts to control his emotions brought on the exact symptoms he hoped to avoid. Dizzy, he leaned against the dodger and brought one hand to his forehead.

"*Señor, está bien?*

Mitch took two slow breaths before answering. "*Si, estoy bien, gracias.*"

When the dizziness faded, he bent under the dodger and stepped to the companionway. Rarely had he been aboard *Walden* absent the sounds of conversations, or meals being prepared, or a movie playing on the VCR. Now she was quiet, with only the creaking of teak steps as he reluctantly descended the companionway. A cloud of flies lifted into the air as he entered the galley. He swatted at them, shooing them away from his face, not wanting to inhale one. He moved slowly forward into the cabin.

All of the beige settee cushions had been removed except the few that had little or no bloodstains. The Persian design carpet runner was also missing from the cabin sole. Only vague outlines remained on the floor where blood once pooled. Someone had cleaned the cabin, erasing the worst reminders of the violent deaths that had occurred there.

Although diminished in strength, the sickening odors still lingered. They could not be confused with anything other than what they were. It would take a thorough scrubbing of the interior with disinfectants and weeks of ventilation to eliminate them. Perhaps there would always be a vague aroma that would remain a mystery to the yacht's future owners. The thought of *Walden* belonging to anyone but Henry was inconceivable. It made as much sense to Mitch as Henry being married to someone other than Jill. The boat had been part of Henry's identity.

A beam of sunlight caught his attention where it slanted through a porthole and reflected off a brass plaque mounted on the forward bulkhead. He read the words again.

I went to the woods because I wished to live deliberately, to front only the essential facts of life, and see if I could not learn what it had to teach, and not, when I came to die, discover that I had not lived.

Henry David Thoreau

The first time Mitch had gone aboard *Walden*, she was brand new, still being commissioned in the boatyard. Henry had shown him the freshly engraved plaque and said: "All you have to do is substitute 'sea' for 'woods' and Thoreau's philosophy becomes my own."

Thoreau was Henry's prophet, and the boat bore the name of the philosopher's famous pond in his honor. The irony of Henry's death in a place known as The Pond dawned on Mitch for the first time. The reality of it brought him back to the present and to the task at hand.

The books, papers and other items Mitch had found strewn around the cabin that unforgettable morning were now neatly stacked on the chart table. He began his search for Jill's journal there, shifting books and manuals from stack to stack. In addition to navigational texts and equipment manuals, there were piles of paperback novels. Mitch adjusted the stacks as he searched, facing bloodstained edges toward the hull.

Not finding the journal on the chart table, he started through the lockers and bookshelves backing the settees on both sides of the boat. He found video tapes, canned goods and boxes of diskettes for the laptop computer.

All three of *Walden*'s sleeping berths had large bookshelves beside them. He went to the forward cabin first, where Jill and Henry normally slept when they were in port or at anchor. Mitch felt uncomfortable entering the privacy of what had recently been their bedroom. Bookshelves lined the hull, converging forward toward the chain locker. He carefully searched the contents of each shelf.

At the very end of the starboard shelf, he found Henry's copy of *Walden and Other Writings by Henry David Thoreau*. He pulled it from the shelf and made one final scan of the other books. The leather-bound diary was not among them.

He didn't expect to find the journal in either of the aft cabins, but he had run out of places to look. His search of their bookshelves yielded only more paperbacks, stashed away for the day when fresh reading material would be hard to find.

He considered the possibilities. The fishermen wouldn't have taken it. Maybe in their frenzied search for valuables they threw it overboard. But if the divers had recovered anything resembling a journal, Martinez would have said something, or would he?

He thought to look for Henry's log. He cleared the chart table, lifted the hinged top until its large spring support snapped into place. *Walden*'s deck log sat atop a pile of neatly folded and numbered charts. He picked it up and thumbed through until he came to the last page with entries. Henry's terse penciled printing recorded *Walden*'s anchoring in The Pond more than a month earlier.

Mitch turned around and scanned *Walden*'s cabin for likely hiding places. A methodical search starting at one point and working his way around the hull through all the cabins was his only option. He'd either find her journal or satisfy himself that it was not on board.

It required more than two hours to find and search every one of *Walden*'s lockers, cubbyholes and hidden compartments. When he gave up, it was nearly 5 o'clock. Taking Henry's log and the Thoreau book with him, he emerged into the fresh air. The young police officer inspected the books, made notations in his pocket notebook and wished Mitch a good evening.

On his way back to The Pond, he pulled in at the Opequimar boatyard to phone Martinez. The detective had left for the day. Mitch left a message saying he would see him in the morning.

Vivian waited at the boarding ladder as he coasted up to *Houdini* and killed the outboard. "What happened? I was ready to swim ashore and come looking for you."

"I couldn't find the journal."

"What's that in your hand?"

"Henry's log and a book he was always after me to read."

"You've been looking for the journal all this time?"

"Except for a stop at Opequimar to call Martinez. Viv, I went through everything on that boat. If Jill's journal is on *Walden*, it must be fiberglassed into the hull because I looked everywhere else."

"What would anybody want with her journal?"

He'd started asking himself the same question a few hours ago. He tied the dinghy's bow line to the stern cleat before answering. "I don't know, I can't figure it out either." That was a lie. An uncomfortable feeling, a dull ache from deep in his bowels grew stronger by the minute. He could think of a reason why one person might have wanted it.

That night, he lay awake long after Vivian's breathing assumed the slow rhythm of sound sleep. One of the last things he'd heard Jill say kept running through his mind. She'd said she'd been catching up her journal in *Walden's* cockpit when Bill came by looking for Henry. Unbeknownst to Jill, that would have been shortly after Bill discovered Marjorie aboard *Silver Cloud* in her freshly ravished state. Jill stated that Bill had muttered some ambiguous comments and left. Bill's comments probably seemed much less ambiguous to him. Or perhaps they were in fact quite clear, and Jill felt uncomfortable repeating them.

Mitch's chest ached from involuntary tensing of the muscles around his ribs. He owed Martinez an explanation. He hadn't told him everything. And it was probably time for a confession to Vivian as well. He wasn't looking forward to either session, particularly the latter.

Yet it was an even more disturbing prospect that kept him awake and started the tear forming in the corner of his left eye. The possibility seemed remote, but the odds made it no less terrifying. If Bill took the journal, it was highly likely that he also killed Henry and Jill. It also meant that Mitch's act of adultery had triggered the murder of his two closest friends.

Wednesday, May 1

Mitch waited outside Martinez' office in the shade of the Strangler fig. It wasn't yet noon but already he felt sluggish from the heat and lack of sleep. At breakfast he had toyed with his oatmeal, searching for plausible reasons why Vivian ought not to accompany him to the police station. He assumed she would want to hear what Martinez made of the missing journal. Unfortunately, she would hear his own theory of its significance as well. Martinez' office was not a good place for Vivian to hear that story for the first time. And maybe, just maybe, the detective had knowledge that would invalidate his theory of the journal's connection with the murders.

Vivian saved him from subterfuge by asking if he minded if she stayed aboard. She wanted to compose a letter to Jill's parents, telling them how happy Jill and Henry had been the past few months, somewhat filling in the gap created by the missing journal. She also admitted to a craving for chocolate chip cookies and planned to bake a big batch after finishing the letter.

"Señor Sanford," hailed a familiar voice, "please come in." The tall detective filled the doorway to his office. Mitch entered, sat in one of the two chairs and placed Henry's log in the other.

"You found Señora Fullerton's journal?" Martinez asked.

"No, I'm afraid not," Mitch replied.

"I see." Martinez placed his elbows on the desk and clasped his hands. "Then what is that, may I ask?" He used his chin to point toward the empty chair.

"This is Henry's logbook. I thought it might be of use to you."

Martinez settled into his swivel chair and crossed his legs. "I have read it."

"You've read this?"

"Yes, Señor Sanford, even in Mexico, we are sometimes competent."

Mitch felt his face grow suddenly warm. "I'm sorry, I didn't mean..."

"No apology necessary, Señor. Do you mind?" Martinez shook a cigarette from his pack.

"No, go right ahead." The match ignited before Mitch finished answering.

"There is nothing in Señor Fullerton's navigational log relevant to this case." Martinez punctuated his sentence with a stream of blue smoke aimed at the ceiling. "It hadn't occurred to me Señora Fullerton might have kept a diary."

"Until Frank Fullerton called you."

"Precisely. I had Ortega search for it yesterday morning. When he failed, I thought perhaps you might know of a secret hiding place."

"That's one of the things that's been bothering me. Jill didn't hide her journal. She left it lying out. She liked to add to it several times a day."

Martinez said nothing. He stroked his chin with the hand that held the cigarette, his gaze fixed on Mitch. "Señor Sanford, I have this feeling I sometimes get when I believe people have something they wish to tell me."

Mitch looked down at his feet. "The fishermen still haven't confessed?"

"No, not yet."

"I may not have answered all your questions as completely as I should have."

"How so, Señor?" Martinez stubbed out his half-smoked cigarette.

"I told you about the incident, the fight, between Bill and Henry at the yacht club."

"You, and many others as well."

"Yes. Well, what I didn't tell you is that Bill suspected Henry of seducing his wife later that morning."

Martinez tucked his chin and squinted. "Señora Schneider? And Señor Fullerton? Why would...?" The detective's eyes opened wide. "Ah, *poner los cuernos a el!*"

"Excuse me?" said Mitch.

"Señor Fullerton seduced Señora Schneider to put the horns on Señor Schneider, to make him the *cornudo*. What is the English word...?"

"Cuckold?"

"Ah." Martinez took a pencil from his desk drawer and wrote in his pocket notebook. He then settled back and began rotating the pencil between the tips of his thumbs and index fingers. "I do not understand why you would not tell me this before. Señor Fullerton was your close friend, no? Why would you want to conceal Señor Schneider's possible motive for the crime?"

"When I saw how Jill and Henry were murdered, and all the things that had been stolen, I assumed they'd been robbed. Plus Bill and Marjorie were at the restaurant with us. Then Carlos and Manuel were arrested. But now..."

"Señor Sanford, how do you know Señor Schneider suspected Señor Fullerton of seducing his wife?"

Mitch cleared his throat. "After the confrontation at the yacht club, Marjorie wanted to return to her boat." Mitch painfully recounted an abbreviated but nonetheless embarrassing summary of the events that had transpired on *Silver Cloud*. Martinez' pencil stopped rotating. His stoic expression dissolved, his jaw sagging millimeter by millimeter as Mitch went on to recite his conversation with Marjorie that evening at *Los Arbolitos*. "She told me Bill was convinced it was Henry instead of me."

"And did Señor Schneider exhibit any hostility toward Señor Fullerton at *Los Arbolitos*?"

Mitch nodded. "My wife commented that he was glaring at Henry. It was about that time that Jill mentioned her journal. She said she was writing in it when Bill came by, acting strange and looking for Henry."

Martinez sank back into his chair and recommenced the rolling of his pencil. He seemed to appraise Mitch carefully for the first time. "So it is possible that Señor Schneider, having discovered his wife's indiscretion, went to the Fullerton vessel seeking satisfaction. Instead, he finds Señora Fullerton alone. Perhaps he makes some vague threats, which he later regrets, having noted Señora Fullerton making notes in her diary."

Mitch felt as if he were physically shrinking in the detective's steady gaze. "If only I'd...but I still can't see how Bill could have done it. He and Marjorie were still at the restaurant when Vivian and I left. Even if he is her husband, wouldn't Marjorie have said something if Bill left the boat that night and returned acting suspicious?" Mitch searched the detective's face, hoping for a hint of agreement.

Martinez swung his swivel chair to his left and began speaking to the wall as if dictating facts into a tape recorder. "Señor Schneider deposited his wife at their vessel at approximately ten-thirty. He told his wife he was returning to Marina Vallarta for a drink at one of the bars. But, according to his private statement to me, he did not stay at the marina. Instead, he claims he went back into town in search of a prostitute, found one, transacted his business, and returned to his vessel some time after midnight." Martinez swung his chair to face Mitch.

"Ho-ly shit," Mitch whispered.

"I beg your pardon, Señor?"

"You say he *claims*—no one saw him, he has no witnesses?"

"Two taxi drivers—and of course, the prostitute. I shall never forget his description of the taxi drivers—'typical Mexicans.' His more detailed description of the prostitute matches none of the known working ladies of Puerto Vallarta. Prior to arresting the two fishermen, we began questioning all taxi drivers in Puerto Vallarta. None of those we questioned remembered taking a lone *Norteamericano* man to or from the marina at those hours. After the arrests, we didn't bother questioning the remaining taxi drivers."

Mitch propped his downcast face between his thumbs and forefingers. "Then it is possible."

"I'm afraid it is, Señor."

Mitch looked up. "Bill did seem intensely nervous that evening when you came to the marina to show us the pictures. When you kept him by himself and then sent Ortega and those two uniformed police officers to get him, I almost thought you were going to arrest him."

"That was exactly what I wanted him to think. Prior to the arrest of the fishermen, I considered him the prime suspect, even without the knowledge of what you have just told me. If he were indeed the murderer, I was hoping he might panic and confess, or try to escape—before he found out about the arrests."

"Did you ask him why he was so nervous?"

"He said he was afraid I was going to tell his wife about his business with the prostitute."

"Did you?"

"I could not see what that would accomplish."

Mitch glanced at the ceiling. "Maybe this explains Marjorie's strange behavior."

"Explain, Señor."

"While we were waiting for you to arrive at the lighthouse that evening, Marjorie seemed...jumpy, apprehensive...more than just saddened and shocked by the murders. Maybe she suspected Bill but was afraid to say anything."

"Señora Schneider impressed me as a very meek woman. And from what I have learned about Señor Schneider, I find it hard to understand why such a bellicose man would be worried about his timid wife finding out about his infidelities. Did he strike you as the type of man who would tremble at such a possibility?"

"No." Mitch looked Martinez in the eye. "So Bill could have gone to *Walden*, killed Henry and Jill and then pretended to Marjorie he was coming back from a bar at the marina?"

"Yes, a cunning person could have done it."

"But, the knife, with Carlos' name on it."

"In Señor Schneider's statement, he claims to have seen the fishermen around the anchored yachts and in the marina. Let us assume he is determined that Señor Fullerton pay with his life for the insult he has suffered. Señor Schneider realizes suspicion will surely fall on him unless it appears, convincingly, that someone else—with a reasonable motive—is responsible for the crime.

"The fisherman, Carlos, claims the knife was in his boat that evening. He left the boat tied to K-dock near the public launch ramp. He and his amigo then made their rounds, checking the garbage containers at each dock until the harbormaster chased them out of the marina. When we arrested him, he claimed not to know his knife was missing."

"According to Señor Schneider's statement, he left his own small boat at the very same dock when he and his wife went to *Los Arbolitos*. It may be that he passed by their boat, spotted the knife, realized its potential, and stole it for later use as the murder weapon."

"Wouldn't Marjorie have seen him take it?"

"It would have been a simple matter for him to make an excuse to return to the dock alone and transfer the knife from the fishermen's boat to his own."

"But how could he have surprised Henry in the cabin of his own boat?"

Martinez leaned over his desk and concentrated on the twirling pencil. "That is troubling. It would have been a bold stroke. Perhaps Señor Schneider went to the Fullerton's boat under the pretext of making amends for the altercation at the yacht club that morning. Señor Fullerton is not unduly suspicious since he is unaware of the recent infidelities of Señor Schneider's wife."

Mitch shook his head in self-disgust.

"Seizing the most advantageous moment," Martinez continued, "he stabs Señor Fullerton through the heart with the fisherman's knife then grabs Señora Fullerton and cuts her throat before she can cry out. It would be a difficult feat for one person. A knife is an uncertain weapon in the hands of the inexperienced." Martinez leaned back. "Do you know the type of business Señor Schneider owned?"

Martinez' words created a mental picture of Bill in the act of murder, momentarily dazing Mitch into stunned silence. "It was a meat packing business wasn't it?"

"Correct. He built it, as you say, 'from scratch.' He made a point of telling me what an independent, self-made man he is."

Mitch stared quizzically at Martinez, not comprehending the connection. When it dawned on him, Martinez resumed. "Yes, Señor Schneider started his business with a small slaughterhouse, doing everything himself. Knives and cutting instruments were the tools of his trade."

Mitch sat up, leaned back in his chair and looked at the ceiling. "So, after he kills them, he rips Jill's clothes, takes a few things, makes it look like robbery and rape."

Martinez nodded. "On his way out he throws the knife in the water beside the boat. Leaving it aboard would be too obvious. He takes the stolen items and puts them in a trash receptacle near the dock where the fishermen tied their rowboat, hoping they will find them, exactly as they claim they did the following morning."

Mitch slumped forward, resting his forearms on his knees. "What can we do?"

"What can *we* do, Señor? If you had told me everything in the beginning, then perhaps I could have done something. Now, I can do very little. Señor Schneider's vessel is somewhere in the Pacific Ocean, I have no dead woman's journal, and even if neither of those things were true it might not change anything. What you and I have suggested is mere supposition." Martinez enumerated the facts with the fingers of his right hand. "It was the fishermen's knife, *they* possessed the stolen goods, *their* fingerprints are on the victim's boat and they have no alibi. In other words they had the means, the motive and the opportunity."

Mitch cradled his forehead in his hands, his fingers branching through his hair. Martinez was silent, allowing him time to fully absorb the expanding nature of the tragedy for which he was responsible. Two possibly innocent men would soon be convicted of murder.

"Before you condemn yourself, Señor, recognize it may just as easily be true that these men are indeed guilty. Or, it could even have been someone else, someone from one of the other yachts. In fact, that was my first theory, until I learned of the animosity that existed between the deceased and Señor Schneider."

Mitch sat up. "It was? Who? Which boat?"

"The couple from the vessel *Phoenix*."

"Jim and Litea? Why them?"

"It troubled me how quietly they left before sunrise, the same morning you discovered the bodies. We had our Navy search for them with orders to escort them back to port. The patrol vessel and two helicopters made a thorough search but found no trace of the vessel *Phoenix* anywhere within a reasonable distance of Puerto Vallarta. Their disappearance remains a mystery."

"I can't think of any reason why Jim would want to kill Henry and Jill. And why would he take the journal?"

"As I said, it was only my initial theory, a reaction to circumstances. However, it could be the answer to your question is in the missing journal. You, and others, described the vessel *Phoenix* and her captain as not being well-prepared for the voyage they were about to undertake. It occurred to me Señor D'Autremont might have sensed an opportunity to acquire some navigational equipment before his departure. Did I mention we have yet to recover the stolen GPS navigation device?"

"No. Jim didn't seem like the type who would steal from another yacht, let alone the kind of person capable of murder."

"People can surprise you, Señor Sanford. I have learned that almost anyone is capable of murder in the right circumstances. When we could not locate the vessel *Phoenix,* I contacted the police in Oakland, California. I was curious, and hoping they had his fingerprints on file. They did. Señor D'Autremont has a clean record. However, the officer I spoke with told me something interesting. He had once arrested Señor D'Autremont for burglary. The charges were dropped when the witness, who had previously identified him, changed her mind. It was written off as a case of mistaken identity."

"I see what you mean."

"Yes, even you have surprised me."

Mitch tried to swallow but his throat was dry. "I surprised myself."

"Don't be too hard on yourself, Señor Sanford, we are all human. The unpredictability of human behavior is what makes my job interesting. What are your plans?"

"We were thinking of going north to La Paz, or staying here through the hurricane season. Now, I'm not sure."

Martinez gazed out the window. "I would rather be in another place."

"Why's that? I understand you're considered somewhat of a hero for having solved this case so quickly."

"This is true. But I will take no pleasure in it if two innocent men are convicted of murder, while a guilty man escapes justice."

"Wouldn't my story and the missing journal help their case?"

"In a US court perhaps. In Mexico, our laws are based on the Napoleonic code. The burden of proof is on the accused to prove his innocence. The evidence against these men is strong and, as you know, there is a great deal of pressure to resolve the matter quickly and quietly. How would it look if I suddenly accused American tourists of committing this crime?"

"I see your point. Still, I'd like to help Carlos and Manuel if I can."

"I will inform their attorney of the missing journal, and if you wish, you can amend your statement."

"Yes, I'd like to do that."

"I will give the information to Señorita Torres today. It will be ready for your signature tomorrow." Martinez stood and offered his hand.

Mitch accepted the detective's handshake. "Thanks." He hesitated before turning to leave. "I'm curious. Where would you rather be than Puerto Vallarta?"

"My fantasy, Señor Sanford, is to be standing on the shore of an island in the South Pacific, waiting to greet persons aboard certain yachts as they arrive after their long voyage from Puerto Vallarta."

Vivian slid a cookie sheet into the oven, sucked a dab of cookie dough from her thumb and turned toward Mitch. "You're saying that, based solely on a missing journal, Martinez thinks Carlos and Manuel may be innocent and that Bill killed Henry while claiming to be in town boffing some hooker?"

Mitch sat on the starboard settee, leaning forward against elbows propped on his knees. He wound a rubber band around the base of his left index finger. "I haven't finished. There's more to it than that."

"Bill's a jerk—no doubt about that—but I find it easier to believe he was in bed with some prostitute than on *Walden* committing murder. Bill wasn't fond of Henry—everyone knew that—but what makes Martinez think he was angry enough to kill him—and Jill—for heaven's sake?"

Mitch tightened the rubber band until his finger felt cool and started turning blue. "It's possible Bill suspected Henry of having sex with Marjorie."

"Henry and Marjorie!" Vivian laughed. "Where did Martinez come up with that?"

"He didn't, actually."

"*You* suggested it?"

Mitch felt his lips getting dry and licked them. "Yes, I did."

"Where did you get it?, not from Henry, I can't believe Henry would..." Vivian twitched her eyebrows suggestively.

Mitch shook his head. "No, it didn't come from Henry."

Vivian scooped a dollop of cookie dough from the bowl and plopped it in her mouth. "I mean, just because they once engaged in a little risqué dancing doesn't prove anything. And Henry wasn't the type to seduce another man's wife out of spite. He may have had a roving eye, but—Marjorie? If the woman in question had been Sharon, maybe, just maybe, I could believe it. When is this unlikely romp supposed to have occurred?"

A lump formed in his throat and he swallowed. "While Bill was at the golf course."

Vivian paused, as if thinking it through. "So Henry finishes changing oil on *Walden,* then goes to *Silver Cloud* and ravishes Marjorie while you and I are with Jill at the Plaza?"

"That's probably what Bill *thinks* happened."

"Mitch, you're confusing me." Vivian stopped tidying up the counter and looked at him. "What are you saying, Marjorie made up a story that she had sex with Henry just to get even with Bill?"

"No, I'm not saying that." He involuntarily bit at an imaginary hangnail on his thumb.

Vivian's eyes followed his thumb to his mouth. It was a familiar habit of his, one that she had learned to interpret. "Besides," she said, "Henry wouldn't have had time...we took a cab back to the marina right after you..." What had really happened came to her in an instant, falling into place like tumblers in a vault.

Mitch watched Vivian's eyes flare wide open and shift from hazel to dark green. "Now, Viv..."

"Oh...my...God."

Mitch sat up and raised his palms. "Viv, it's not—"

"It was you!" she screeched, "You fucked her! You son of a bitch, you actually *fucked* her!"

It was going to be even worse than he imagined. Vivian never used the F-word. "Viv, keep your voice down, there's still one boat nearby."

"Don't tell me to be quiet, you bastard!" Vivian's eyes darted around the galley counter. She saw the bowl, grabbed a handful of cookie dough and threw it. The large glob hit Mitch in the left eye and hung there like an eye patch.

"I can't believe it! Mitchell Sanford, Marjorie is old enough to be your mother!"

Mitch began scraping the dough from his eye. "She is not. And besides, it's partially your fault it happened."

"*My* fault?"

Oh shit, wrong thing to say.

"How the hell is it *my* fault?"

"Well, you did volunteer me to take her back to her boat."

"I didn't expect you to provide *stud* service! You *asshole*! I can't believe it. I even complimented you for comforting her!" Vivian's hand came to her forehead. "I had no idea how far you'd gone to cheer her up."

Mitch got up and started toward her. "Viv, wait; let me tell you what happened; it's not like what you're imagining." He tried to take her shoulders in his hands, but she chopped them away with a sweep of her wrist.

She cocked her arm for a slap. Mitch flinched but didn't raise his guard, preparing himself to accept the blow. She checked her swing. "How do you know what I'm imagining?" Storm clouds drifted through her eyes. "I *cannot* believe this." She stared at him in silence for several seconds. "I'm not sure I want to hear this."

"It happened almost exactly the way I told you. When we got to *Silver Cloud*, she started crying on my shoulder; I was just comforting her; she kissed me, we—"

Vivian raised a hand. "That's enough. Stop. I definitely don't want to hear this." She turned her back on him and looked through the porthole above the stove. "I can't believe it; shy, demure little Marjorie?"

"Viv, she was on the verge of an emotional collapse. I was afraid she was going to hurt herself. It was just one of those moments when—"

"I *said* enough! Keep the Polaroids to yourself, I *get* the picture."

Vivian watched a chalk white cruise ship moving away from the wharf across the harbor. Mitch waited in silence. A minute passed. She bowed her head, supporting it with her right hand. When she finally raised up and turned to face him, tear streaks marred both cheeks.

"Oh, Viv, I'm sorry. I really, really am." He tried again to move closer. She put the heel of her palm in front of his face. "I didn't mean to hurt you," he said.

"Yeah, right. Get out of my way. I'm leaving." She stiff-armed him in the chest and moved past to the settee.

"You're leaving? What're you saying...that you're going to go get on a plane or something?"

"No, stupid, I'm taking the dinghy and going for a walk. But thanks for the suggestion, I'll seriously consider it." She didn't bother lacing up her shoes, snatched her straw hat from the settee and stood to leave.

Mitch blocked her path. "Come on, Viv. I know how you feel. It didn't mean anything."

Vivian refused to look him in the eye and spoke toward the deck. "If you do not get out of my way, I will scream until the port captain hears me."

Mitch's shoulders sagged. He stepped aside into the galley. Vivian darted up the companionway.

"What about your cookies?" he called after her.

"Fuck 'em; let 'em burn!"

He moved to the chart table and slumped into the seat. The tension that held him rigid gave way to nervous exhaustion. With the fatigue came conflicting feelings of remorse tinged with relief. His confession lessened the burden of his guilt but it brought the knowledge that he had hurt Vivian and scarred their relationship forever, perhaps ending it.

———

For the first half hour Vivian alternately cursed Mitch and Marjorie with every vile name she could think of. Yet the farther she walked, the more worry and self-reproach diluted the purity of her anger. She began to cry. Maybe there was more to it than Mitch had said, or more than he knew. Maybe he had become bored with her. Maybe he was ready for anyone new, even an older woman. First Henry and Jill, and now this. Was God punishing her? Perhaps her own close call with infidelity and her failure to disclose it had finally caught up with her. At least Mitch had confessed, or was about to when she guessed. She weighed their separate circumstances. She had not gone through with her affair, but had kept it a secret, betraying Mitch's trust. Mitch had gone through with it, but at least had tried to come clean about it. But would he have if it hadn't been for the murders and the missing journal? *And has he told me everything?*

Her own secret, once a festering sore deep inside, had almost been forgotten until Jill brought it up at the Plaza. *Damn!* If this had happened two years ago she might have understood it. But in the last several months she and Mitch had been as frisky as teenagers and almost as silly; billing and cooing at each other, making love in the middle of the day. It just didn't make sense.

Mitch was sitting at the chart table when she returned. He'd turned the oven off and a sheet of golden cookies rested on the cold burners. He sat hunched over the table, leaning on his forearms, as if studying something intently, but the teak surface was bare. She moved to within reach of him, but he didn't turn.

"Mitch?"

"What?"

"Will you tell me the truth about something?"

"What?"

"Whatever I ask."

"Yes."

"Do you love me?" She managed to keep her voice even and unstrained.

His head raised a notch and turned halfway toward her. "Do *I* love *you*? I should be asking you that question. Of course I love you."

"Really?"

"Yes, really."

"Did you have an affair with Kathy Hale?"

"No! No, of course not. Good God, Vivian, not you, too?"

"Under the circumstances, I felt I had to ask. Have you ever had an affair with *anyone* besides Marjorie?"

"Vivian, it was not an affair, it was..."

Vivian raised her voice and cut him off. "I know what it was, Sir Lancelot. Now answer the god-damned question."

"No, I have not." Mitch looked back down at the table. "Okay, here's the deal. *Look at me.* I'm not saying I forgive you, and I'm not saying I don't. I need some time to...to let this work its way through my system. Maybe then I'll have something to say. Until then, let's drop it and try to move on. Okay?" When Mitch looked her in the eye, she could see that he'd been crying too. It took all her willpower to keep from losing her resolve.

Mitch sucked in his upper lip and glanced away. "Yeah, fair enough."

The silence that followed was softened only by the sound of wavelets lapping against *Houdini*'s bow. Vivian studied him, and as she did she felt some of her anger drain away. Fury, in its pure state, was hard to sustain when contaminated with even a small measure of empathy. She picked up a spatula and began moving cookies from the sheet to a paper towel spread out on the counter. In a softer voice she said, "What else did Martinez have to say?"

"About what?"

She paused. "About how Bill could have committed this crime when all the evidence points to Carlos and Manuel?"

Mitch sat up and swiveled the seat around until he faced her but held short of meeting her gaze. Slowly, and without emotion or emphasis, he recounted Martinez' theory of how Bill seized upon the idea of getting his revenge when he saw Carlos' knife. He concluded by telling her about the holes in Bill's alibi.

"Is that it?" Vivian asked. "You look as though there's something else. I have to know everything, Mitch."

"It's nothing like that." Mitch looked her in the eye for the first time. "It's something else Martinez said."

"What?"

"He said it bothered him that two potentially innocent men might pay for the crime of another man."

"I hadn't thought about that side of it." She pictured Carlos and Manuel standing beside *Houdini* in their small boat. "When you told me how you found Jill—and that knife, ugh!—I remembered the day Manuel brought me the sea shells. What's going to happen to them? Could they be executed?"

"I don't think Mexico has capital punishment, but from what I've heard, it might be preferable to life in a Mexican prison."

"What they've suffered already is an injustice if they're innocent."

"And, if so, the person who really killed Henry and Jill is getting away, free as an albatross gliding over the ocean."

"Another injustice."

"And I'm responsible for all of them." Mitch looked away, staring blankly up through the open companionway.

For the first time, Vivian comprehended the treble nature of the guilt that was weighing on Mitch's mind. In her own distress she had forgotten that others had suffered more serious consequences as a result of his actions. It must be ripping him apart. "You don't know what really happened."

"And probably never will. But I'd sure like to. Martinez said he'd like to be waiting in Hiva Oa when *Silver Cloud* arrives."

Vivian moved toward him until she was standing within reach. "Couldn't he contact the French authorities and have them do something?"

"What could they do, ask Bill a few questions and hope he panics? Martinez tried that already. From what Martinez said, it sounds as though the Mexican government wants to keep the lid on the whole incident and bury it as soon as possible. Accusing an American on flimsy evidence would keep the adverse publicity alive. That wouldn't help the tourist business. From their perspective, two poor fishermen are a small sacrifice if it appeases public opinion and prevents further damage being done to a major segment of their economy. Besides, Martinez' superiors are satisfied the evidence sufficiently proves Carlos and Manuel are guilty."

"And if they're not—Bill gets away with it?"

"That's the distinctly shitty outlook. Unless..."

Vivian studied the far away look in Mitch's eyes. "Unless what?" She resisted an urge to put her hand on his shoulder.

"Unless he *does* panic."

"From what you just said, that's not likely to happen, is it?" Mitch didn't answer.

"Wait—are you suggesting Bill might do something rash and expose himself if someone were to show up in Hiva Oa and start asking questions about knives and journals...and Mexican prostitutes?"

"Something like that."

"Are you saying you might want to sail to the Marquesas after all?"

He tilted his face up toward her. "The idea is beginning to have a certain perverse attraction."

"It's late in the season to be leaving, and Henry won't be around to bail us out of trouble." There was no fear in her voice, only caution.

"Believe me, I've thought about that."

"If it *was* Bill, it could be dangerous to go snooping around after him."

"Henry wouldn't have hesitated an instant to do the same for us."

"No, he wouldn't; neither he nor Jill would have rested until they knew the truth. But *Silver Cloud* has a week's head start."

"Bill doesn't think we're coming. He won't be in a hurry. He'll cruise the Marquesas for a few weeks before continuing on to Tahiti."

"Mitch, what if it wasn't Bill?"

"Martinez said Carlos and Manuel had the motive, the means and the opportunity to commit the crime. Well, so did Bill. Unless Jill's missing journal is a bizarre coincidence, my money is on him."

"He did sound unusually relieved that evening at the lighthouse when he found out Carlos and Manuel had been arrested."

"Exactly. And some other things he said after the murders bothers me."

"Such as?"

"I ran into him the morning I went to the port captain's office to call Frank. He expressed his sympathies."

"That's doesn't sound like Bill."

"Especially, if he thought it was Henry instead of me who..."

Vivian paused for a deep breath. "Bill would be more likely to dance on Henry's grave. And Jill's remarks to him at the yacht club wouldn't have endeared her to him either." She turned, walked to the foot of the companionway and gazed out into the cockpit. There were a couple of scores to settle. She turned and sat down on the steps. "Okay, let's go make trouble."

"Are you serious?"

Her long eyelashes lowered, veiling her eyes. "Deadly."

During dinner they negotiated a plan and a division of labor. Mitch would visit the port captain first thing in the morning to obtain their clearance papers while Vivian made a run to the *Comercial mexicana* for a supply of fresh fruit and vegetables. They would rendezvous at the marina and stop by *Walden* on their way back to take off a few dry provisions and Henry's guidebooks for French Polynesia.

"While we're aboard *Walden*, remind me to find Henry's box of computer disks," said Mitch.

"What for?" asked Vivian.

"If Martinez will let us have Henry's computer, can't we hook it up to the ham radio and use it to receive weather faxes?"

"You're right."

"We'll need the weather fax software, which is probably still on *Walden*."

"Speaking of the radio, something just occurred to me. If I check in every evening on the Pac Maritime Net's roll call, Bill will almost certainly hear me and know we're coming."

Mitch's eyes shifted back and forth. "Then we won't check in."

"What if we get rammed by a whale, or what if *Houdini* springs a leak and sinks out from underneath us? Who would know where to start searching for us if I haven't been reporting our position every day?"

Mitch dropped his fork. "*Damn!*"

"What? Is it that bad?"

"No, I know what we can do."

"So what's the problem?"

"I was supposed to ask you to contact Frank on the Mañana Net about setting up a radio sked so he could stay in touch with Fred and Chuck when they come to take care of *Walden*. When I couldn't find the journal, I forgot."

"How does that solve our roll call problem?" Vivian asked.

"Can't we set up a radio sked with Frank for an odd time and frequency?"

"I get it, only Frank will know where we are and where we're headed. You think he'll be willing to do that?"

"When he finds out we're going—and *why* we're going—he'll insist."

"I'll call him on the Mañana Net tomorrow."

"Better not. If I were Bill, I might still be monitoring the Mañana Net to keep track of any news about the case against Carlos and Manuel. Better call Frank from a pay phone at the Plaza when you go shopping at the *Comercial.* Tell him about the journal and set up the sked."

Thursday, May 2

The clerk at the port captain's office prepared *Houdini*'s clearance certificate in record time. Mitch's luck held and he caught Martinez at the police station just as the detective was getting in his Ramcharger to leave. Mitch informed him he was not just there to sign his amended statement, but to say good-bye as well.

"So, you are sailing for the Marquesas? I admire your motives but fear for your safety. You can expect no aid from the French authorities, you know."

"Yes, we know."

"No crime has been committed in their jurisdiction, and if they contact us, all we can tell them is that we have the accused murderers under arrest."

"They haven't confessed, have they?"

"No, but we are transferring them to Guadalajara today. It would not surprise me if one or both of them confessed very soon."

The somber look on Martinez' face conveyed the deeper meaning in his statement.

"Señor Martinez, we both know those men aren't guilty."

"What I know and what I think are two different things." Martinez looked over Mitch's shoulder toward the open door of his office. He lowered his voice. "Señor Sanford, if you were a thief and a murderer, would you try to sell your stolen goods within hours after killing the American tourists to whom those items belonged?"

"No, I wouldn't."

Martinez nodded. "These two fishermen are not educated men, but I do not think they are stupid. Furthermore, their fingerprints were found only on the outside of the victim's boat. If they committed these murders, they carefully removed their fingerprints from inside the cabin. While they are not stupid, I do not think they are that smart."

"Have you mentioned these inconsistencies to your commander?"

Martinez glanced toward the door again. "Señor Sanford, if you were not going where you are going, I would not be telling you these things."

"Would it be possible to see Carlos once more?" asked Mitch.

Rather than delegate the task to Ortega, Martinez personally escorted Mitch to the basement holding cell.

"Do they know they're being transferred to Guadalajara?" Mitch asked as they approached the metal door.

"Yes. We notified their families this morning. They are coming to visit them before the transfer."

Martinez inserted the large key in the lock and opened the door. There were now only four men in the lock-up, which made it seem much less crowded, although it was only two less than on Mitch's previous visit. Martinez said a few words in staccato Spanish toward the direction of the pale green metal bars. A figure rose from the bench at the rear of the cell. As he came forward into the light, Mitch recognized Carlos. But it was a different man than he had seen on his last visit. Carlos' face showed sadness and the strain of incarceration, but the look of shame Mitch had seen before was gone. As Mitch moved to meet him at the bars, Carlos met his gaze without flinching.

"*Buenos días, Carlos.*"

"*Buenos días, Señor,*" Carlos said, taking hold of the bars.

"*Cómo está?*" said Mitch, placing his hands on the cool bars below Carlos' hands.

"*Estoy inocente, Señor.*" His quiet tone expressed no plea, no emotion, merely a simple statement.

Mitch looked into Carlos' dark, unblinking eyes. "I believe you." When Carlos made no reply, Mitch looked over his shoulder at Martinez for help.

"*Entiende?*" said Martinez.

"*Si, entiendo,*" said Carlos.

Manuel came up behind Carlos.

Mitch looked to Martinez again. "Can you tell them what we're going to do?"

"Do you think it wise to raise their hopes, Señor?"

"I suppose you're right."

Martinez studied Mitch for a moment then spoke to Carlos and Manuel in Spanish. "I simply told them you are going to try to help."

Mitch extended his right hand through the bars. Each man shook his hand.

"*Buena suerte,*" said Mitch.

"*Vaya con Dios, Señor,*" said Carlos.

Mitch followed Martinez from the main building back to the detective's office. Ortega stood by two women sitting on the low wall beneath the Strangler fig. Each woman had bundles of what appeared to be clothes resting on their laps. The younger of the two, not yet twenty Mitch guessed, held an infant in her arms. Two adolescent boys and three small girls flanked the other woman. Martinez tossed the key ring to Ortega who then turned to the ladies motioning for them to follow. As they rose, the younger woman gave Mitch a look of hate that was hard to miss.

Señorita Torres came into Martinez' office carrying Henry's notebook computer and small printer. Martinez motioned for her to give them to Mitch. Mitch read the amendment to his statement and signed it. He thanked her and she left.

"My advice, Señor Sanford, is to be extremely cautious; trust no one. You will be on your own, far from help. Don't add your own life and that of your lovely wife to this misfortune."

"We'll be careful," said Mitch. "If we find out anything that might help Carlos and Manuel, we'll contact you."

"Adios, Señor. May we meet again in happier times."

Mitch found Vivian waiting for him beside the Marina Del Rey condos when he arrived at the marina. He grabbed half of her collection of grocery bags. "What did Frank have to say?"

"He tried to talk us out of it at first. He thinks of you like a son. He doesn't want to lose you, too."

The flatness of Vivian's tone did nothing to raise Mitch's hopes for a quick reconciliation. "But he doesn't want Henry and Jill's murderer to get away either."

"Right. When I told him you couldn't find Jill's journal and what that implied, he changed his mind."

"Did you set up your clandestine radio sked?"

"Yes; we picked a frequency at the low end of the 15-meter band. Both the Mañana and Pac Maritime nets are on 20-meters. For a time, we picked oh-one-thirty Greenwich. It's a good time of the evening for Frank but not too close in time to the other nets. Other people may hear us, but the chance of one of them being Bill is exceedingly slim."

"He's got no reason to be suspicious. Besides, he'll be busy sailing *Silver Cloud.*"

At *Walden,* Vivian readily accepted Mitch's advice that she not go aboard. He quickly found the computer disks. From his earlier searches, he had a general idea where most provisions were stored. He grabbed two plastic, one-dozen egg carriers and several Tetra-pak cartons of assorted fruit juices. *Walden* was bulging with provisions that would go to waste, but there was little room for anything more on *Houdini.* From the bookshelf over the chart table he took two navigational guides for French Polynesia and a tourist's travel guide for the South Pacific. The one other piece of gear he would like to have had was Henry's Magellan GPS. But as Martinez had told him, the GPS was one of the items that had not been recovered.

By 12:15 p.m. they'd stored the additional provisions, had lunch and closed and dogged all of *Houdini*'s watertight hatches and ports. They brought the dinghy aboard, washed it, deflated it, and lashed it to the forward grab rails in its storage bag. After checking the oil and water, Mitch turned the key and started *Houdini*'s diesel engine. A familiar voice spoke to him from within. He opened the engine compartment again and looked at the fuel filter vacuum gauge. It was in the green; fuel was flowing freely. *Thanks for the reminder, Henry.*

Vivian appeared at the top of the companionway. "Are we ready?"

He turned to the main power panel and flipped several switches. "Are the instruments on?"

She scanned the depthsounder, knotmeter and wind indicator. "Yup, all on."

"All that's left is a stop at fuel dock, and then, as Henry used to say, it's time to rock 'n' roll."

With *Houdini* now the only remaining boat in The Pond, and no one around to observe his mistakes, it came as little surprise to Mitch that he and Vivian were able to retrieve both stern and bow anchors without incident. Nevertheless, his knees shook as he turned *Houdini*'s bow up-channel and began motoring slowly toward the fuel dock.

Both anchors and their rodes were heavily fouled with mud and marine growth from their long submersion in the harbor's excessively fertile water. Vivian returned from the bow, holding up her muddy hands. "What a stinky, slimy mess. I'll clean the foredeck after we refuel."

In twenty minutes they took on sixty-one gallons of diesel, filling *Houdini*'s 110-gallon tank. A teen-aged Mexican boy helped them cast off and they were on their way back down the channel. Mitch took one last look over his left shoulder. Like a mare in her stall, *Walden* rested patiently in her O-dock slip. He couldn't help feeling that a piece of the universe was out of kilter. *Walden* and *Houdini* had become almost as much an inseparable pair as he and Henry had once been. It didn't feel right—slightly unfaithful—to leave her behind. He absolved himself with the knowledge that he was sailing to avenge her owners and whispered as much to her under his breath before he turned away.

Only the derelict charter boat remained anchored in The Pond. The one-legged pelican, it seemed, had vanished for good. Mitch took a final look at *Houdini*'s former anchorage as they passed by and entered the main harbor.

Vivian left the cockpit to go forward, then stopped. "I just thought of something we forgot."

"What's that?"

"Shouldn't we have topped off the number one propane tank?"

Mitch paused, considering her question. It had been two-and-a-half weeks since he and Henry had taken their tanks to be filled. "What's left in number one should last until we reach the Marquesas. The number two tank will last at least another month or two after that, plenty of time for us to reach the gas supply in Nuku Hiva."

Vivian nodded and continued making her way to the bow. Mitch turned *Houdini*'s steering wheel a quarter-turn to the right and the sloop's bow came around, following the contour of the low shoreline to starboard. Within minutes they passed the empty cruise ship wharf, the jetty and the red and green entrance buoys. The afternoon winds were light and *Houdini*'s slow pitching motion was barely noticeable in the low swell on Banderas Bay.

Mitch breathed in the ocean's fresh air and took note of the time for his log, almost 2 p.m. A speedboat towing a para-sailing tourist dangling from a red and yellow chute completed a wide turn and headed toward the crowded downtown beach, Playa del Sol. To the south, a half-mile off rocky Mismaloya Beach, a cruise ship lay at anchor. Several local yachts and a turquoise trimaran charter boat out day-sailing crisscrossed wakes on the whitecap-free bay. Mitch had forgotten how pleasant and relaxing the ocean could be under the right conditions. He watched Vivian sluice down the muddy foredeck with clean seawater brought up in a bucket at the end of a short length of rope. Though she evinced no outward hostility toward him, he sensed she was taking care to avoid close contact, not an easy task within the confines of *Houdini's* forty foot hull.

Half an hour out, a high-pitched engine alarm jolted him out of his musings as Vivian fed the last of the cleaned anchor chain into its forepeak locker. The engine's temperature gauge commanded his immediate attention. *220? How the hell could it overheat so fast?* He pulled the kill switch. The diesel stuttered and rumbled into silence.

Vivian joined him. "What's up?"

"The engine overheated."

"Great. Now what?"

"I don't know. I checked its water and oil just before we left." He went below and opened the engine compartment. The fifty-horse Mercedes radiated heat like a New England wood stove. Clearly, it was not a false alarm. The voice was there again. He checked the seawater cooling system's strainer. The water behind the glass was clear; no eel grass or other foreign material had clogged the wire mesh basket. The problem had him stumped until he looked at the rubber hose leading from the strainer to the through-hull fitting. The flattened hose resembled an empty tube of toothpaste. Only one possibility suggested itself: the sea water cooling pump had sucked something into the through-hull opening and the resulting vacuum had collapsed the hose, cutting off cooling seawater to the engine's heat exchanger.

Vivian watched as he stood up and stripped off his T-shirt. "What is it?"

"Looks as though we've sucked something into the seawater intake."

By the time Mitch found his mask, snorkel and fins, *Houdini* had glided to a standstill, rocking slowly from side to side in the gentle swells. As he prepared to enter the water, Vivian re-rigged the boarding ladder at the starboard lifeline gate.

Holding his snorkel in one hand and covering the mask's face plate with the other, he stepped off the caprail, hitting the water feet first. The long, lemon yellow dive fins made a loud smack as his feet hit the surface.

A cloud of tickling bubbles surrounded him as he rose. He removed the mask, spit into it and wiped the saliva over the inside surface of the face plate.

"How's the water?" asked Vivian.

"Warmer than I expected and it's a heck of a lot cleaner than in the harbor." Mitch slipped the mask on, adjusted the strap and inserted the snorkel's mouthpiece into his mouth. With a wave at Vivian and a deep breath he dove like a seal beneath *Houdini*'s hull.

A week ago, when he'd gone down holding on to *Silver Cloud*'s boathook, he could barely see his outstretched hands. He wouldn't call this visibility good, but it was more than adequate for the task at hand. He could just make out the underside of *Houdini*'s bow, bobbing up and down thirty feet away.

It took a second to reach the sea water intake. The half-inch diameter hole exited in the curve between the bilge and the long fin keel that extended six feet below the surface. Just above the hole, a long white scar in the blue bottom paint served as a vivid reminder of *Houdini*'s close call at Sacramento reef.

Something pink within the hole caught Mitch's eye. He pulled it with a thumb and forefinger. A small amount of thin plastic ripped loose, leaving nothing exposed to grab.

Mitch popped to the surface below Vivian and held up the piece he'd ripped loose.

"Plastic bag?" said Vivian.

Mitch removed the snorkel mouthpiece and tipped the mask back on his forehead. "Yeah, and it's way up inside the through-hull. I need something long and skinny with a little hook on one end."

Mitch held on to the boarding ladder until Vivian returned a minute later. She handed him a coat hanger with its hook straightened except one little L-shaped kink she'd made in its end. "How's this?"

He reached up and took it. "Perfect." He pulled down his mask and dove again.

The improvised tool quickly did its job. He managed to remove the remainder of the bag in one piece. He was making a final inspection of the hole when he felt a strange sensation. It was like a cool current had passed over him, like the bow wave of a submarine.

He looked down. An involuntary reflex jerked his knees to his chest. The last half of a dark sinuous shape passed less than six feet below him. It seemed to go on forever. The body tapered to an asymmetrical tail whose long, scimitar-like upper half fanned the water in rhythmic sweeps, nearly touching the underside of *Houdini*'s keel.

Mitch coiled himself against the keel to spring up for the ladder. One split second before he committed himself, the huge shark made a quick turn at the limit of visibility and headed back toward the ladder. Out of breath, his only recourse was to surface on the other side of the keel. He grabbed the prop shaft and pulled himself through the gap between the prop and the rudder.

He broke the surface, pulled the mouthpiece out and yelled, "Shark!" Immediately, he jammed the mouthpiece back in, took a quick breath and dove. He had to keep track of it.

Vivian lunged from the starboard side of the cockpit to port. "Where!" By then, Mitch was gone.

Mitch hugged the port side of the keel, holding on to the prop shaft. Cautiously, he peered around the propeller to the other side. He came face to face with a gaping mouth like a trash can rimmed with shards of glass. He shrank back behind the keel. A merciless eye turned briefly toward him. Gill slits and great pectoral fins came next, followed by the fish's monstrous body. It reminded him of the Philadelphia subway.

He let go of the shaft and drifted up the port side, watching the shark swim aft until it disappeared beyond his range of visibility. He took the mouth piece out. Vivian waited on deck above him. "Did you see him?" Mitch gasped.

"No!"

"Look aft. He should be aft. Tell me if you see him."

Vivian leaped to the stern in time to see the shark's dorsal fin break the surface. The size of the animal stunned her. She hurried back to Mitch. "He's about thirty feet astern and going straight away!"

Mitch took a deep breath, dove and pulled hard, heading under *Houdini* as fast as he could swim.

Vivian rushed aft just in time to see spray fly high into the air as the shark reversed course with a violent thrash of its tail. "Hurry, Mitch!" In the next instant, she heard the sound of him exhaling through his snorkel. She lunged to meet him at the ladder.

"Mitch, hurry, hurry! Get out!" He was too far down for her to reach.

The last rung of the ladder hung two feet below the surface. His long dive fins wouldn't let him get his foot high enough to step in. There wasn't time to take them off. He grabbed the sides of the ladder as high as he could reach and pulled himself up with every ounce of strength he could will into his arms.

Vivian saw the shark less than ten feet away, charging for the ladder.

Mitch thrashed his legs, trying desperately to get one fin through the rung.

Vivian reached down for his shoulders.

The tip of one dive fin caught a rung.

Mitch exploded out of the water flinging his upper body over the caprail, knocking Vivian backward. Her relief turned to horror as she heard the crash of the shark's massive jaws and saw Mitch yanked away.

In a desperate survival reaction, Mitch threw his left arm around the closest gate stanchion and seized his left wrist with his right hand. Vivian could do nothing. The shark stretched Mitch out toward the bow. The force caused *Houdini*'s bow to slue to port.

Mitch's body jerked spasmodically as the enraged shark whipped its head from side to side, attempting to shake its prize loose. Mitch suddenly went limp. He hung vertically by his elbow from the stanchion, not moving.

Vivian froze, momentarily unable to move. When he began moving, slowly trying to lift himself over the side she rushed to him, pulling at him, clawing at his armpits, inching him over the side. Her profession had accustomed her to the sight of blood. She steeled herself for what she was about to see.

Mitch half rolled, half flopped on to the deck. Vivian saw the fin missing from his right foot. The shark had missed.

His death grip on the stanchion had so weakened him that she had to remove the snorkel from his mouth and push the mask away.

Mitch said nothing, taking slow deep breaths that collapsed suddenly at the end.

"Honey—Mitch, are you okay?"

"Big..." he breathed.

"What?"

"Tiger," he said with the next breath.

She kept massaging his head, waiting for him to catch his breath.

"Big...fucking...shark..."

Vivian sniffed and wiped the corner of one eye. He was going to be all right. If anyone was going to bite his leg off it would be her and not any God damned shark. Looking around, she saw no sign of the giant fish or other boats nearby. They were in no further danger. She let *Houdini* take her own lead, drifting slowly downwind.

"Did he...get me?"

"No, just your fin."

"Couldn't tell...can't feel anything...."

"Take it easy. Just rest."

Fifteen minutes went by before he could sit up and another ten before he could lift himself up to a sitting position on the cabin roof. The elbow and left shoulder of his right arm ached from nearly being dislocated. Vivian took off his remaining fin and helped him carefully make his way to the cockpit.

"What'll we do?" she asked.

"Buy different colored fins," he groaned.

"You know what I mean."

"Start her up," he said, "Let's go."

"Back to the harbor?"

"No, let's go. I'll be okay."

"Are you sure?"

"Just keep an eye on the temperature gauge."

Vivian started the diesel and waited for the idle to smooth out before pushing the shift lever forward. Once *Houdini* gathered way, she brought the bow around to a heading that would clear Cabo Corrientes. After resting another ten minutes, Mitch joined her in the cockpit.

"You were right, it was a humongous shark," she said. "It must have been close to twenty feet. I didn't know sharks got that big.

"Tiger sharks can grow to over twenty feet—when they're well fed."

"Maybe the shark and the plastic bag are omens, Mitch. Perhaps we should stop and think this through a bit more."

A random vision came to Mitch of the one-legged pelican, hopping up its chain. "No, I'm not giving up that easily."

"*That easily*? Mitch, right now you could be cruising around Banderas Bay in the belly of a shark, for Pete's sake. Did you get a look at what he did to the swim ladder?"

He shook his head.

Vivian reached down and picked up the aluminum ladder from behind him. "The shark ate your fin and the bottom rung, and left the rest of it like this." A one foot section of the right hand rail was bent sideways at a 45-degree angle.

"That just proves that luck is on our side." Mitch massaged his left shoulder with his right hand.

"*Luck? Is on our side?*" Vivian looked at him as if an alien had suddenly taken up residence in her husband's body. "Do you think you can even raise and set sails in your condition?"

"Between you, me, and the autopilot, I think we can manage."

"Okay, hot shot, let's find out. Shall I engage the autopilot?"

Mitch glanced at the instrument panel. The wind speed read eleven knots from the northwest. "*Houdini* is a sailboat, let's sail."

"What's our course?"

"The first leg is 225."

Vivian concentrated on the magnetic compass as she turned *Houdini*'s steering wheel rapidly from left to right in short increments making fine adjustments to *Houdini*'s heading. When satisfied, she flipped a cam lever that tightened a belt attached to the steering wheel and a small electric motor. She then pressed a red button on a small black box near her left knee and released the wheel. After a moment's pause, the autopilot's motor chirped once and the wheel jerked to the right. A few seconds later, it chirped and whirred, spinning the wheel six inches to the left.

"I stand relieved," said Vivian. "Now what?"

"We'll reverse the way we normally set sail. You go to the mast and raise the main. I'll stay here and trim the sheet."

Vivian arched one eyebrow at him, but left the cockpit and went forward without comment. It all went easier than she expected. When she was ready, Mitch pushed another red button on the autopilot's control panel nine times causing *Houdini* to turn ninety degrees to starboard, directly into the northwesterly wind. Hand over hand, as fast as she could, Vivian pulled the halyard line down, causing the heavy dacron mainsail to begin its ascent. When she could pull it no higher, she wrapped the line around the halyard winch and turned its handle until the sail's luff was taut.

"Okay, fall off," she yelled. The stiff white sail flogged noisily in the increased apparent wind.

Mitch pushed the opposite button nine times and *Houdini* returned rapidly to her original heading. He used his good arm to ease the mainsheet, letting the boom and foot of the sail move out over the port rail. The sail quieted as the wind filled and molded it into its proper airfoil shape. He added two wraps of line around the mainsheet winch and winched it tight. He slowed the engine to idle, shifted to neutral and pulled the kill switch. With the burden of propulsion shifted to the mainsail, *Houdini* slowed from six knots to four.

After coiling and cleating the main halyard, Vivian returned to the cockpit. "All right, *mon capitaine,* ready for the big guy?"

"I'll ease its furling line," said Mitch, " and you sheet it in."

Setting the large, 600-square-foot genoa jib was a task made less demanding by its roller-furling system. When not in use, the sail rolled up around the headstay wire like a gigantic window shade. Vivian took one turn of sheet line around the port primary winch. "Say when."

"When!"

The ratcheting winch gears sang as Vivian's hands leapfrogged each other, hauling the line in quickly, trying to keep up with the rapidly filling sail. It unfurled instantly, crackling and snapping as it luffed. She sheeted in as far as she could by hand before resorting to the winch. As the powerful two-speed winch pulled the genoa into a smooth, tight curve, *Houdini* heeled to port, yielding to the wind's pressure against her full spread of sail.

Mitch glanced at the knotmeter. "Back up to six knots and better. Keep it up, *Houdini* girl, we need every tenth of a knot you can give us."

Vivian wiped perspiration from her forehead and took a Scrunchy from her shorts pocket. She pulled her hair through the frilly piece of elastic cloth, forming a long full ponytail. "I guess that wasn't so bad."

"Can you watch things for a minute while I go start the log and set the SatNav?" asked Mitch.

Vivian gave the horizon a 360-degree scan. "Doesn't look as though anyone's around to run me down." As Mitch descended into the cabin, she added: "Bring me a Diet Pepsi when you're finished, okay?"

Vivian always looked forward to the initial contrast between the rumble of the diesel engine and the relative silence of sailing. It amazed her that an object as large as *Houdini* could move so stealthily.

Once the hammering sound of the diesel quit echoing in her ears, she heard the individual sounds of sailing: the curling waterfall of the bow wave; the hiss of foaming bubbles rising in the wake; and the occasional creaks from cabin woodwork, as *Houdini*'s fiberglass hull flexed like the skin of a large sea creature, adjusting to the pressure of the sea.

She turned aft to survey the panorama of Banderas Bay in *Houdini*'s wake. Puerto Vallarta had become an impressionist's painting of randomly organized splotches of red, white and green. The rising horizon already obscured the sands of Playa del Sol. The only positive landmark she could still make out was the distinctive metal crown atop the old cathedral. The gold ball at its apex glinted regally in the late afternoon sun. The bay's southern shore from Mismaloya to Cabo Corrientes presented a solid green wall of steep, jungled cliffs.

She could not avoid the thought that this beautiful stretch of Mexican coast might be the last bit of land she'd ever see. Ahead lay thousands of miles of unpredictable, unforgiving ocean. She redirected her overactive imagination, canceling the unwanted thought by fantasizing the gray-green Sierra Madres to be her first glimpse of tropical Hiva Oa rising off *Houdini*'s bow.

Mitch pulled his logbook from the bookshelf and sat down on the nav station's swing-out seat. At the top of the next unused page were several labeled blank spaces: time and date of departure, port of departure, port of destination. He filled in all but the last. He'd developed a superstitious habit of not filling in the destination until after he'd safely arrived. Fate was not to be taken for granted, and now was not the time to tinker with a successful system. He began filling in the log details, guessing at the times he wasn't sure of.

Time	Entry
1355	*Departed Puerto Vallarta Harbor en route Hiva Oa, Marquesas*
1430	*Engine Temp Alarm—220 degrees*
1450	*Removed plastic bag from cooling water intake*
1500	*Attacked by rather large shark*
1545	*Engaged autopilot, set main and genoa, steering 225M at 6.3 knots*
1555	*All systems normal*

Henry had a saying: if it was easy, everyone would be doing it.

Mitch turned his attention to a small, gray electronic box. He pressed two buttons on its keypad and waited for the green digital display to change. He had entered the latitude and longitude of Hiva Oa's eastern tip into the SatNav's memory over two weeks earlier. Now it obediently displayed the direct course and distance from *Houdini*'s present position to Hiva Oa: 221° magnetic; 2,690 nautical miles. *Houdini* would actually sail closer to 3,000 nautical miles as he planned to follow Henry's dog-legged route to avoid getting caught in the calms and squalls of the InterTropical Convergence Zone. He pressed more keys and entered *Houdini*'s present course and speed.

While noting the figures in his log, he gave a silent prayer that he would be seeing the comforting green glow of the SatNav's display all the way to Hiva Oa. If he had Henry's GPS, he could have had both units operating side-by-side, backing each other up. But now, if the SatNav failed in the middle of the Pacific, he would have to rely on his untested skill with a sextant to guide *Houdini* safely to her destination. In his practice sessions with Henry, he had never obtained a reliable position.

The sun had been down two hours when *Houdini* passed Cabo Corrientes and entered the open Pacific. A bright flash from the cape's cliff-side lighthouse pierced the darkness reassuringly once every five seconds. A tricolor light at the graceful sloop's masthead broadcast her own signature, sending out a steady beam of green to starboard, red to port, and white astern.

Alone in the cockpit, Mitch sat behind the wheel and scanned the horizon for coastwise shipping that might cross *Houdini*'s path. When neither his eyes nor the radar screen's phosphorescent sweep detected a single ship, he allowed himself to take in the night sky. Without the polluting, electric glow of civilization, the stars glittered like grains of agate sand on an indigo beach. The foggy, galactic trail of the Milky Way meandered from horizon to horizon. Dead astern hung the Big Dipper, *Ursa Major*. Henry had pointed out its three bright navigational stars and taught him their names: Dubhe, Alioth and Alkaid.

He winced as *Houdini* rolled and he braced himself reflexively. His shoulder had stiffened since the attack to where he could no longer rotate the arm without experiencing a stabbing pain. He rubbed the shoulder and watched the black swells roll away to port. He made a silent resolution: he resolved to stay out of the water if the sharks promised to stay out of the boat.

He heard Vivian's footsteps on the companionway ladder and turned. She paused on the middle step, looking from left to right. Her eyes had not adapted to the darkness.

"Mitch?"

"Right here."

"Jeez, you startled me. For a minute there—are you wearing your safety harness?"

"No. I'll put it on before you turn in. Did you listen to the Pac Maritime Net?"

"Yup."

"Did you hear Bill give his position?"

"Yup. Are you ready for a surprise?"

Mitch assumed from her question that *Silver Cloud* must be much farther, or much closer, than he would have guessed. "Where are they?

"That's not what's unusual."

"They just changed course for Panama...or Hawaii?" Mitch guessed.

"No, the surprising thing about his report was that tonight is the first night he's checked in."

"You mean they've been sailing for a week and he just now reported *Silver Cloud*'s position for the *first* time?"

"That's right. When the net controller got to the end of the roll call and Bill hadn't checked in, I thought maybe he was playing our game. But then the controller asked if there were any new boats wishing to join the roll call and up pops Bill with his position, requesting to be listed on the roll."

"Did he say why he hadn't checked in before?"

"No, and the controller was too busy to ask. He had two other boats waiting to join the roll."

"So Bill didn't report his position until they were several hundred miles at sea?" Mitch glanced aft over his shoulder. He didn't speak again until he saw the flash from Cabo Corrientes. "It doesn't sound like we're on a wild goose chase. Better try to get a couple hours sleep before your watch." Vivian handed him his safety harness and waited in silence until he put it on.

As she disappeared into the darkened cabin, Mitch recalled the previous night when Vivian had chosen to sleep alone on the settee in the main cabin rather than with him in their double berth. At sea they would be standing alternating three-hour watches until they anchored in the Marquesas. He would not again have the opportunity to sleep beside her until that day. That would have been hardship enough under normal circumstances, but one he could have endured, knowing her feelings toward him were as they had been before the disclosure of his infidelity. Sensing that she preferred this circumstance of quasi-celibacy imposed by short-handed passagemaking created a sadness within him that would be as difficult to ignore as the pain in his shoulder.

During the remainder of his watch, Cabo Corrientes Light grew faint and sank closer to the ill-defined horizon. He knew when he relieved Vivian at three in the morning it would be gone. And in the past, when he had relieved her on one of their rare overnight coastal passages, Vivian could usually point to *Walden*'s stern light a mile or so ahead. Tomorrow morning, *Walden* would not be there either.

Following the sea wind's normal pattern, it eased off as the night progressed. Mitch found himself in an atypical mindset; he wished for stronger winds. *Houdini*'s speed dropped steadily each quarter hour until it hovered between 4.5 and 5.0 knots. As the digital speed display dropped each tenth of a knot, he contemplated the ramifications: the duration of the voyage increased, a murderer slipped further away, and the time of hurricanes drew nearer.

PART THREE

THE PACIFIC

Like a tiny leaf in a vast desert, *Houdini*'s taut sails pulled her through a seascape of undulating hills and valleys. Rays from the rising sun pierced ridges of translucent turquoise wave crests. A long, low swell, rising like Neptune's respiring chest, approached from fifty yards astern. The smooth mountain of water overtook her. The yacht's transom lifted, two feet, four feet, six.

In a moment the swell would pass and she would descend into the valley behind it. But for a few brief seconds, *Houdini* ignored the laws governing flat-water boats. The unseen hand of gravity tugged at her stream-lined hull and with the aid of forward momentum she broke free.

Her bow dipped. She hovered a moment. Then came a fleeting flash of acceleration. She raced down the face of the steepening swell, a thoroughbred released from the gate. Her hull and keel harrowed the sea's surface into a wide ribbon of sizzling foam. Surfing into the trough, she spent the gift of gravity, outran the wind and stalled her sails. The swell overtook her, lifting her once again, this time passing harmlessly underneath, continuing its resolute journey. A clone approached from astern, ready to begin the cycle again.

In the week since leaving the Mexican coast, *Houdini* had averaged 127 miles a day, a respectable pace considering the northeast trade winds were already in their summer decline. Her crew fell closer in step with the ocean's cadence with each passing day as they became accustomed to the monotonous routine of passagemaking.

After two days at sea, Vivian had gained control of her queasy stomach. The pain in Mitch's shoulder and elbow subsided, allowing him to sleep more than fifteen minutes at a stretch.

On the third day, as *Houdini* passed ninety miles south of Soccoro Island, they felt well enough for a collaborative effort to connect Henry's computer to the ham radio, making possible the reception of facsimile weather charts. After a few garbled screens and several adjustments, the first of several detailed weather maps transmitted from San Francisco and Honolulu appeared on the laptop's display.

A guest came aboard the evening of the fourth day. A brown booby, a large, albatross-like seabird, landed on *Houdini*'s stern rail. Sitting almost within reach of the yellow-footed bird, Vivian froze, fearing she would scare it away before Mitch could take its picture. In the next twenty-four hours three more of the nun-faced birds came to share the roost. Vivian realized her concerns had been premature. She and Mitch took turns posing for group photos with the hitchhikers.

Each morning the birds took wing, soaring around *Houdini*. They strafed the troughs for flying fish and dive-bombed from altitude for prey beneath the surface. One by one, they returned to *Houdini*'s stern rail each evening, to preen, sleep, digest and defecate. After two days of the latter, Mitch was ready to revoke their crew privileges and chase them off. Vivian responded with a threat of mutiny and a promise to clean up after them. "Besides," she told him, "don't you know it's bad luck to kick them off?" Mitch hadn't heard this particular nautical superstition, but it had an irritating plausibility. He concluded it wasn't worth violating as long as Vivian erased the foul smelling white streaks that decorated *Houdini*'s transom every morning. Secretly, he enjoyed the bird's company as much as she did.

Like the birds, Mitch and Vivian took their meals on the wing, eating outside in the cockpit rather than below. At sea, the sealed cabin was cramped and stuffy while the cockpit was light and airy, and usually dry in the warm, fair weather. Neither of them felt comfortable remaining below for very long without a lookout on watch. With the steaming speeds of modern freighters, a ship hidden just over the horizon could run them down in fifteen minutes.

After the evening meal, Vivian kept her scheduled radio contact with Frank. She gave him *Houdini*'s latest position, course and speed along with local weather conditions. Hearing Frank's voice every evening helped her forget how alone they were in the ocean's midst. And, provided her radio signal was strong enough, he patched her into the phone system and called her mother or Sonja, her slightly daffy, sex therapist sister. The ham radio was her umbilical cord to home.

Later in the evening, before her first off-watch sleep period, she listened to the Pac Maritime Net for Bill's report of his current latitude and longitude. In the morning, Mitch plotted *Silver Cloud*'s position on his chart. Using dividers, he then measured the distance between *Silver Cloud* and *Houdini*.

Unlike Mitch, Bill hadn't followed Henry's longer, west— south—west dogleg route and it had cost him. He had sailed *Silver Cloud* the shorter rhumb line route, straight for the Marquesas and entered a wide section of the InterTropical Convergence Zone, an area of calms, squalls and thunderstorms that gradually narrowed to the west. The ITCZ's contrary winds slowed *Silver Cloud* considerably. *Houdini* had made miles on her every day. The total gained after one week came to 132, the equivalent of one good day of sailing.

Sailing more west than south had kept *Houdini* out of the convergence zone, but at the same time it also kept her north of the hurricane breeding zone. As long as she stayed north of ten degrees north latitude, she remained in the potential path of any tropical storm that formed south of her. If they weren't chasing *Silver Cloud*, Mitch might have turned south and crossed the ITCZ earlier, settling for a slower but safer passage. Thus far the gamble paid off, keeping *Houdini* in fair weather and reliable winds. Nevertheless, the longer they stayed north, the more Mitch felt an increased pressure to turn south.

Frequent practice with his sextant, taking observations of the sun and stars, had helped to keep his mind occupied. In the afternoon of their sixth day out, he had called Vivian down to look at his chart work. His morning and noon sun sights had produced a fix of their position that, for the first time, agreed closely with the SatNav's electronically derived position. She had congratulated him with a one-armed hug and a brief look into his eyes that hinted her feelings toward him might have begun to thaw. Despite the hope this small show of affection stirred within him, he felt a simultaneous pang of sadness at being unable to share the news of his newfound skill with his teacher, Henry.

This morning, trouble appeared on the horizon, figuratively if not literally. The previous night's weather fax chart showed a continuation of the benign northerly winds. But now that *Houdini* approached the waypoint where Henry's dogleg route called for a turn to the south, the ITCZ's belt of unstable weather had suddenly expanded from a width of 120 miles to nearly 500 miles. Its northern boundary moved up to less than two degrees of latitude south of *Houdini*'s current position.

Mitch watched the knotmeter register *Houdini's* rapid acceleration as she surfed down the advancing slope of another swell. While waiting for Vivian to receive the latest weather chart, he considered their options. Once they reached the waypoint they could turn south according to plan and head into the ITCZ, or they could gamble and continue sailing southwest for another one or two more days, hoping to find a narrower place to cross the ITCZ's river of bad weather. But Henry had been very specific; if he went too far to the west before making the turn, the southeast winds and west setting currents below the equator would make it impossible to reach the Marquesas without many extra days of hard sailing against the wind. A few days earlier, Vivian told him of hearing one yacht's skipper report to the Pac Maritime Net that he had made that very mistake. He was giving up on reaching the Marquesas and altering course for Tahiti. Perhaps the morning fax would bring more encouraging news.

The expression on Vivian's face when she emerged from the companionway was not what he'd hoped for. "No change?" he asked.

"No fax," she answered. "Very weak signal and lots of static. The chart was a mass of streaks and dots."

"You couldn't even make out the ITCZ boundaries?"

"Zilch."

Mitch glanced at the southern horizon and then back to the knotmeter.

"Looks like we've slowed down," Vivian said.

Mitch nodded. "Our average is down to just over four knots. The wind's been easing ever since I assumed the watch. If we make the turn to the south, the wind will be coming from dead astern, its apparent speed will drop, and we'd be going even slower. And, if nothing's changed since last night's chart, we'd be in the convergence zone by tomorrow morning. Bill's out of it now and making better time."

"How far did you say they're ahead of us?"

"640 miles, as of last night. We've closed the gap to about five days, but we'll lose what we've gained very quickly unless we keep our speed up."

"And how do you propose we do that?"

"Stay on this reaching course another day or two and hope for an improvement in the ITCZ before we have to turn south. And try the spinnaker."

"The *spinnaker*?" Vivian called it the S-word. Just the mention of the temperamental twelve-hundred square-foot sail gave her anxiety pains. "We've used it only two or three times on the ocean, Mitch. You said yourself you're only comfortable using it in light seas and close to land. Now you want to try it in these swells?"

"No, but I think we could be going thirty to fifty percent faster if we do. I've been studying our movement. These swells are as regular as corn rows, and with the wind angle close to the beam we're not rolling much. With the spinnaker pulling, it should steady us even more."

Vivian scanned the long rows of swells stretching to the horizon in either direction. "Do you promise we'll douse it if the wind picks up?"

"Cross my heart. If we don't like the way it acts once it's set, we won't even wait for a wind increase."

Within half an hour they had the genoa jib furled around the headstay wire and the large nylon spinnaker ready for hoisting on the foredeck. To make setting of the big sail easier for a crew of two, a snake-like sock contained the sail until it was fully hoisted.

Vivian crouched in the cockpit by the port primary winch, ready to trim in the sheet line when Mitch gave the word.

From the base of the mast Mitch yelled, "Ready?"

Vivian took a deep breath. "Whenever."

Mitch pulled down on the spinnaker halyard, causing the dark blue sock to begin its ascent. The one-foot diameter tube offered little resistance to the wind, making the hoisting process no more difficult than if he were hauling a watermelon to the masthead. He cleated the halyard and took hold of the cord that raised the sock.

"Viv, start sheeting in as soon as the sock passes the halfway point." Mitch pulled on the cord. The sock accordioned as it rose, exposing a rainbow of brightly colored panels of rip-stop nylon sailcloth. The sail quickly captured the wind and spread outward, causing the sock to shoot skyward faster than Mitch could pull the cord. "Trim, trim!" he shouted.

"I'm trimming, I'm trimming," Vivian grunted. She fought to get a third turn of sheet around the winch.

Houdini heeled ten degrees farther to leeward under the force of the huge sail. Now full, it resembled one half of a hot air balloon. Mitch braced himself against the mast. He could feel *Houdini's* 24,000 pounds accelerating. It felt like the *Millennium Falcon* of *Star Wars* making the jump to light-speed.

"How much more?" yelled Vivian, slowly cranking the two-speed winch in low gear.

"That's good," Mitch replied. "What's our speed?

Vivian glanced over her shoulder. "Six-point-eight."

"Whoa, big difference!" Mitch finished coiling the spinnaker halyard and made his way back to the cockpit.

"Just remember your promise," Vivian said.

He nodded. "Isn't it gorgeous?" The mainsail shaded half the spinnaker. The other half of narrow yellow, orange, red and lavender panels glistened in the morning sunlight. From its apex near the masthead, the hemispherical sail stretched to lower corners at the bow and several feet to port out over the water.

"I admit it's pretty, but it's Beauty and the Beast rolled into one as far as I'm concerned."

"Can you watch it for a second while I log the sail change and plot the latest SatNav fix?"

"Don't leave me out here alone with this monster for very long. I won't be held responsible for the consequences if you do."

The wind's strength and direction remained almost constant throughout the morning. With *Houdini's* increased speed through the water, came greater response to the rudder, easing the autopilot's job of steering a straight, efficient course. Gradually, Vivian relaxed enough to return to the dog-eared copy of *Pillars of the Earth* she'd been reading. She hid from the sun's hot overhead rays in the one corner of the cockpit shaded by the awning.

After his morning sextant observation of the sun, Mitch alternated his attention between the spinnaker and pages of

The Prince of Tides. There was little else to watch out for. They were far from the heavily traveled shipping lanes, and despite their vigilance, hadn't seen a single ship since leaving the Mexican coast.

Vivian folded the paperback on her thumb. "I forgot to tell you what I heard this morning."

"What's that?" asked Mitch.

"While I was waiting for the fax broadcast time to roll around, I tuned into the Christian Science Monitor frequency."

"What's happening back on planet Earth?"

"Mostly the Gulf War; some little software company is suing the big one for megabucks; and the stock market is up seventeen points. But what was interesting was a report on NAFTA. Have you heard of it?"

"North American Free Trade Agreement?"

"Right. The announcer said members of congress are predicting a long battle over ratification because of Mexican immigration, pollution, crime and civil rights issues."

"Unfortunately, they're probably right."

"Do you think it might have negative consequences for Carlos and Manuel?" asked Vivian.

"It's more likely the reverse will happen."

"What do you mean?"

"It's more likely the crime they're accused of will be detrimental to the agreement. It wouldn't surprise me if NAFTA opponents are already using Henry and Jill's murders as another argument to sway votes against the agreement."

Vivian studied the horizon. "So if we prove it was another American, and not two Mexicans who killed Henry and Jill, it might help Mexico as well as Carlos and Manuel?"

"That's quite a stretch, but who knows; larger fates have turned on smaller feats."

By mid-afternoon *Houdini*'s speed slowed to five knots. With each drop in wind velocity, Mitch felt more smug about his decision to set the spinnaker. Had they stayed with the genoa instead of setting the spinnaker, they would have been wallowing along at closer to three knots. On a short run, a one-or-two-knot difference was not much to get excited about. But on a long passage, a one-knot difference meant twenty-four miles gained or lost in one day. If a one-knot gain could be sustained for five days, it equaled one hundred twenty miles, the equivalent of one less day at sea. Mitch hadn't forgotten Henry's maxim: the longer you stay at sea the more chances you give it to swat you.

Houdini's slower pace forced the autopilot to work harder to correct the boat's heading. The sloop yawed and rolled to the rhythm of the passing swells. The sinuous course caused the fussy spinnaker's leading edge to collapse and fill with a sudden pop, like the snapping of a towel.

After one particularly loud pop, Vivian lowered her book. "Maybe it's time to douse it, ya think?"

Mitch looked at his watch and then the sail. Despite its occasional complaints, the sail still pulled well, not yet fully collapsing as it would if the winds grew much lighter. "We'll be taking it down in about an hour anyway. Let's try to carry it that much longer."

"By the same logic, one more hour won't—" A loud beep from the cabin interrupted her. It was the SatNav's alarm, signaling a satellite had passed overhead and provided a new fix of *Houdini*'s position.

"Okay," Mitch said, "I'll plot this fix first and then we'll take it down. How's that?"

"Fair enough," said Vivian. "While you're down there, how about checking the neighborhood with the radar?"

Mitch turned on the radar to let it warm up while he plotted *Houdini*'s updated position. Because of its heavy electrical consumption, he followed Henry's practice of turning the radar on only for brief periods. Using it continuously would require running the engine to charge batteries two hours a day, consuming fuel reserves they might need to power *Houdini* through calms and into port.

After plotting the fix he punched the radar's button that expanded the range of distance displayed on the phosphorescent green screen. He stopped at the twelve-mile setting and watched the sweep rotate. *Hello.* "Hey Viv, we've got a contact."

Vivian's gaze snapped around in fear she had let a ship sneak up behind them while she was reading. "Where?"

"Port beam, eight-point-three miles."

Vivian looked toward the southeast. "I don't see anything."

"He's over the horizon at that distance. But judging by the size of the blip, he's big."

"Which way is it headed?"

"Too early to tell. Give me a few minutes and I'll have a rough idea."

Mitch noted the blip's range and bearing after a three-minute interval and then used techniques Henry taught him to plot the ship's movement relative to *Houdini*. He called up from the cabin: "If we both maintain course and speed, he should cross our bow seven miles ahead—in other words, no problem."

"So he's passing us?" asked Vivian.

"Right. Probably out of Panama, headed for Japan. Ready to take down the spinnaker?"

"Yes, more than ready, except now it's almost time for the San Francisco weather fax."

"Get the fax and then we'll douse it."

While Vivian received the latest tropical weather chart, Mitch scanned the southern horizon with binoculars, searching for the source of the radar echo. There it was, like a gigantic submarine, only its black-rimmed white smokestack and black-tipped cargo booms protruding above the horizon. In the short time since he had first detected it on radar, the ship had already covered half the angular distance between *Houdini*'s beam and bow.

"Mitch," called Vivian, "if it's safe, you should come down here for a second and look at this."

He took one last look at the freighter as it disappeared behind the spinnaker's trailing edge before laying the binoculars on the main hatch and descending the companionway ladder. "What's up?" He moved behind Vivian where she sat on the swing-out chair at the nav station.

"Take a look at that." she said pointing to a small object on the laptop computer's screen. "Is it what I think it is?"

Mitch leaned over her shoulder for a closer look. "Son of a bitch. Where the hell did that come from?"

The object in question was a small circle with two tails curving in opposite directions. The tails symbolically represented the bands of clouds that extend outward from the wall of a hurricane's eye. The symbol rested on the tenth parallel of latitude, north of the ITCZ. The storm's emblem continued to creep up the screen while the rest of the chart's detail filled in from the bottom.

"There was nothing indicated on the last chart was there?" asked Mitch.

"I didn't get the last chart, remember?" Vivian answered.

A small box containing hand printed characters began to emerge in the lower portion of the screen, directly below the storm symbol. They watched in silence as words in the box became readable.

T.S. ANDRES
10.5 N, 116 W, WSW @ 4 kt
MAX WIND 60 kt

"'A' is for Andres, first tropical storm of the season," said Mitch.

"It's pretty close, isn't it?"

"Judging by those coordinates, about a hundred and fifty miles southeast of us. I can't believe it's headed west-southwest. Henry said they almost always head northwest once they form."

"Maybe Andres is a bad boy who doesn't follow the rules."

"At the moment the little shit is almost paralleling our course and speed."

"What now, Kemosabe?"

"He'll undoubtedly gain speed and overtake us. I guess our best bet is to turn south and hope he turns north like he's supposed to—or that we at least cross his path well before he reaches our longitude. How soon will we get another fax?"

"The next tropical analysis is not until tomorrow morning, but there's a satellite photo later tonight."

"That won't show us which way he's headed or how fast, but it might give us an idea how organized and how big he is."

"I can start monitoring the Coast Guard's voice broadcasts—"

Houdini yawed to port and heeled hard to starboard. Mitch stumbled against Vivian, crushing her against the chart table.

"What the...?" The thunderous rumble of the collapsing spinnaker drowned out his voice.

He regained his balance and leapt up the companionway with Vivian right behind. They quickly surveyed the surrounding sea. There was nothing, no ship, no sudden change of wind speed, just a train of steep, closely spaced cross-waves rolling in from the southeast.

The autopilot whirred and chirped, turning the wheel to the right in larger and larger increments. The spinnaker collapsed and swung like an empty hammock in the windshadow of the mainsail. Mitch dove for the autopilot control box, pushed the standby button and flipped the cam lever. He spun the wheel until it rebounded off the rudder stop at hard right.

His eyes riveted on the spinnaker. "Come around, *Houdini*, come around, baby." There was a sound he wanted to hear more than anything else, the sound of the spinnaker popping full. Vivian removed one turn of the sheet line from the winch.

Before *Houdini* could head up and fill the spinnaker, another of the cross-waves caught her. She rolled hard to starboard. The limp, half-filled spinnaker dipped behind the headstay and made one tight wrap around the furled genoa. Another roll, another wrap.

"What should I do, Mitch!"

"Try to sheet it in!"

The words had barely escaped his mouth when the lower half of the spinnaker inflated with a bang. The sudden load jerked the sheet from the winch, burning Vivian's left hand before she realized it. Mitch watched dumbfounded as the snarling, snapping spinnaker coiled itself around the furled genoa in seconds. It sucked its tangled, flailing sheets into its folds like Godzilla eating spaghetti.

Vivian clutched her red-streaked palm.

"Are you okay?" Mitch asked.

"I'll be all right," she said.

He steered while trying to see the spinnaker from under the cockpit awning.

"What do you want me to do?" asked Vivian.

"I don't know. Let's drop the awning. I can't see."

Vivian unzipped and untied the awning, letting it fall into the cockpit well. With it down Mitch could see the spinnaker.

The top half was wound around the furled genoa jib in tight wraps alternating with distended bulges. As *Houdini*'s bow swung into the wind, the lower half of the spinnaker inflated explosively, sending a shudder through the rigging, shaking *Houdini*'s mast like a fishing rod."

Vivian instinctively ducked in reaction to the sound and shock wave. "Mitch, I don't think the mast will take too many of those!"

The wind's force increased with every ten degrees of heading change to windward. Mitch hoped the increased relative wind would somehow loosen and unwind the spinnaker. Instead it caused the upper half to constrict itself more tightly around the captured genoa, and the lower half to collapse and fill more violently.

"I think you're right." He spun the wheel left, slowing the bow's swing, eventually reversing it. As *Houdini* turned back downwind, the relative wind strength eased. The spinnaker's writhing and snapping became less violent. He continued turning downwind until the snarled spinnaker was back in the windshadow of the mainsail.

"Mitch, did you see those waves?"

"You mean the ones that did this? Yeah, I saw them."

"Did they come from the storm?"

"No, it was the wake of that freighter."

Mitch steadied on a downwind, southerly course and re-engaged the autopilot. He took a closer look at the spinnaker. Even in the reduced wind it resembled a grotesque Medusa-like creature, with lines flailing wildly from its bulging, snarled mass. He wouldn't have blamed Vivian for giving him a good "I-told-you-so." Instead, she stood quietly beside him, surveying the angry mess. "Let me see your hand," he said.

Vivian opened her left hand for him to inspect. A crimson stripe crossed her palm.

"I'll bet that hurts. You'd better go put something on it. Meanwhile, I'll try to figure out how to get us out of this hole I've dug."

He couldn't believe how tangled the spinnaker had become. It and its sheets had tightly wrapped themselves around the furled genoa. Having both the spinnaker and the genoa jib out of commission limited their propulsion options to the mainsail and the engine. Under main alone their speed had dropped to three knots. They could motor at six knots, but they still had two thousand miles to go. They would run out of fuel long before they reached Hiva Oa. And no fuel would eventually mean no electricity for navigation instruments and lights.

The bigger problem was Andres. At its present course and speed Andres would overtake them in little more than a day. If the storm hit them before they were able to get the spinnaker down from the headstay, the consequences were unpleasant to think about. The partially wrapped spinnaker presented an immense resistance to any wind and its height above the water gave it tremendous leverage. Storm force winds could easily force *Houdini*'s mast into the water and capsize her—unless she was dismasted first. One way or another, the spinnaker had to come down.

Vivian returned with a large gauze pad taped to her palm by three rings of adhesive tape. "What's the verdict?"

"We've got to get it down."

"Can we cut it away?"

"Its wrapped too high up." The spinnaker's loose folds inflated, punctuating his sentence with a hull shaking pop as if expressing its feelings on the matter.

"Isn't there some way we can at least prevent it from doing that?" asked Vivian.

"Let's go forward and take a closer look."

"Okay, but don't forget what happened to me," she said, holding up her bandaged hand.

A cacophony of crackling sail cloth, whipping sheet lines and seas hitting the port bow surrounded *Houdini*'s foredeck. The slow speed and new course heading accentuated the rolling and pitching, forcing them to work their way forward in small increments, crouching from handhold to handhold to avoid being catapulted over the side.

Reaching the foredeck, Mitch held on to the bow pulpit's steel tubing with one hand while shielding his face from the thrashing sheets with the other. Vivian huddled beside him, holding on to the lifelines.

Mitch picked a time immediately after a swell had passed, when the mainsail's windshadow momentarily quieted the sail. He lunged to grab one of the sheet lines attached to the clew, the spinnaker's free flying corner. In a lucky grab, he caught both port and starboard sheets. He pulled the clew in rapidly. If he could wrap it around the furled genoa before the wind caught it again, he might have it under control. The next swell caught *Houdini's* stern, yawing her to windward. It was enough to cause the breeze to fill the lower, unwrapped third of the sail. Enough to place a huge load on the sheets.

Mitch used all his strength, trying to muscle the clew to the headstay. In the attempt, he failed to notice he'd held on too long. His feet left the deck an instant before he realized it. He felt himself lifted up and over the lifelines. It was too late to let go.

To Vivian's horror she watched Mitch swing out over the water, suspended below the spinnaker's clew. In their rush to gain control of the sail, neither of them had donned their safety harnesses or life jackets. If Mitch dropped into the water, *Houdini* would be past him in seconds, well before she could get to the cockpit, disengage the autopilot, start the engine and turn to get him. She'd never be able to keep track of him in the eight-foot swells.

Mitch lifted his feet to keep them from dragging in the water. He pulled himself up the sheets to the clew on arm strength and adrenaline. His toes skimmed the water's surface and he swung away as *Houdini* rolled to port. At the end of the swing he glanced back at the bow. Vivian crouched helpless and speechless in the pulpit.

He would have laughed out loud at his predicament and her wide-eyed expression if *Houdini* had been in Puget Sound and not the middle of the Pacific. The roll back to starboard began. The sail lifted him six feet above the water and ten feet out from the bow. His weight and the mainsail's windshadow caused the spinnaker to collapse. Like Tarzan coming home to Jane, he swung toward *Houdini's* bow.

"Look out, get away!" he shouted, afraid he would mistime his drop and knock her overboard. Vivian lunged out of the way. He released the sheets and landed against the anchor windlass.

Vivian was at his side at once. "Are you hurt?"

Mitch's lips stretched taut across his teeth, his eyes closed tight. "I think I broke my ass and strained my shoulder again."

Once he was safe on board and apparently not seriously injured, her concern turned to nervous anger. "What kind of dip-shit, macho stunt was that? Don't you *ever* leave me alone in the middle of an ocean!"

"I'll try my best." He massaged his right buttock. "If you've got a better idea how to corral this thing, I'm ready to hear it."

"What if we set the tack free?"

"What, and let the whole bottom of the spinnaker loose?"

"All the strain is caused when it suddenly snaps full of air," Vivian argued. "If we release the tack, it can't fill. It won't have any power; it should just flag in the breeze."

"So it's flying out over the water, then what?"

"If we turn a little more downwind, putting it in the lee of the main, maybe it will come close enough for us to grab it."

"When did you think of this?"

"Just now."

"I wish it had been ten minutes ago, because it just might work. We'll have to be careful not to gybe the main." An accidental gybe would send the heavy boom crashing from one side to the other, putting more strain on *Houdini's* overtaxed rigging. "What the hell," said Mitch, "it can't get much worse than it is."

The strategy worked exactly according to Vivian's prediction. The sail's freedom was short-lived. The angle of the wind pushed the lower half of the flagging sail toward the lee of the mainsail where it settled docilely against the lifelines. For one split second they stared in disbelief that the plan had actually worked. Then Mitch saw the dangling sheets about to go under water and wrap themselves around *Houdini's* prop. Simultaneously, they lunged to corral the sail, pulling it on board before another gust of wind could carry it out of their reach.

"Now what?" said Mitch. They hugged armfuls of billowy nylon sailcloth and pulled its trailing sheets aboard.

Vivian looked up to where the rest of it wound tightly around the genoa like ribbons around a May pole. "What if we twist it, like we're wringing out a wet beach towel?" She looked at Mitch for his reaction.

He looked back, and without a word they took hold of the sail's foot and began twisting. Within a minute the spinnaker's lower half had been wound into a multi-colored candy cane. Now completely under their command, they walked the tightly twisted sail back to the bow, passed it around the headstay several times, making descending spirals around the furled genoa. Using the sheets, Mitch tied the spinnaker to the headstay, keeping the sail locked in position.

"Can we leave it like that until Andres has passed?" asked Vivian.

Mitch looked at the upper half of the spinnaker. "Too risky," he said. "Strong winds could rip it open. We'd be knocked over like a bathtub toy. Besides, it's trapping the genoa. Without it, and the extra speed it gives us, we're sitting ducks."

"I don't think I want to hear the solution."

"I'm going to have to go to the top and release the sail from its halyard."

"I knew I didn't want to hear it." Vivian looked to the top of the mast. "Mitch, you can't go up there now. It'll be dark in a few minutes."

"First thing in the morning. Maybe Andres will give us a break until then."

"You've already re-injured yourself."

"It has to be done. It's just strains and bruises, I'll be okay. You're the one that's going to need strength, to winch me to the top."

"With Andres coming, and now this, maybe I should check in with the Pac Maritime Net tonight to let them know our situation."

Mitch considered the suggestion. "No, I don't want Bill to know we're coming. We've got things under control. Just let Frank know. By tomorrow we'll have it all straightened out." He looked at the masthead fifty feet overhead, swinging against a backdrop of thickening clouds. "Besides, what could possibly go wrong?"

Friday, May 10

The early morning high seas weather report was not encouraging. The Coast Guard short-wave broadcast from Honolulu reported Tropical Storm Andres becoming more organized and increasing in intensity. They projected the system's movement over the next twenty-four hours as due west at seven knots. Yesterday's friendly cotton balls of cumulus clouds had disappeared, replaced by telltale wisps of cirrus.

At the storm's predicted rate of advance, Mitch believed they would feel its touch very soon. Vivian relieved him of the watch for his early morning sleep period, but instead of curling up on the settee, he quietly went about searching through lockers, pulling out the items required for his trip to the masthead: the bosun's chair, his good knife, wire cutters, an aluminum carabiner, kneepads, and a foam life-vest.

The pieces of equipment made a small pile in one corner of the cockpit. He stood halfway up the companionway steps studying them, trying to think of other tools the task might require. One trip to the top of the fifty-foot mast at sea would be bad enough. He didn't want to make a second.

He thought of Henry. In his calm, slow way, Henry would have talked him through the procedure over the radio. An irrational urge came over him to go below and turn on the radio.

Instead, he leaned back and looked up through the spray dodger's windshield at the upper half of the mast. *Houdini* rolled more today with just the mainsail up than she had yesterday with either the spinnaker or the genoa flying with it. He sensed Vivian watching him, waiting to hear his plan. But when he turned, he found her scrutinizing the air bubble traveling through a curved glass tube mounted on the cockpit's forward bulkhead. "How much are we heeling?" he asked.

Vivian watched the bubble in the inclinometer through another roll.

"Twenty-five degrees."

"Twenty-*five*?"

"*Twenty-five*, port and starboard."

The wind had risen overnight to fifteen knots from dead astern, increasing *Houdini*'s speed to five knots under mainsail alone. At seven knots, Tropical Storm Andres gained two miles on them each hour. Although white foam now topped nearly every wave, their overall pattern was uniform, giving *Houdini* a somewhat predictable motion. As each swell lifted her stern, she pitched downward, yawed to the right and began a slow roll to starboard.

Mitch rotated his left arm. The pain and stiffness from the shark encounter in Banderas Bay was back as a result of yesterday's impromptu spinnaker ride. With his other hand, he massaged his bruised posterior. "I think we'll have to take the mainsail down in order for me to go to the top in these conditions."

"Won't that make us less stable?"

Mitch moved to Vivian's side in the cockpit. "I'm hoping for just the opposite; but the real reason I want it down is so I can wrap my legs completely around the mast at all times, except when I have to go over the lower shrouds and spreaders." He pointed to the metal arms that spread like albatross's wings, holding the shroud wires away from the aluminum spar. *Houdini*'s mast had two pairs of spreaders; one pair a third of the way up and another pair two-thirds up.

"So we'll have to motor while you're aloft?"

"Right. I think if we go close to full speed and square with the waves, it should help to stabilize the boat and make it easier for the autopilot to keep her on track. The last thing I want to have happen while I'm up there is a broach."

Vivian hadn't even considered that possibility. The only sailboat broach she'd ever seen was on a videotape about heavy weather racing that Mitch once brought home from the library. In her mind she pictured *Houdini* streaking down the face of a steep wave, losing rudder control and swerving violently to starboard, putting the tips of the spreaders in the water. What would it do to Mitch if he were at the masthead when that happened? "Are you going to rig a safety belt to keep from being pulled away from the mast?"

"I'd have to undo the belt each time I passed over the spreaders and the lower shroud wires. I'll run the spare genoa halyard to the base of the mast as a safety line." Mitch held up the carabiner. "Then I'll clip the bosun's chair to it with this. That should keep me close to the mast, but not slow me down. When I'm done, I want to come down fast."

With the engine running, and Mitch at the base of the mast, Vivian disengaged the autopilot and swung the helm hard right, bringing *Houdini* smartly into the wind. The mainsail and its snake-like reefing lines crackled and flogged angrily until he lowered the sail and tied it to the boom. While he finished furling the mainsail, Vivian steered *Houdini* back to her original downwind course.

Using hand signals, Mitch gave her course corrections from his forward vantage point until *Houdini* steadied on a course perpendicular to the crests of the following seas. At his signal, Vivian re-engaged the autopilot. With mainsail furled it was relatively quiet. The low clicking rumble of the diesel engine blended with the wind whistling through the empty rigging, and the bubbling hiss of the frothy wake. The motion felt better, the rolling less severe.

"What's the inclinometer reading?" Mitch shouted.

Vivian watched the bubble as *Houdini* heeled to port and starboard through half a dozen rolls. "Mostly tens, fifteen once," she yelled back.

"I don't think we can do much better than that. Let's go."

Vivian joined him at the mast. He stepped into the canvas bosun's chair and put his knife and wire cutters into its pockets. A foam life-vest went on over his T-shirt. Rather than for flotation, it was there to protect his ribs from being cracked against the mast. Flotation, he hoped, would not be needed. Kneepads provided similar protection for bare knees.

The morning temperature had already topped eighty. More clothes than his cut-offs and T-shirt would cause him to overheat and restrict his movement.

He checked to make sure the main halyard was securely shackled to the bosun's chair. When he was ready, he stood up and held on to the boom. Vivian took up the halyard's slack, put three turns of the half-inch line around the mast-mounted winch, and fed the tail into the self-tailer. With his feet still on deck, Mitch tested the chair with his weight.

Vivian stood close beside him, wiping strands of windblown hair from her face. She held on to the mast for support as

Houdini rolled rapidly from side to side. "I didn't like winching you up the mast, even when we were tied to the dock in the marina back home."

"I wasn't particularly crazy about it myself." Mitch fought to keep his mind off what lay ahead, concentrating on the moment at hand, visually checking the halyard shackle one last time.

"You're sure there's no other way?" Vivian asked.

"None that I can think of. Let's get it over with." *Before I change my mind or lose my nerve.*

The winch's self-tailer freed both of Vivian's hands and arms to rotate the winch handle. With most of Mitch's weight still on deck, she cranked the winch handle in the high-gear direction to take up the strain. When his feet lifted off, she reversed direction, automatically switching to the slower but more powerful low gear. The one other time she'd winched him to the masthead, more than a year ago, she'd had to stop for rest several times. But now, with all the physical exercise she'd had since they'd started cruising, she found she had the strength to keep cranking continuously. The adrenaline pumping into her system helped.

As soon as Mitch rose above the furled mainsail, he switched his grasp from it to the mast, locking his legs and ankles around the cool aluminum spar. He clipped the carabiner on the bosun's chair around the halyard safety line that ran taut along the mast.

At ten feet above deck the motion wasn't bad. He clung to the mast with little effort. The following wind carried up the smell of diesel exhaust fumes. As he rose higher, glancing down at Vivian and *Houdini* rolling under him, the first sensations of nausea reached his head and stomach. He shifted his gaze to the more stable horizon, which moved farther away as he inched upward.

At deck level the waves had a variety of features like pedestrians on the sidewalks of Manhattan at rush-hour. But at forty feet the seas appeared as regimented as the rows and columns of a vast army. Helmeted in white, identically clad in uniforms of grayish blue, they marched in perfect unison across an endless parade ground.

Three feet from the top, Mitch clutched the mast fiercely, preventing his weight from pulling him free as *Houdini* rolled to starboard. The life-vest cushioned his chest and ribs as G-forces at the end of the opposite roll to port pressed him hard against the mast.

His eyes came level with the top of the mast. "Whoa!" he shouted to Vivian.

Vivian cleated the halyard and moved aft to the dodger where she had a better view. It was also safer than standing directly under him if he should drop a tool.

Mitch held on for three complete rolls to adjust to the carnival-ride motion. The addition of his weight at the masthead reduced the yacht's stability and increased the degree of heel in each roll. From side to side, his body inscribed an arc through the air more than forty feet in length. At the end of one particularly long roll to port, he forced himself to look down. *Holy Shit!* He was well out over the water.

Neither his strength nor his churning stomach would hold out for long. He turned his attention to the head of the spinnaker. From its head to midway down the headstay, the rainbow-colored sail wound in ever tighter wraps around the furled genoa like a giant python climbing a jungle vine. To release its grip, he must trip the snapshackle securing the sail to its halyard. Mitch realized he would have to let go of the mast with one hand and stretch out with the other toward the headstay to find the snapshackle hidden somewhere in the accordioned material of the snuffing sock, then pull the shackle's release pin. *Damn it, Henry, you never said there'd be days like this.*

Mitch waited for a mild roll to port that would push him toward the mast rather than away from it. When it came, he let go of the mast with his right hand. Leaning backward toward the bow he made a blind stab into the snuffing sock and caught the snapshackle's lanyard on the first try. He jerked it open and retreated instantly to the security of the mast. The sail slumped a few inches and stopped.

He clipped the freed halyard shackle to the bosun's chair and was about to reach out again to untwist the sail from around the headstay when he saw the problem. The light cord that hoisted and lowered the snuffing sock had snarled itself in a Gordian knot around the headstay and the spinnaker. He'd have to cut the cord to free the sail.

Hugging the mast again, he removed the knife from the bosun's chair. His hands were sweaty. The thin stainless-steel folding knife felt warm and slippery in his grasp. If he dropped it he'd have to go down for another one or have Vivian somehow send one up. He unfolded the sharp serrated blade with care.

He looked astern of *Houdini*, sizing-up the approaching swells. Again he let go with one hand and leaned back at a forty-five-degree angle away from the mast. It was no good. The snuffing sock hid the control cord where he needed to cut it. Mitch grabbed the mast before the opposite roll pulled him away from his precarious perch.

Concentrating on the snarled control line, while swinging through the long arc, brought back the motion sickness. Just clinging to the mast was draining his energy. If he failed to get the spinnaker loose on the next try he doubted he would have the strength or the will to make another attempt. His face contorted with rage and fear.

"You son-of-a-bitch," he yelled at the spinnaker, "what the hell do you want from me!"

To cut the sock control cord away from the headstay he would have to let go of the mast with both hands. He glanced down at Vivian and swallowed.

From behind the dodger, Vivian watched Mitch sweep through the air and out over the water at the end of each long roll. "*Please, God*, don't let him fall."

Terrible thoughts pried their way into her consciousness. What would she do if Mitch fell overboard? What if she lost him and found herself alone in the middle of the Pacific? Could she sail and navigate *Houdini* by herself? Would she even want to try; or, would she give up and join him?

Mitch clung to the masthead, waiting through one more roll. He felt the need to say something to Vivian, anything, just so she would hear his voice and he might hear hers. He spaced his words to keep them from smearing together and flying away with the wind. "I'm...going...to...have...to...let...go... with...both...hands."

"Mitch!"

Mitch circled the mast with his legs. Waves of nausea surged in his stomach, pushing up against his diaphragm like expanding magma. He pursed his lips and swallowed hard, constricting the muscles in his neck. Whoever killed Henry and Jill would pay for this.

He no longer had the luxury of biding his time, waiting for a moderate roll. He unclipped the carabiner from the safety line.

On the next roll to port he reached for the headstay. One hand, then the other. His ankles locked around the mast. He stretched out. Now horizontal, back to the deck, he looked to the sky. His right hand clutched the knife and headstay. The left clawed the snuffing sock. *Damn sock; get the hell out of my way.*

He sensed the end of the roll to port. *Need both hands.* He improved his grip near the top of the arc and held on for the roll to starboard.

"Mitch, be careful! Please!"

Vivian couldn't bear to watch but neither could she look away. Mitch was stretched like a prisoner on a medieval torture rack between the mast and the headstay. He would be bashed and beaten if he failed to hold on. Vivian silently cursed her vivid imagination that presented an image of her lowering Mitch's unconscious body as he slammed against the mast and rigging wires.

At the end of the starboard roll, Mitch went to work furiously pulling at the nylon sock. It opened, exposing the control cord. One determined slash of the knife and the spinnaker slid free. When the cord gave, he nearly lost his grip. He caught the headstay wire with his right hand—a second before the roll to port could throw him free. At last the spinnaker was loose. With strain-stiffened fingers, he folded the knife and slipped it into the bosun's chair pocket. In the next two rolls, he removed two wraps of the spinnaker from around the headstay. The lightweight sail eased its constrictions around the furled genoa and slid halfway down the stay, pulled by its own weight.

"VIVIAN!"

"WHAT!"

"Pull on the spinnaker!"

Vivian rushed toward the bow, grabbing lifelines and handholds like an Olympic cross-country skier poling for the finish line. A cross-swell struck *Houdini* on the beam. Its spray curled over the lifelines, drenching her to the skin. Within seconds of reaching the bow, she pulled the big sail to the foredeck and stuffed it into the bow pulpit.

His task completed, there was nothing to distract him from his nausea and the swell of acid rising from his stomach. He gagged once, then again, but held short of vomiting into the wind.

Vivian had the presence of mind to tie the sail to the pulpit so that it wouldn't slip over the side and be sucked into the spinning prop.

"DOWN, DOWN, DOWN!" Mitch shouted.

"I'm *coming!*" she yelled, fighting her way to the mast across the rolling deck. She uncleated the mainsail halyard and began carefully taking the line out of the self-tailer's jaws.

"DOWN!" Mitch yelled again.

Vivian ignored him and eased the line around the winch drum, being careful not to let the line jam in an override. She allowed herself one quick glance at her husband as the line slipped slowly through her fingers.

Mitch felt himself descending. It gave him the willpower he needed to gain control of his flip-flopping stomach. He closed his eyes and rested his head against his right shoulder as the mast slipped through his upraised arms.

When his feet touched the upper spreaders, Mitch opened his eyes and unlocked his legs to pass around the wing-like metal arms. His kneecaps were even with the spreaders, almost to the point where he could re-lock his legs around the mast. *Houdini* rolled hard to starboard. Before he could again circle the mast with his legs, his lower body swung into space.

"VIVIAN!"

The steep angle of heel and the terror in Mitch's voice broke her intense concentration on the winch drum. She looked up at the precise moment he lost his grip on the mast. "No!"

Stretching out, trying to regain his grasp, he nearly turned upside down in the chair. *Houdini* rolled past twenty degrees of heel. The carabiner—he'd forgotten to re-clip it to the safety line.

At twenty-five degrees of heel he swung out like a plumb bob, thirty feet above the water. *Houdini* lingered at the end of the roll. He forced himself to look down. *Houdini*'s course was not perpendicular to the crest of the wave that lifted and rolled her. Something was wrong. She'd somehow turned twenty degrees to the left.

"We're turning! We're turning!" he shouted, as *Houdini* slowly began to right herself.

Vivian looked back to the cockpit. From the mast it was impossible to see if the autopilot still had control. She cleated the halyard and scrambled aft.

As the next pyramid-shaped wave moved under *Houdini*'s keel, the yacht rolled faster. Mitch braced himself for the impact as he swung toward the mast. As if seeing everything in slow motion, he realized he would miss it. He would fly right past the mast as *Houdini* healed to port.

Desperately, he grabbed for the mast as he went by, misjudged the distance and cracked his right elbow. He began to spin.

At thirty degrees of heel to port, he hung well out over the water, twirling in the air like a circus performer. He cradled his numb elbow close to his body while his left hand gripped the halyard to keep him upright.

"Mitch, the autopilot's belt broke!" Vivian shouted, as she took the wheel and spun hard to starboard.

Part of him heard her, the other part concentrated on locating the mast. The next swell lifted and heeled *Houdini* back to starboard. The yacht's bow dropped toward the forming trough. The forward pitch changed the angle of his return swing. He hit the port spreader with his left shin and crashed into the mast with his chest and head. The impact dazed him but halted his swing long enough for his left arm to slide around the mast. Straddling the port side of the mast, he avoided another ride to starboard.

Tears of desperation ran down Vivian's cheeks as she willed *Houdini* back to her proper course. The bow came around square to the waves and the next roll to port was less severe. Vivian couldn't think what else to do except steer. She was trapped at the wheel, unable to lower Mitch or go below to retrieve the spare belt.

"Mitch, what should I do!"

Mitch hung on. "Let me...rest a second." The reduced heeling enabled him to hold on with just his arms. The spreaders still prevented him from getting his legs around the mast. He considered his options. The big question was, did he have the strength left for any course of action?

He calmed himself with a deep breath. He flexed his tingling right arm, testing it. Shouting as distinctly as he could, he told Vivian his decision. "Set the wheel brake. Then come to the mast, uncleat the main halyard, and hurry back to the wheel."

"You'll fall!" she shouted.

"No! I'll hold on to the safety line and lower myself."

"Mitch..." Vivian pleaded.

"Do it!" he yelled, feeling his strength draining away through every pore.

Vivian glanced at the swells overtaking *Houdini*. They looked ominous, but she could not foresee any immediate improvement. After steadying the boat square to the next wave, she centered the rudder and turned the wheel brake until it was tight, locking the steering wheel in position. In five seconds she was at the mast uncleating the halyard. Before taking the wraps of line off the winch drum, she looked up. "Are you ready!"

Mitch's inner voice encouraged him, like a coach sending in the quarterback with a suicide play. He let go of the mast with his arms and grabbed the safety line. "GO! GO! GO!" he shouted. His hands took the strain of his weight as Vivian threw the turns of rope off the winch and then dashed back to the cockpit to retake control of the wheel before *Houdini* drifted off course.

Mitch lowered himself in cautious, hand-over-hand increments. The instant his knees were below the spreaders he locked his legs around the mast, taking half the burden from his weakened arms. Like an inchworm, he painfully descended, holding first with his legs, letting his upper body slump and then sliding his legs down the mast while gripping the safety line.

Relief flooded Vivian's over-stressed nerves as he reached and cleared the lower spreaders. In another minute he passed the boom and his feet touched the roof of the cabin. His legs collapsed under him and he crumpled to the cabin roof, motionless beside the mast.

"Mitch, are you all right?" Vivian shouted.

"Just let me lie here for awhile, but don't go anywhere; I may want you to shoot me."

Mitch felt as if every connection between his brain and muscles had been switched off. Unfortunately, the same was not true for his stomach. No longer overshadowed by other worries, the waves of nausea and convulsions returned. Buried inside him though, a new emotion was growing. Pride. He'd faced danger and shown courage. His fear was gone.

Then he remembered Andres.

Throughout the morning, the wind backed slowly from northeast to west. Once again under full sail, *Houdini* forged her way southward through the building seas on a course Mitch hoped would be perpendicular to, and directly away, from Andres' most likely track. If the cyclone's path lay north of her, *Houdini* would be in what textbooks called the storm's 'navigable semi-circle' and the counterclockwise wind-flow would push her away. But if the storm's track passed south of her, she would be in the 'dangerous semi-circle.' The monstrous whirlpool of wind and cloud would pull *Houdini* into its path, drawing her toward the eye.

A small sailboat might survive a hurricane's near miss with winds of less than seventy miles-per-hour. But at the perimeter of the eye, the wall, where winds often exceed one hundred miles-per-hour, the chances of avoiding a catastrophic capsize or pitchpoling in steep breaking seas were only slightly better than those of winning a state lottery.

Henry had told him: "It's the seas and not the wind you have to watch out for. The wind may scare you shitless, but it's the seas that'll kill you."

The weather service still designated Andres a tropical storm. Early season tropical depressions often fizzled, never achieving the full rank of hurricane. Mitch prayed that would be Andres' fate. He rested his battered body in the cockpit and gnawed the corner of a thumbnail, scanning the eastern horizon. The shifting wind and parade of changing cloud forms told him

Andres was closing in. With *Houdini* fully canvassed, there was little else he and Vivian could do except listen to the weather broadcasts and prepare for hurricane force winds and heavy seas.

Houdini had taken good care of them thus far. Mitch spoke to her silently, exhorting her to live up to her name. He thought of Vivian's mother. She was very close to her two daughters. He envisioned her sitting at home watching TV, nervously awaiting her regular evening call from Frank Fullerton, telling her that her daughter was alive and well. Mitch felt a total determination to see Vivian delivered safely to the Marquesas. He had to get *Houdini* through this storm. After that, if it came to it, Vivian was capable of sailing the rest of the way on her own.

He heard footsteps on the companionway. Vivian popped up through the main hatch and offered him a sandwich swaddled in a paper towel. "Thanks. What's the barometer reading?"

"1003, down eight millibars from last night."

"After lunch, let's make sure we've got everything prepared for rough going."

"Think it's going to hit us?"

Mitch spoke with more confidence than he felt. "The center will miss us but we'll get gale force winds and big seas."

Vivian brushed the hair back from his forehead. "How are you feeling?"

"Like I played pro football in a jockstrap. It only hurts when I breathe."

Vivian gave him a forced smile that conflicted with the concern in her eyes. "You're going to be a big help."

"It's only bruises, and I'm not seeing spots anymore."

"What kind of preparations do we need to make?"

"We can start by seeing that everything below is securely stowed in a locker or tied down, absolutely nothing lying around loose. Henry told me most injuries in a knockdown or rollover are caused by flying objects."

"Lovely image. What else?"

"Double check to see that all the hatches and ports are dogged down tight. And let's take the cowl vents off deck and put in the deck plates."

"It's so humid and stuffy below already, I wonder if we'll be able to breathe down there without them."

"If we don't seal the cabin tight, it could get a lot more than humid."

By mid afternoon, *Houdini* charged southward at over seven knots in the rising winds. Rain showers slanted to the sea surface from the charcoal gray underbellies of anvil-shaped thunderclouds marching along the northeast horizon. Mitch studied the dark line of squalls, trying to get a sense of their relative movement. Somewhere beyond them lay Andres, a massive engine of nature, fueled by the heat of the tropical ocean. A long-period swell rolled in from the east, opposing wind-driven seas, whipping them into steep, irregular shards of water.

Below, Vivian struggled in *Houdini's* rolling, airless cabin to keep her balance. She gripped the chart table with one hand while pressing computer keys with the other. Concentrating on the small keyboard amidst all the movement made her woozy. If she hadn't duct-taped the laptop and its small printer to the table, they would have long since flown across the cabin.

When the weather chart image filled the screen, she pressed a key and waited while the tiny ink-jet printer made a paper copy. She leaned against the bulkhead, hiding her eyes from motion in the crook of her elbow until she heard the printer stop. She ripped the sheet of paper from the printer and half-staggered, half-charged her way past the galley and up the companionway.

She sucked in a deep breath of fresh air as she emerged underneath the dodger. "Here's the bad news." She handed Mitch the print-out and crawled aft on her hands and knees to the exposed area near the helm. She turned, letting the strong cool breeze hit her in the face.

"So, Andres has made the major leagues," Mitch said.

HURRICANE ANDRES
10.5 N, 117.7W W @ 7 kt
MAX WIND 75 kt

He studied the chart.

"There is some good news. They're no longer saying he's headed west-southwest, just west."

"And it hasn't gained speed since the Honolulu voice broadcast this morning," Vivian added.

The previously isolated hurricane symbol now appeared in the bull's-eye of a target formed by three isobar rings of decreasing barometric pressure. The innermost ring bore the label, '96', the abbreviation for 996 millibars. The outer ring, 1004 millibars, encompassed *Houdini's* current position.

"How close do you think he'll get?" asked Vivian.

"Assuming no major changes in his course or ours, I'd guess about sixty miles."

"Sounds close."

"It is."

With sunset came time for Vivian's radio contact with Frank. *Houdini* lurched and slid down the growing seas, most of which now sported breaking crests. She waited until the last possible moment before leaving Mitch and descending into the cabin. To prevent more spray from finding its way below, she closed the main hatch behind her. Inside the dimly lit, sealed and stuffy cabin she felt like a maraschino cherry in a cocktail shaker.

She pushed the ham radio's power button and turned the dial until the ice-blue numbers read 21.380. Already, the first tendrils of nausea invaded her brain and stomach. She sat on the chart table's swing-out seat and rested her head on her forearm.

At exactly 0130 Greenwich time she heard Frank's voice, crackling with static, asking if the frequency was in use by other stations. After a brief pause, he said Vivian's call sign three times followed twice by his own. Vivian keyed her hand mike and answered his call sign with hers.

"*Vivian, I can barely copy you. Much worse than yesterday. Take it slow.*"

Vivian spaced her words. "It's probably due to the weather. We have some bad weather near us."

"*I know. How close is it to you, and what is your position?*"

"It's about one hundred miles southeast." She continued, giving him *Houdini*'s latitude, longitude, course heading, boatspeed and wind and sea conditions.

"Too much static, Vivian. I copied the storm one hundred miles southeast. The rest, garbled. Are you and Mitch both okay?"

"Yes, yes, we are okay," said Vivian, raising her voice. "We had problems with the spinnaker yesterday but it's fixed now." She covered her eyes.

"Understand you had some kind of problem but it's okay now. Roger?"

"Roger, roger."

"Your mom sends her love. Any messages?"

"Tell her we're fine and that I love her too."

"I'm losing you, Vivian. Anything else?"

The first convulsion rippled up her abdomen. "No. That's it. Thanks, Frank."

"Martinez called. The trial starts tomorrow. Copy?"

"Roger...roger, Frank, I copy." Another convulsion; she clutched her throat.

"Okay, you two keep 'er snugged up tight and right side up. I'll be here tomorrow. Roger?"

Vivian acknowledged and signed off. She dropped the mike, punched the power button and headed for the companionway.

"Did you get him?" Mitch asked.

She ignored his query and lunged for the lee rail. Gathering her hair in one hand, she leaned over the side and retched the contents of her stomach into the ocean sliding by, inches from her face as *Houdini* rolled hard to port.

Mitch tentatively massaged the back of her neck. "I gather it's not too pleasant down there."

Vivian paused, wiped her mouth and dipped her hand in the sea. "One more second and I would have barfed on the mike." She sat up and glanced at a tubular cresting wave off the port quarter, then at the taut, metallic looking sails and finally the windspeed indicator. "Twenty-five knots! Mitch, we can't keep carrying all that sail in this amount of wind."

"I know; the autopilot's going nuts. We've been surfing to ten knots, even hit eleven once. We need to either hand steer or shorten sail."

"For God's sake, let's reef. It'll be dark soon."

"The speed is taking us out of the storm's path, but you're right. We'd better do it."

Furling the large genoa in the strong winds was a struggle. At least the roller furling system allowed them to accomplish the task from within the relative safety of the cockpit. Reefing the mainsail, however, required that one person go forward to the mast. Mitch took four sail ties from the lazaret.

"Are you sure you're up to this?" asked Vivian. "Maybe you should let me put the reef in." She had reefed the main herself only twice before, in relatively light conditions for practice. She wondered if Mitch had regained enough strength after his masthead ordeal to hold on to the boom and corral the stiff, heavy sail.

"I think I'm up to it. Rather find out now than later."

"Okay, but can we go for two reefs while we're at it?"

Three rows of reefing points divided *Houdini*'s mainsail into four horizontal slabs. Each reef reduced the mainsail area exposed to the wind by twenty percent.

"That'll really slow us down."

"But if the wind keeps rising, we won't be slowed for long." Vivian pleaded with her eyes. "And if we don't do it now, we'll have to reef again in higher winds and darkness."

Mitch looked at her and then studied the sails and windspeed indicator before answering. "Okay, two reefs it is."

With the sail ties draped around his neck, he crawled and inched his way to the mast, working from hand-hold to hand-hold. Spray from the bow curled up and over the rail, drenching the back of his T-shirt. The warm water felt cold in the wind, causing him to shiver.

He winched the topping lift, raising the boom end to put slack in the sail's leech, then lowered the sail and began tying the excess sailcloth to the boom. He was over half way to the end of the boom, cinching the third tie, when Vivian noticed he hadn't attached the tether of his safety harness to the base of the mast. She started to yell a warning but held her breath as he moved out to the fourth reef point. *Houdini* heeled to port placing Mitch over the rushing water.

He finished the last of the four ties and pulled himself back along the boom. Vivian breathed again.

The first fat drops of rain arrived, dappling the darkened surface of the sea. Mitch hurried below, handed up Vivian's foulweather jacket and bib overalls. He then changed into dry clothes and his own foulweather suit. He poked his head out the main hatch. "You hungry?"

"Maybe. Not sure if I can keep anything down, though."

He disappeared again for ten minutes. When he re-emerged, he carried two large mugs.

"What is it?" Vivian asked.

"Beef stew. Fresh out of the can."

"That brown mush? Cold? How can you eat that stuff in these conditions?"

"Either I'm getting my sea legs, or I'm too hungry to care. Don't you want to try some?"

"Are you kidding? Just the sight of it makes me nauseous. Mitch, I just noticed something."

"What?"

"The birds are gone."

Vivian had the small satisfaction of seeing her prediction come true. *Houdini* initially slowed to six knots and then five with only the double-reefed main. But as the rain fell harder and squalls overtook them, the windspeed climbed into the thirties, gusting higher. And with it, *Houdini*'s speed crept back into the sixes, sevens and eights.

It was a night she wouldn't likely forget. Squalls like monstrous herds of buffalo stampeded over them in the darkness, heeling *Houdini* wildly left and right. Lightning bolts flashed all around, illuminating the slanting showers and thunderclouds from which they came. Between peals of thunder, the only sound that interrupted the sizzle of rain striking the sea and the whoosh of *Houdini*'s wake was the roar of crashing waves that broke close astern every few seconds.

She shined her pocket flashlight on her watch. It was almost ten, an hour into her first watch of the night, and yet Mitch was still with her in the cockpit. The spray dodger, which spanned the cabin roof and covered the main hatch, afforded them some protection from the pelting rain. She nestled between Mitch's upraised knees, her head against his chest. Though their circumstances forced their intimate huddle, she couldn't ignore the plain fact that it pleased her. "You need to get some sleep," she said.

"I'll be okay."

"No, really. We're both going to need rest, and I can't sleep when it's my turn unless I know you've had at least a couple of hours yourself."

"Sure you can handle it alone?"

She hadn't the vaguest idea. "The windspeed seems to have stabilized. I can manage."

"Okay, but don't leave the cockpit without telling me, and call me if the wind strength starts building."

"Have no fear about that." Vivian raised up to let him move.

"I may not hear my alarm." Mitch said, as he climbed over the companionway weather boards. "If I'm not out here by midnight, give me a shout." Vivian nodded, and he disappeared beneath the sliding hatch.

The SatNav's display and the power panel's indicator lights bathed *Houdini*'s darkened interior in a dim mixture of green and red. Normally Mitch would have removed his clammy foulweather gear at the foot of the companionway to keep the rest of the cabin dry. Instead he staggered his way forward and collapsed onto the port settee. Being fully dressed and ready to dash on deck took precedence over comfort and protecting the cushions.

Heeled on starboard tack, the L-shaped port settee was on the low side. Gravity pressed him into the corner between the seat and back cushions. The drawback of sleeping on that side was noise. At anything over five knots, the whoosh of water sliding along the hull was like a roaring cataract. The fiberglass skin amplified the noise and made it sound as if the boat were going twice its true speed. But hardly a minute passed before an ingenious feature of the human brain relieved him. It filtered out the ambient noise in his fatigued and semiconscious mind. Simultaneously, he fell sound asleep.

Outside, Vivian crouched beneath the dodger, hugging her knees to her chest on the higher, windward side of the slanting cockpit. If Andres cooperated, Mitch might get two hours of undisturbed sleep. If he didn't hear his alarm, she'd let him sleep an extra hour.

To keep her thoughts trained on what was happening, rather than what might happen, she developed a scanning routine. Starting with the knotmeter, she noted boat speed, then glanced at the wind indicator for wind speed and direction. Next she peeked from under the dodger and put the flashlight's beam on the double-reefed mainsail, searching its seams for rips and satisfying herself that it hadn't shaken loose its reef ties.

She strained to scan the horizon on each side from bow to stern in search of ships. The chance of seeing anything, or being seen, in the driving rain and darkness was almost laughable. With the autopilot working so hard, they couldn't afford the constant power drain of the radar. The magnetic compass was the last check in her system. Although at times *Houdini* fell as much as fifteen degrees off course, the autopilot gamely fought a running battle to bring her back to the programmed heading of 160 degrees magnetic.

During the ten minutes Vivian allowed between each scan, her thoughts bounced erratically between paranoid wonderings of Andres' movements and random memories. Her foul weather suit felt cold and clammy against bare arms and legs. Even with the protection of a turned up collar and sou'wester hat, strong winds from the quarter drove sufficient rain against her exposed face and hair to soak her T-shirt to the skin.

Two days earlier she'd been lazing in a sunny cockpit. Between chapters in her book, she'd imagined her former co-workers toiling at the dental clinic and pitied them. Suddenly, the humdrum routine of a dentist's office didn't sound so dreary. In fact, Muzak and floors that didn't move sounded wonderful. And a warm, king-sized waterbed—sleeping in till noon on the weekend, that was heaven.

A more distressing thought arose; if she and Mitch hadn't come along, Henry and Jill might still be alive. Henry's original plan had been to be in Zihuatenejo in time to leave for the Marquesas on the first of April. She and Mitch had slowed them so much they had barely made it to Puerto Vallarta by that date. Henry and Bill might never have met if *Walden* had been free to sail according to Henry's schedule.

But, if they hadn't come, where would that have left her and Mitch? The rift caused by Marjorie would have been avoided, but if not for this trip...would there be any relationship left to ruffle? If forced to make a choice, she'd relive the revelation of his affair with Marjorie rather than go back to the emotionless limbo they'd been in two years ago. At least now there were sparks and flames.

During her night watches since leaving Mexico, she'd evolved a more complex view of the sin of adultery than the simple, one-dimensional offense she'd drawn narrow boundaries around in the past. She now viewed this particular sin as having varying degrees of severity, similar to those of murder. If one actively, and with premeditation, pursued an illicit relationship for no other reason than sexual gratification, they were guilty in the first degree. Period. Neither Mitch nor Marjorie, or herself for that matter, were guilty in the first degree. She could not conceive herself committing that crime, nor could she see herself forgiving it in others.

If, in a moment of pent-up lust or passion born of deprivation, one person seduced another person, causing one or both parties to break their marriage vows, the seducer was guilty in the second degree. This was Marjorie's crime.

But for the one seduced, it seemed a lesser offense, perhaps the third degree, depending on how much he or she resisted. She supposed that some might even argue that, depending on the circumstances, the person in this case is, in one sense, a victim, not an adulterer. This was Mitch, and, had it not been for a narrow escape, herself as well.

She thought a person of average morality should have no trouble avoiding the sin in the first degree, or even the second. But how many people, whether happily married or not, could avoid it in the third degree if subjected to a determined, all-out assault by a reasonably attractive, sympathetic, and desperate admirer? The majority of men probably never had to face such a predicament. But for women, dealing with sexual advances, improper or not, was a fact of life. Women had more at stake, and through experience, developed appropriate ways of deflecting unwanted attention at an early age. Nevertheless, from her own close call, she knew it was virtually impossible for a person—man or woman—to know with absolute certainty, that under no circumstances would they fall from that precipice. One only gained that self-knowledge at the moment of truth.

She hadn't yet forgiven Mitch, but as each day passed, the hurt and anger faded by degrees. Having nearly lost him, first to the shark and then the spinnaker, made her realize that such pain could not displace the deep seated love she still felt for him. In time the hurt might remain only as a small ember hidden beneath the ashes, a reminder of the importance of fidelity.

Houdini heeled sharply to a stronger than average gust and she started her next scan.

Saturday, May 11

Mitch tried to yell a warning, but as if in the vacuum of space, no sound escaped his mouth. He watched helplessly as the knife flashed from behind Bill's back and plunged into Henry's heart. Jill's piercing scream came too late. It ended abruptly in a gurgling hiss as Bill whipped the thin blade around and cut her neck to the vertebrae in one clean movement.

Mitch sat up, covering his ears, shielding them from the sound of Jill's struggle for one last breath through her severed throat. Three seconds passed before he realized it was the sound of water streaming past *Houdini*'s hull. He grabbed his wrist and pressed a button on his watch. The illuminated display read 00:10. He'd slept through his alarm. Vivian had let him sleep.

Though the wind didn't sound much worse than when he'd come below, it occurred to him *Houdini* now heeled more—a lot more—than she should with the wind on the quarter. The wind must have backed further as Andres approached.

He swung around to a sitting position and ran his fingers through his hair and down his face, wiping away the last vestiges of the gruesome nightmare. He staggered across the tilted, rolling cabin to the chart table and punched a button on the SatNav. Green numerals displayed the time of last position fix. *Good; less than half an hour ago. At least we know where we are.* He wrote the coordinates down and pressed another button. The speed- and course-made-good since last fix appeared; 6.9 knots, 232 degrees magnetic. 232? *Vivian, where the hell are you going?* We're supposed to be heading southeast. *You're paralleling the hurricane's course, for Christ's sake.*

He flipped up the jacket's hood and headed for the cockpit. Even the dim glow of the SatNav and power panel lights was enough to partially impair his night vision. He slid the main hatch open. Looking to his left he waited for Vivian's huddled form to appear in her usual position. Normally, she said good morning before he saw her, but tonight she was silent.

"Viv? What's going on? How come you changed course? "

The autopilot chirped spasmodically, obediently following the unceasing commands of its electronic compass. The cockpit's outline became visible. Vivian was not in it. Maybe she slipped past him to use the head while he was asleep.

He twisted around and yelled into the cabin. "Vivian! Are you down there?" No answer.

A tingling sensation spread over his face and became a shiver that flowed down his neck and back. He turned back, groped for the pad-eye where her safety harness's tether line should be attached, felt the snap hook, grabbed the smooth nylon rope and followed its white trail through the darkness with his eyes. The taut line stretched from the pad-eye to where it bent the port cockpit lifeline into a broad V.

She's overboard!

He prayed he wasn't too late. He vaulted over the companionway weather boards and dove to the lee rail in one motion. It was nearly awash. He saw her instantly.

She was at the end of the nylon tether, not more than five feet away. Her body slid over the top of a passing bow wave, became partially airborne and crashed hard into the face of the next one. He could not see her face. The way her body undulated and moved so passively told him he was too late. She was completely limp.

Her boots and socks were gone, legs spread slightly apart. Her arms, where were her arms? He saw them—folded across her chest. She's holding on; *she's holding on to the harness!*

"Vivian, I'm here!" he shouted "I'm going to get you. Hang on!"

He tried pulling on the tether. It might as well have been an iron bar. The weight and drag of Vivian and her wet clothes was too much. Even if he hadn't been weakened and bruised from the masthead trip he couldn't have hoisted her aboard against the tremendous pull.

Think! If he tried to winch her in he'd have to disconnect the tether from its pad eye. He might lose her trying to get the heavily loaded line around the winch. He had to slow *Houdini* down. If he lost her in the dark at this speed she'd be gone in an instant. She was alive and still attached to the boat. Whatever he did, he mustn't make matters worse.

He groped for the autopilot's control box, found it, brailled his way to the buttons and pressed the ten- and one-degree-right buttons simultaneously, a combination which initiated a one-hundred-degree tack to starboard. *Houdini* turned slowly into the howling wind. The mainsail's leach slatted and snapped like a sidewinder on amphetamines. He winched its sheet in tight, calming the gyrating boom.

Houdini lost her forward momentum, barely completing the tack. Speed dropped to two knots, then dead slow. Mitch punched the pilot's 'Standby' button and locked the wheel hard left, putting *Houdini* in a heave-to configuration, stalled, with her rudder and sail in opposition.

Vivian trailed on the sloop's windward side. The wind and sea pushed her toward the hull. The speed that had prevented Mitch from pulling her in had also kept her on the surface. When *Houdini* stopped, Vivian sank.

Mitch's heart came to his throat when he saw the ghost-like form of a red-trimmed, white foulweather suit beneath the dark water. Only the top of her sou'wester hat broke the surface. He grabbed the tether and pulled. He fell backwards in the pitching cockpit, narrowly avoiding going overboard to starboard. Vivian had been trying to pull herself up. He had jerked the wet line through her weakened hands.

He leaped back. She was completely under. He seized the tether again, this time taking up the strain slowly until he felt her full weight. Her hat broke the surface, head tilting to one side. Her arms hung motionless.

Devoting every ounce of strength, he managed to get her shoulders above the water, but no more. *Please, God, let me get her up.*

He held her there, racking his brain for a solution. He'd have to use a winch after all. A breaking wave crashed against *Houdini*, slamming Vivian against the hull, drenching him, and filling the cockpit well. He held on. At the same instant, he felt a momentary easing of the strain on the tether. He took in the slack. *Come on, you bastards, give me another one!*

He worked Vivian alongside the hull to the lifeline gate. A smaller wave came. He gained another six inches. He wrapped the tether's slack around a stanchion with one hand and quickly opened the lifeline gate with the other. The carabiner attaching the tether to Vivian's harness was now within his reach. If he could grab it, he'd have a better purchase. To reach it, he'd have to lean far over the side. He hesitated. If he went overboard, it would be the end of both of them.

He wedged himself against the gate stanchions, reached down and grabbed the carabiner. Pulling on it caused Vivian to rotate toward the hull. He saw her pale, lifeless face. A surge of fear-driven adrenaline rippled through his body. A breaking wave approached off the beam. *Come on, come on, you big son-of-a-bitch, come on!* Bracing his feet against the caprail he waited for the wave's impact. It hit and curled over him. He heaved on the carabiner with everything he had.

Houdini rolled away from the breaker, heeling past forty-five degrees. For an instant Vivian lay flat against the smooth fiberglass hull. Mitch used the wave's energy and hauled her over the rail.

As *Houdini* righted herself, he dragged Vivian by her armpits to the protection of the cockpit. He skipped the CPR preliminaries and immediately began breathing for her. After two breaths, he checked her neck for a pulse. A wave of relief swept over him. He felt the unmistakable throb of her carotid artery.

"You're gonna make it, Babe, you're gonna make it." He pinched her nose and breathed for her again. Once, twice. She coughed, then sputtered. It was the most beautiful sound he'd ever heard. He braced himself in the rolling cockpit, trapping her tightly against the seat back.

"Viv, can you hear me?"

She coughed, spraying seawater and mucous in his face. She moaned. It was brief, almost inaudible. But it was her voice, a voice seconds ago he thought he might never hear again.

She tried to swallow; she coughed. "My throat," she murmured.

"You swallowed a lot of seawater. Take it easy."

Flashes of lightning periodically illuminated her face as twenty-foot waves lifted and rolled the 40-foot sloop like a toy, yawing the hull left and right. Large curling breakers crashed menacingly on all sides.

Mitch ignored the chaos. He didn't care how unseamanlike or risky it was. For the moment, his only concern was for Vivian's well-being and comfort. He wiped wet strands of hair away from dazed, half-lidded eyes. He brushed his cheek against her mouth and felt her warm breath.

She whispered into his ear, "I knew...you'd get me."

"God, Viv, how long were you out there?"

"Don't know."

"Did you scream?"

"Once. Got mouthful."

Houdini rolled hard to port. He caught himself from falling against her.

"Got to sail her, Mitch."

"Soon as I get you below. Can you help?"

"I'll try."

Like one drunken sailor bringing another back from an all night binge, Mitch managed to half-carry, half-drag Vivian below and onto the starboard settee. He rigged the lee cloth to immobilize her in the berth.

He knelt beside her. "Everything's gonna be okay, Babe. Just rest."

"Sorry."

"What for?"

Her eyes closed. Her voice was dreamlike. "Worst time for this."

"Don't worry; it's okay. What happened?"

"Autopilot lever flipped off. Jumped over to push it down...started coming back to course. Wave hit, boat heeled. Fell over lifelines.

"Thank God for your harness."

"Tether's too long. Started spinning. Spread my legs to stay on my back."

"You did good, Babe."

Her eyes half opened. "Can you...manage?"

"I'll get us turned around, and we'll be gone before Andres knows we're here."

She almost smiled. "You don't fool me."

"I know."

"No you don't. You think you're only pretending to be brave." Her eyes opened and fixed upon his. "Mitch...I love you."

Mitch bowed his head against her shoulder. He kissed her cheek. "I love you, too."

Her eyelids fluttered and closed. He watched her breathe for a few seconds before leaving the relatively secure, comparatively quiet cocoon of *Houdini's* cabin and returning to the chaos outside. While rescuing Vivian, he had shut out everything else. Stepping into the cockpit, his senses experienced the full onslaught of the maelstrom's growing fury. It was raining hard, but in the rising wind it was difficult to distinguish rain from wind blown spray. As waves crested and broke, gale force winds carried away their tops in horizontal sheets that flew away like wraiths into the blackness downwind. Within his small dome of visibility, Mitch could see the white crests of graybeards all around him. Only random chance had prevented another large breaker from capsizing them while he was below. Such luck would not hold; he could not leave *Houdini* to fend for herself.

He had to reduce sail. He checked the windspeed indicator. It was now holding at thirty-five knots and creeping higher with each gust. No sense going for a third reef; furl it; go bare poles. *Houdini* would derive enough power for steerageway from the windage of her mast and rigging.

Even with the assistance of engine and autopilot, furling the main took twice as long and was three times as dangerous without Vivian's help. The boom snapped viciously from side to side, trying to fling him overboard as he worked his way aft from the mast to the dodger. Each time the yacht crested the ridge of an approaching wave and fell down its backside, he held on against negative G-forces that threatened to lift him from the deck. Slowly and deliberately, he tied the remaining loose sailcloth to the boom. He cinched each reef knot until his fingers ached. Once finished, he crawled on his stomach along the cabin top, to the deck and back to the cockpit.

The wind-driven rain hit with such intensity and volume he had to shield his mouth to breathe. Even the briefest of glances to windward stung his face with BB shots of salt spray that prevented his eyes from opening for more than a split second. *Should have brought my ski goggles.* He remembered his dive mask. It was still in the lazaret.

He snatched the dive mask and snorkel from the lazaret and put them on. He turned to face the wind. He could see—sort of—and he could breathe. He checked the wind indicator;

forty-to-fifty steady, and gusting higher. He reached down, pressed the autopilot's standby button and flipped the cam lever, giving him control of the wheel. He turned it a quarter-turn to the left. He looked to starboard. At the limits of his impaired visibility he saw a thin white fuzzy cloud above where he visualized the horizon should be. Instantly, he realized it couldn't be a cloud; it was the crest of a freak wave bearing down on him—two waves piggybacked to form a single monster.

He pushed the throttle to the stop and spun the wheel hard over. The diesel raced. *Turn, baby, turn!*

The sloop came around, stern to the wave, a second before it engulfed her. Mitch held his breath as everything around him turned white. Giant hands pushed down on his shoulders, slamming him into the helm seat. As fast as it had come, it was gone. *Houdini*'s engine labored to get her moving up the backside of the huge rogue. He stood in foaming water to his crotch. Slowly the sloop gained way. Several hundred pounds of sea water slowly drained over the coaming and out through the scuppers. One of the spray dodger's steel support arms dangled in mid-air, ripped loose from its attachment.

Mitch looked over his shoulder at the next approaching wave. *Come on, Houdini girl, give me some speed, just a little more speed, baby.* His eyes fixed on the knotmeter. The rumbling Mercedes smoothed and the boat's speed rose to two knots, then three. Now he could steer. Within seconds he was going too fast. The boat surfed wildly down the steepening slope. He cut the throttle, shifted into neutral. *Houdini* didn't slow; he killed the engine. With the strong wind at her back, she charged into the trough at over six knots with only her mast for a sail. He tore off the mask and snorkel.

Half an hour later and the wind still rising, *Houdini* was hitting eights and nines, skidding and swerving down the steep faces of each overtaking wave. Too often, one caught her flat-transomed stern and yawed her to one side, momentarily exposing her vulnerable beam to the oncoming seas. Each time, Mitch fought to head her back down-slope before the tubular crest hit her broadside and rolled her.

He knew he had to somehow slow the boat down. Fatigue, inexperience, or bad luck would eventually cause a mistake;

Houdini would broach and be capsized instantly. It was time for the drogue. Henry told him he'd never see conditions rough enough to use it.

He waited for the best possible conditions, re-engaged the autopilot and clawed the drogue out of its storage place in the starboard lazaret. The drogue, similar in form and function to a jet airplane's braking chute, consisted of a three-foot diameter hoop of stiff wire cable and a large open-weave basket constructed of two-inch nylon webbing. A heavy doughnut-shaped ring of flat steel weighted the bottom. He quickly checked to make sure the drogue's tow line was securely shackled to its swivel and eased the limp basket over the transom and into the water. It inflated immediately. The drag was tremendous, more than he could hold. The tow line streamed out as though he'd harpooned a whale. He scrambled to get a turn around the large stern cleat. Half the drogue's 250-foot tow line ran out before he gained control. *Houdini* slowed from six knots to five. When seventy-five feet of line remained on board, he took two wraps around the starboard genoa winch and cleated it. *Houdini*'s speed fell to three and four knots. *Jesus, Henry, you'd think I knew what I was doing.* He disengaged the maniacally chirping autopilot and began to steer.

Wind velocity increased to fifty-five knots, gusting frequently to seventy. He estimated the seas at thirty feet, but it was impossible to see from crest to crest except when lightning flashed. He found he could almost steer by sound. The closest and biggest breakers roared a warning of their approach. On hearing one approach, he snapped his head around to face the hail-like spray long enough to spot the wave then dodge left or right as necessary. When not in the midst of evasive action, he concentrated on keeping *Houdini* on a track that quartered away from the ridge of each new crest like a surfer staying in front of the curl.

In the first hours of hand steering he was absorbed with learning how to maneuver in the horrendous seas. Gradually, his senses and reflexes tuned into the hidden pattern. His body became an automaton, a machine separated from his brain. It freed his mind to think of other things. He knew he should be terrified, as terrified as he was when he came on deck after securing Vivian in her berth. But a strange exhilaration came over him, and an almost quixotic feeling of invincibility.

The mountains around *Houdini* turned white beneath a blanket of spindrift.

Sunday, May 12

He thought he was hallucinating until he realized it was simply the first light of dawn, shifting black to gray. He'd almost forgotten other worlds existed besides the dark, tempestuous hell he'd sailed through for the last several hours. Vivian's bodiless face suddenly floated above the companionway weather boards. The vision spoke to him.

"How are—" She cleared her throat and tried again. "How are you doing?" she yelled.

Her voice was barely audible above the shrieking wind. "Great!" he shouted back, smiling. Lack of sleep, fatigue and seeing her up made him feel giddy.

Vivian glanced to the left and right of him, taking in the steep, foam-streaked waves that approached off both quarters. "The sea's driven you insane."

"It's not as bad as it was. I'm just glad to see you up. Are you okay?"

"Better. I have a monster sore throat and bruised armpits. Want me to relieve you?"

"No, just keep me company for a little bit."

She disappeared, returned quickly, tying her sou'wester in place as she came up the steps. She snapped her tether to her harness, climbed over the weather boards and joined Mitch beside the wheel. "Have you been hand-steering all this time?" she asked.

"Yeah, it's too much for the autopilot. Here, stand in front of me."

Vivian slid behind the wheel between his outstretched arms, whose robotic movements mimicked the autopilot's short, precise, course corrections. She put her hands on the wheel beside his. He heard the rushing sound and sensed the familiar light in his peripheral vision that he'd learned to detect. He snapped the wheel hard right and turned sharply away from a wall of white foam. When it had passed, he gently resumed his quartering course and jerky, minute corrections. Satisfied, he lifted the brim of Vivian's hat with his nose and snuggled his lips next to her ear for a fleeting kiss. "I thought I'd lost you last night. I never want to have that feeling again."

Vivian rolled her head so that his lips moved along her cheek until they met the corner of her mouth. "Me either."

He resumed his vigil, but kept his mouth close to her ear as he spoke. "Viv, I'm sorry for everything. Can we start over?" Her silence wasn't what he'd hoped for.

Finally she answered. "Yes, but there's something I need to tell you when we're out of the storm."

"Tell me now." He heard a wave coming and spun *Houdini*'s wheel a quarter turn to the right.

She cleared her throat. "That week Kathy Hale quit and you almost resigned?"

"Yeah?" He jerked the wheel to the right, then back.

Vivian's chin tilted down. "I did something that week," Vivian paused as *Houdini* accelerated down the face of a wave, "that I'm...that I should have told you about."

Mitch recalled the unaddressed interoffice envelope he'd found on his desk. His chest muscles tightened. "What?"

"I went to lunch with one of my patients that week. I went to a motel room with him, but nothing happened, Mitch, and I never saw him again, I swear it."

"Nothing happened?"

"No. I ran out."

He took a breath, kissed her on the neck and said his thought out loud. "So it wasn't a hoax."

Vivian pulled away. "What hoax?"

He heard the anger rising in her tone. "No, not you. That following Monday, I found an anonymous note on my desk. Said something like, while I was having Kathy Hale, someone else was having you at such and such motel."

"Someone did see me." Vivian took one hand from the wheel and covered her eyes. "You never said anything."

"I didn't believe it—couldn't. Figured it was some jerk wanting to give me a zinger on my way out the door. And I guess I thought, if it were true, I was mostly to blame." He straightened the wheel as a wave broke against *Houdini*'s transom. "I tore up the note, threw it in the trash. That's when I called and asked if you wanted to go with Henry and Jill."

Vivian shook her head and leaned back against him. "You mean you quit for us, so that we could be together?"

"I did say that; more than once, Babe."

"I thought you were saying it just to convince me. All this time I thought it was really because of all the crap you were going through at work." The wind shrieked in the empty rigging as *Houdini* rose on the exposed crest of a passing swell.

"That was part of it." Mitch turned the wheel left two spokes, paused, then right one. "But the note made me realize my priorities were upside down. I moved you, us, having a life, to the top."

Vivian turned around. Her moisture-filled eyes glinted in the growing light. She embraced him tightly. "Can we pick up where we left off a month ago?"

He broke his trance-like concentration on the sea long enough to meet her kiss. New strength rippled down his shoulders and arms.

Vivian held herself hard against him for a long minute in silence before she turned and looked at the monstrous seas charging after them. She leaned her head back against his shoulder and spoke in his ear. "Do you think we've seen the worst of it?"

Friday, May 24

Aboard attack submarine, *USS Houston*, SSN-713, Commander Neil Palmer Anderson III leaned over Senior Chief Sonarman Eddy Lee's shoulder. "Whatcha got, Chief?"

"Small surface contact, Captain. Doing six knots, heading 225. No screw noise, just a depthsounder. My guess is a sailboat."

"Sailboat, huh? Headed southwest...wonder if they tangled with that hurricane up north couple weeks ago. C'mon, Chief, let's go have a look, make sure they're okay."

Anderson addressed his Executive Officer in the control room. "XO, take us to periscope depth; hundred yards off the contact's port beam."

"Aye, aye, Captain."

Anderson removed his wire-rimmed glasses and fitted his eyes to the periscope's eyepiece. "Lessee what we got here. Right as usual, Chief. It's a sloop; beige hull, red sheer stripe, 'bout forty feet. Name is...*Houdini*. Under full sail; everything seems to—" Anderson pressed the button starting the video tape system.

The XO's brow furrowed. "What is it, Skipper?"

"The crew are on deck, and they are *definitely* okay. In fact, that may be the healthiest woman I've ever seen."

"Is she naked?" asked the Chief.

"Most definitely, Chief. Most definitely."

The XO moved next to Anderson. "Are they...?"

"Not exactly. He's lying on his back on top of the cabin. She's facing the opposite way, kneeling over him. At the moment, I'd say they're communicating in Latin."

Now it was Chief Lee's brow that wrinkled. "Latin?"

Anderson stepped aside. "Here Chief, have a look."

Eddy Lee jumped to the scope. Ten seconds passed before he spoke. "Man-oh-man, is she ever—wait—she's up...she's turning around. She's in the saddle. There she goes. Ride him, sugar! Ride him hard, baby!"

The XO leaned toward Anderson and whispered. "Skip, could I...?"

"Chief, let the XO have a peek." By now every eye in the control room was riveted on the periscope. Chief Lee waited until the last possible second before relinquishing it to the exec.

The XO slid in and made a quick adjustment. "*Un*believable. She's...magnificent."

Four other officers and twelve enlisted men each spent a timed minute at the scope. The rest of the crew would see the unabridged videotape after the evening movie.

Vivian lay on top of Mitch, her legs straddling his, her head resting on his chest. His strong fingers massaged each of her vertebrae as his hands traveled up and down her spine. Since Hurricane Andres passed and the seas resumed their normal size and pattern, she and Mitch had made love in warm sunshine on top of *Houdini's* cabin almost every afternoon. She loved how Mitch's lovemaking didn't stop when the sex was over. He always held her close and caressed her for a long time afterward.

"It's been awhile since we've done that," he whispered.

"I thought it would be appropriate to reintroduce it to our repertoire on your birthday."

"Mmm, nice gift."

"There's something primitive about making love outside, exposed to nature. Makes me go a little crazy."

"I've noticed," Mitch winced.

Vivian chuckled and stroked his arm. "Ooh, did I hurt you?"

"Yes, thank you. Better take a look around."

"I keep forgetting that's why we moved the cushions up here." Vivian raised the upper half of her body and let her gaze slowly sweep the horizon from quarter to quarter. "Nope, we're all alone." She eased back down on him, brushed his hair with her fingers and gently kissed each closed eyelid.

"Ready for your shower?" Mitch asked.

"You said I could have a nice long one today, right?"

"No need to conserve water with only one day left at sea."

While Vivian went below to get her shampoo, creme rinse and towel, Mitch attached the spare genoa halyard to the five-gallon solar shower and hoisted it up the port cap shroud, seven feet above deck. The device consisted of a satchel-like bag made of heavy vinyl plastic, clear on one side, black on the other. Filled with water and left exposed to direct sunlight for two hours, the bag could heat water until it was too hot for comfort. A red plastic shower head at the end of a two-foot hose hung from the bottom of the bag.

Vivian joined him at the port shrouds. "Just leave enough for me to soap up and rinse off," he said.

Vivian leaned against him. "We could shower together, like yesterday?"

"No, you go ahead and enjoy it. Besides, I'd rather watch."

"Pervert."

Mitch returned to the cockpit as Vivian began her shower. She held the shroud wire in the crook of one elbow for support and pulled the shower head down, opening the push-pull valve. *Houdini* pitched and rolled mildly over low, wind-rippled swells, making it only moderately difficult for her now-experienced sea legs to maintain her balance. She moved the shower head around, thoroughly wetting her long hair. The hot water streamed down her face and neck, turning into tiny rivulets that meandered and criss-crossed her honey-colored body to the deck. The past several days of nude sunbathing had nearly eliminated the tan lines that remained from Mexico.

Mitch stood naked behind the dodger, watching her work in the shampoo, building up a Marie Antoinette mass of lathered tresses. It was Vivian's self-assured sense of humor that first made him truly fall in love with her, and not her voluptuous figure, but in all the years he had known her, the sight of her naked form had never failed to mesmerize him. Against a backdrop of light blue sky, cobalt ocean and the sloop's white sails, this portrait of her was possibly the most stunning of all. In a moment of erotic daydreaming, he imagined her to be a mermaid princess who had leaped aboard and ravished him; and now she had been transformed into a woman by bubbles of magic soap that flowed around her breasts and down her waist and thighs. He considered getting a camera but settled for burning the image into his memory.

When she finished and began toweling herself dry, her hypnotic spell eased enough to permit him to shift his focus to the band of horizon between her and *Houdini*'s bow. Would that view really change tomorrow? After twenty-two days at sea it seemed a fantasy that anything could disturb the horizon's clean sharp edge. What would a tropical island look like when it first appeared on the horizon? Would it even be there? After their recent experience with hurricane Andres, he wondered how anything other than a massive continent survived the relentless battering of the Pacific Ocean.

Since crossing the equator more than a week ago, *Houdini* had entered the steady southeast trade winds and experienced near perfect weather from that time on. Short of using the spinnaker again, they kept her under maximum canvas twenty-four hours a day, barreling down the rhumb line toward the Marquesas. In the past two weeks she had gained an average of more than twenty-five miles per day on *Silver Cloud*. According to Bill's last report to the Pac Maritime Net, *Silver Cloud* had made her landfall on the island of Hiva Oa yesterday morning. And early this morning, *Houdini*'s SatNav declared the waypoint off Hiva Oa's eastern tip to be 125 nautical miles straight ahead. Despite his irrational doubts, Mitch had to accept the idea the Marquesas were really out there somewhere, and that he and Vivian would see one of them tomorrow morning.

He would have been more certain of this if it were Hawaii or Tahiti over the horizon. Jetliners full of tourists flew to those islands. Therefore they *had* to exist. But until Henry described the Marquesas, Mitch had never heard of them. If very few people know that a place exists, maybe it doesn't—like the tree that falls silently in the forest because no one is there to hear it. Perhaps it's a hoax, a geographical joke perpetrated by mischievous cartographers and perpetuated by duped sailors who arrive to find only a large buoy with a *ha-ha* sign. Mitch found the sea to be an infinite source of fantasy.

The Marquesas had fascinated Henry, more so than any other islands in the South Pacific. He'd said he was in good company because they had also enchanted the likes of Melville, Heyerdahl and Gauguin. The writer, the adventurer and the painter had all found inspiration and the answers to some of life's questions on the half dozen sparsely populated islands of this remote archipelago.

According to Henry, there was not much that was boring about the Marquesas, culturally or geologically. The adolescent islands ranged in age from one to six million years, near the same age as their Hawaiian cousins to the north. But while the origins and distribution of those islands were straight-forward and well understood, scientists found the Marquesas' arrangement and structure inconsistent with most other Pacific Island groups. In addition to the crustal plate movements, volcanism and erosion, which shaped the other island chains, the Marquesas' complex morphology resulted from the added effects of massive faulting.

One of Henry's books showed relief maps of the three largest Marquesan islands. They all exhibited classic volcanic cones with distinct calderas, but with one consistent anomaly: each island appeared to have been sliced in half, as though God baked three pies and ate half of each. The sheer cliffs resulted from immense faults that uplifted half of the island, leaving the other half below water, splitting volcanic peaks as easily as mounds of whipped cream. Before completing their rise from the sea, several hundred thousand years of wave action had sheared off most of the tops of the two largest islands, Hiva Oa and Nuku Hiva, leaving broad plateaus two thousand feet high around the flanks of the highest, razor-backed ridges.

The first people to inhabit the Marquesas were close to the roots of the Polynesian family tree. Archaeological studies had shown them to be the undoubted ancestors of early Hawaiians, the Maori tribes of New Zealand and the mysterious Easter Islanders.

"Hoping to see land already?" asked Vivian, rejoining him in the cockpit.

"I was thinking about the first people to sail to the Marquesas. They sailed there from Samoa or Tonga two thousand years ago."

"I don't suppose they had SatNav or radar."

"Not even a compass. And it's two thousand miles, upwind, with no engine, just sails made of woven mats."

Vivian studied the forward horizon. "Why would they leave their homes and risk drowning or starving at sea when they had nice big islands like Samoa and Tonga?"

"Overpopulation, lack of food, or losers in war maybe."

"Refugees. Some things haven't changed."

"Perhaps they just loved the sea and had a natural curiosity to find what was beyond the horizon."

"If they had to come so far, not many must have made it."

"Probably not, but they must have been prolific breeders. I read there were once as many as 200,000 Marquesans, in dozens of independent warring clans. Then European explorers, missionaries and whalers arrived. They brought weapons, disease and slave ships. With better weapons the Marquesans became more successful at killing one another. But small pox, measles and venereal diseases took most of them. By the 1920's, their numbers dwindled to less than two thousand."

"Two thousand? How many are there now?"

"Six or seven thousand, sprinkled over the six big islands. It's ironic that so few of them survive and remain—none of pure Marquesan blood—in what was once the center of the Polynesian world."

"Considering what's happened to them, I wouldn't be surprised if they saw visitors like us as their enemies."

"Let's hope not. It wasn't that long ago that they ate their enemies."

Vivian leaned over and pretended to sniff at Mitch's shoulder. "Whether they do or not, you'd better take your shower."

PART FOUR

HIVA OA

The eastern cape of Hiva Oa rises like a medieval castle. Its forbidding walls are perpetually dark and misty. The headland narrows to a long promontory jutting into the Pacific, curving smoothly to the northeast in phallic defiance of the constant trade wind driven waves that assault it. The French call the finger of land Cap Balguerie. Marquesans ignore the French appellation, referring to it by its aboriginal name, Matafenua, the Eyes of Land.

Teiki reined his pony to a halt. He gave another tug on the left rein and the sturdy bay stallion turned 180-degrees to the east. It was the brief twilight before sunrise. Only the brightest of stars lingered in the fading darkness. From the crest of the ridge above the valley of Puamau, he gazed out over Matafenua and the ocean. The faraway horizon appeared as an indistinct charcoal gray boundary between blue-black water and sapphire sky.

This was his favorite moment in his routine trips to Atuona. He always left the valley floor in Puamau in time to arrive at the ridge crest before sunrise. He never tired of watching the sun make its appearance from beyond the sacred cape. He knew that a country named Peru lay several thousand miles in that direction. That *haoe* people sailing from that country had brought the first horses to Hiva Oa four hundred years ago, was one of the few interesting things he could recall learning during his turbulent days as a recalcitrant youth in the French Catholic school system. He rubbed his horse's withers and spoke to him in the Hiva Oa dialect of Marquesan. "Kehu, your ancestors came from the land out there." The stallion snuffled an acknowledgment and shook his long black mane.

It was significantly colder on the exposed ridge crest than on the valley floor, two thousand feet below. The body heat of the perspiring horse felt good against Teiki's bare thighs. This day he had chosen to leave his wooden saddle in Puamau for the ride to Atuona.

He rubbed the cold away from a left thigh that was copper brown, smooth and almost hairless. A vivid blue maze of parallel lines and geometric shapes covered the right leg in a massive tattoo that stretched from under the white-fringed hem of cut-off jeans to his ankle. A rectangle in the center of the design framed a wild-eyed tiki figure. In each corner of the frame, a circle enclosed an inverted Y.

Though cool to Teiki's skin, the morning winds were light. Only sparse whitecaps flecked the ocean's surface. The eastern horizon's colors shifted vertically from sapphire to magenta, then orange. The blurred horizon slowly focused into a definite sharp line. Large clouds approached from the south. "It will rain before we reach Atuona, Kehu." A golden glow announced the sun's imminent appearance. Maybe this new day his third child would come into the world.

Teiki wheeled the stallion around to leave but stopped. Something out of place in this familiar vista caught his eye. A breaking wave? No, the white speck stayed constant, did not fade away. Sails? Yes. From this distance, the boat seemed barely moving and very close to Matafenua.

More *haoe*. If they are French, let them crash against the cliffs. We have more than enough French in *te Fenua Enata*. At least these *haoe* have courage and skill. They come in small boats with sails in the way of our ancestors. The *haoe* who come in planes from Tahiti have money but little else. They stay in groups, talk among themselves. They are afraid of us. They look at us as strange animals. But they are the ones who sweat and do not bathe. They smell very bad. *Haoe* men use their money to *titoi* with our women. These *haoe,* the ones who come to *te Fenua Enata* from across the sea in small boats are not as bad. They stay longer. Some even greet us with *ka'oha* instead of *bon jour*.

Teiki stretched himself up straight as the sailboat closed the gap with Matafenua. A pleasant thought occurred to him. Maybe it's Roger, finally coming back from America. How long was it? Twenty years?

The moment the sailboat appeared as though it would crash against Matafenua, the upper limb of the sun broke the horizon, forcing Teiki to shield his eyes. He squeezed the stallion's ribcage with his legs, reined him around and started down the trail to Atuona.

Mitch liked his pre-dawn watch. The antelucan hours were like gift wrappings, that both concealed and presaged the pleasures or disappointments contained in the new day. Like a child on Christmas eve, his anticipation of the imminent landfall on Hiva Oa had made it difficult for him to fall asleep when Vivian relieved him at midnight. Minutes prior to her taking the watch he had detected the first vague glow of the island's echo on the radar screen at a range of twenty-two miles. When he returned to relieve her at three, she pointed out a white light, low off the starboard bow, blinking in the distance, as *Houdini*'s rise and fall caused the apparent horizon to eclipse it. Before going below, she'd made him promise to wake her the moment he sighted land.

Now, at five after five, the beam of light remained fixed and the radar displayed the sharp image of Cap Balguerie only three miles to the southwest, straight ahead, somewhere in the night's lingering blackness. Checking the compass bearing of Vivian's light against his chart of Hiva Oa, he determined it must be coming from the village of Puamau. Even one electric light seemed too civilized for so remote a place.

Morning twilight would arrive in a few minutes and he would see land. Although he thought it possible for the SatNav to deceive him, he trusted the Furuno radar completely. The SatNav's black box relied on frequent updates sent by humans to the system's satellites. The radar did not rely on ongoing human intervention. If the Furuno said land was ahead, then land was ahead. Alternately looking under the boom to starboard, and then left of the headstay, he searched the assumed horizon for a telltale sign, a shadow, something different to interrupt the endless continuity of the ocean they had lived on for twenty-three days.

He shifted his gaze upward and he saw an outline, darker than the night. A thunder cloud? He checked the radar screen again. No squalls anywhere. It was a vague outline of something. He hurried below to check the chart of Hiva Oa. *You stupid—that's it!* The chart indicated Cap Balguerie was 300 *meters*, not 300 *feet*. He hadn't paid close attention to the elevation. Because of the long promontory's narrowness, he'd assumed it to be a low-lying peninsula.

He moved to the settee and shook Vivian gently by the shoulders. "Viv!, Viv!, it's land, Babe!"

Suddenly he remembered the autopilot was steering *Houdini* straight at the vision he'd just seen. He charged back to the cockpit, dove for the autopilot control box and punched the minus-ten button. The sloop obediently headed up, putting the high headland on the starboard bow. Mitch winched the main and genoa sheets in tight, trimming them for the new heading. The sails were now close-hauled. If she couldn't slide past the cape on this heading, he'd have to tack away to the southeast.

Vivian came up the companionway and turned to look over the canvas dodger. "Where is it?"

"It's behind the sails now," he said. "We were going to run into the damn thing."

Vivian peeked under the boom. "Hiva Oa," she whispered. She glanced back to the instrument panel. "Mitch, look at the depthsounder."

For days on end the depthsounder had constantly displayed two dashes, its enigmatic way of saying, "no bottom," when in fact the depth simply exceeded its 400-foot range. During much of the passage, the depths had exceeded 10,000 feet. Despite its uselessness as a navigation tool at sea, Mitch kept it on, hoping it might warn an unsuspecting whale of *Houdini*'s approach. The sounder's minimal current draw seemed a reasonable price to pay for the protection of both species. Now the LCD display registered a number. The depthsounder's infrasonic ping echoed back from volcanic rock, 270 feet below.

"Yow!, it's coming up fast," Mitch said. "I just looked at it a minute ago and it still hadn't found bottom."

Without her harness, wearing only shorts and an oversized sweatshirt, Vivian moved forward along the port deck, grabbing cabin-top handrails and lifelines as she went. Unwilling to miss out on their first tropical island landfall, Mitch unsnapped his tether's carabiner from his harness and followed.

Vivian reached the bow, stood upright and braced herself against the headstay. Now she could see around the genoa. Mitch came up behind and took hold of the bow pulpit and headstay for support. *Houdini* rose and fell rhythmically, in time with the four-foot southeast swell rolling under her. Morning's light gathered quickly and the cape was completely visible.

"It's breathtaking but not at all what I had in mind," Vivian said, raising her voice so Mitch could hear over the roar of the frothing bow wave.

"It's so dark, and hostile," Mitch said.

"Yeah, exactly. I was expecting palm trees and jungles."

The massive promontory remained somber in the growing light, its sheer vertical face and southern walls devoid of vegetation. The eroded edges of hundreds of layers of black and dusty lava rock appeared scorched and burned. A handful of stunted, leafless trees perched atop the monolithic point of land like singed hairs on a balding head.

Mitch pointed to starboard. "See that large cone-shaped valley over there. That's where your light was coming from." The upper rim of the shadowed valley caught and reflected the first rays of morning sunlight.

Within seconds, the tip of the cape eclipsed the valley. Mitch felt the warmth of the sun on his neck. He put his left arm around Vivian's waist. She rested her hand on his. Together they watched Matafenua's barren cliffs glide by. Waves crashed against huge slabs of fallen lava rock, sending plumes of spray and foam high into the air. He spoke in Vivian's ear. "We're getting too close. I'd better go see if we can pinch up a little more."

"Is it all right if I stay and watch?" asked Vivian.

"It's a once in a lifetime experience, soak it in."

"Thanks."

Vivian watched Matafenua give way to Hiva Oa's southern coast. Although nearly as steep and high as the cape, the beige cliffs rising from the water were now speckled with occasional patches of green.

The long coastline formed a gigantic natural seawall stretching unbroken to the west. However, it soon gave way to a sharp V-shaped canyon that sliced straight inland and up toward the island's spine, a central east-west ridge. The steep-sided chasm revealed a cornucopia of lush trees, shrubs and vines in verdant contrast with the sterile cliffs and high plateaus above it. The pompon heads of lofty coconut palms clustered like bouquets of chartreuse dahlias in the canyon's stream-carved notch. Halfway to the plateau above, they thinned and disappeared. The canyon terminated at the base of the roof-ridge line of jagged peaks.

Deflected and disturbed by the island barrier, the wind eased, becoming variable in both speed and direction. Whirlpools of thermal air currents circulated between the land and sea.

Vivian hadn't realized how twenty-three days of ocean air had sensitized her sense of smell, gradually cleansing away Mexico's redolent mix of land and shoreline odors. The heady, fertile fragrance of the canyon's foliage filled her nostrils and lungs. The effect was like breathing the nitrous oxide they used at the clinic. A sudden feeling of well-being and impending pleasure soaked through her, filling her to the brim. She felt an urge to dive overboard and swim toward the aroma's source. She watched with regret as the savagely beautiful canyon passed astern.

She hadn't turned forward for more than a minute when she had to rub her eyes. She must be suffering from sleep deprivation. They were approaching the same canyon again. She glanced astern and saw the first canyon still barely in sight, disappearing behind the belly of the curving genoa. A blunt headland separated the new ravine from its twin. Clumps of bushy trees and yellow-green shrubs dotted the upward sloping grassy plateau between the two chasms. She began to understand why Gauguin left Paris.

Houdini passed two more canyon valleys cutting into the high plateau in the same manner as the two before them. No plumes of smoke or other signs of human habitation marred their pristine beauty.

Gray clouds gradually banked up against the ridge crest and spilled out over the water. The sails flogged and slatted complaints against the light, fluky winds. Mitch started the engine and Vivian came back to help him furl the main.

Three miles from the village of Atuona the first large raindrops smacked against the stiff cloth of the furled mainsail as Mitch finished cinching the last tie. He still wore his foulweather suit. Vivian hurried below to don hers. When she rejoined him, the pelting rain descended with such force and volume that it was impossible to look up. It was one of the rare instances Mitch was glad to be motoring instead of sailing. With the autopilot steering easily in the declining swells, he and Vivian stayed under the protection of the spray dodger, occasionally peeking around its side curtains to check their progress toward Atuona and Taahuku Bay.

Mitch checked the chart. The fourteen miles of Hiva Oa's southeast shoreline ended in a mountainous hook of land surrounding Traitor's Bay, a name given by early European navigators. The large open body of water faced the onslaught of prevailing southeasterly swells, making it nearly useless as an anchorage except for ships too big to enter the smaller, more protected Taahuku Bay, which sits conveniently close to Hiva Oa's main village of Atuona.

The favorable conditions during their last week at sea permitted Mitch's thoughts to focus on how best to use *Houdini*'s unexpected arrival to Bill's disadvantage. At times, especially during long night watches, he fantasized surprising Bill and dispatching him in ways that ranged from crushing his head with a rock to hanging him from *Silver Cloud*'s mast by a halyard. But each day, as *Houdini* cut the distance to the Marquesas by another one-hundred to one-hundred-fifty miles, he concentrated more rationally on how to use his advantage to startle Bill and bluff him into revealing his guilt. He debated whether it was better to make the bluff elaborate or stay close to the facts, much as Martinez had laid them out. Now with *Houdini* less than thirty minutes from entering the harbor where *Silver Cloud* was reportedly anchored, the reality of the impending confrontation and its possible consequences sent an involuntary shiver down his back. Maybe Bill's reaction to their arrival would make any bluffing or plotting irrelevant.

The need to find the narrow entrance to Taahuku Bay put his imagination in check. He took a spiral bound sailing guide to French Polynesia out of a protective plastic bag and spread it open on top of the main hatch. He quickly found the page with a chartlet of Atuona, Taahuku Bay and its approaches. It showed the small narrow harbor guarded by two points of land projecting into the larger Traitor's Bay; Black Point to the left of the opening and Flat Point to the right. Just inside, a rock jetty that extended out from Flat Point cut the width of the entry in half.

Mitch peeked from under the dodger and looked forward off the starboard bow. Trying to identify the two points in the steady rain shower felt like searching for a stranger in a steam room. "I think I see it," he said. "See what you think." He let Vivian squeeze in front of him. "See that dark rocky headland, right there?"

"Kind of low, with something white up above it?"

"Right. I'll bet that's what the guide calls Black Point and the white thing is the light that's supposed to be on it. Then right in front of that, see the point gradually rising from the water to a low hill?"

"I think so."

"I bet that's Flat Point; the chart calls it Point Tearoa."

A mile from Black Point the shower ended and the clouds began to lift. Mitch stood on the starboard cockpit seat and braced himself against the dodger. Vivian stood on the opposite seat. Out of the misty air materialized distinct features in the lush volcanic crater valley of Atuona. A series of buildings came into view from behind Black Point; two of them large, modern looking, windowless buildings set near the beach. Further up the slope, a handful of smaller buildings with rusty roofs peeked out through dense vegetation. On either side of the broad valley, tall white crosses on foothill pedestals sat like parentheses that bracketed the village. Far to the left of town and near the beach, a slash fire burned. Nearly doused by the downpour, it sent up billowing clouds of white smoke.

"Good God, Mitch, look at that mountain," said Vivian. Above the plume of smoke a knife-edged ridge stair-stepped up the side of the valley and disappeared into the slowly fading rain clouds.

"That has to be Temetiu," Mitch said, looking at the guide. "Henry's book said Temetiu is all that remains of the rim of the massive volcano that created this end of the island. It's almost 4,000 feet to the top."

"This is more the tropical paradise I had in mind."

The face of the mountain was sheer to the point that, if it were not for the green-carpeted talus slope at its base, it would plunge vertically into the sea. Clumps of tenacious foliage bearded the precipitous face except one wide, and apparently sterile, band of lava striping the mountain wall immediately below the veil of clouds.

Even with the village of Atuona in full view, the immensity of Hiva Oa made the small village resemble little more than a collection of large boulders that had rolled down from the cliffs. Without the distant bonfire, there was little to suggest the presence of any inhabitants.

"Mitch! Look!" Vivian pointed off the starboard bow toward Flat Point. As *Houdini* moved closer, a forest of sailboat masts seemed to grow in height, rising like Jack's bean stalk out of the low promontory. The tip of the rock jetty and then the first of the sailboats came into view. Mitch reached down and pressed the autopilot's buttons bringing *Houdini* to a heading that would take her to the mouth of Taahuku Bay.

Vivian grabbed the binoculars and trained them toward the entrance. "Incredible; there must be over twenty boats packed in there. From the chart I didn't think there'd be room for more than ten."

One hundred yards from the breakwater Mitch disengaged the autopilot and took the wheel.

"There's *Dream Lover*," said Mitch, pointing toward the far inside edge of the harbor. The immaculate Maple Leaf 54 sat quietly, moored bow and stern.

"And there's *Phoenix* right next to her," added Vivian. "That's one mystery partially solved."

"If you'll take the helm, I'll go forward and get the anchor ready."

Vivian put down the binoculars and moved behind the wheel.

"Take it slow," said Mitch, "until we get the anchoring situation figured out. You're right about it being crowded."

Mitch arrived at the foredeck as the bow passed the green pole beacon standing at the tip of the stone breakwater. He thought it should be red until he remembered Henry had said the world was divided into two buoyage and marker system conventions. Almost every country outside of North America used the opposite standard of green to starboard and red to port when approached from the open sea. The J-shaped jetty consisted of large, squarish blocks of dark gray basalt arranged in neat, close-fitting layers, of which three were above water. As they entered the relatively calm waters of the harbor, *Houdini* ceased her rolling and pitching motions for the first time in twenty-three days.

Inside, Mitch saw that Vivian's initial estimate was close to the mark. At least two dozen sailboats, flying ensigns of Great Britain, Holland, Germany, France, Canada and the US, had anchored in three neat parallel rows, more in the first, and only five or six in the last row, near the narrowing end of what might have been more properly designated a large cove. All boats were moored with secondary anchors astern, keeping their bows uniformly pointing toward the bay's entrance. He and Vivian had learned from experience, that if everyone had anchored using a particular system, they needed to anchor *Houdini* using the same method. This monkey-see-monkey-do behavior usually had a good reason behind it, and in this case it was obvious that one reason was the tiny harbor's lack of swinging room, as was the case in The Pond at Puerto Vallarta.

Mitch hurried back to the cockpit. "We're going to have to set a stern anchor," he said, opening the cockpit lazaret.

"What do you want me to do?" Vivian asked.

"Just go slow and cruise around until I get it rigged."

Vivian glanced left and right as *Houdini* ghosted between a sheer rock face and a steel Dutch ketch at the end of the first row. "Cruise around? Where the heck am I going to cruise around in this shoe box?"

Mitch stopped pawing through the lazaret for a quick look. He pointed to a relatively open area in front of the anchored boats. "How about over there, between the jetty and that wharf?"

"Now you tell me. There's not enough room to turn around."

"Just go down one row and come up the other side," Mitch said without looking up from his efforts to dig out the 18-pound stern anchor.

"Yeah, right," Vivian muttered, as she spun the wheel hard right, bringing *Houdini*'s bow around smartly to a course between the first and second line of anchored boats. A gauntlet of anchor chains and stern rodes stretched out from each row, narrowing her path.

"Mitch, what if it isn't deep enough to turn between the last boat and shore? If it isn't, we're screwed because there's definitely not room to turn around here. I'll hit somebody or run over an anchor rode for sure."

Mitch popped up for another glance. Seeing that Vivian was not exaggerating, he stopped and stood beside her at the helm as they approached the last boat in the front row, Jim and Litea's *Phoenix*.

"Just cut it close around *Phoenix*. I'll stand by to fend off, just in case."

Vivian spoke to his back as he went forward. "Your confidence is reassuring." Vivian gave the depthsounder a quick glance. It read 23 feet. She slowed the engine to an idle and turned toward *Phoenix*. "18 feet, Mitch."

"You're okay, keep coming."

Vivian watched the depthsounder's reading count down to ten feet before it began to creep up again. She let escape the breath she was holding as *Houdini* slid slowly past a quiet and apparently unoccupied *Phoenix* and into the open. *Dream Lover*'s white inflatable bobbed lazily beside the big cutter's boarding ladder. The depthsounder readings rose into the twenties. Mitch resumed getting out the stern anchor and its 15-foot chain lead. Vivian made a slow circle in the open area while he coiled the half-inch nylon stern rode behind her in a series of overlapping figure-8's.

"Wonder why no one's anchored out here?" Vivian asked.

"It's probably where the ships turn around that use that wharf," Mitch said, gesturing toward a long concrete pier backed by a flat area of reclaimed land. "Okay let's do it."

"Where?"

Mitch looked through the first row of boats packed closely together from shore to shore. "There, in the second row, almost to the far inside end. See the gray boat flying the big French ensign? Looks as though there's a good-sized gap between it and the last boat in the row."

"How do you want to approach it?"

"We'll go down the entrance side, turn between the second and third rows and come up into the gap. If it looks good, we'll drop the stern anchor going in, pay out lots of stern rode until we're far enough forward to drop the bow anchor. Then you pull in on the stern rode while I ease out the chain. Simple."

"Right," Vivian said skeptically.

"What could possibly go wrong?"

Vivian rolled her eyes. She straightened the wheel and headed for the narrow channel between the end of the rows and the black basalt cliff.

To Vivian's mild amazement, it went exactly according to Mitch's plan. He tossed the stern anchor and its chain over the stern as she turned into the designated gap. She kept an eye on the nylon rode, snaking its way over the transom as Mitch scrambled to the foredeck. When the sloop's bow emerged into the fairway between the first and second rows, Mitch gave the hand signal for neutral and yelled for her to snub the stern rode. The stern anchor took a solid bite, halting *Houdini*'s forward motion like a slow-motion bungee jumper. Mitch simultaneously sent the 44-pound bow anchor splashing down with its chain rattling out in hot pursuit.

Vivian led the stern rode to the starboard genoa winch and began grinding. Slowly, *Houdini* fell into place beside an unpainted aluminum French sloop to starboard and an American cutter to port. Scanty underwear and colored plastic clothespins decorated the lifelines of the otherwise austere French yacht.

After setting the bow anchor's shock-absorbing snubber line, Mitch returned to the cockpit, shedding his foulweather jacket as he came. Inside the hill-rimmed harbor, the ocean's cooling breeze was absent. The rain shower left muggy, steamy air in its wake. He tossed the jacket under the dodger. His visions of the South Pacific had led him to expect white sand beaches and crystal clear water. Instead, the water around *Houdini* was a turbid brown and the beach terminating the bay, charcoal black. Still, it made sense. The water's murkiness no doubt stemmed from the runoff, and the sand's blackness from its volcanic origins.

Vivian came to mock-attention and saluted him. "Nicely done, Captain Sanford."

"Come here, Babe," he said, holding out his arms.

She met him at the edge of the cockpit. He pulled her so close she had to lean back to look into his eyes. "We made it," she said.

"Hey, what a team, huh? I love you." He kissed her.

"I love you, too." She hugged him close and then it dawned on her. "Mitch, I didn't see *Silver Cloud*."

"She's right over there," he said, turning her around until she looked off the starboard quarter. "You were too busy steering to notice." The ketch's black-striped clipper bow protruded from the far end of the last row of boats in the anchorage.

"I guess the gang's all here then."

"Look's that way," Mitch replied.

"Did you see any sign of Bill or Marjorie?"

"No, but they must be on board. I saw their dinghy trailing astern."

"What now, *mon Capitaine*?"

"Check in with the gendarmes, I guess, and then get some rest."

"Are you going to tell the police about our suspicions?"

"Seems like the prudent thing to do. I can't see how it can hurt as long as I'm discreet about it. I wish the rules allowed you to come with me."

"As much as I'd like to set foot on land, I'd also like to open all of *Houdini*'s hatches and ports, air her out and make our bed with fresh clean sheets. By the time you get back, I should have everything tidied up and ready for us to take a nice long nap—*together*."

"I'll come straight back, unless there's anything you want me to pick up."

"Just our mail. Grocery shopping can wait."

While inflating the dinghy, Mitch watched the crew of another yacht row their tender around the end of a rip-rapped sea wall at the end of the reclaimed land. Given the short distance, he opted to row as well rather than bother to unlash and mount the outboard motor.

Upon rounding the end of the wall, he had expected to find the other dinghy and several more, either beached or tied to a dock. Instead he found the riprap made a 90-degree turn and continued straight toward shore. There wasn't another dinghy in sight. The mystery quickly ended as he found a hidden small-craft launching ramp cut into the sea wall. 'Launching ramp' was a generous description. It was little more than a sloping gap in the rip-rapped wall. Numerous sharp rocks poked up through silty water, some capable of slicing open the inflatable's Hypalon tubes.

Despite the hazards, two other inflatables and three hard dinghies rested high and dry near the top of the ramp. None of them looked familiar except a wooden lapstrake job with the name *Phoenix* hand painted on its transom.

Mitch stepped out in knee-deep water, locked the oars and lifted the motorless inflatable, supporting one tube on his shoulder like a duffel bag. He felt his way cautiously among the slippery rocks, testing his footing with each step before shifting his weight. When well above the high tide line, he eased the dinghy down and leaned it against the sloping rockwork sides of the ramp.

With the inflatable safely situated, he paused beneath the shade of a nearby tree. The commercial wharf and warehouse seemed deserted. He removed the chart-guide from the waterproof sports pouch and studied the chartlet of Taahuku Bay. To reach Atuona, he had to follow the road from the wharf, around the head of the bay, along the other side, over Black Point and then a short stretch into the village.

It felt strange to walk on solid ground. His feet clomped like a deep sea diver's weighted shoes. He laughed inwardly at his awkwardness, but exhilarated in it at the same time. It was undeniable proof that he and Vivian had brought *Houdini* 3,000 miles safely to her destination, an item he could now enter safely in his log without risk of breaking his taboo. Feeling hard, motionless earth beneath him, seeing neon green tropical foliage in every direction, smelling airborne scents of fragrant flowers, he understood for the first time what Henry had tried to convey to him about the unique rewards that accrue to sailors who endure the hardships of a long voyage. The simplest of sights, the subtlest of smells were as rich and shocking to him as if he had landed on a strange, jungled planet in another galaxy. His gaze ricocheted from tree to tree and plant to plant as he started up a short-cut trail that led to the road. He marveled at the variety of species, wondering their names and what use the inhabitants made of them.

The narrow paved road skirting the bay was quiet and undisturbed by traffic. Since the road ended at the wharf, he reasoned it must be busy only when a copra ship arrived to load and unload cargo. Tall trees on either side grew together overhead, forming a high-roofed tunnel of green lace and creating an Eden-like atmosphere of peace and well-being. And yet the solitude and tranquility disturbed him almost as much as it pleased him. The look Vivian gave him when he told her he planned to tell the French police about the murders in Puerto Vallarta, was that penetrating look she used whenever she suspected he was saying less than what was on his mind. It had occurred to him that if they were to have an unfortunate but plausible accident, and meet with an untimely death in the Marquesas, the gendarmes might not look too deeply into the circumstances—unless he gave them reason to be suspicious.

At the head of the bay he passed a three-way intersection. The map indicated the intersecting road led up to the plateau and the island's aircraft landing strip. From there it continued on to the bays and villages on the northeast side of the island. Just beyond the intersection, a bridge crossed a wide, shallow stream that flowed from Taahuku Valley into the bay. Half way across the bridge, Mitch heard the unmistakable sound of hooves clopping on pavement. Turning to look back at the intersection, he saw a bare-chested rider guiding a small bay horse on to the main road.

As the horse and rider drew nearer, he could tell from the sheen on the man's black wavy hair that it was still wet from the recent downpour. A soaked shirt lay draped across the pony's withers. Bare feet and legs dangled without benefit of stirrups. By the time Mitch realized he was gawking at the man, it was too late to turn and resume walking without appearing rude. The rider reined the stocky animal to a halt beside him, almost pinning him between the horse and the bridge's low railing. Mitch guessed the man to be ten years his junior, though with Polynesians, he had no basis for his estimate. And he couldn't tell if it was the man's natural expression, or if he was in fact scowling at him. The only Polynesian word he could think of was the Hawaiian *aloha*. His

French was only slightly less limited. He forced a smile and hoped the man would speak first, enabling him to grasp his meaning from context or a gesture. Instead, the Marquesan continued to scowl. Unable to stand the tension of the awkward silence any longer, he offered, "*Bon jour.*"

"*Ka'oha,*" grunted the horseman.

"Huh?"

The Marquesan looked away, as if summoning his patience. "*Ka'oha, Tu parle Francais?*"

"A little—*un peu,*" Mitch replied.

"*Americain?*"

"Yes—*oui.*"

The Marquesan's eyes narrowed. "Where you from?"

"You speak English!" said Mitch, breaking into an unrestrained smile.

"Yes, speak English, speak Marquesan, no *Francais.*"

"But you...no *Francais?*" said Mitch.

The man frowned and shook his head. "You from California?"

Mitch felt as though a judge were staring down at him from his bench. "No, I, that is we, my wife and I, we're from Washington."

"Ah, Washington; President Bush." The Marquesan looked away and nodded knowingly, "Desert Storm."

"No, no, Washington *State*, near Seattle, on the west coast."

The frown softened. "Ah, West Coast; California, yes. Good. You know Roger?"

"Roger?"

"Roger from California."

"No...at least I don't think so."

"When you come Hiva Oa?"

"Today, just now," replied Mitch. "It's really beau—"

"You pass Matafenua this morning?"

"Matafenua? Oh, the cape! Yes, yes, we passed it earlier this morning. How did you know?"

"I see you. I am above my village on Kehu looking down."

"Are you from Puamau?" asked Mitch.

The rider's frown disappeared altogether, shifting to amused puzzlement. "How you know Puamau?"

"We saw a light from there last night as we approached Cap Bal—uh, Matafenua. And I read about it in a book."

"What book? American book?"

"Yes, a guide—"

"Where you go now?

"To the Gendarmerie. I have to—"

"Long walk. You ride with me." The Marquesan extended a heavily muscled forearm for Mitch to grab.

Mitch noticed the man's leg. A bizarre, savage-looking tattoo covered everything except the foot. "No, that's okay, I don't want to trouble you. I can—"

"No trouble. Kehu small but strong. Come." He motioned with his hand for Mitch to clasp arms.

Mitch glanced down the road toward town. "Well, if you insist." Taking the man's forearm in his own, he hesitated briefly and then vaulted upward, fully expecting not to make it. But the Marquesan expertly used his own weight to lever him on to the horse's back.

Mitch fumbled to keep from dropping the sports pouch in his other hand while not losing his balance as the stallion began walking.

"What your name?"

"Mitch, what's yours?"

"Teiki."

"Tiki?"

"No, *tay-iki*. Mitch?"

"Right."

"Sound like 'bitch.'"

Mitch smiled. "Right."

Mitch felt the wetness of the horse's coat soaking through his cotton shorts as they rode past a soccer field laid out in the valley's flood plain. A shiny white Toyota, four-wheel drive pick-up came around a curve and passed them in the opposite direction. The truck's Marquesan driver extended his hand from the cab in a brief wave. If Teiki returned the greeting, Mitch didn't catch it. Seeing a car, and not some World War II vintage Citroen, but a brand new Toyota, came as another blow to his image of the Marquesas as a remote archipelago inhabited by primitive natives who only recently gave up eating human flesh.

After a long silence, Mitch asked: "Where did you learn to speak English?"

"Roger."

"Who's Roger?"

"American man. Came to live in Puamau."

"Really? What was he doing there?"

"Hiding."

"From what?"

"Viet Nam. You go Viet Nam?"

"Yes."

"At first I don't like Roger. Man should not be afraid of war."

"But you changed your mind about him?"

"Roger not afraid of big Marquesan sharks. He dive for fish, work hard. Help people of Puamau. Teach me English, tell stories of America California."

"That's quite a tattoo you have. Are those peace symbols?" Mitch said, pointing to a circle at one corner of a square set in the tattoo."

The Marquesan glanced at his leg. "Mark on Roger's hat. *Tuhuka patu tiki*, tattoo man, put two on Roger's ass."

"I see," laughed Mitch. "Roger sounds like an interesting guy. I'd like to meet him."

"Not here. Went back to America California."

"How long ago was that?"

"Twenty years, more. He say, someday come back, take me on sailboat to Tahiti and Bora Bora."

Another four-wheel truck streaked by, this one a silver four-door with two young Marquesan girls standing in the bed holding on to the roll bar. Their long dark hair flowed behind them in the wind. Teiki seemed not to notice.

"Do you always ride your horse from Puamau?" Mitch asked.

"No. Drive father's truck when bring fruit and vegetables to sell. Today come visit wife."

"She lives in Atuona?" said Mitch, tentatively.

"No. She stay with my sister until baby born."

"So, you're expecting a baby! Do you have other children?"

"One boy, one girl. You?"

"No, no children," said Mitch.

"Why? You don't like?"

"No, it's not that. It's just that we never wanted to have children of our own. We like other people's children. When is the baby due?"

"Today, tomorrow, next week."

"Your English is very good," Mitch said. "Do you get many opportunities to speak it since your friend left?"

"Speak English every week," Teiki said proudly.

"With who?"

"Cousin is minister. He learn English at Christian missionary school in Fiji. We talk English every Sunday."

"He's a Protestant minister?"

"Yes."

"I thought most Marquesan's were Catholics."

"Most are. Easier to be Catholic."

"Easier?"

"Be Catholic, speak French, get lazy government job, buy new truck. Easier."

"I see. I thought I read somewhere that tattoos were banned by the church?"

"Tattoos okay now. Cousin teaches us the old ways. We learn chants and songs of our ancestors."

"Instead of hymns?"

"One hymn, one chant."

"Interesting."

"You come tomorrow."

"To your church?"

"Cousin meet you and wife with truck at Taahuku."

"We'd love to if other problems don't interfere."

"What problems?"

"It's a long story."

After crossing over the headland forming Black Point, Mitch saw the first signs of a town. A low building with a corrugated metal roof started one end of the long main street that ran through town. Large white letters on a green awning proclaimed *Snack Make Make* and shouted the praises of Heineken beer. Three four-wheel-drive pick-ups and two gaudily painted motorcycles were parked randomly in the restaurant's gravel parking lot. A couple in the telltale worn and casual dress of blue-water sailors enjoyed a midmorning croissant and what appeared to be demitasses of espresso on the establishment's shaded wooden deck.

A short distance further Teiki pointed out the post office and the local branch of the Westpac Bank set back from the road, partially screened by flowering shrubbery. Beginning at the post office and running on into town, a low masonry wall of smooth-faced stones ran along the seaward side of the road. Foliage from high colorful bushes spilled over the wall onto the street. Multi-colored croton competed with trumpets of bright red hibiscus and fragrant white frangipani. Tall coconut palms, breadfruit and mango trees cast cooling shadows on the road, which carried a variety of mostly four-wheel-drive vehicles.

Teiki brought the stallion to a halt beside a blue metal gate, above which hung a red, white and blue sign. "Gendarmerie," he said, pointing at the small, one-story white building behind the gate.

Mitch carefully slid off the side of the horse, taking care not to get behind the animal. "Thanks for the ride, Teiki. I enjoyed meeting you."

"You come dinner tonight."

"Dinner? But your wife, the baby—"

"My sister's house. You come. No problem. We have too much food."

Mitch felt his lack of sleep pressing down on him, but he sensed in Teiki's tone and facial expression that a rare honor had been offered. To refuse without explanation would belittle the invitation. A full explanation, considering the language barriers, seemed impossible. "Are you sure it's okay? I mean, shouldn't you check?"

"No problem. I meet you and wife here at sunset. Take you to sister's house."

"Well...if you're *sure*..."

Teiki gave what passed for the beginnings of a smile, nudged the stallion forward with his legs and turned his attention to the road.

Vivian tuned the ham radio to one of the Voice of America frequencies and listened to US and world news while changing into clean clothes and trying to do something with her rain-dampened hair. She stood at the vanity across from the forward berth and made a vow to herself in the mirror that as soon as she found someone competent to do the job, she would grit her teeth and have her hair cut short for only the second time in her life.

She'd have trusted the task to Jill. They had cut each other's hair once a month since sailing out of Puget Sound. It dawned on Vivian that she had known Jill better—in some ways—than her own sister. Besides a dear friend, Jill had been a role model that any woman could look up to.

Damp, mildew-smelling clothes, foulweather suits, and rubber boots lay strewn about on *Houdini*'s cabin sole and around the folding dining table. She bagged the clothes and straightened up the cabin. Although all hatches and ports had been closed throughout the entire passage from Mexico, saltwater nevertheless managed to find its way below, dripping from foulweather suits or floating down the main hatch and companionway in an invisible mist. Saltwater seemed to take forever to dry unless exposed to direct sunlight. With a sponge and a bowl of fresh water, she went all around the cabin, wiping down wooden bulkheads and lockers, Formica counters, and the teak and holly sole. She finished by sponging off both pairs of foulweather suits and taking them outside to dry.

On deck, the seductive scent of Hiva Oa called to her again. She looked astern, up Taahuku Valley and imagined finding a jungle canyon with a waterfall pool where she could sit on smooth black rocks beneath the falling water for hours on end. But simply being still, resting quietly at anchor, neither rocking nor rolling, was a luxury in itself. The prospect of going to bed that night at a reasonable hour and sleeping—in a real bed—until well after dawn the next day, sounded like an act of devilish indulgence.

With the foulweather suits draped over the boom, she turned to survey her surroundings. Mount Temetiu's uppermost peak still hid in a veil of clouds, but sunlight now dappled its flanks and cast shadows contrasting with shades of green that would rival any national park in the world. In the opposite direction, high on the hill above the wharf side of the harbor, a series of small A-frame cabins clustered together in what appeared to be a small resort. Although dinghies trailed behind or rested alongside most of the yachts in the compact harbor, Vivian could see few people on deck, suggesting that they too appreciated their release from the tyranny of round-the-clock watch standing. The owners of the lingerie-decorated French yacht, immediately to starboard, were one of the few crews apparently ashore. However, as Vivian studied the aluminum sloop, a small blonde woman emerged from the yacht's companionway and began removing a pair of panties and a bra from the port lifeline. Vivian squinted to improve her focus. *Marjorie?* Vivian called out, in a raised but tentative voice: "Marjorie, is that you?"

The woman glanced around, not knowing from where the voice had come.

"Marjorie, over here," Vivian shouted, now certain it was her.

Marjorie turned toward *Houdini*, saw Vivian, and appeared to take in the full sight of *Houdini* all at once. "Vivian!" she shrieked, "what are you *doing* here?" Marjorie's hands clasped the top of her head, as if to keep it from falling off.

Vivian did her best to manufacture a diplomatic smile. "We decided to come after all." She hadn't expected the woman to be happy to see her, but Marjorie's reaction was even more disconcerted than she'd anticipated. "What're you doing on that boat?" Vivian asked.

"Where's Mitch?" Marjorie shouted, ignoring the question. Without waiting for an answer, she turned and looked behind her.

The little bitch has more nerve than I gave her credit for. "He went into town to clear us in. Why?"

"Oh, no! No. No." Marjorie kept repeating the word over and over as her small face contorted inward. Marjorie looked back in the direction of *Silver Cloud*, leaning left and right, as if looking for something behind the ketch. "Oh, Vivian, *Vivian!*" Marjorie said, clasping her hands against her chest..

"What is it, Marjorie? What's wrong?"

Marjorie's attention shifted to the other boats nearest her, checking each in rapid succession. "Oh, damn!" she yelled. She moved quickly to the aluminum yacht's lifeline gate, kicked off her flip-flops and dove head first into the brown water wearing yellow shorts and matching T-shirt. Vivian watched incredulously as Marjorie swam determinedly toward *Houdini*, her arms wind-milling through the water like a riverboat's paddle-wheel. She covered the fifty feet between *Houdini* and the French yacht, lifting her face to take a breath only once. Vivian moved to the ladder to meet her.

Marjorie started talking while still gasping for air as she grabbed the swim ladder. "When did you...get in?"

"About two hours ago. Be careful, the ladder's missing the bottom rung. Didn't you see or hear us anchor?"

"No, I slept in," Marjorie said, struggling to get her foot on the rung that was barely six inches below the water's surface.

"You didn't have to swim over in your clothes, Marjorie. We could have—"

"How long has Mitch been gone?" Marjorie's right foot caught the rung and she stood up. "Can I come aboard?"

"Yes, of course. He's been gone an hour maybe. Why do you want to know? You're beginning to make me...nervous."

"I'm dripping wet."

"It's okay. Let's sit in the cockpit."

Marjorie stepped aboard and sat down in *Houdini*'s cockpit without looking Vivian in the eyes. She wiped her wet hair back and let her face fall into hands supported on her knees. "Vivian, I don't know where to begin."

"You can skip Puerto Vallarta," Vivian said flatly.

A pained, high-pitched groan emanated from Marjorie's throat. "Mitch told you."

"Eventually."

Marjorie still did not look up. "Oh God, Vivian, I don't know *what* to say. What must you think of me? I'm so sorry. It was all my fault, not Mitch's."

During the passage, Vivian had thought several times about what she would say to Marjorie at this moment. She had vacillated between a mature, regal approach and a good raking with all claws fully extended. Now that the object of her disgust sat a few feet across from her, dripping wet and crouching pathetically on the cockpit seat, the fury that had once burned inside her felt more like yesterday's scattered coals. Maybe the hurricane took it out of her. More likely it was that she and Mitch had put the incident behind them, coupled with the knowledge that she had come close to committing a similar offense. "Is that why you swam over here, to apologize?"

"No, no," sobbed Marjorie.

"Marjorie, what the hell is it?"

Marjorie looked up but avoided Vivian's eyes, gazing into the distance beyond her. "Mitch is in danger."

"Did Bill find out it was Mitch?"

Marjorie nodded and looked directly at Vivian for the first time. "Not until just before we got here." Vivian leaned closer, resting her elbows on her knees. "Bill hounded and pestered me all the way across the Pacific. I told him several times it wasn't Henry and he gradually came to believe me, but he knew I'd been with somebody. He wouldn't let up. He was driving me crazy. He said he wouldn't let me off the boat until I told him who it was. I was desperate to get some time away from him. I thought Mitch was safe in Mexico." Marjorie looked down again. "So I told Bill what really happened."

Vivian's right hand cradled and squeezed her forehead. "Oh, shit."

"Vivian, if Bill runs into Mitch, I'm afraid he might do anything. He...he swore he'd kill Mitch if he ever saw him again."

"Right now Bill's on *Silver Cloud*, isn't he?"

"I think so; the dinghy's there."

"Marjorie, did Bill ever say anything about Henry and Jill's death? Anything that might indicate that he...you know..."

"No. He won't talk about that night. I've tried asking him about it. He just gets angry and says he was at the marina having a drink. But I can tell when he's lying. I don't know what to think anymore."

Vivian rubbed her face and after a pause asked: "How did you wind up on the French yacht?"

"After we arrived, Bill broke his promise and left me stranded on the boat while he went to clear us in. I was pacing the deck. I must have looked like a caged animal. I'd have jumped overboard and swam ashore right then if I could have figured out how to take some things with me. Then Bertrand and Yvette rowed by in their dinghy. They saw that I was in distress. They were the first friendly faces I'd seen in twenty-seven days."

"What'd you say to them?"

"I can't remember. It must have sounded like gibberish. I guess I told them Bill and I weren't getting along and that I was desperate to get away for awhile."

"So they took you in?" asked Vivian.

"Bertrand insisted. He said he'd seen this happen to husband and wife crews before. I threw some clothes and toiletries in a bag and they took me to their boat. This is the first time I've been off it since then. I still haven't been ashore. I'm afraid to go as long as Bill is around."

"What happened when Bill came back and found out you'd left *Silver Cloud*?"

"It took him a while to find me. When he did, he got into a heated argument with Bertrand. Bertrand's big, like Henry. He told Bill to keep away and that I was welcome to stay with him and Yvette as long as I wanted."

"What'd Bill do?"

"He left, finally, but told Bertrand he was in for trouble and that if I didn't return to *Silver Cloud* with him right then, it would be much worse for both of us later."

"Where are Bertrand and Yvette now?"

"They rented a Jeep and went sightseeing. I don't expect them back until late this evening."

Mitch shifted his weight from foot to foot, working the stiffness out of his thighs. He tugged the inside hem of wet shorts plastered to his butt and crotch as the Marquesan horse and rider continued down the main street of Atuona. The bay pony whipped its black tail impatiently from side to side. The stallion had begun a trot on its own and Teiki had quickly reined him back to a stately walk.

Passing through a narrow entrance between the blue vehicle gate and a high hedge of red hibiscus, Mitch noticed the French tricolor and the flag of French Polynesia hanging motionless from twin flagpoles in a courtyard to the right of the small police station. A short park bench sat in the shade of the eaves to the left of the open doorway. The need for the bench became obvious the moment he entered. The gendarmerie's reception area and counter might accommodate two lines with no more than two persons in each line. At the moment, however, Mitch had it all to himself. The open area behind the counter accommodated four desks, all of them unoccupied save one in the far corner. He glanced at his watch as it dawned on him today was Saturday. The arbitrary days of the week had lost their tenuous significance at sea. Perhaps the gendarmes didn't conduct business on Saturdays. As soon as Mitch laid his sports pouch brief case on the counter, a stocky, sandy-haired Frenchman wearing khaki shorts and a military-creased shirt rose from the desk and approached the counter. His almost beardless face was smooth and freckled.

"*Bon jour, monsieur. Puis-je vous aider?*"

Mitch answered as he searched the pouch for his Berlitz phrase book. "Uh, *parlez-vous Anglais?*"

The young gendarme smiled. "A little. You have arrived on the yacht, Monsieur?"

"Yes—*oui.*"

"*Eh bien,* welcome to *Polynésie Française.* You are *Americain,* Monsieur?"

"Yes, it's that obvious, is it?"

"*Oui,* American English is very...different."

Mitch noticed the man's nose and upper lip twitch like a rabbit's. "Oh, sorry, I was given a ride into town on a very wet horse."

"Ah," the gendarme said with comprehending smile and nod. He reached below the counter and produced a three-page photocopied form stapled together at the corner. "Please complete this questionnaire, Monsieur, *bien?*"

"*Merci,*" Mitch said, relieved it was easier to communicate than he'd feared. The gendarme returned to his desk and resumed stamping forms in one pile, turning them over, and stacking them neatly face down in another pile.

The bilingual questionnaire asked for essentially the same information as had Mexican clearance documents: *Houdini*'s tonnage and measurements, his and Vivian's vital statistics. More probing inquiries asked about the presence on board of narcotics, pets, living plants or firearms. He answered 'no' to each. While filling out the form, he heard the voices of two men coming from an enclosed office partially hidden from his view behind the wall at the end of the counter. They laughed frequently and talked in a rapid river of flowing French that sounded almost like singing or poetry. Mitch stole a glance toward the half-opened door and saw a distinguished, fiftyish looking man seated behind a wooden desk. He wore the same military-style khaki shirt as the younger gendarme. Mitch could neither see nor distinctly hear the source of the other voice, but it had a familiar ring, like someone well known. Maybe it was that goofy French actor, Gerard Depardieu, whom Vivian thought was so sexy.

On finishing the form Mitch held it up, catching the young gendarme's attention. The police officer took the questionnaire and transposed the bulk of Mitch's entries to a large green tri-fold card, which he explained would be *Houdini's* boat passport. While in French Polynesian waters, the law required captains to present their boat passports to the local gendarmerie at every island in French Polynesia where their vessel called. The gendarmes at each island would stamp and annotate the document with the dates and times of *Houdini's* arrival and departure from their jurisdiction. The gendarme finished the clearance procedure by stamping both Mitch and Vivian's individual passports, recording their entry into *Polynésie Française.*

Handing the passports to Mitch, the gendarme smiled and said, "*Voila*, Monsieur, as citizen of USA you are permitted thirty days in *Polynésie Française* without visa. With visa you may stay six months. To obtain visa you must secure bond equal to airfare for you and your wife to USA. The bank across the street can process bond for you on Mondays and Thursdays. That is clear?" The speed of the short, French-accented speech indicated numerous repetitions in the past.

"Yes, that's quite clear," Mitch said. "*Merci beaucoup.*"

"*De rien*, enjoy," said the man, with a barely perceptible bow from the waist and a slight nod of the head. As the man started to turn away, Mitch opened his mouth to speak but couldn't find the words.

"Yes, Monsieur?"

"Is their somewhere we can talk in private?" Mitch asked.

The gendarme's freckled forehead twitched. He looked out the window. The bench was empty. He raised a hinged section of the counter next to the wall. "This way." He led Mitch around the wall to a second office, next to the one occupied by the other gendarme.

After closing the door, the gendarme seated himself behind the desk and motioned for Mitch to take the chair opposite him. "Is there a problem, Monsieur?" he asked.

Mitch told him the story of the murders of Jill and Henry Fullerton. He tried to avoid biasing the man, withholding his own theory, telling the young police officer only the facts of the case as clearly as he remembered them.

The gendarme frowned. "If the police in *Mexique* have arrested the two fishermen, and the evidence against them is as you say, what have we in Atuona to do?"

Mitch leaned closer to the desk and slightly lowered his voice. "The day of the murders there was an incident, an attack on Henry Fullerton by a man who's now here in Atuona, on another boat."

The gendarme paused, studying Mitch carefully. "You saw this...fight?"

"Yes, along with my wife and two other couples who are also here on their yachts."

"You suspect this man of the murders, and not the fishermen?"

"Yes, because whoever did it, took Jill Fullerton's journal."

"*Journal*? I do not understand, Monsieur. What does a *journal* have to do with it?"

"Jill Fullerton kept a detailed journal, a diary. She would have recorded the details of the fight and—"

"Pardon monsieur, but you said there were many witnesses to the fight. What difference would a journal have made?"

"Jill told us at the restaurant that night that Bill Schneider, the man who hit Henry, had come by their boat looking for Henry while she was sitting the cockpit writing in her journal. She seemed upset when she told us. I think Bill may have threatened Henry and then noticed her journal. And why would the fishermen take it? It had no value to them, they couldn't speak English. I doubt they would have known what it was." Mitch held his breath, waiting for the gendarme to ask why Bill had attacked Henry. He hoped to avoid bringing Marjorie into the discussion.

"*Interessant*. This journal, the police never recovered it?"

Mitch exhaled. "No."

The gendarme opened the desk drawer and removed a tablet of writing paper. "What is the name of this man's yacht?"

"*Silver Cloud.*"

"And the other witnesses?"

"*Phoenix* and *Dream Lover.*"

As he finished writing the third name, the gendarme said: "And you say the fishermen are now on trial for the murders?"

"Yes."

"And please, the names of the victims again?"

Mitch spelled Jill and Henry's names. "Do you want the names of the others?"

"Not necessary. We have their information in our files, such as you have just provided. I will speak to my chief, Monsieur, but I suspect there is little we can do. We are only three gendarmes on Hiva Oa, and we are responsible for the islands Fatu Hiva and Tahuata as well. Without official request from *Mexique*, I can offer you little hope of assistance except to say I have noted your comments and will place them in your file, and will make notations in the files of the other three yachts. Perhaps we can radio headquarters in Papeete to learn if requests for information about this man's yacht have been received from the police of *Mexique* or USA."

Even that offer surprised Mitch. As he heard himself relate the story, he felt slightly ridiculous. "*Merci beaucoup,*" he said, rising from his chair. "I felt I should tell someone, just in case."

"*Oui*, I understand. The death of close friends is difficult." The gendarme paused before opening the door to allow Mitch to exit. "Monsieur, for the safety of you and your wife, I hope you will leave police matters to us."

"Of course," Mitch said, extending his hand.

The young gendarme gave Mitch's hand a firm shake. "We hope you enjoy your stay in *Les Marquises*, Monsieur Sanford."

It was almost noon. The bank was closed but perhaps the post office would be open. Mitch waited for a truck to pass before crossing the street. Two stout Marquesan women in brightly-colored ankle-length dresses crossed in the opposite direction. They both carried large pandanus leaf baskets filled with yellow-green papayas. Farther down the main street he saw a dozen or so other pedestrians milling about, all of them locals, judging by their dress and brown skin.

A walkway of smooth river stones embedded in concrete led from the street through tall, multi-colored croton and red bougainvillea to a pale yellow building with the word 'POSTES' in raised block letters directly beneath the soffit of its unusual roof, which blended modern construction with Polynesian design. At the counter inside, Mitch wrote his and Vivian's name on a piece of paper below the words *Poste Restante* and handed it to a gigantic Marquesan postal clerk, who disappeared for two minutes before returning with a large padded envelope containing mail from their forwarding service in Seattle.

On his way out, Mitch noticed an unlabeled glass telephone booth at the opposite end of the counter. The phone had neither a dial nor buttons, just a handset. He'd seen phones like it before in *Larga Distancia* offices in Mexico where multi-lingual operators placed your call and you paid the charges when you'd finished. That there were any phones in the Marquesas surprised him. Vivian would be pleased to know she could call her mother.

The smell of melted cheese and frying onions drifted to the road from *Snack Make Make* as he walked by. It reminded him that he hadn't had anything to eat since the night before. Under more normal circumstances, and if he'd had any of the local currency, he'd have considered stopping to order a couple of sandwiches to go. But these were not normal circumstances and food was not his first concern. He didn't like leaving Vivian alone. He'd have something to eat as soon he got back. His next priority would be to get some sleep before confronting Bill. *Teiki. Oh boy.* What would Vivian say when she found out he'd committed them to having dinner that night with a tattooed Marquesan horseman?

His hope of hitching a ride back to Taahuku soon dimmed. Despite the apparent traffic in Atuona, once he passed the restaurant at the edge of town, not a single car passed him for several minutes. It occurred to him that all the trucks he'd seen looked very similar. Perhaps the same three or four vehicles were going back and forth, cruising the 'strip,' such as it was.

His legs needed the exercise anyway, and walking did have one other benefit: it helped him think. Despite his promise to the gendarme to stay out of police matters, he disliked the idea of simply waiting for Bill's reaction to his and Vivian's surprise arrival. Although he'd rarely followed it, he'd always admired General Patton's philosophy: Any action boldly taken is better than no action at all. In this instance, the General's advice seemed particularly appropriate. He could start by telling Bill that it was he, not Henry, who'd had sex with his wife. That should cause a reaction. If Bill didn't hesitate to beat the tar out of him, then maybe he was innocent of the murders. But, if Bill acted out of character, if he appeared reasonable—in the presence of witnesses—then it was time to start watching out for an ambush at those times when he and Vivian were alone.

Depending on how far he wanted to push it, and on how Bill reacted to the first stratagem, he could turn up the intensity with a bluff: *You killed the wrong man, Bill. I told the police about your fights and arguments with Henry. They know about Jill's missing journal. They've talked to every taxi driver and hooker in Puerto Vallarta. Your alibi doesn't hold water. When we left Mexico, Martinez was going through diplomatic channels to have you arrested and returned to Mexico.* That should do it.

Upon crossing over Black Point, he saw *Houdini* and the rest of the boats anchored in Taahuku Bay. Framed in palm fronds and slender pandanus leaves, the eclectic fleet reminded him of a flock of sleeping ducks. He heard a car approaching and turned, extending his hand and thumb, hoping the signal didn't have any profane or disrespectful connotations in Marquesan culture. It was one of the trucks he'd seen parked in front of *Snack Make Make*. The truck seemed to slow the instant he stuck out his hand and then immediately speed up, accelerating as it went past. The driver ignored Mitch as he went by, looking down toward the gear shift lever instead. It appeared to Mitch the man had only pretended not to see him. It disappointed Mitch to find this good-ol'-boy style of humor not limited to the back roads of America.

After several more minutes and no more cars, he rounded the end of the bay and passed the intersection where he first saw Teiki. Shortly beyond the intersection, he entered the tunnel of overhanging trees. The sound of something rustling the bushes at the bottom of the steep embankment beside the road caught his attention. He continued walking, peering down as he went, trying to catch a glimpse of whatever it was. He'd read in Henry's guide book that a rare, flightless ground dove lived only in the Marquesas. When he heard the soft footfalls behind him it was too late to turn.

Instinctively, his shoulders hunched. The attacker's blind-side tackle knocked him off his feet, snapping his head backward. Together they flew over the edge and plunged into the dense undergrowth, tumbling over moss-covered rocks, caroming off boughs of small trees as they slid to the bottom of the embankment. Mitch struggled to break the vacuum in his lungs. Before he could take a breath, the assailant's fist came through the brush, catching him high on the right cheek. Dazed and unable to see his opponent, he flailed and kicked aimlessly.

A hand came at him. It grabbed for the collar of his T-shirt.

Mitch rolled hard right, tearing the hand loose, sliding downhill.

He managed half a breath. He drew back his arm, cocking it against his chest. A leaping form from above descended. Mitch timed his blow. His assailant anticipated it, blocking it easily with his right forearm. The man landed on Mitch's midsection like a movie cowboy leaping from a hotel window to his saddled horse. Mitch groaned as his air left him once again.

He opened his eyes and saw Bill sitting on his chest, using knees to pin his arms to the ground. A Buck knife suddenly appeared in Bill's right hand. In a smooth, one-handed motion, the six-inch folding knife opened against Bill's knee and the curving point moved to Mitch's throat, touching the skin next to his pulsing carotid artery.

Bill's chest heaved. He stared straight into Mitch's eyes. The look on his face was pure hate. His upper lip curled up exposing teeth and gum. The skin of his forehead wrinkled back revealing the hidden whites of his eyes. "I've got you now you son-of-a-bitch."

Mitch tried to speak. Bill's weight on his midsection allowed little chance to regain his breath.

"Your ass is mine, pal. Your swingin' dick days are over."

Bill pressed the point of the Buck into Mitch's throat, depressing the skin.

Mitch struggled to get enough air in his lungs to speak. "You...killed...Henry." he gasped.

"You pansy-assed sheep turd; so that's what gave you the balls to show up here. You'd like to think I killed him just so you can justify dicking my wife!"

"You...thought...it...was him. That's why...you...killed him."

"I did at first, but not anymore."

Mitch managed to suck in a full breath. "Did you have to kill him?

"I *didn't* kill him, scumbag. You're not listening."

"Martinez knows you took the journal."

"Journal? What the hell are you—I could care less what that Frito Bandito thinks he knows."

"Martinez checked with all the taxi drivers and prostitutes. He knows you lied about your alibi."

"That does it." Bill kept the knife at Mitch's throat while inching his buttocks down onto Mitch's thighs.

"If you're going to kill me at least tell me the truth."

"I didn't kill him—and what makes you think I'm going to kill you? No-no, that would be all wrong. The punishment has to fit the crime. No pal, I'm going to show you what we do with the little boy pigs back in Kansas."

Mitch's eyes opened wider as Bill inched backwards.

"That's right, I'm gonna cut your balls off and toss 'em in the creek for the crawdads to feed on. And then I'm gonna go one step further and cut your dick off an inch at a time and make you eat it until there's nothing left but a bloody stub. You'll never fuck another man's wife as long as you live!"

"You *didn't* kill Henry?"

Bill looked at him as if he were the dumbest person on earth. "I couldn't believe it when I saw you go by the restaurant on the back of that horse. It was a gift; like God saying, 'Here, Bill, you punish this one.' All I had to do was sit and wait."

"Bill, you really didn't—" The knife pressed harder.

"No asshole, how many times do I have to say it! Thanks to you, Marj jumped ship and joined the harem of some slimy-dicked Frog." Bill slid down until he sat on Mitch's knees. "One move, stud, and a gallon of your blood will be flowing down river."

"Marjorie...left you?"

Bill raised his free hand to strike. "You don't say her name. She's probably spreading her legs for that snail-eating, twat-licker right now. That's another reason why this is going to feel so good." He lowered his hand and unbuttoned the top button of Mitch's shorts.

He's telling the truth. "Bill, wait. I didn't mean for it to happen. I—"

"She told me it was her doing." Bill jerked the zipper of Mitch's shorts with his left hand while still holding the knife at Mitch's throat.

Shit, he's serious, he's really going to do it. Mitch felt a baseball-sized stone under his right hand. "Bill, honest to God, I felt terrible. I told Vivian and—"

"You told her?" Bill pulled down Mitch's shorts, exposing his underpants.

"Yes." Mitch let his fingers settle slowly around the rock.

"Great, now every cruiser in the South Pacific will hear about it." Bill jerked Mitch's underpants down, unveiling his genitals. Mitch winced as Bill encircled his scrotum with the thumb and forefinger of his left hand, squeezing until the skin stretched drum tight.

"In just a second, pal, you'll get to kiss your balls good-bye."

Mitch sensed Bill timing the movement of knife from throat to groin. His only chance was to go with the rock the instant the knife left his throat. If he went too soon, Bill would see it coming and it would be all over. His fingers tightened around the stone.

Bill glanced from Mitch's face to where his hand lifted Mitch's testicles. Beads of sweat ran down Bill's forehead and hung from his eyebrows. Mitch felt Bill's grip relax.

"I can't do it," Bill said. He removed his hand from Mitch's groin.

Mitch groaned and eased his grip on the rock.

"You fucking deserve it, but I can't do it," Bill said, still holding the Buck at Mitch's throat.

Both were silent for several seconds. Mitch closed his eyes and listened to the sound of his breathing and the burbling of the nearby stream. Bill withdrew the knife, resting its hilt on his thigh.

"Is it okay if I pull my shorts up?" Mitch asked, eyeing the knife.

Bill paused. "I'd like nothing better than for you to try something cute." He let his statement hang in the air for a moment and then rocked back and rose to his feet, still straddling Mitch.

Mitch rubbed his neck and where the knife had been and checked his fingers for blood. There was none. Bill backed away. Mitch looked down to make sure everything was still there before quickly hiking up his underpants and shorts. As he zipped and buttoned the shorts, he kept an eye on the hand that held the knife. He made no move to get up. He had no desire to provoke Bill. He propped himself up with his elbows and rested in a half-reclining position. He felt a dull pain below his right eye. The corner of his left eye was wet. He wiped it with the back of his hand, which came away smeared with blood.

Bill turned his back on him and raised his left hand to his face. It looked to Mitch as if he might even be crying.

"I even *liked* you, you son-of-a-bitch," Bill said, his voice cracking with emotion.

"I didn't plan it, Bill; neither did Marjorie. It just happened. I'm not proud of it. Except for Vivian and Martinez, I haven't told a soul."

"Martinez, that superior son-of-a-bitch. I'll bet he got a hoot out of that story."

"Not really. But he was pretty sure it was you who killed Henry and Jill, and not the fishermen."

"But I didn't." Bill half-turned and tossed the knife on the ground next to Mitch's right hand. "You might as well finish the job you started in Puerto Vallarta."

Mitch sighed. "Honest to God, Bill, if I could go back and change what happened I would. It didn't exactly do wonders for my marriage either."

"What the hell am I going to do? I can't sail *Silver Cloud* by myself."

"Is that all you care about?" Mitch quietly picked up the knife, folded it and slipped it in his pocket.

"No." Bill seemed to lose strength, kneeling down on one knee. "Marj is all...I love her. I'm afraid she's gone for good."

Mitch sat up, staring at Bill's back in silence a moment before speaking. "If you love her so much, why do you treat her the way you do?"

"I don't know. It started a long time ago. I was afraid I'd lose her."

"You were afraid you'd lose her? So you started putting her down all the time? You'll have to explain that one."

"I wouldn't expect you to understand. You obviously don't have the same problem."

"Problem?"

Bill raised his head but didn't answer.

"What problem, Bill?"

"I can't let her get close to me."

"Why not?" Mitch said, scooting closer.

Bill wiped his face and looked up toward pinpoints of sunlight twinkling through the leaves that gently illuminated the shady surroundings.

"Why can't you let Marjorie get close to you?"

"You *are* a dumb shit."

Mitch saw that Bill wasn't going to help him out. He began thinking out loud. "You're mean to Marjorie...because you can't let her get close to you...because...because what, you've got VD, AIDS?" Bill remained silent. "I don't have the same problem. Oh. *Oh.*"

"Finally getting the picture, Einstein?"

"You're...impotent?"

"I *hate* that fucking word."

"But, all that talk. Your stories about you and Marjorie." Mitch suddenly remembered Marjorie's words, '*It's been years, Mitch.*'

"That's what it was all right, talk."

"What about the prostitute in Puerto Vallarta? Was that just an alibi?"

"That bastard, Martinez, said he would keep that confidential. Did you tell Marj?"

"No, and I won't. Martinez didn't tell me about that until after you'd sailed. So, was it just a story?"

"No." Bill sighed. "After I'd found out what Marj had done, I was furious, wanted to get even, and I thought, maybe with another woman, someone I didn't know or care about...but..."

"It didn't make any difference?"

Bill shook his head. "She kept my money anyway. I heard her laughing about it with a whore down the hall."

Mitch remembered Bill and Marjorie had two grown sons. "When did this start, Bill?"

"If you think I'm going to play True Confessions with you..."

"Have you ever told anyone else about this?"

"What do you *think*? Is this ironic or what?" Bill gazed up as if speaking to the trees. "Look who I'm talking to, for Christ's sake."

"There are people, therapists, who can help people in your situation. My sister-in-law—"

"Well, I'm not talking to anybody. Besides, what's the point? Marj is gone."

"She's still in Atuona, isn't she?"

"Yeah, but she told me she'd swim home to the States before she'd get back aboard *Silver Cloud*. She never talked back to me like that before—thanks to you."

"It's not too late, Bill. Just tell her what you told me."

"What?"

"That you love her, you're afraid of losing her and you want her back."

"Like that's going to make her jump into my arms."

"You'd be surprised the effect a little humble honesty can have. Tell her you and I had it out; that you had the chance to get even, but you didn't and instead you forgave me. You tell her that and I'll bet she'll listen to whatever else you have to say."

"Who the hell said I forgave you?"

"Well then, lie."

"In truth, it wasn't all your fault or hers; it was mine as well."

"That's close enough; quit while you're ahead."

"This cruise is my life's dream, but I'd leave the boat where it sits and fly home tomorrow if that's what it took to get Marj back."

"Tell *her* that." Mitch stood, removed the knife from his pocket and held it out to Bill. "I've got to get back to the boat. You coming?"

Bill took the knife. "No, I think I'll sit here for a spell."

"How'd you get ashore? I saw your dinghy tied to *Silver Cloud.*"

"Caught a ride in with some other folks. I'll catch a ride out."

The twenty-fifth-floor view through a tinted glass façade took in a commanding sweep of San Francisco Bay from Alcatraz to Yerba Buena. An eight-foot slab of white-veined black marble on angled stainless steel legs formed an executive desk that nearly bridged the apex of the large corner office. Two black leather chairs set three feet back from the desk faced the converging windows, obliging guests to appreciate the superb and expensive vista.

The polished desktop was devoid of clutter except the current week's copies of *Barron's* and *PC Week,* and an ebony phone-set. The device chimed once and a small red diode began flashing.

The man in the high-backed chair behind the desk put down the legal document he was reading and picked up the handset. "Yes? Oh really? Put him on." He waited until the familiar voice spoke. "Yes, well, we're working six and seven days a week, trying to meet the deadline for the next release. How's it going down there? I suppose you're calling to tell me how boring paradise is. You sound a million miles away."

"I doubt this is a very private line; bear that in mind."

"You sound troubled."

"Someone unexpected has turned up here."

"Who might that be, Old Chum?"

"Friends of your former business associate."

"Those same friends you mentioned when we last spoke?"

"Correct."

The man behind the desk held the phone to his ear with a shoulder and tugged one cuff of his white silk dress shirt until a diamond stud cufflink emerged from the sleeve of his charcoal gray Armani suit. "Perhaps they simply changed their plans."

"That was my hope, too. However, I overheard the end of a private conversation he had with one of the locals."

"Don't keep me in suspense, Old Chum. You know how that annoys me."

"The local expressed his sympathy but told the man it would be better to leave matters in the hands of professionals."

"By 'locals' and 'professionals,' whom do you mean?"

"Assume the worst."

"I see. That is bad news."

"Yes. I managed to steal a glance at a piece of paper on which the local had written the names of three yachts, including ours."

"Well, at least the field hasn't been narrowed to one."

"That is the only reason I took the chance to call. We may still have time to...clear matters up."

"What do you have in mind, Old Chum?"

"I think you should send a specialist."

"A technician?"

"Yes, exactly."

"You handled the matter before. Why not now?"

"There was no choice then, no time."

"Damn! Do you realize that yesterday the case was decided in our favor? On top of everything else, *they* are going to have to pay damages to *us*!"

"How much?"

"I don't think it would be wise to mention a specific figure, let's just say you could have afforded a much nicer boat."

"Really? All the more reason to tie off loose ends here. What can you do on short notice?"

"As it happens we may be in luck. I believe one of the parent company's people is in Los Angeles at the moment."

"By the by, are they upset about PV?"

"No, not all. In fact, they were rather impressed with your initiative. They didn't think you had it in you. I have to admit,

Old Chum, I was completely dumbfounded myself. It's a side of your nature I would never have dreamed existed."

"The specific details would surprise you even more. Sometime in the distant future, when we can risk seeing each other in person, I'll fill you in."

"If an opportunity should present itself, I don't think you should wait for our man. It's risky to wait, you know."

"I'm well aware of that. We've survived one coincidence. I'm not sure we can survive two."

"Do what you have to do, Old Chum, and in the unhappy event that you should get caught, there's no need for the whole thing to unravel."

"Absolutely. You just be sure the technician is sent to repair only what needs fixing. And before you take offense, it's not you I'm worried about."

"You've proved yourself. You have nothing to fear from them. What about travel arrangements?"

"Los Angeles to Papeete, and from there to Hiva Oa. He may have to purchase his ticket for the flight from Tahiti to Hiva Oa from another passenger. I'm told it's booked well in advance by teachers and government officials.

"I'm told he's very resourceful."

He's likely to stand out in the crowd."

"What would you suggest?"

"If he were say, a professor of archaeology on his way to visit Marquesan ruins, it would attract less attention and give him an excuse to visit areas not frequented by run-of-the-mill tourists."

"It wouldn't surprise me if archaeology were one of his many interests. Is there a hotel or someplace where he can stay?"

"There are several small bungalows on the hill overlooking Taahuku Bay where we're anchored. I'll try to leave a message and directions should we have to leave before he arrives. What name should I use?"

"Hold on one moment," the man swiveled his chair to the left and scanned the book titles on the shelf behind his desk. "Ah, how about Vanzetti?, yes, *Professor* Vanzetti. I do hope you and your friends will try to stay in the area until he arrives, Old Chum."

"We'll do our best."

"Be careful. No one's asking questions about you here, so I think we're safe—as long as you see to it that no one *else* connects us."

"That was a one-in-a-million chance, Philip. I won't make that mistake again, especially now, with all the publicity you must be getting."

"Yes, some of it is right here on the desk in front of me. Next time we talk I must tell you about my new car; almost six figures."

Mitch sat quietly while Vivian ministered to him in the cockpit. After cleaning the wound and dabbing it with Betadine, she carefully placed a butterfly bandage on the cut over his left eyebrow. "Takes care of that one. Not much I can do for the other except make an ice pack. From the looks of it, you're going to have a pretty good shiner."

Mitch tentatively touched the puffiness below his right eye. "My first fight, if you could call it that. Getting hit in the face wasn't so bad. It happened so fast I didn't feel a thing. All I remember is not being able to breathe."

Vivian glanced at his lap. "Sounded like getting hit in the face was the least of your worries."

Mitch held up a thinly gapped thumb and forefinger. "Bill came this close to severely curtailing my contribution to our sex life."

"And yet you think he's not the one who killed Henry and Jill?"

"He had me dead to rights, Viv. He could have killed me. He couldn't even bring himself to do what he intended—thank God."

"The impotency story is so out-of-character it's almost believable. Bill doesn't seem the type who'd make up a story like that."

Mitch leaned back and looked up, his gaze orbiting an imaginary point in the sky.

"What is it?" Vivian asked.

"I just realized what this means."

"What *what* means?"

"If Bill *isn't* the one who murdered Jill and Henry, then I didn't cause their deaths."

"That's true, but if not Bill, then who? Carlos and Manuel?"

"Maybe." Mitch looked forward toward *Phoenix* and *Dream Lover*. "Did I tell you Martinez first suspected Jim?"

"No. As you may recall, we got into a rather heated discussion shortly after you began telling me Martinez' theories."

"That's right, I guess we did."

"Why did Martinez suspect Jim?"

"Initially, because *Phoenix* slipped out so early and quietly that morning, and later because of the GPS that was never recovered."

"But what reason would Jim have had for taking Jill's journal?"

"Martinez didn't have an answer for that. Maybe in the struggle Jim left bloody fingerprints on it and threw it over the side to be safe. Who knows?"

"You could have spared me the bloody fingerprints image." Vivian peered through the dodger's windshield toward *Phoenix*. "If it was Jim, it *would* explain his odd behavior this morning."

"You saw him?"

"While Marjorie and I were waiting for you to return I saw him rowing back to *Phoenix*."

"I didn't see him in town. He must have passed Bill and me while we were resolving our differences down in the bushes. What'd he do that was so odd?"

"Rather than stop by, he rowed behind that boat," Vivian pointed to the American cutter between *Houdini* and shore, "crossed our bow and continued past *Phoenix* to *Dream Lover*."

"What's so unusual about that?"

"Let me finish." Vivian shot him an arched eyebrow. "It was like he was going out of his way to avoid us. I caught his attention anyway, and waved. He just smiled, nodded and kept rowing. Don't you think it's a bit strange that he didn't stop to at least welcome us to the Marquesas after not seeing us for a month? After all, we had become pretty good friends with them."

Mitch nodded pensively. "He and Litea did come over to welcome us when we arrived in Mazatlan after crossing the Sea of Cortez."

"And that was only a two-day passage."

Mitch looked over Vivian's shoulder. "Here comes Victor." The large white inflatable sped out from the beach at the far corner of the harbor, skirting past *Silver Cloud* and the other boats anchored at the ends of their respective rows. Victor appeared to be headed out the harbor entrance, but upon passing the last boat in the front row he made a sweeping turn and approached *Dream Lover* from the bow. Mitch watched until Victor reached the big cutter's stern and killed the engine. "Seeing Victor reminds me, we've been invited to dinner."

Vivian's brow's knitted. "On *Dream Lover*?"

Sharon waited on deck at the top of the steps molded into *Dream Lover*'s reversed transom while Victor tied the dinghy's painter to one of the large stern cleats. He could sense she was upset. For once, he was prepared for her disapproval.

"Well?" Sharon said.

"Well, what?" replied Victor.

"Victor, I'm not in the mood. What happened? Didn't you meet Mitch? I saw him just now watching you return."

Victor handed her his hand-held marine VHF radio. "Landing the dinghy on the beach and getting up that hill to the road is not as easy as it looks."

"I'm not interested in your Walter Mitty heroics. Did you meet him or not?"

"No, I didn't meet him, I—"

"You got cold feet and stayed hidden in the bushes. *Really*, Victor, after what you've done, I'd have thought you could manage this."

Victor moved up the transom steps, placed a hand on Sharon's shoulder and pushed her backwards out of his way, causing her to trip and nearly fall on the low aft cabin roof. "If you'll give me one goddamned minute, love, I'll tell you what happened."

Sharon regained her feet, collected herself and glanced at the nearby boats. "Victor!, they might have seen that."

"And what they or anyone else would see is a husband giving his wife the discipline she desperately needs. You're always insinuating—rather ironically—that I'm not manly enough to suit you. I should think you'd welcome a little husbandly dominance."

Sharon bristled. "You know we mustn't do anything to attract undue attention." She moved forward and sat in the rear of the large center cockpit. "All right, I'm sitting here, patiently waiting to hear of your derring-do." She crossed her legs, folded her arms and, with a practiced flip of her head, fanned her long blond hair across the back of her white silk midi.

Victor followed and sat on the starboard seat a few feet away. He removed a pair of sunglasses and wiped perspiration from his receding hairline with a handkerchief. "While I was beside the road, waiting for Mitch to come around the bend, I had a thought."

"How utterly novel."

Victor ignored the dig. "Suppose Mitch and Vivian *are* here because of the murders, *but,* what if they suspect someone else. We always said, if suspicion were to shift to anyone other than the two Mexicans, Bill was the most likely candidate, right?"

Sharon inhaled a deep breath and exhaled slowly. "Yes; so?"

"I realized that by pretending to run into Mitch in order to gauge his attitude towards us I was running the risk of attracting his suspicion when in fact he might not have the slightest inkling of our involvement."

"So pray tell me, dear husband, what did you do?"

"I went to the gendarmerie ahead of him."

Sharon's normally arched eyebrows lifted higher still. "You *what*?"

"It was a gamble, I admit."

Sharon pointed to a bulge in the large front pocket of his military style shorts. "You went into the gendarmerie with *that* in your pocket? You must be out of your mind!"

Victor extracted a small automatic from his pocket and laid it beside him on the seat. "Don't be ridiculous. Of course I didn't take it with me. I hid it in the rocks beside the trail leading from the road down to the beach."

The lines of disapproval eased from around Sharon's eyes. "On what pretense did you go to the gendarmerie?"

"First, I ran to the store just down the block and bought a writing tablet. I hurried back to the gendarmerie, arriving hardly more than two or three minutes ahead of Mitch. Fortunately, the gendarme on duty was not the same one who cleared us in, so I didn't have to worry about him remembering me. He allowed me to speak to the chief gendarme. I told him I was a free-lance travel writer doing an article about the Marquesas and wanted to interview him regarding Hiva Oa."

"And he bought it?"

"Without hesitation. That I was a *Canadien,* who spoke fluent French, and that he had an ego of immense proportions, certainly helped. When I rattled off the names of Canadian and French travel magazines as though I conferred with their editors every day, he had no doubt I was the genuine article. And why should he?"

"But didn't Mitch see you?"

"On our first visit to the gendarmerie to clear in, I remembered seeing the chief sitting in his corner office talking to someone else. The angle was such that I couldn't see the other person sitting across his desk. Mitch may have heard my voice, but I spoke French the whole time, and no louder than necessary for the chief to hear me."

Sharon re-crossed her tanned legs and leaned forward, propping her chin with a forearm. "Why, Victor, my brave and clever little spy, whatever did you find out?"

Victor glanced aft toward *Houdini* before he answered.

With fingers laced behind her neck, Vivian listened as Mitch finished recounting the highlights of his encounter with Teiki. "He sounds fascinating, and it's nice he gave you a ride into town, but—."

"It was funny how he suddenly took to me after first seeming so hostile."

"Mitch, I'd love to meet some Marquesan people and sample the local cuisine, but *tonight?*"

"Viv, this is a rare invitation. This guy is the genuine article, a real Marquesan. I'll bet this is the first time he's ever invited foreigners home to meet his family."

She dropped her arms, leaned forward and rubbed his knee. "I was hoping we could go to bed, *now,* and not get up for at least two days. Aren't you exhausted?"

"Yeah, and sore all over, too. But there's no way to contact this guy even if we wanted to. He'll be standing there, waiting for us in front of the gendarmerie at sunset. If we don't show, Viv, it'll confirm his low opinion of foreigners." Vivian slumped as he continued. "Look, we can nap for a few hours before we head in. We won't stay any longer than we absolutely have to. Promise."

Sharon shifted to the seat beside Victor and massaged the back of his neck. "At least they haven't narrowed it down to one boat. You said we're third on the gendarme's list?"

"Almost Philip's exact words," said Victor.

"I wonder what caused Mitch to shift his suspicions away from the Mexicans?"

"Yes, that is puzzling. Perhaps I should have asked Philip to send someone to Puerto Vallarta to check into that."

"Nevertheless, your instincts were impeccably accurate, darling. It's a good thing you *didn't* encounter Mitch on the road. Now we have more time. When is this...Vanzetti?, due to arrive?"

"With luck, two or three days." Victor glanced toward *Houdini* again. "Something else just occurred to me: if Mitch and Vivian had to sail all the way here from Mexico to raise their suspicions with these backwoods gendarmes, it means that whatever it was that aroused their suspicions must not have been material enough to cause the Mexican authorities to contact their peers in Papeete."

"You're absolutely right," Sharon said. "That's splendid thinking." She stared off toward the commercial wharf. "I'll bet it was that damned journal. I told you you should have simply cut out the one page and thrown the book over the side with the knife. Chances are none of it would have been readable by the time they found it."

"As I recall, dear, it was a bit late by the time you offered that suggestion."

Sharon kissed him on the cheek. "I'm sorry; let's not start pointing fingers again." She started and sat up straight. "Damn!"

"What?"

"*Phoenix* is leaving tomorrow."

"I thought they weren't leaving until Monday."

Sharon shook her head. "Jim stopped by to tell us on his way back from town."

"I'm not sure I see why their departure is cause for concern. Might it not make them look suspicious; leaving immediately after *Houdini* arrives?"

Sharon stood and moved to the port side of the cockpit to look at *Phoenix,* anchored midway between *Dream Lover* and the shore. "Suppose *Phoenix* and *Silver Cloud* were both to leave but *Houdini* stayed here. That would probably mean Mitch and Vivian suspect us. Then this thug of Philip's shows up and they meet with an unfortunate accident. Who do you suppose your gendarme friend is going to want to talk to first?"

Victor nodded. "I see what you mean. But *Silver Cloud* arrived only, what, two or three days ago? And as practically everyone in the harbor must know by now, Marjorie has jumped ship, so Bill is not likely to be going anywhere soon. And as we've agreed, he's Mitch's most likely suspect."

"And therefore, the one Mitch is most likely to invalidate first. It's possible we don't have much time after all."

"I see what you mean. We need a contingency plan. We can't simply sit and wait for Philip's man to arrive."

"We either have to solve the problem ourselves, while at least one of the other suspects is nearby, or somehow keep them here until Vanzetti arrives to take care of it for us."

"I did tell Philip we'd try to handle it ourselves if given the opportunity."

She pressed a breast against his arm. "Perhaps there's hope for you yet."

Victor responded, sliding his hand up the inside of her thigh. "I suppose it's well within your inestimable powers to convince Jim that now is not a good time to leave Atuona?"

"Victor! First spying and now pimping. You're positively a revelation today. I'm suddenly aroused by this new you."

"Really?" His hand moved to her crotch. "Perhaps we should move our strategy session to the aft cabin."

"Yes, let's. But first, why don't you pay a visit to *Phoenix* and invite Jim and Litea over for sundowners. Judging by the way Jim looked at me when he stopped by this morning, I doubt he'll refuse."

"Why don't you come along to make sure?"

"I *am* sure. And besides, I want to have everything ready for you in the aft cabin when you return."

"*Every*thing?"

"Like I said, darling, I am *very* aroused."

Victor kissed her abruptly, nearly chipping a tooth. "Hold that thought, Love, I'll be right back."

She licked and touched her teeth as Victor stood and made his way aft toward the transom. "Darling, why don't you go by *Houdini*, too, and invite Mitch and Vivian while you're at it?"

Victor froze. "Do you think that wise?"

"*Think*, Victor. How will it look if we don't appear delighted to see them?"

Victor turned and backed down the steps into the inflatable. "You're right again. God, this is getting to me, too. I'm as crazy as you are. I'll be ready for you when I get back."

"I wouldn't be too sure," countered Sharon. "You've been a naughty little girl and I think you're in for a rough afternoon."

Mitch lay beside Vivian in the forward berth staring at the overhead. "What're you thinking?" she asked.

"Just the irony of it all."

"What do you mean?"

"Henry was the one with the dream; the one with parents and brothers. On the other hand, if it had been me..."

"Mitch! What about me?"

"I wasn't making a wish, I just think it's ironic."

"Close your eyes and try to get some sleep." Vivian rolled away and buried her face in her pillow.

Mitch had barely dozed off when she nudged him. "What's that?" she asked.

"What's what?"

"Sounds like an outboard motor coming alongside."

Mitch raised up on his elbows and listened. "You're right, it is." He swiveled and hopped off the berth, stumbling aft as he tried to get a foot into his cutoffs. A series of raps sounded on the aft deck.

"Ahoy, *Houdini*, anybody home?"

Victor. Mitch dropped the cutoffs and went up the companionway in his briefs. "Vic, hi, how's it going?"

Victor stood in his dinghy holding on to *Houdini*'s caprail and reached out his hand. "Welcome to the Marquesas, Mitch! Congratulations on your passage." A frown creased Victor's forehead. "What happened to your face?"

"Oh, wasn't watching where I was going and took a little fall on the way back from town." Mitch took Victor's offered hand and gave it a firm shake. "How long have you and Sharon been here?

"Let's see, we arrived on the sixteenth, so that's what, almost ten days ago?"

"Wow, you had a fast passage."

"Twenty-one days; nothing spectacular for a 54-footer. How about you?"

"Twenty-three," Mitch said.

Victor gave an approving nod. "Not bad! When I came back from town I said to Sharon, 'Look who's behind us!' She nearly fell over the side. When did you two sneak in?"

"Early this morning. Not many people were up and about."

"After that terrible business in Puerto Vallarta, we were afraid we might have seen the last of you."

Mitch glanced down at his feet for a moment. "After we had time to think it over, we realized Henry would have wanted us to finish the voyage the four of us started together."

"You're absolutely right. You're going to circumnavigate then?"

"No, we'll probably have to head home from Tahiti or Bora Bora, but at least we've made it to the South Pacific."

"You certainly have, which is why I'm here, actually. Sharon and I wish to invite you and Vivian to join us, along with Jim and Litea, aboard *Dream Lover* for sundowners this evening to celebrate your successful passage."

"Sounds great, Vic, and really thoughtful, except we already promised a Marquesan friend we'd have dinner ashore with his family tonight."

"A dinner invitation already? You certainly don't waste time making friends. I suppose it will be too late to pop over for a nightcap by the time you get back?"

"I'm afraid so. Vivian and I are both dead tired. We hope to be heading back to *Houdini* by nine or ten at the latest. We'll probably sleep all day tomorrow."

"How stupid of me! I'll bet I interrupted a nap."

Sharon removed a large hat box from the foot of Victor's hanging locker. She opened it and laid out the contents on his side of the bed: a large pair of white, brief-style panties; a large bra with small cups; a short, red pleated skirt; and a white knit sweater with a large red megaphone emblem on the front.

She put the empty box away, slipped out of her blouse and shorts, and moved across the cabin to her own lockers. From a hanger, she pulled an embroidered chambray shirt with pearl-buttoned pockets and from the foot of the locker she grabbed a pair of fancy-stitched western boots with caps of silver on sharply pointed toes. She opened a drawer beneath the bed and took out a pair of light blue denim jeans with a saguaro cactus appliquéd on each knee.

She laid the jeans and shirt on the foot of the bed, reached into the drawer again and took out a pink and purple-striped object hidden beneath a stack of dress shorts. It formed two erect and opposing penises joined at the hilt, one short and curved the other long and straight. She tossed the dildo on the bed and after removing her bra and panties laid down beside it. From a small drawer built into the headboard behind her, she removed a tube of K-Y. After applying some lubricant to the curved shaft, she raised her knees and inserted it into her.

Sharon closed her eyes and relived the prior night's exquisite experience. Her youthful partner had been understandably reluctant, perfectly so. The young Marquesan girl's virginal reticence was what had made the orgasm so seismic, the after-shocks rippling back and forth between them, turning minutes into hours. The remembrance echoed through her; she sighed pleasurably and ceased the movements. She sat up, slipped into the slim-fit jeans, carefully folding the dildo's other half out of the way as she pulled the zipper. Standing before the mirror over her vanity, she twisted at the waist, studying her bare breasts in profile from the left and right. Satisfied, she caressed the obvious bulge in her jeans. She preferred not to use the dildo on Victor, but then, he had shown rather daring initiative today, and deserved his favorite reward. She wouldn't disappoint him. Vivid memories of last night's conquest would see to that.

Their nap, though free from further interruptions, lasted less than three hours. Nevertheless, Mitch felt more spring in his step this second time ashore. Vivian laughed at her initial wobbliness. "I feel like a baby who's just discovered it can walk," she said. Mitch felt as though his siesta had delivered double the revitalizing effect of an equal amount of the fitful, often interrupted sleep periods they'd grown accustomed to at sea. By the time they reached the point on the road where Bill had ambushed him, the mountains above Atuona already cast a carpet of shadows over Taahuku Bay. He continued his guided tour for Vivian and pointed toward the intersection farther up the road. "There's where I first saw Teiki on his horse."

"So that road goes to Puamau?" asked Vivian.

"Right. But Teiki said once you pass the air strip it's more of a wide trail than a road, which probably explains why I have yet to see anything other than four-wheel-drive vehicles and motorcycles."

Vivian touched his arm. "Look at those two people coming across the bridge. It has to be Jim and Litea."

"You're right, it is."

Jim and Litea both carried bulging plastic grocery bags in each hand. Jim spoke as the distance between them closed. "*Bon soir mes amis, comment ça va?*"

"Hi, Jim," Mitch said, coming to halt at the edge of the road. "I should have guessed with a last name like yours, you might speak French. Hi, Litea."

Litea sat her two bags beside the road. "Hi, Mitch, hi, Vivian, we're sure glad to see you here; a little surprised, though." Her happy expression reversed itself. "We were shocked beyond words when Victor told us about Jill and Henry. It must have devastated the two of you."

"'Devastated' pretty well sums it up," Vivian said. "We're somewhat surprised to find you two here, too."

Jim's brows lowered. "Why's that?"

Mitch answered. "The Mexican Navy went out looking for you the day you left. They couldn't find a trace."

"Why...why were they looking for us?" Jim asked.

"The police wanted to question everyone who knew Henry and Jill, especially people like us and the two of you who had been in contact with them that last day."

"Oh yeah, sure. They would want to talk to us," Jim said.

"We thought maybe you'd changed your minds at the last minute and headed south to Costa Rica," Vivian said.

"We were at Ipala," said Litea.

"*Ipala*?" Mitch queried.

Jim cleared his throat. "Yeah, the day we left PV the wind died and I didn't want to use up a lot of fuel motoring right at the outset of the long passage, so we ducked south of Cabo Corrientes and anchored in the little cove at Ipala. After two days, the wind picked up and we took off."

"I guess the Mexican Navy didn't think of that possibility," said Mitch.

"Unless they approached the cove from the south or flew right over top of us, they'd never have seen us," Jim said.

"We were completely oblivious of what happened in Puerto Vallarta until we arrived here and talked to Victor and Sharon," said Litea. "They didn't mention anything about the Navy looking for us."

"I doubt they knew," Mitch said. "I only found out after most of the boats had left."

"Did *Dream Lover* beat you here?" asked Vivian.

"Almost," Jim answered. "We pulled in only two or three hours ahead of her."

"Mitch, what happened to your eye?" asked Litea.

Mitch instinctively felt for the bandage over his eye. "Oh, I wasn't watching where I was going and took a little fall.

Nothing serious. How'd your celestial navigation go, Jim? You made it here, so I assume it went well."

"Yeah, yeah it did." Jim glanced at Litea. "Everything went fine, no problems."

Vivian looked down at the bags of groceries and fresh produce. "Looks like you might be leaving soon."

Litea nodded. "Sometime Monday."

"Maybe," Jim added. "We haven't decided for sure."

"You came in at a time when the bay is calm," said Litea. "It's like being in a washing machine in here when the seas outside begin to build. Well I'd like to find some place a little calmer and more protected."

"I noticed a little swell starting up when we rowed ashore," Vivian said.

"You haven't seen anything yet," said Jim. "The day after we got here I was working on the engine. It was so rough I got seasick—at anchor!"

Litea added: "People on boats that were here before us told us it got so bad the week before we made landfall they all had to pull up their anchors and move over to Tahuata or the north side of the island for two days."

"It was that rough?" Mitch asked.

"Downright dangerous," said Jim. "They said the shore break started right behind the last row of boats. Litea's right; you entered on a rare day, so be alert."

Vivian asked Litea, "When you leave, where are you headed?"

She glanced at Jim before answering. "Ua Pou, initially, and then on to Nuku Hiva."

"Did you clear out today?" Mitch asked.

"Uh, no. Yesterday afternoon." Jim glanced at his wristwatch. "Since you're headed toward town, I assume you're not coming to *Dream Lover* for sundowners."

"No," Mitch replied, "we're having dinner in town, and if we don't get going, we'll be late."

"Us, too," said Jim. "Perhaps we'll see you tomorrow."

Vivian waited until Jim and Litea were well out of hearing range. "Mitch, is it just my imagination, or did Jim seem a little nervous?"

"More than a little."

After taking a long, hot shower, Sharon changed into her costume for the evening: a pink spandex body-suit with scooped neck, sans bra; a silk, midnight blue ankle-length pareo tied in a knot over her right hip exposing a long wedge of bronzed thigh whenever she moved and, to complete the tropical ensemble, a mist of *Gardenia Passion* at the base of her neck.

In *Dream Lover*'s galley she arranged alternating rows of crackers and cheese slices on a serving tray as Victor watched. "Rather plebeian hors d'oeuvres," she said, completing the last row, "but considering the time allowed and the guest list, they'll suffice."

Victor sidled up behind her, putting his hands on her hips. "The way you look and smell, Love, I doubt you'll have much trouble bringing Jim under your spell, although I suspect you'd prefer to exercise your magic on a more challenging subject."

Sharon let a telling moment of silence lapse before she answered. "I'm sure your immense charm will be sufficient to distract Litea long enough for Jim to develop the unmistakable impression that certain rewards are forthcoming if he doesn't stray too far."

Victor's hands slipped around her waist and inched upward. "You'll be discreet, of course."

Sharon twisted from his grasp and moved toward the companionway. "It's interesting that you should bring up the subject of discretion, Victor dear, after your assignation with the town strumpet last week."

Victor's face turned to stone. "I thought we'd agreed not to talk about that anymore. Besides, I have a notion you evened the score last night. Where the hell were you, anyway?"

Sharon spoke over her shoulder as she made her way carefully up the companionway steps. "Don't for a second think you could *ever* get even with me playing that game, Victor."

"Yes. Yes, you're quite right, Darling. You more than proved that this afternoon. I'm still numb with ecstasy. So let's stop this bickering."

"Jim and Litea are rowing this way, Victor. Hand me the pitcher of martinis."

Teiki led Mitch and Vivian through Atuona to the house of his sister, Tahia, and her husband Maurice. Along the way, he proudly pointed out the landmarks of Atuona. "White church over there, Catholic. Cousin's Protestant church down that road."

Mitch observed Teiki glancing away whenever the two made eye contact. The cause of this behavior became evident when Teiki tentatively asked him about his facial contusions. Mitch gave him the same fabricated, but simple and discreet explanation he'd given Jim and Litea. Teiki, unable to stifle his chuckling, broke into unrestrained laughter, reaching a state of near drunkenness, pantomiming Mitch looking for a ground dove and then stumbling and falling off the road. When he regained his composure, he looked at Vivian and said, "I think...I think maybe you angry because Mitch make you come to dinner."

Now it was Vivian who laughed. "You thought I did this?" she said, pointing at Mitch's marred face.

Teiki nodded and once again convulsed with laughter. Vivian joined him.

Mitch glanced at the two people on either side of him. "I don't think it's *that* funny."

Vivian put her hand on his shoulder. "I'm sorry, it isn't." She slowly managed to stifle her giggling, then relapsed. "Yes, it is!"

Her laughter set Teiki off again and the two of them wobbled down the road hanging on to Mitch's shoulders. He felt as though he were returning a pair of lunatics to the asylum.

At the end of a short dirt road serving half a dozen homes, they came to a small three-room house of white clapboard with a rusting corrugated metal roof. In the center of the front yard grew a round, low tree with large green leaves and several fruit hanging from its branches, the likes of which Mitch had never seen. The dark green fruit were the size of grapefruit. From their color and skin texture, he imagined they were some gigantic species of lime. As Teiki led them inside and began the introductions, the small house seemed to bulge with smiling Marquesan children and adults.

Teiki's wife, Annette, was easy to identify. The shy Marquesan woman, wearing a bright yellow shift, sat in the room's one easy chair, cradling her distended belly in her hands. A beautiful Polynesian woman stood beside Annette. Her resemblance to Teiki left no doubt that she was his sister, Tahia. Teiki's brother-in-law, Maurice, introduced himself in French, shook Mitch's hand and kissed Vivian's. His shifty eyes and thin mustache gave Mitch the impression of the villain in a martial arts movie. Next came Teiki's seven-year-old son Pohu and nine-year-old daughter, Meto. Pohu was an imp with wildly tousled hair, bright eyes and a mouthful of white teeth. Meto took refuge from the strange guests behind her mother and aunt.

When Teiki finished introducing his nieces and nephew— Jeanette, thirteen; Marie, eleven; Paulette, eight and Rene, six—Maurice spoke several words in Marquesan while looking at Vivian.

Teiki turned to Mitch and Vivian to translate. "Maurice says you are lucky man, Mitch, because Vivian is *vehine po'otu oko*, a very beautiful woman."

"*Merci*," said Mitch, smiling at Maurice. Vivian blushed under Maurice's lascivious gaze.

Teiki explained Mitch's injuries, bringing on yet another chorus of snickers and laughter that Mitch accepted with good-natured grace.

When Tahia, Jeanette and Marie finished setting out the table, everyone took a seat with Teiki placed between Mitch and Vivian. Teiki said grace, first in Marquesan and then in English. As large steaming bowls of food made their way around the table, Teiki explained their contents, "This taro, this breadfruit, this green papaya."

"This looks like chop suey," said Vivian, as she took a large porcelain bowl from Maurice filled with bean and bamboo sprouts, water chestnuts, mushrooms and what appeared to be large chunks of pork.

"Yes, chop suey," said Teiki, handing Mitch a large bowl of rice. "Pork from Maurice's *puakas*."

To Mitch the boiled taro tasted a lot like potato, yet starchier. The breadfruit was bland and flavorless. He was glad he'd taken a large helping of chop suey.

"Try this, very good," said Teiki, handing Vivian a shallow bowl containing chunks of white meat in a milky liquid. "*Poisson cru*; raw fish soaked in juice of lime with onion and green pepper, covered with coconut cream."

"How do you eat it?" asked Vivian.

Teiki reached over to the bowl, took out a small filet with his fingers and plopped it in his mouth, swallowed it and smiled. Vivian followed suit. "This *is* good. Try it, Mitch, it's delicious."

The idea of eating raw fish didn't appeal to him, but not wanting to offend his hosts, Mitch tried a small piece. It was cold, but tasted as if it had been cooked in a delicious sauce. "You're right, it is good."

———

The foursome clustered in an aft corner of *Dream Lover's* capacious square cockpit underneath a tent-like awning, the mainsail's boom serving as its ridge. Victor and Litea sat facing each other at the corner's apex with their respective mates close beside them. While Sharon's distance from Jim minimized opportunities for ostensibly unintentional contact, it offered compensations. Sharon had explained to Victor before their guests arrived that the arrangement would allow Jim the opportunity to look as often and for as long as he liked without fear of being noticed by Litea, who would be sitting in front of him. She concluded her tutorial by telling him that while he had Litea's attention, she would make sure to have Jim's.

The pitcher of martinis had made three rounds by the time Sharon found it necessary to turn on the small red Chinese lantern that hung from beneath the boom. The dim, rubescent light gently illuminated the four faces, subtracting years from each of them with the exception of the younger Litea.

Athough Litea sipped infrequently from her glass, Victor filled it to the brim each time he filled his own. Sharon made sure Jim's glass was never empty and whenever she leaned over to fill his glass, she gave his eyes a drink as well. Rather than simply ignore these casual exhibitions, Victor abetted them. He engaged Litea in the center-stage conversation with a series of seemingly genuine and sincere questions. At frequent intervals, Sharon re-crossed her legs, adjusting her pareo with feigned modesty. It annoyed her that it had grown nearly dark before Jim caught on that the show was not accidental. Once he had, it boosted her morale to note that he could barely take his eyes off her long enough to make sure Victor wasn't glaring at him. Satisfied she had completed phase one, she waited for a pause in the conversation. "Litea, it occurred to me that you and Jim have been aboard *Dream Lover* two or three times now, but have never been below. Would you care for a tour?"

"Are you kidding?" said Litea, "I've been dying for a chance to go below."

"Why didn't you say so!" Sharon leaned forward and put her hand on Litea's knee. "Please forgive my bad manners. We've had so many guests lately I've lost track of who's been given the tour and who hasn't." Sharon rose, and as she did, Jim began to rise as well.

Victor spoke as Litea passed in front of him, "Jim, hold on; I'll give you your own private tour, and while the ladies are occupied there are a couple of questions I've been wanting to ask you."

Jim slowly settled back onto his seat, glancing between Victor and Sharon as she descended the companionway behind Litea. "Questions?"

"Yes, about your passage from Mexico." Victor allowed himself a trace of smile as he waited for Jim to snap out of his trance.

"Sure, what do you want to know?"

"When we first met in Puerto Vallarta, I recall you telling Henry you'd be navigating the passage strictly by celestial means. I'm curious as to how many sights you typically shot each day."

Jim paused before answering. "The embarrassing truth, Victor, is hardly any."

"I don't understand." Victor's puzzled frown transformed to open-mouthed amazement. "Don't tell me you managed to make landfall based on *dead reckoning*?"

"No, I had a GPS."

"GPS?, I thought...didn't I hear you say you'd been unable to acquire a GPS or SatNav just prior to your departure?"

"Yes, but I managed to trade for one the morning we sailed."

Victor leaned back slowly and rubbed the back of his neck. Was it possible? "Really? With whom did you trade?"

Jim moistened his lips and glanced away. "Maybe you can give me some advice."

Steady, try to remain calm. "Be glad to, Jim, if I can."

"The morning we left PV, as we were taking in our anchors, a couple of Mexican kids rowed up to us in their father's boat. They showed me a battery-powered Magellan GPS and asked me what it was. I tried to explain it, but they didn't understand. I think they thought it was just a big calculator. They asked me if I wanted it. Naturally, my immediate reaction was 'yes.' They pointed at my old saltwater rod and reel and suggested a trade. At the time, I thought, 'hey, no-brainer,' and gladly made the trade. But now I realize I may have made a mistake."

Victor fought to keep from laughing and restricted himself to an appropriately baffled smile. "Mistake? It seems to me like you struck a fantastic bargain. What's the problem?"

"Well, you see, I knew these kids."

"So?"

Jim cleared his throat and glanced toward the companionway. Neither Litea or Sharon were in sight. "Victor, they're the sons of one of those two Mexican fishermen you told us was arrested for the murders of Jill and Henry."

Victor forced himself to pause for more than enough time for even limited powers of reason to suggest the implication. "Oh, my God. Now I see what you mean. It must have been Henry's GPS."

"I didn't ask any questions." Jim frowned. "Thought I was being smart."

"But at the time, you didn't know what had happened. In fact, you didn't even learn of the murders until we arrived in Atuona."

"That's true and it never occurred to me that someone might have been hurt, but I was pretty sure the GPS had to be hot. I mean, you don't find a perfectly good GPS in a trash can."

Want to bet? "Yes, but there you were, virtually on your way out to sea." Victor leaned forward, adopting a fatherly demeanor. "You had no time; you had to make a snap decision. Were I to have been in your shoes, I would not have hesitated to do the same thing. In these waters, a GPS can be the difference between life and death."

"Thanks, but I feel like I should have tried to contact the Mexican police right after you told us about the murders. I could use a cigarette. Do you mind?"

"Not at all. There's an ashtray right behind you."

Jim pulled a small white bag and a folder of cigarette papers from his shirt pocket.

"Don't be too hard on yourself," Victor continued. "If you were to contact the Mexican police now, you'd only be adding to the mountain of evidence they have already."

"That's sort of what I told myself after the shock wore off."

"I recall how surprised you were—a natural reaction to such tragic news—but you seemed so thoroughly stunned. I thought to myself that I hadn't realized how close you were to Henry and Jill. Now I see there was more than friendship behind your reaction."

Jim nodded. "I had almost stopped thinking about it until *Houdini* showed up this morning."

"*Houdini*? Ah, yes. That was a bit of a surprise, wasn't it? I can see why it might cause you some concern, what with Mitch and Vivian being Henry and Jill's closest friends. Yes, Mitch might not be too pleased to know how you came by your GPS."

"Yeah, which is where I could use some advice. We ran into him and Vivian today. He also asked how I made out with the celestial. If the subject had come up later, I think I'd have told him the truth, but he caught me by surprise and I more or less lied."

Thank God. "You didn't tell him about the GPS?"

Jim shook his head. "Now I'm thinking I should go see him tomorrow and come clean. What do you think?"

"That is a tough question. Let's ponder it for a moment." Victor looked at the lights on shore and tried to run through all the possibilities. He gulped the half martini remaining in his glass and looked back at Jim. "No, I don't think you should. Think about it: Mitch and Vivian are carrying on with their lives, trying to put it all behind them, just like the rest of us. If you were to tell Mitch about the GPS now, it would reopen wounds that perhaps are just now beginning to heal."

"I guess that's true. I hadn't looked at it that way." Jim relaxed. "I like Mitch and Vivian. I don't want to hurt them any more than they have been already."

Victor nodded his concurrence. "Ab-so-lutely."

"On the other hand, I'm not sure how long I can keep Mitch from finding out about the GPS as long as we're around each other. Unless I continue to lie about using celestial, and hide the GPS every time he and Vivian come over for a visit, one of them is bound to get wise sooner or later."

"Is Litea aware of the GPS's origin?"

"We've never discussed it; I've avoided the subject. But I think she must have guessed where it came from when you told us about the murders." Jim shook his head vigorously. "Shit!, why did it have to be Henry's? If Mitch somehow finds out about it before I tell him myself, it won't look good. I think maybe I'd better tell him the next time I see him. He's a reasonable guy. I think he'll understand."

Victor leaned back and took a deep breath. He glanced toward shore, then back at Jim.

"What is it?" Jim asked. "You look as if there's something I'm not considering."

"It's just..."

"Just what?"

Give me a second, for Christ's sake! Wait, yes, that might work. "It's just that when you mentioned Mitch being reasonable, it triggered something in my memory I couldn't quite put my finger on until now."

Jim shook his head. "I don't follow."

"I was in town this morning, running errands, when I happened to see Mitch leaving the gendarmerie. By the time I was able to disengage myself from the business at hand, Mitch had already left town and I was unable to chat with him. I assumed he'd been to the gendarmerie to clear in. I had some business there myself, and while I was waiting to be helped, I observed a pad of paper on the counter. On it was written one word: *Phoenix*."

Jim sat up straight and slowly rubbed his hands on his cut-offs. "I'm afraid I don't see what..."

"Were you at the gendarmerie today?"

"No, I checked us out of the Hiva Oa district yesterday. Why?"

"It just struck me what an odd coincidence it is that I should see Mitch come out of the gendarmerie, and then upon going in immediately after him, spot the name of your boat on a pad of paper at the counter where he must have been standing a few minutes earlier."

"What...what are you saying? That Mitch might have talked to the gendarmes about me? Why would he do that?"

Victor again fell into his fatherly tone. "It probably *was* a coincidence. That pad of paper could have been sitting there since your visit yesterday afternoon. However, we can't overlook the likelihood that the GPS now in your possession was undoubtedly taken during the commission of two ghastly murders."

Jim's eyebrows knitted and his gaze darted around the cockpit floor. "I don't remember the gendarme that cleared us out writing down *Phoenix'* name. You don't think Mitch suspects me of...murdering Jill and Henry?"

"The odds are against it, but—to be safe—it might be wise to hold off telling him about the GPS for a few days."

Jim took a last drag from his cigarette and stubbed it out. "Victor, you won't mention this to anyone, will you?"

Victor leaned back and folded his arms. "Jim, rest assured, this conversation never happened."

"Thanks, I—"

"Ah, looks like tour number one is finished," said Victor, glancing to his right as Litea came up the companionway.

"She's an incredible boat!" exclaimed Litea. "Jim, you won't believe it."

Victor spoke to Sharon as she came up the steps behind Litea. "Love, would you mind giving Jim the tour rather than me, you do a much better job of it."

Sharon raised an eyebrow and smiled at Jim. "Beware Jim, this is Victor's way of getting time alone with Litea." She backed down the steps. "Come on down, have a look."

Dream Lover pitched and rolled gently to a passing swell as Jim rose from his seat. He stumbled awkwardly to his right and nearly fell in Victor's lap.

"Careful Jim," said Victor jovially, "I fear it's starting to get bumpy again,".

"I think it's the martinis I need to be careful of."

Sharon waited at the bottom of the companionway ladder where a small overhead spotlight conveniently illuminated her décolletage.

Mitch surprised himself by eating something of everything and finishing everything on his plate. After dinner, Teiki suggested he and Mitch go outside with Maurice for a cigarette. Although Mitch didn't smoke, he went along to be social, assuming it was the custom for the men to get out of the house after dinner so the women could do their work.

Vivian reined in her feminist sentiments in recognition of cultural diversity and stayed to help Tahia and her daughters clear the table and do the dishes.

When the three men stopped beside the tree in the front yard, Mitch spoke while Maurice went about making a cigarette. "Teiki, I've noticed that members of your family have Marquesan names, while Maurice and his family have French names. Why is that?"

"All children get Marquesan name at birth and most get French name before start school. Use Marquesan name at home, French name at school—and with *haoe*, foreigners. But my father and mother never give me, Tahia, or my brothers French names.

"But you do speak French, right?" Mitch smiled.

Teiki tried to scowl but couldn't completely suppress a grin. "Know *how*, but do not *speak*." Maurice grunted and Teiki appeared to translate the conversation into Marquesan. Maurice nodded as he rolled a long, slender cigarette in a piece of paper torn from a newspaper and handed it to Teiki. "Only speak Marquesan and English."

"But you started to speak French to me this morning."

"Maybe sometime, to *haoe*, but never to Frenchman."

"Never?"

"No. Unless emergency."

Teiki spoke rapidly to Maurice in Marquesan. Maurice replied, laughed and lit their ultra-thin cigarettes with a disposable lighter.

"Almost no one speak Marquesan," said Teiki. "Hard for Tahitian to understand Marquesan. In Atuona, Marquesan men tell joke about Frenchman and *haoe* visitors while stand right beside them."

"Like a game, eh?" said Mitch.

Teiki laughed. "Yes, Marquesan game." He rattled off a long series of syllables that all sounded like vowels to Mitch. Maurice ejected a puff of smoke and laughed.

"Are you doing it right now?" asked Mitch, smiling tentatively.

"No, no. Just tell Maurice what you say. You learn some Marquesan words. People think maybe you understand. Then they make no jokes about you. Tomorrow, I write some Marquesan words for you and give to you at church."

"Thanks," said Mitch, "I'd like to learn some of your language. *Ka'oha* means hello, right?"

"Good. And *ka'oha oe* mean 'hello to you'."

Tahia's scream abruptly ended the lesson.

───────────

Sharon felt a moistness in her palms. Her below decks tour of *Dream Lover* was half over and Jim had yet to make the slightest advance. What in God's name had Victor done to him? After the way Jim had ogled her in the cockpit, she was certain he'd make a play for her when she forced him to brush past her in the narrow passageway leading to the forward cabin. It was the berth farthest from the cockpit, and therefore, the best place for their encounter. Was it inconceivable this bullet-headed, perspiring slab of muscle could be immune to her? For the first time she could recall, doubt of her effect on the opposite sex entered her mind.

As they reentered the main cabin, Jim paused at a bulkhead covered with framed photos. For several seconds, he studied a thin, glass-covered wooden case containing a large silver medal suspended from a ribbon pendant. "Is that really an Olympic Silver Medal?" Jim asked.

"Yes, that's Victor's brag wall."

Jim shifted his attention to a large black and white photo of a much younger Victor leaping from a high-dive platform. "He must have been pretty good to win an Olympic medal."

"According to him, he still is. If you're ever anchored nearby some place where the water's a bit clearer, you're bound to see a performance. There's absolutely nothing Victor likes more than an audience to dive for."

"What does he do, find a cliff?"

"Oh no. He's had special little steps welded to the tips of the lower spreaders. He climbs the mast steps and walks out to the spreader tips."

"He *walks* on the spreaders?"

"Heights don't faze Victor. He holds onto the cap shroud until he's set. Then, it's showtime."

"Amazing." Jim scanned the other pictures of Victor, then turned to follow Sharon.

"Watch your head," she said, leading the way aft from the galley. Midway along the passageway, she tapped a small double doorway to her left. "This is the engine room. If you'll excuse me, I'll let Victor show that area to you another time." She entered a large aft stateroom dimly lit by one small reading lamp beside the bed. "And here, we have the master cabin, or *master's* cabin as Victor prefers to call it."

Jim gazed around the compartment, his eyes settling on the king-sized berth. "It's huge. It's more like a bedroom."

"Which is why I saved it for last."

Jim's head snapped to look Sharon in the eyes. "Excuse me?"

Sharon let a pleasant smile suffice for an answer, turned and opened a locker door behind her. "*Voila*, the washer and dryer."

Jim stared as if she had opened a garage door and revealed a full-sized Rolls-Royce. "No shit, a washer and dryer?"

"No shit," Sharon echoed.

"Oops, pardon my—"

"Don't bother." She closed the locker door and opened another door to her right. "And finally, we have the aft head." The bathroom compartment took up one corner of the stateroom. Sharon stood next to the entrance, holding the door open. "Take a look inside and you'll find another surprise."

Jim slid sideways past her, into the narrow doorway and peeked into the unlit compartment. "No way. Tell me that isn't a bath tub."

"I'm afraid it is. It's not very practical at sea, and we shower most of the time anyway, but in port it's a nice luxury every now and then."

Jim stepped all the way in. "How much fresh water do you carry?"

"Five hundred gallons, but we have a water-maker, too."

"*Five hundred*? For two people? We go a month or two on *Phoenix*'s one hundred twenty."

Sharon wiped the perspiration from her hands on her pareo. She stepped into the doorway, blocking it as Jim turned to come out. "Sometime when you're in the mood, you'll have to come over and have a tub. I might have to scrub your back, though. I doubt you can reach it with those arms." She reached out and ran the fingertips of her left hand from the crook of his right elbow, up his smooth biceps and underneath the sleeve of his shirt.

The expression on Jim's face reminded her of a rabbit frozen in the headlights of an onrushing car. He stuttered. Before he could speak, she placed her other hand across his mouth to silence him. She removed her hand and kissed him, opening her mouth invitingly while gently closing the head door behind her with her foot. Her time of nervous uncertainty ended as his arms surrounded and pulled her to him. His tongue sought hers and she tasted the harsh tobacco of his hand-rolled cigarette. She offered no resistance, letting herself be crushed against him in the dark compartment.

Sharon allowed him to kiss her with predictable macho fervor for what seemed like enough time to touch up her nails. Gradually, she wondered if he somehow missed the message she was not likely to resist whatever liberties he might wish to take. The monotony was cut short when she felt his left hand leave her back and slide down her right hip. *That's a good boy.* He searched for the opening in her pareo. He found it and she rewarded him by teasing his tongue with her own. His hand slipped in, curving under her naked posterior, then sliding up and over until he touched the thong of her body-suit.

He withdrew his hand and grabbed the loosely tied knot of her pareo. He jerked roughly and threw the silk garment into the empty tub.

His hand immediately sought the intersection of her thighs. He found the snaps and clawed them open. *Aren't you clever.* She went wild, licking his mouth, moaning softly, mindful of Litea sitting a few feet above them. His fingers probed then withdrew. She sensed him unbuttoning his cutoffs and pushing them down. *So soon?*

The unpredictable moment had arrived. If she drove him too far and lost control she'd lose her advantage. His hand returned to the back of her left thigh and tugged it outward.

She reached down and took him in her left hand. *My God, what a log!* She stroked then pulled, urging him closer until she felt its head slide against her wetness. His other hand slid down her right thigh. He began lifting her on to the counter beside the wash basin. *That's enough.* She squeezed hard and pushed down as though power-shifting her Porsche into second gear. She covered his mouth with her own, swallowing his anguished groan. She pulled back. "Not here, not now," she whispered.

"But—"

Her free hand slapped over his mouth. "They're right above us. We'll make too much noise." She maintained a firm grip but eased up on him. The small dark room choked in a smothering gardenia scented fog.

"I'll be quiet," he gasped.

"Maybe you can be quiet," she licked his lips and kissed him recklessly, "but I can't. I'll scream the moment I feel you in me." She smelled his gin and tobacco as he gulped and panted in her face.

His breathing slowed. "When?"

"Tomorrow."

"But...we're leaving for Ua Pou, I've told—"

She shushed him. "Stop at Tahuata on your way. I'll get Victor to follow you. Wait for me there."

Mitch ran behind Maurice and Teiki as they sprinted toward the door. At first he could not see the cause of Tahia's anguished wailing, only her frightened face clasped between her hands. He moved from behind Maurice and saw Annette kneeling on the floor in front of Teiki's son, Pohu. Vivian, on her knees behind Pohu, had the boy in a bear-hug with her hands clasped beneath his rib cage. The boy's wide unfocused eyes stared wildly from their sockets; his open mouth emitted neither sound nor breath.

"Come on Pohu," growled Vivian, as she used her right hand to push her left fist abruptly up into the boy's upper abdomen for the fourth time. A large piece of gristly pork ejected from Pohu's mouth, hitting his pregnant mother on the shoulder. Vivian eased her hold on him and the boy immediately gasped for air and collapsed from his involuntarily rigid state.

Vivian stepped back, allowing the tearful Annette to comfort her dazed child. "Your son was choking on a piece of meat," Vivian said to Teiki. "I think he'll be all right."

Teiki shook his head. "Many years ago, cousin on Tahuata die like that. I tell Pohu, 'eat slow, chew food.' Maybe he listen now." Teiki clasped Vivian's right hand between his two big, dark hands. "Thank you for my son's life." He released her and knelt beside Annette and Pohu.

Mitch moved over behind Vivian, encircled her shoulders with his arms and kissed the crown of her head. "You done good, kid."

Vivian put her hands on his arms. "All that first-aid training at the clinic finally paid off."

Victor returned Litea's wave as Jim tugged at the oars, pulling their dinghy toward the vaguely perceptible form of *Phoenix,* silhouetted against the few lights illuminating the warehouse and wharf beyond her. Sharon put one arm around Victor's waist and waved with the other. "It's getting late," she said. "You'd better leave as soon as they go below."

"Dare I ask what took so long with Jim?"

"What in God's name did you two talk about? I felt as though I were having to start over."

"I can understand why our conversation might have made your task more difficult. It somewhat unnerved him, but it brought—"

"You were supposed to engage him in light conversation, talk about the passage, not jolt him out of the mood."

"If you will let me finish, I was about to say that my chat with him brought incredible news."

Sharon rolled her eyes. "What news?"

"You'll never guess who has Henry Fullerton's GPS."

Sharon turned to face him. "You're not serious? It's there? aboard *Phoenix*?"

Victor nodded.

"How did—don't tell me he beat the Mexicans to the refuse bins?"

"No, he traded for it, with the older one's sons."

"Victor, this is wonderful!"

"I had a feeling you'd be pleased."

"After the tragedy, we'll be forced by our consciences to tell the good gendarmes about the GPS and our reluctant but dreadful suspicions."

"I was thinking that with Jim in possession of Henry's GPS, perhaps there needn't be a tragedy."

She considered his suggestion briefly. "Too risky. We don't know how much Mitch and Vivian know. It's possible they already know about the GPS, and how Jim acquired it."

"What about Litea? Wouldn't she back up Jim's claim of a trade?"

"She'd be looked at as a potential accomplice. It would be her word and Jim's against the two Mexicans. And, if Mitch and Vivian have met with untimely deaths while in Jim's and Litea's company...no, I'm afraid you're not going to get out of this, Victor. We're wasting precious time. I'll get the bag, you check the ashtray."

They waited half an hour, to be sure Pohu had fully recovered. Mitch touched Teiki's shoulder to tell him it was time for him and Vivian to start the long walk back to Taahuku Bay, but before he could speak, the Marquesan turned from his wife and son and said, "You tired, sleepy. I take you to Taahuku in Maurice's truck."

Teiki insisted they wait while he gathered presents for them. Maurice helped him draw a one-liter bottle of fresh Fatu Hiva honey from a twenty-liter keg. From trees in Tahia's backyard garden, he filled two plastic shopping bags with limes and green oranges. From the odd tree in the front yard, he picked a half dozen of the large green fruit that had puzzled Mitch when they first approached the house.

"What are those?" Mitch asked as he and Vivian watched Teiki put them in the bed of Maurice's maroon Mitsubishi.

"Pamplemousse. Roger say they like what you call grapefruit, only sweet, not sour. Tomorrow, I cut bananas. Bring to you at Taahuku."

"That's really not—"

Teiki waved away the objection. "Only way get bananas. Store don't sell because everyone have banana tree."

Annette came out of the house, towing Pohu with her. The heavily pregnant woman embraced Vivian awkwardly, crying and repeating the word 'merci' nonstop. Vivian's eyes misted up as she peeked at Mitch over the shorter woman's shoulder. Teiki spoke softly to Annette, gently pulling her loose from Vivian and pointing her toward the house. Loaded down with fruit and honey, Mitch and Vivian joined him in the cab of Maurice's pick-up.

When Teiki brought the truck to a halt on the commercial wharf and turned off the key, he said, "Tomorrow morning, bring bananas, take you to church."

"What time?" asked Mitch.

"Eight-thirty."

Mitch looked at Vivian. She shrugged her shoulders.

"Okay, Teiki. See you tomorrow."

Mitch watched the pick-up's red taillights flicker and disappear behind the trees lining the road before turning to walk toward the launch ramp.

Vivian picked up the bag of oranges and hurried after him.

As Mitch rowed them through the eerie darkness and increasing swells of the unfamiliar harbor, Vivian found she could not suppress the persistent feeling that someone watched them as they approached *Houdini's* starboard lifeline gate. After stepping aboard, Mitch handed her the fruit and honey, which she set on the cockpit seats. She took the painter from him and walked it aft to the starboard stern cleat. After letting out several feet of the yellow line, she began making overlapping figure-eight turns around the cleat. Although still relatively early by the standards of civilizations addicted to late-night television, it appeared that every crew had turned in. She could not see a light burning in a single cabin, including *Silver Cloud's*. That surprised her. From what Mitch had told her, she would have guessed Bill might be having difficulty sleeping. If he were drinking himself into oblivion, he was doing it in the dark.

Mitch opened the companionway door and slid back the main hatch. He picked up a bag of limes in his right hand, descended two steps and stopped. He cocked his head slightly left. Something wasn't right. He hunched down and peered into the cave-like darkness. He sniffed the air and sensed a hint of something sickly, yet familiar. He looked for the red glow of the propane indicator light. It was off. Joints in the teak cabinetry creaked like an old rocking chair in time with *Houdini's* gentle pitch and roll. He steadied himself and half-turned toward the cockpit. "Viv, were you using the stove this afternoon?"

"No." She secured the line and turned forward. "I haven't cooked a thing since we arrived. Why?"

Mitch lifted his foot to descend to the next step. "Something's weird down here."

He did not hear Vivian's, "Wait!", nor did he feel the light resistance of taut monofilament fishing line beneath his running shoe. Instead he caught a fleeting glimpse of a small bright flash near his foot and immediately heard a sound like a bag of cement mix falling on pavement. The last thing his eyes registered before his eyelids slammed shut was a neon blue cloud spreading over the cabin floor, reaching up to envelope his ankles and calves. A blast of hot air sent him sprawling back against the steps. As quickly as it formed, the vaporous flame disappeared. A tingling numbness crawled up his legs. Dizziness set in.

"Mitch!" Vivian shouted.

He tried to stand and back his way up the steps. Nausea and shock overtook him. His legs crumpled. He slid into a heap on the cabin sole. Limes scattered and rolled forward.

Vivian ignored the danger and descended into the dark cabin. "Mitch, are you all right?" She cradled his neck in her hand.

"What happened?"

Vivian looked where the propane valve's indicator light should be. It wasn't on. She reached out, found its panel and felt for the switch. Her fingertips brailled the rocker switch a few seconds before they convinced her the switch was in the 'on' position. How could the switch be on and the light off? She flipped the switch off and felt for the burner controls. From right to left, she tried each knob. All off. She checked the oven control. It was on; all the way. She turned it off and opened the oven door. A slight whiff of unburned gas greeted her. She grabbed a kitchen towel and fanned furiously. Holding her hair back, she edged her nose into the oven and sniffed until satisfied no more gas was entering the cabin. Her attention returned to Mitch. "How are you feeling?"

"I think I'm okay, but I might throw up."

"Just lie still. Are you burned?"

"My legs feel tingly."

Vivian stood to turn on the overhead light. She paused to take one more long sniff and then flipped the light switch. Mitch lay curled up on the sole in a fetal position with one wrist shielding his eyes from the light. Vivian knelt beside him and inspected his legs below the knees. The unpleasant odor of burned hair filled her nostrils. The flash of flame had singed every hair on the front of Mitch's hairy shins into tiny black stubs and curlicues. She brushed them gingerly and they fell away like tissue paper ashes.

"Ow!"

"Sorry."

The cloud of flame had reddened the tanned skin of his shins and ankles. Vivian gently forced him to stretch out on his back. After putting a throw-pillow beneath his head, she pulled two clean dishtowels from a drawer, soaked them in fresh water and placed one on each shin. "How's that?"

Mitch inhaled a deep breath. "Good. Better."

She made another compress for his forehead and when five minutes had passed, cooled each one under the tap and replaced them.

Mitch took the wet towel from his forehead and wiped his face. "I think I'm okay now."

"Can you stand? If you can make it to the cockpit, I want to flush your legs with fresh water."

With Vivian's assistance he rose in stages and made his way stiff-legged up the companionway steps. She filled a large sauce pan with fresh water and poured it slowly over each shin.

Mitch leaned back against the coaming. "That feels good."

Vivian refilled the pan twice more and was going for another when Mitch stopped her. "That's enough. It doesn't feel much worse than a bad sunburn."

"I'm not taking any chances. One more pan of water and then I'm going to put some Silvadene on them."

After delicately coating each shin with the anti-microbial ointment, Vivian put the lid on the tube and sat down beside him. "The propane switch was on but the light was off. And the oven control knob was turned all the way up. I didn't leave it like that. Someone came aboard and turned it on."

"And somehow rigged it to ignite when we came aboard."

"Why didn't we get blown to bits?"

"Good question." He pondered it in silence. "I guess there wasn't enough gas to sustain an explosion."

"Then whoever did it must have left minutes before we returned, otherwise the cabin should have been filled."

"True. Wait—check the tank."

"What?"

"Look at the gauge."

Vivian opened the lazarette underneath the helm seat and shined a flashlight on the pressure gauge. "It's empty! We must have been almost out when we sailed in."

Mitch chuckled. "They didn't think of *that* possibility, did they!"

"I think the blast has made you a little punchy. If we'd filled that tank in Puerto Vallarta, or run out yesterday and switched to the other tank, we'd be toast right now."

"Yeah, the top half of *Houdini* would be scattered in bits all over the harbor." He laughed nervously and swept his arm in a circle. "And the other half would be on the bottom."

"You *must* have a concussion. How can you sit there and make like it was a practical joke?"

He tilted his head back and looked at the swarm of stars overhead. "Viv, I am simply glad we are alive and that *Houdini* is in one piece."

"Do you think it did any damage? Other than to you I mean?"

"Let's have a look." He raised himself up and carefully made his way below to the chart table and nav station. Vivian went about turning on cabin lights. The SatNav and main power panel looked unaffected.

"The only thing I can see," said Vivian, "is some yellowing and rippling of the varnish on the cabin sole. Uh oh, what's this?" She pointed her flashlight at the foot of the companionway steps.

"What's what?" Mitch moved to where Vivian knelt.

Vivian pointed. "Look at this."

Mitch inspected a small piece of folded sandpaper in the jaws of a wooden clothes pin attached with duct tape to one side of the companionway. Something else caught his eye. From beneath the bottom step he picked up a piece of kinked and brittle fishing line and a partially burned wooden match. Using a series of tiny hitches, someone had tied the fishing line to the match. On the opposite side of the step, at the same height as the clothes pin, he found more of the shriveled monofilament line tied and rolled around another match stick taped to the teak stairway.

"Pretty crude," said Vivian.

"But quick and effective," Mitch countered. "Whoever rigged it probably didn't count on anything being left around to inspect."

"Or didn't care if there was."

Mitch looked at the control panel for the propane tank's solenoid switch. "There's why the indicator light wasn't on." Its red lens and tiny light bulb were missing.

Vivian felt a shiver run down her back. "It should have worked."

Mitch nodded. "Exactly what its designer must be thinking right about now."

Vivian met Mitch's eyes and sensed he was having the same thought. In silence they made their way topside. They looked forward over the dodger toward *Phoenix*. The shadowy forms of *Phoenix, Dream Lover* and the other boats in the front row rocked and pitched slowly to the rhythm of the incoming swells. To starboard, Marjorie's French yacht bobbed peacefully. Wavelets lapped hulls, loose halyards slapped metal masts, small waves rustled on the black sand beach.

"What now?" asked Vivian.

"Sleep—before I pass out on my feet."

"Mitch, how can you sleep, knowing someone just tried to *kill* us? Whoever it was might decide to try again."

"I seriously doubt that. Whoever rigged it now knows we're in the game."

For the second or third time since turning in, Vivian pressed the button on her wristwatch illuminating its digital display. 2:34 AM. Mitch lay on his back breathing a slow, even cadence. How can he sleep so soundly? She doubted she had slept longer than five minutes in a single stretch. She'd slept better at sea. A lot better. And as though the night's events were not enough to spoil her slumber, the unceasing swells entering Taahuku Bay kept the fore and aft tethered *Houdini* pitching and rolling in an irregular pattern to which she was unaccustomed. The hobby-horsing motion caused a cacophony of troubling sounds. The cabin woodwork creaked and groaned a nonstop conversation. A snapshackle overhead, at the end of a slack halyard, rattled in its pad-eye like a mouse in a pantry. Bottles and glasses slid and tinkled as though a poltergeist housekeeper labored to reorganize her galley.

If Mitch hadn't fallen so fast asleep, and if not for his burns, she would have climbed over him and set about silencing the maddening sounds. And it seemed that whenever her brain did manage to filter out the innocuous noise and let her begin to lapse into unconsciousness, a wavelet would choose that precise moment to slap the hull next to her pillow. She cataloged the rational and harmless explanations for all these noises and yet she was unable to force the thought from her mind that the next creak might be caused by a foot landing softly on *Houdini*'s companionway step.

Sunday, May 26

Through half-lidded eyes Vivian watched a porthole-shaped spot of sunlight slowly waltz back and forth across varnished hanging locker doors as *Houdini* twisted to port and starboard between her moorings. Yawning, she pulled back the loose strands of hair from her face and glanced at her wristwatch; seven thirty-five. Not right. She hadn't yet adjusted it to the local time zone—nine-and-a-half hours behind Greenwich. How odd. She removed the watch and pressed buttons until the display read 7:06.

Taking care not to wake Mitch, she sat up and looked out the rectangular porthole set in the port side of the cabin roof. Shielding her eyes from the bright sun rising above the hills to the east, she could see the American cutter directly to port and the wharf beyond. The angle forward was too sharp for her to see *Phoenix* off the port bow.

She wanted Mitch to have all the sleep he could get, and yet her anxiety was getting the better of her. She distracted her impatience by lying down again and studying the constellations of small moles on his back.

She put a hand on his shoulder. His skin was warm and dry.

Slowly, he rolled toward her onto his back and rubbed his eyes. "What time is it?"

"Almost seven-thirty. How are you feeling?"

"Not bad."

"How about your legs?"

He lifted a leg, looked, then reached down and touched a shin. "Still sensitive, but better than last night."

"Shouldn't one of us get up and have a look around? I mean, whoever rigged our propane surprise last night is bound to be getting antsy, don't you think?"

"I'd say that's a fair assumption."

"What about informing the police?"

"Yeah, I think we now have a story that is closer to home and a little less hypothetical." Mitch sat up and pivoted his legs over the edge of the berth.

Emerging into the cockpit, soothing heat from the morning sun soaked into his arms and shoulders. He turned forward, paused, then leaned down to yell into the cabin. "They did it to us again, Viv."

She stood bent in half beside the vanity, brushing her hair forward from the back of her head to where it nearly touched the teak and holly floor. "Who did what?"

"*Phoenix* is gone. So much for leaving 'sometime Monday.' I barely caught a glimpse of her stern disappearing behind the breakwater." Just ahead, *Dream Lover* rode majestically to the rise and fall of the incoming swells. Her large white inflatable bobbed and weaved behind her stern.

A familiar high-pitched voice came from across the water to his right. "Good morning, Mitch."

Mitch flinched. "Oh, hi, Marjorie." He placed a hand on one hip, and with false nonchalance resisted the urge to cover his one brief item of clothing with his hand. He took some relief in seeing Marjorie had to shield her eyes from the low morning sun. "I didn't see you there."

"Just came out," she shouted. When Mitch failed to end a long pause, she added, "Did you and Vivian catch up on your sleep last night?"

"Ah, yes, yes we did. Thanks."

"Isn't it wonderful to be able to sleep in and not have to stand watch every night?"

"Yeah, great, wonderful. Well, I've got to...start breakfast." Marjorie waved as he backed underneath the dodger and down the companionway.

"Talking to someone?" said Vivian, meeting him at the foot of the steps.

"Just Marjorie."

"Uh huh." Her gaze yo-yoed down and up.

"Hey, I was looking for *Phoenix* and *Dream Lover*, I didn't—"

"Relax, stud. So, *Phoenix* left early again; you think it means Jim is definitely our man?"

"It could be coincidental, I suppose, but Litea said they weren't leaving for Ua Pou until *tomorrow*."

"To which Jim quickly added a 'maybe.'"

"And I took that to mean maybe later, not maybe sooner."

"Yeah, that's how I read it, too. But Mitch, I'm still not convinced about Bill."

Mitch shook his head. "As much as I believed it was him before, I can't believe it now, unless yesterday was an extremely elaborate ruse."

"What's that?" Vivian stared out the companionway and pointed toward the aft end of the cockpit.

"What? I don't see what you're looking at."

"Right there, in the corner of the cockpit behind the steering wheel. It's either a cigarette butt or a cockroach."

Mitch headed up the steps. He knelt in the cockpit and retrieved the small brown object with his thumb and forefinger. "Shit-oh-dear, it is a cigarette, hand-rolled."

"I guess that settles it."

Mitch nodded. "I can't believe Jim would be so stupid as to toss a butt in our cockpit."

"He probably didn't think there'd be anything left of the boat, or maybe he flipped it over the side and the wind blew it back."

"Mitch looked perfectly healthy to me." Sharon sat on the edge of the king-sized berth. "And not terribly concerned while he was talking to Marjorie."

Victor replied over his shoulder from the head compartment. "Oh, he's concerned all right. He knows what's going on. I don't understand it. It should have worked."

"Perhaps the match didn't light."

"No, it lit. I saw a bright flash, like a camera. But for some bloody reason, the damn boat didn't explode."

"If we had simply flown to Spain and bought a villa on the Costa Del Sol, like I wanted to, instead of indulging your ridiculous Captain Cook fantasies, none of this would have occurred. We'd be sitting on our terrace, having our morning café and reading the *Herald Tribune*."

"You've made that point, dear, several times now." Victor finished zipping his fly, turned and stood in the doorway.

"If they go ashore, Victor, we can't risk letting them get to the gendarmerie."

"It's Sunday morning. It'll be closed and they might have a hard time tracking one of them down."

"They'll locate one sooner or later. If they head in, Victor, you'll have to stop them. That's all there is to it."

"Why? They may well suspect Jim. They may even find the cigarette butt. I admit I thought the idea a bit overdone at the time, but now I must confess it was a subtle stroke of genius."

"Victor, *Dream Lover* was on the list Mitch gave the gendarmes. Even if Jim becomes their prime suspect, the gendarmes would hold us for questioning for who knows how long. Do you want to risk the consequences of that?"

Victor glanced down and shook his head. "Maybe Mitch won't go to the gendarmerie. If *Houdini* were to leave soon, we might assume he and Vivian suspect Jim."

Sharon paused to consider his point. "Nevertheless, you'd better get ready for a quick trip to the beach, just in case."

"We could simply leave, and head for South America."

"Victor, you know as well as I do, if we run it's like screaming our guilt. And if the French Navy didn't catch us, every port in the Pacific—the world for that matter—would be notified to watch for us. We'd only be delaying the inevitable. We have no choice but to end this; here, now."

———

"Mitch, we can't take off after *Phoenix* without letting the police know what's going on."

"How do we even know if Jim's really going to Ua Pou? Unless we get out there right now, Viv, we may never know where he's headed. They could go anywhere; Pitcairn Island, or some uninhabited atoll."

Vivian grabbed Mitch's arm. "Teiki!"

Mitch glanced at his watch. "Shit, I forgot."

"No, don't you see? We can have Teiki tell the gendarmes what happened last night and where we're going."

"Right!" Mitch looked at his watch again. "He's supposed to be here in about twenty minutes. I'll throw some clothes on, row ashore and be waiting for him. You get *Houdini* squared away and ready to go the minute I get back. Check the engine oil and water."

"Water—what about water—and fuel?"

"We still have plenty of fuel; and for water we can survive on our Mexican beer if we have to. How about food?

"Nothing but eggs and canned meals, but lots of both."

Sharon looked over Victor's shoulder at a chart of the southern Marquesas spread out on *Dream Lover*'s chart table. "What we need is some place not too far from Atuona, but not so populated."

"How about this?" Victor pointed at a large bay near the western tip of Hiva Oa. "Hanamenu."

"Let's see what the guide book has to say." Sharon thumbed through a spiral bound book. "Here it is, Hanamenu; semi-protected anchorage in 30-40 feet...ancient ruins...small deserted ranch...beautiful spring-fed waterfall pool." Sharon opened a second book. "Look at this map of Hiva Oa. There are two trails to Hanamenu from Atuona, but no road."

"Damn."

"No, that's good. No one lives there, and no roads means no cars passing by. Vanzetti can hike it and the gendarmes won't be able to get there too quickly if there's a problem."

"Hanamenu it is then. Let's hope we get that far. Do you want to write the note to Vanzetti or shall I?"

"You're the copy writer, dear. You write it, I'm going to check on *Houdini* again." Sharon laid the guide book on the chart table and disappeared up the companionway and into the cockpit. She was back at the head of the stairs in an instant. "Victor, hurry, I think Mitch and Vivian are getting ready to go ashore."

"Right there. Almost finished."

"Sign it 'J,'" said Sharon.

"Jay?"

"As in Jim, in case the note should fall into the wrong hands. It may prove mildly confusing to Vanzetti, but people in his line of work are used to receiving cryptic communications."

"Genius again, my dear." Victor added the large initial with a flourish. "There, that's got it." He folded the note, put it in an envelope and addressed it to 'Prof. Vanzetti,' in care of the *Baie de Taahuku Resort*. He slipped his small .380 automatic into his pocket and snatched the handheld VHF radio from its charger.

"Mitch is rowing ashore alone, Victor. This calls for different tactics."

Teiki arrived in the maroon Mitsubishi as Mitch rowed the last fifty feet to the launching ramp.

"*Ka'oha*," hailed Mitch, as Teiki waded in to catch the inflatable before it could touch the sharp rocks.

"*Ka'oha oe*," Teiki replied. Together they carried the inflatable up the ramp. "Where Vivian?"

"On our boat. Teiki, I'm afraid we can't come to church with you today. I'm really sorry; something's come up. Is Pohu all right?"

"Pohu fine. Your legs red; no hair. What happen?"

"We had a fire, an explosion really, after we got back to the boat last night."

"Boat burn?" Teiki seemed as if he might lose his balance and reached toward Mitch. "Vivian okay?"

"She's fine. The boat didn't burn. Everything's okay."

"How fire start?"

"Cooking gas."

"Ah." He nodded knowingly.

"Teiki, I need your help."

"Vivian save Pohu's life. I do anything."

"Thanks." As quickly and simply as he could, he told Teiki the story of the murders, pointing out *Silver Cloud* and *Dream Lover* as he mentioned them. He wrote *Phoenix'* name in the dirt with a stick to help Teiki remember it.

"But now you think man you fight with not kill your friends?" Teiki asked.

"Right. We think the man, who left this morning on *Phoenix*, did it and then tried to kill us last night with the explosion."

Teiki nodded. "Your duty to punish man who kill your friends. Not Christian way, but Marquesan way."

The look Teiki gave him sent a shudder down Mitch's back. "Right, well, we want to make sure he doesn't get away."

"You go after him?"

"Yes. We think he may be headed for Ua Pou, but we're not sure. We want to follow him. Is there a gendarmerie on that island?"

"Yes, at village of Hakahau."

"Could you tell the gendarmes here what's happened and where we're going? They already know what happened in Mexico."

"I tell them now." Teiki paused. "Maybe better you wait for gendarmes. Man who try kill you, try again."

It occurred to Mitch that if they waited for the gendarmes to arrive, they might restrict *Houdini* from leaving. "Do the gendarmes have a boat?"

"Yes, but at Fatu Hiva now. Not come back Atuona for two days more."

"If someone doesn't go after him right now, Teiki, the man who killed our friends will get away."

"Yes. You right. You go. I tell gendarmes."

Teiki hoisted a huge stalk of green bananas out of the pick-up on to his shoulder and headed toward the launch ramp. They launched the dinghy and as Mitch rowed away Teiki called out, "Mitch, you protect Vivian."

Mitch called back, "I will."

Teiki waved, turned and sprinted toward the Mitsubishi.

"Holy cow, Mitch. There must be over fifty bananas here." Vivian took the heavy bunch from him and set it down in the cockpit.

"Looked like you had a visitor while I was gone."

"Victor. He came by right after you left. Said he was going to town on a mail run. Wanted to know if we had anything ready to mail to take along, provided you weren't already headed in yourself."

"A mail run? on Sunday?"

"I asked him about that. He's not going to pick up mail, just drop what he has in the slot. He said he and Sharon are thinking of leaving today."

"Have they checked out?"

"No. He said they aren't leaving the Hiva Oa district, just going out to visit some of the other bays and islands in the southern group."

"Did he say where they're headed first?"

Vivian nodded. "Tahuata, and get this, to rendezvous with *Phoenix*."

"Tahuata? What happened to Ua Pou?"

"I don't know, but doesn't this sudden change of destination have a familiar ring?"

"Yeah, it's the same trick Jim pulled when he left Mexico."

"Right, instead of leaving Puerto Vallarta and heading out to sea, he hid around the corner in Ipala for two days until the search was over."

"Victor didn't by any chance mention exactly where on Tahuata they planned to rendezvous?"

Vivian raised her eyebrows and gave him a self-satisfied smile. "No, but I asked: Hana Moe Noa."

"My wife, the budding detective. Did you tell him we might be leaving, too?"

"Yeah, I fibbed and said, 'What a coincidence. We're heading to Tahuata as soon as Mitch returns from his visit with our Marquesan friend.'"

"What'd he say to that?"

"He was happy; said he hoped we'd anchor at Hana Moe Noa because the one regret he and Sharon had about leaving Atuona was that they hadn't yet had a chance to spend any time with us. I'm glad at least one other boat will be around besides us and *Phoenix*."

"Wasn't he surprised to hear we were leaving Atuona after only one day's rest from our passage?"

Vivian nodded. "He asked about that. I told him we were hoping to find a less rolly anchorage, where we could sleep better."

"Good thinking."

"I didn't make up that part. *You* slept last night, not me."

"Oh, sorry. Hey, *Phoenix* may pull another fast one and not head for this Hana Moe Noa place either. We'd better pick up our hooks and get going."

"Stern anchor first?"

"Right."

"Dream Lover, this is Dream Lover mobile, do you copy?"
Sharon leaned forward and snatched the VHF radio mike
from its holder. *"Dream Lover* mobile, *Dream Lover.* Where
are you?"
*"I'm up on the road, looking down on you, about to make
the turn towards town."*
Although tempted to ask Victor what he'd learned from
Vivian, Sharon knew there were always one or two busybody
boats monitoring the ship-to-ship VHF frequencies. "Any
problems...getting ashore?"
*"None. If you'll look out the port in my direction you'll see
Houdini passing by."*
Sharon rose from her seat in time to see the beige sloop
gliding away toward the harbor entrance. *"Houdini's* leaving?
So soon?"
*"Yes, I spoke to Vivian, and as luck would have it, they too
are headed for Hana Moe Noa."*
"You don't say? How marvelous." Sharon settled back into
the navigation station's high-backed swivel chair. "Well then,
hurry back."
"Righto. Be ready to leave."
"Roger, *Dream Lover* out."

Vivian negotiated the narrow exit and steered *Houdini* into
the exposed reaches of Traitors' Bay. Mitch labored on the
foredeck to lash the still-inflated dinghy to the cabin top
forward of the mast. Beyond Point Teaehoa, off *Houdini's*
starboard bow, the island of Tahuata loomed large on the
southern horizon, so large that had Vivian not studied the
chart, she might have mistaken it for an extension of the larger
Hiva Oa. The earthy scent of land dissolved quickly, replaced
by the fresh smell of sea air. Vivian leaned left to see around
the mast and called to Mitch, "I don't see *Phoenix* anywhere."
Mitch cinched the last strap holding the dinghy down and
glanced forward. "They've rounded the point already." He
turned and looked off the port beam. "Unless they changed

their minds and sailed that way." He shook his head. "No, if they sailed east, we'd still be able to see them."

"Are we going to raise sail?"

"Wind's too light. Better keep motoring. Otherwise, they'll get away from us."

"Is it okay then if I use the autopilot?"

"Sure."

Satisfied *Houdini* had steadied on a course that would clear Point Teaehoa, Vivian knelt down, flipped the cam lever and punched the 'Auto' button. As she stood and gazed to starboard, the fortress-like islet of Anakee slipped along the starboard beam. The village of Atuona receded off the quarter.

In the late morning sun the steep face of Tahuata hung across the southern horizon forming a tapestry of ash browns and variegated greens against a weft of hundreds of thin bands of black lava rock. The garland of puffy cumulus surrounding the highest peaks accentuated an uncommonly dark blue sky that Vivian attributed to the absence of civilization's pollution. She sat down on the cockpit's port seat as Mitch rejoined her in the cockpit and wordlessly went about finding a piece of line and then using it to hang Teiki's stalk of bananas from the backstay. "Guess what I saw as we were leaving?" she asked.

"What?"

"I saw Bill in his dinghy on the other side of the French boat talking to Marjorie."

"Really?"

"Yeah, and he wasn't even yelling at her. In fact, he even looked somewhat contrite, if that's possible."

"Maybe there's hope."

"I'm not sure I care," mused Vivian. "I guess I do."

"Damn!"

"What?"

I just realized. Teiki doesn't know we're going to Tahuata. He thinks we're headed for Ua Pou. Nuts!"

"If he tells the gendarmes and they radio ahead, how soon will they expect us at Ua Pou?"

"It's a one-day sail, two at most. Could you call them on the ham radio?"

"Even if we knew the frequency, Mitch, I doubt it's one our ham radio can transmit on. We could use the VHF to call one of the boats back in Taahuku."

"Right." Mitch started for the companionway. "Wait, Jim's probably monitoring VHF. There's a good chance he'll overhear. We don't want him to know we've left Atuona, let alone what we're up to."

"How about this: Jim doesn't have a ham radio and I still have my sked with Frank. We can have Frank call the gendarmes on the phone."

"Good thinking. What time's your sked?"

"Zero-one-thirty GMT." Vivian looked at her watch. "With the time zone change that makes it two in the afternoon Marquesan time."

"Okay, assuming *Phoenix* is at Hana Moe Noa like she's supposed to be, we'll anchor and play it cool until you make contact with Frank and let him know the situation."

"Then we sit tight and wait?"

"Unless Jim takes off again, in which case we'll have to follow. Hmm, I have another idea."

Sharon strained to see ahead, clinging to the mast with one hand, shading her eyes with the other. Since clearing Taahuku Bay in pursuit of *Houdini* and *Phoenix*, Victor had kept *Dream Lover*'s turbocharged diesel whining at maximum RPM. After rounding Point Teaehoa and crossing the two-mile-wide Haava Channel to Tahuata's northern shore, Sharon moved forward for an elevated vantage point. The main halyard winch served as a small step, allowing her to stand beside the mast, three feet above the cabin roof.

Victor shouted from the wheel. "We should have spotted them by now."

Sharon made one last scan of the horizon before jumping down. "They had a one-hour head start. They're probably around the bend, hugging the shore like us." She made her way aft from handhold to handhold as *Dream Lover* rolled to the rhythm of the following swells made steeper by the strong current funneling through the relatively narrow channel.

When she rejoined Victor at the wheel he said, "I wish you'd sent Jim directly to Hanamenu."

"How could I? We didn't know Hanamenu existed until this morning."

"We should have thought about the possibility of needing an alternate rendezvous with Vanzetti last night, before Jim and Litea arrived.

"Last night, *dear*, we thought the whole matter would be resolved. My only concern then was keeping Jim somewhere nearby so we could tell the gendarmes where to find him. Besides, it will take Philip's man at least another day to get to Atuona from Papeete."

"Yes, that's true."

"As a matter of fact, Victor darling, it's fortunate I *didn't* suggest Hanamenu to Jim. That little half-truth you told him about Mitch mentioning *Phoenix* to the gendarmes made it certain he'll be less than thrilled when he sees *Houdini* arriving close on his heels."

"That was necessary, to keep him from telling Mitch about the GPS and how he acquired it."

"Agreed, but nevertheless, Jim will want to move on the minute he sees *Houdini*. By going to Hana Moe Noa first, I'll have one more chance to send him in the direction we want him to go. If I'd sent Jim directly to Hanamenu, and he bolted when *Houdini* arrived, what would we do then?"

"Yes, I understand your strategy; I just think it's dangerously complex."

"You scoffed at the cigarette butt idea, too, and yet Mitch and Vivian followed Jim out of Atuona, not us."

"Touché."

"Furthermore, Hana Moe Noa, like Hanamenu, is reported to be uninhabited. If there are no other boats there besides *Phoenix* and *Houdini*, I think we should handle the problem ourselves, if given the chance."

"Sharon, for God's sake, you're talking about *four* people. If we wait for Vanzetti, he'll make it possible for us to return to Atuona and establish an alibi."

"We have no guarantee he'll even show up at Hanamenu. And what if we arrive there and find half a dozen other boats anchored? Sharon placed a soothing hand on his shoulder.

"Victor, each day we let go by, the more likely this whole thing will fall apart in so many pieces we'll never put it back together."

"Damn. If fucking Philip had answered his phone this morning we'd know where Vanzetti is. Philip's probably at the track, picking a horse for the next race without the slightest regard for what we're going through down here. Maybe we should try a radio-telephone call to him on the SSB?"

"Too much risk of being overheard. We simply have to hope Vanzetti's on his way. And in the meantime, take advantage of any opportunities that arise, just in case he isn't."

Victor eased the wheel left as *Dream Lover* cleared Tahuata's northwest point. "I'll concede we could probably take Jim and Litea by surprise, but Mitch and Vivian—look there." Victor pointed to the left of the bow. "Is that a mast on the horizon?"

Sharon moved to the cockpit chart table and lifted a pair of binoculars. "Yes, it is. And it's *Houdini*." She scanned to the left, paused, then back to *Houdini*. "That's odd."

"What?"

"I think I see the entrance to Hana Moe Noa, and if so, *Houdini* is beyond it."

"You mean passing it? Are you sure?"

She handed the binoculars to Victor and took the wheel. "Look for yourself."

Victor trained the binoculars on *Houdini*. "I think you're right. Why would they keep going?"

"Maybe Jim didn't stop." Sharon paused. "However, I suspect it's Mitch being clever."

"In any case, love, it makes it rather difficult for us to handle matters ourselves." Victor lowered the binoculars and turned to Sharon.

She hated that smug tone he used whenever he was right. "I'll bet you *Houdini* is anchored in Hana Moe Noa before sundown."

"Do you think Jim saw us go by?" asked Vivian.

Mitch laid the binoculars under the dodger. "No. There was no one on deck."

"So now we sail around until after my radio sked with Frank?"

"Right. We'll motor down the coast a little way, then turn around and come back after your contact. The later we arrive, the less likely it is that Jim will leave before tomorrow morning.

Victor concealed his relief as they nosed *Dream Lover* into the small bay of Hana Moe Noa and found two unfamiliar yachts anchored a short distance from *Phoenix*. The American Stars and Stripes flew from the backstay of one, the British Red Duster from the stern staff of the other. Victor noted Sharon made no comment, in itself a telltale of her disappointment.

Though hardly more than a large indentation in Tahuata's crenelated northwest coastline, Hana Moe Noa's location in the island's lee made it seem placid as a mill pond compared to rolly Taahuku. *Phoenix* lay to her bow anchor on the far right, close into and facing a white sand beach which stretched between two low rocky bluffs bordering the bay.

As they motored slowly toward their intended anchorage, Victor left Sharon at the wheel and moved forward to prepare the anchor. He eased the windlass brake, allowing the thirty-kilo anchor to slip from its roller until it hung one foot above the blue water sliding underneath. While Sharon idled *Dream Lover* forward, he studied the two yachts that would lie between them and *Phoenix*. The closer of the two, a navy blue ketch as large as *Dream Lover,* hailed from New Haven, Connecticut. He could just make out the port of registry on the transom of the hard-chined British sloop lying off *Phoenix*'s port beam. Bristol. How many years had it been? At eighteen he'd left the southwest of England for the southwest of Canada with a cardboard suitcase and barely enough money for winter session at UBC. He hadn't been back since. Under different circumstances he would love to have had the yacht's owners aboard *Dream Lover* to hear news of his nearly forgotten homeland. Perhaps in another day or two, this wretched business would be behind them. *Dream Lover* could then resume her role as the center of impromptu social gatherings for the international yachting community. Sharon yelled 'neutral,' forcing his attention to return to the windlass.

Two hours later, *Houdini* had yet to return. Over a late lunch he and Sharon discussed the possible interpretations of this unexpected development and the courses of action that lay open to them. Victor set his wine glass down on the marble inlayed teak dining table and looked at his watch. "It's nearly 2 o'clock; in another hour or so we'll have no choice but to wait and see what tomorrow brings."

Sharon stood in the galley refilling her wine glass. "I think we have to proceed on the assumption that Mitch and Vivian will return. If they don't, it won't harm anything if we've needlessly sent Jim and Litea off to Hanamenu. Frankly, if *Houdini* doesn't return, I haven't the slightest idea what our next move should be, nor whether it makes any difference."

"Well then, I suspect we'd better pay *Phoenix* a visit soon or Jim may think you've changed your mind. We don't want him sailing off should *Houdini* suddenly come steaming around the bend."

"I'm somewhat surprised Jim hasn't paid *us* a visit."

Victor knew better than to offer a smart reply. "You haven't told me how you plan to convince him to move to Hanamenu?"

Sharon frowned. "How do you think?" She took a long drink from her glass and moved to the starboard settee.

Victor rolled his eyes. "I mean, how are you going to get him *alone* again? Litea's liable to get suspicious if you offer him another tour of the aft cabin."

"I have one idea." Sharon turned her back to him and looked out the ports toward *Phoenix*. "I learned something about Litea the night we met her aboard *Walden* in Puerto Vallarta. At the time, I didn't give it much thought. Now, it may prove useful."

"Do I have to guess?"

She downed the rest of her wine. "Come, I'll tell you about it while we launch the dinghy."

Vivian adjusted the ham radio's volume to its mid-range setting. "Frank, I copy you pretty well, how me?"

"Vivian, I can tell it's you but I can't make out what you're saying. Try it again and take it slow."

"We—need—you—to—make—a—phone—call. Over."

Static crackled from the radio's speaker for several seconds before Frank responded. *"I'm sorry, Vivian. Propagation conditions must be bad. I can make out a syllable every now and then, but that's it. If everything is AOK, give me a 'roger, roger."*

"No. Everything is *not* AOK."

"All right, Vivian, I heard your 'AOK.' Check your antenna cable connections for corrosion and let's try it tomorrow; roger?"

Vivian looked at Mitch sitting on the settee beside her. He shrugged his shoulders. She keyed the mike. "Roger, Frank, will try tomorrow, will try tomorrow." Vivian listened as Frank signed off with his call letters followed by hers. "Now what?"

Mitch stroked his stubbled chin. "We could return to Atuona and hope that Jim stays here until we can contact the gendarmes and get back. Except..."

"Except what?"

"Teiki told me the gendarme's launch is at Fatu Hiva and won't be back for two days. Even if we were to come back tomorrow morning with a couple of gendarmes on board *Houdini*, it might be too late. Jim could take off at any time."

After a pause, Vivian said, "Then I guess we stick with the plan, anchor a safe distance away from *Phoenix*, and see what happens. Frank should be able to copy me tomorrow."

"It's a mystery to me why we can hear him so clearly, and yet he can't hear you."

"He's got ten times the watts and a huge antenna on a hilltop. There's no comparison."

"Well, let's just hope the propagation conditions improve." Mitch rose from the settee. "I'd better get back in the cockpit before we run into something."

While Victor changed into his swim trunks, Sharon loaded his skin diving equipment into the dinghy. When he returned to the transom he found her holding the white tender close astern by its painter. "I suppose I'm ready," he said, and stepped aboard.

Sharon tossed the bow line into the inflatable as he whipped the starter cord bringing the outboard engine to life in a cloud of blue-gray smoke. She watched him depart for *Phoenix* until he disappeared behind the British sloop. Before going below to change, she loosened her swim fins' straps.

Victor shifted into neutral and killed the engine, coasting the last ten feet to the boarding ladder. "Ahoy, *Phoenix!*"

Jim emerged from *Phoenix*'s companionway. "Victor! Glad you guys decided to come."

Litea came up the steps behind Jim to a level that exposed bare shoulders above the hatch. "Hi, Victor."

Victor felt a sudden disappointment that Litea was not included in their plans. "I do hope I'm not interrupting anything."

Litea laughed at his inference. "No, no, I'm just being lazy and enjoying the weather."

"Yes, of course. Well, our guide book tells us this is one of the few good snorkeling spots in the Marquesas because of its white sand beach."

"If this is an invitation," said Jim, "the answer is 'yes.'"

"What about you, Litea?"

"Is Sharon going?"

"I don't think so. She's trying to shake off a rather nasty headache at the moment."

Litea paused. "Why don't you and Jim go. I haven't worked up my nerve yet."

"Nerve?"

"Sharks scare me to death, even the little ones."

"Are you sure? I know the Marquesas do have a reputation for huge sharks, but I seem to recall reading that it's primarily the black sand beaches and murky waters where you need to watch out."

Litea bit her lower lip. "No, you two go ahead. If you don't see any sharks today, and if Sharon is feeling better tomorrow, maybe I'll go then. How's that?"

"Fair enough. I'm ready whenever you are, Jim."

Now it was Jim who balked. "Gee, if Sharon—and Litea— aren't going, maybe I should wait until tomorrow."

"There'll be more to see tomorrow," Victor said.

Litea gave Jim a gentle push. "Go ahead, Jim. You're always complaining about not getting enough snorkeling time because of me."

Jim looked over his shoulder. "You sure?"

"I'll be lost in my paperback and probably won't even know you're gone."

Already wearing a small red swimsuit, Jim had only to pull his mask, fins and snorkel from a lazaret. Victor motored slowly away from *Phoenix* as Jim settled in the inflatable's bow. Once past the other two yachts, he twisted the throttle and sped up. A loud whistle intercepted them as they passed *Dream Lover*'s stern. Victor gave Jim a puzzled frown and put the dinghy in a tight banking turn.

Sharon stood on *Dream Lover*'s port side wearing a large orange T-shirt with a silk-screened Aztec design, her hair done up in a Swedish braid. As the dinghy came alongside she peered down at the two men through large rose-tinted sunglasses.

"What's up, love?" asked Victor

"My headache's all but disappeared. Is it all right if I go along?"

"Certainly. The more the merrier, eh Jim?"

"Absolutely."

"What about Litea?" Sharon asked.

"She's not too keen on sharks," Jim answered. "She said she might go tomorrow."

Sharon smiled. "Well then, we'll have to go again, won't we?"

Victor maneuvered the dinghy around to the swim step. Sharon came down the transom steps and handed Jim her fins and mask. She turned around to take the step down into the dinghy. As she did, her T-shirt rode up revealing a white triangle of thong bikini that disappeared between bare buttocks. Victor discreetly observed Sharon's choreography was not wasted on Jim.

Victor raced away from the anchored yachts toward the opposite end of the beach. A thirty foot wall of light colored ash-and-cinder rock formed the northern limit of the bay. Over the years, large chunks of the wall had calved off like icebergs from a glacier. They were all completely submerged, except one large boulder whose exposed slanting corner glinted in the sunlight. Victor slowed to an idle a hundred yards from the wall and two hundred yards out from the beach. He turned the dinghy in a tight, slow circle, creating a smooth slick on the breeze-rippled surface that allowed him to see the bottom clearly. Unlike silty Taahuku Bay, the waters of Hana Moe Noa were crystal clear. Encrusted with white and pink coral, the sunken boulders could be seen in complete detail to their bases more than twenty feet down.

Victor shifted to neutral and coasted into somewhat shallower water. "This looks good, love."

Sharon tossed the dinghy's rubber-coated mushroom anchor overboard. Victor killed the engine and began wetting his fins in the water. Jim followed suit. Sharon slipped her foot into one fin and immediately took it off. "Victor, did you use my fins the last time you went snorkeling?"

Victor put on his second fin and reached for his mask. "No, why?"

"They're loose." She took the fin off and began to tighten the strap.

"I seem to recall you loaned them out that day we went out to Lover's Beach at Cabo." Victor slid his mask on, inserted the snorkel and tumbled backwards into the water.

Sharon spoke as if he were still there. "Has it been that long since we snorkeled? I suppose it has."

Jim spit in his mask, wiped saliva on the face plate and rinsed it out in the water.

Victor popped up beside the dinghy and pulled out his snorkel. "It's incredible. Wait till you see the fish!" Without waiting for a response, he turned and paddled away toward the wall.

Jim paused while putting on his mask, to watch Victor depart. Sharon finished adjusting her fin straps and slipped them on. She crossed her arms, grabbed the hem of her T-shirt and pulled it off. She found Jim staring at her unfettered breasts. "I hope you don't mind."

Jim's gaze rose slowly to meet hers. "No, no, I don't mind. Doesn't Victor?"

"In advertising, working around models all the time, he's gotten used to it. Besides, Victor likes to flaunt his possessions."

"I can see why."

"I snorkel this way whenever I get the chance. Makes me feel like one of the fish. Some of the other women, however, don't appreciate my love of nature."

Jim was staring again. "I can understand that, too."

Sharon inserted a thumb underneath the thong's narrow hip strap. "I'd dispense with this, too, but even Victor's tolerance has its limits." She slipped her mask on. "Shall we go?" She took the snorkel in her mouth and somersaulted backward into the water. It was warm but cooler than in Mexico, enough to send a slight rush of adrenaline coursing through her.

She paused to check the seal of her mask before scanning the bottom. Victor hadn't exaggerated. Although the corals were primitive compared to Caribbean species, the schools of fish were like Christmas tree ornaments, surreal in their colors and designs.

Jim splashed down on the opposite side of the dinghy. She waited until he turned and looked at her, then took a deep breath and dove. A solitary trout-shaped fish cruised below her along the bottom edge of a massive coral encrusted block of stone. She pulled and kicked her way to the bottom for a close-up look. A parrot-green body flowed behind a Halloween orange head from which blue-green stripes radiated outward like Indian war-paint from its mouth and eyes. Its fins and tail were rainbows of green, orange and flame red. The fish darted nervously ahead of her as she leveled off behind it. She followed until her lungs complained, giving up the chase in a slow drifting ascent.

At the surface, she searched for Victor and spotted his snorkel well ahead and moving away. A flick of her fins twisted her around. Jim surfaced behind her. She turned and dove again. Upon reaching the bottom, she cruised through a four-foot gap between squarish boulders, standing upright like submerged skyscrapers. Her long yellow fins and tennis-conditioned legs propelled her swiftly along the submarine boulevard. A barrel roll to her back and a quick glance behind found Jim close on her trail. She completed the roll and slowed the rhythm of her legs, making long sinuous kicks. He must be enjoying the view from back there. Would Litea wear a thong? It was really a shame circumstances did not allow for her participation. It would have been exciting to see Litea's petite brown form in the water.

Upon exiting the gap between the rocks, she turned right and stopped. Less than five feet ahead, a small flat-sided fish the color of fresh egg yolk hovered three feet above the bottom. Its face sported a burglar's mask of black combined with the long slender snout of an anteater. Beyond it, four dazzling fish, also yellow but lighter, with thin chevrons of white on their sides, swam in quick obliques with the precision of a military drill team. Full length dorsal fins tapered to thin pennants that trailed behind. She had never seen living creatures this beautiful. Ignoring the little burglar, she moved after the threadfins. They zigged and zagged away. She strained to stay down, surfacing only when her body demanded it. With Jim beside her they shot upward, erupting simultaneously at the surface.

"Did you see them?" she gasped. "Did you see those four I was following? Weren't they gorgeous?"

Jim spit out his snorkel. "Yeah, beautiful."

Sharon could tell he really hadn't seen them. Her initial disappointment was mollified with the knowledge that he had been entranced by beauty in another form. "Come, let's go see if we can find them again."

Reaching the bottom, she glimpsed the four aquatic butterflies flitting around a boulder too far to reach on this dive. She rolled to her back, using slow leg kicks to propel herself inverted along the bottom. Jim pulled down from the glittering surface. She watched until he reached the bottom and leveled out behind her. Her breasts floated up, shifting back and forth with each slow kick.

When the tips of her fins nearly grazed his mask, she locked eyes with him, continuing to propel herself backward like a nautilus. It was clear Jim had little interest in the fish. The task at hand would carry more suspense if there were some doubt as to its outcome. Litea—now she would have been a stimulating and worthy challenge. Her air depleted, Sharon stopped kicking, allowing herself to float upward. Jim came to the surface in front of her.

Treading water, she removed her snorkel and tilted her mask up. Jim followed suit. He was much too beefy for her tastes but he had an angular masculine face and cheap blue eyes that would send shock waves through some women. She waited for him to say something or make his move. He simply stared back. *How much time does he think he has?* Without warning she reached over and fondled the front of his spandex swimsuit. He flinched and searched for Victor.

"He's way over there." Sharon tilted her head sideways toward Victor without averting her eyes.

Jim immediately took a breast in each hand, lifting and pushing them together.

Sharon squeezed him. "That tight little suit of yours is so confining; it must be uncomfortable in your present condition." She pulled out on the waistband and rolled the suit down beneath his buttocks. "How's that?"

Jim cleared his throat. "Much better."

She took him with both hands and felt him continue to grow and harden. His thumbs roughly massaged her erect nipples.

"I've got to have you, Sharon." His head tilted forward to kiss her.

In the water Jim lacked any advantage of weight or muscle and Sharon pushed him away easily, simultaneously increasing the motion of her hands. His eyes closed, head rocked back; he went rigid. "You will have me," she said and stopped.

His eyes opened. "I mean now. God, I mean *right* now. I haven't been able to sleep or think about anything else since last night."

"I'm not interested in a quickie out here, like two sharks in heat with my husband lurking about. I want it slow...I want it long...and I want it deep." She pumped him faster.

Jim sucked in a short breath, his hands left her breasts and clamped her wrists, forcing her fingers open. "When?"

My, he's very strong. "Be patient," she said and smiled soothingly. "Tomorrow, I have it all planned." He released her wrists and she took him again. "Victor wants to go to Hanamenu tomorrow...to explore the ruins."

"Hanamenu?"

"At first I argued for spending more time here. But then I saw how it would serve my needs—and yours—if I agreed. I told him fine, he could go tromp about the ruins all day if he wanted, but I planned to stay on board and write letters. He'll be gone for hours."

"But Litea—"

Her long fingernails dug sharply into his shaft to interject. "I wasn't finished. I'll call you on the VHF as soon as he's ashore and say that I have some kind of mechanical emergency and need your help. You'll come over, leaving Litea on *Phoenix* without a dinghy. We'll then have all the time we want in the privacy of *Dream Lover*'s aft cabin. How does that sound?"

Jim's head snapped to his left. "Shit!"

Sharon looked to see if Victor was making an unscheduled return. He wasn't. "What is it?"

Jim pointed with his nose. "Out there."

A sailboat had entered the small bay from the south. From the distance and her low angle of view, Sharon could see only the boat's mast and cabin top. She recognized it, nevertheless. "Why, it looks like *Houdini*."

"It is. I can't believe they left Atuona after only one day in port."

"Does it bother you that Mitch and Vivian are here?" Sharon asked as she resumed a faster cadence with her hands.

"No, it doesn't...it just caught me by surprise." His frown lines disappeared slowly and his hands recommenced the fondling of her breasts. "Isn't there any way it could be tonight?" His eyes expressed even more desperation than his voice.

"There's no opportunity for us to be alone. I promise I'll make it worth waiting one more day."

"Sharon, you're not...you're not playing games with me, are you?"

For her reply, she gazed momentarily into his eyes, took a deep breath and pulled herself under. The hood of his penis felt strangely cool, its rim rough against her swirling tongue. Should she bring him to climax? It wouldn't be good for him to return to Litea in this state. On the other hand, a simple orgasm now might appease him. Can't risk that. With a parting nip of her teeth, she rose to the surface. "Still think I'm playing games? There's a lot more where that came from."

Jim's hand made a fumbled attempt to grab her thong and pull it down. She parried his wrist easily and backpedaled away with a flick of her fins. "Victor's getting closer." She directed Jim's attention with a shift of her eyes.

Jim twisted and glanced over his shoulder. Victor was still a hundred feet away but headed in their direction. "When are you leaving for Hanamenu?"

"Tomorrow morning. And it would be a good idea if you left first. That way it will appear to both Victor and Litea as though we are following you, just in case either of them should get suspicious."

"Good idea. I'll tell Litea I want to go to Hanamenu soon as I get back."

What a dolt. "Have a beer first, study your charts for awhile."

Jim's eyes narrowed, then he nodded. "Yeah right, right."

Sharon pulled her mask down and prepared to insert her snorkel. "I wouldn't swim too close to the bottom like that. You might run aground."

The spot Mitch chose to drop anchor was practically within shouting distance of Victor and Sharon's anchored inflatable. This put *Houdini* at the opposite side of the bay from the other yachts and as far from *Phoenix* as she could be and still be in the same anchorage. Vivian stood beside him in the cockpit, watching through binoculars as Sharon climbed into the dinghy and began wringing out her braided hair.

Mitch put a hand on the glasses. "Can I have a look."

Vivian brushed his hand away. "Not on your life."

Once Sharon had her T-shirt on, Jim and Victor joined her. Victor started the outboard and they zoomed away. Only Sharon waved toward *Houdini.*

Vivian waved back. "I would have thought they'd at least swing by and say hello.

"What do you want to bet Jim suddenly thought of some pressing need to get back to *Phoenix* in a hurry?"

"I suppose. Perhaps Victor and Sharon will come over later by themselves. Maybe we should tell them, Mitch. They could be in danger too."

"I've thought about that. Something tells me we shouldn't involve them until after we've made contact with the gendarmes. Let's leave it to chance."

"What do you mean?"

"If Victor and Sharon come over, we'll tell them. If they don't, we won't. Jim has no reason to harm them as long as they stay clear of us."

"That's true. What are we going to do tonight?"

"Much as I hate to say it, I think we'd better keep a cabin light on and set a watch, say two hours on, two hours off."

"Good grief. Oh well, I probably wouldn't sleep anyway if we didn't do something like that. At least I'll have a chance of getting three or four hours' sleep, knowing you're on guard. What do you want for dinner, brown mush or Spam and eggs?"

Monday, May 27

Mitch let Vivian sleep even though it had been three hours since he relieved her of the watch. The sun had been up for an hour. He was nodding off, about to drop the mail he was reading when the distant sound of rattling anchor chain jarred him back to consciousness.

He jumped off the settee, opened the companionway doors, and slid back the hatch cover in time to see *Dream Lover*'s anchor break the surface. He went out to the cockpit and looked for *Phoenix*. She was gone. "Damn it!" He glanced at his watch. Her masts had been there behind the other boats not more than twenty minutes ago.

Sharon brought *Dream Lover* around in a wide turn to within fifty yards of *Houdini*.

"Hey, Vic!" Mitch shouted. "Where's everybody going?"

Victor knelt on *Dream Lover*'s foredeck putting a stopper pin through his anchor. He stood as Sharon steadied the cutter on her outbound course and shouted back, "Jim's headed for Hanamenu, back on Hiva Oa." He formed a megaphone with his hands. "Supposed to be interesting ruins there; thought we'd tag along."

Sharon waved. "Come and join us."

Mitch waved back and yelled. "We might do that."

Dream Lover had long since disappeared around the northern headland by the time *Houdini*'s anchor came off the bottom. From the bow, Mitch twirled an upraised index finger in a tight circle, signaling to Vivian that she could shift into forward gear and turn away from the beach. As she increased engine RPMs, she gave the lovely palm-studded beach one last glance and spun the wheel. What a shame, to have to leave this tranquil bay without ever going ashore or taking a swim. She was about to look away when a flash of movement caught her eye. A man far down the beach ran toward them, waving a hand in the air. Vivian thought she heard him whistle or shout. She turned and almost yelled in Mitch's face as he rejoined her in the cockpit. "What's with that guy?"

The Marquesan man in brown shorts and white shirt ran until he reached the midpoint of the beach. He stopped and windmilled his arm in a big circle. Mitch waved. The man jumped up and down shooting his hands toward the sky. "I think he wants us to come back."

"What for?"

"Who knows, maybe he has carvings to trade. We don't have time to go back and find out." Mitch waved again, sending the man into another paroxysm of jumping and signaling. "Sorry pal, maybe next week."

Once they cleared the headland, Mitch spotted *Dream Lover* following *Phoenix* two miles to the northwest. Vivian steadied *Houdini* on their course and engaged the autopilot. "Mitch, can you handle things up here while I take Frank's suggestion and check the ham radio's antenna connections?" Mitch nodded and she went below.

The wind funneled through Haava Channel in substantially stronger gusts today than during yesterday morning's transit. Without her sails up to steady her, *Houdini* rolled from side to side like a metronome in the choppy beam seas. By the time Mitch conceded that he should have raised sail for the twelve-mile passage, they were more than half way there. When Vivian rejoined him in the cockpit, the prominent westernmost tip of Hiva Oa, Kiukiu Point, towered a mile ahead. "You look a little green around the gills, Babe."

Vivian faced the stiff breeze, closed her eyes and filled her lungs with fresh air. "I can't believe I've lost my sea legs already."

"I'm sure futzing with the radio didn't help."

"Why didn't I remember to do this last night while we were anchored?"

"What took you so long?" Mitch asked.

"The cable connectors were clean and shiny, no corrosion. But as I was reattaching them, I noticed a thin streak of rust on one side of the radio housing. I removed the radio from its bracket and found more rust stains on top."

"That doesn't sound good."

"It's not." Vivian wiped her forehead and sat down. "I unscrewed the housing and pulled it off. There were salt crystals on one of the circuit boards."

"How did saltwater get on top of the radio?"

Vivian shrugged. "It must have come down behind the overhead panels and worked its way out through a screw hole."

"All those waves that crashed on deck when we were being chased by Andres probably forced their way in."

"I soaked a paper towel in fresh water and dabbed away the salt and water stains, then put everything back together and tried tuning up. The power meter says it's putting out only five watts on transmit. No wonder Frank could barely hear me."

"Is it still receiving?"

"Oh yeah, the receive side is fine; VOA and the BBC were coming in loud and clear."

Mitch scratched his head. "Maybe we'll have to risk Jim hearing us and call someone in Atuona on the VHF after all."

"Except, VHF works line-of-sight, remember?"

Mitch looked up at the steep cliffs to starboard. "You're right, we're not likely to reach anybody in Atuona over those."

"Frank was able to copy me a little. If propagation is better today, even with only five watts he should be able to hear me well enough to understand a simple message. Or, I can try one of the net frequencies and see if someone else can relay for us."

"We'd better start thinking about an alternate plan. One that doesn't depend on radios."

A knife-blade ridge separates the flooded valleys of Hanamenu and Hanaheku. At the seaward end of the divide, Grosse Tour, a flat-topped 700-foot pinnacle of lava rock guards the cheek-to-cheek bays like a castle on the Rhine. Erosion's patient sculpting has carved the larger, scimitar-curved canyon of Hanamenu into the perimeter of a thousand-foot plateau, itself once a shallow reef, scoured and flattened to its present state by endless trains of bulldozing waves.

Hanamenu valley's eastern slope is as constant and as steep as the flank of an Egyptian pyramid. The western slope is not so uniform. Layers of soft ash and cinder have eroded away, leaving overhanging cliffs and palisades of smooth black basalt hundreds of feet high.

Though anchored well back into the narrow bay and within the island's lee, *Houdini* faced seaward into a light eddy of wind that wrapped around the eastern headland, sending silty brown waves hurrying toward a black sand beach four hundred yards astern. Mitch had selected an anchorage to starboard of

Dream Lover such that the big cutter once again partially obscured the line of sight between *Houdini* and *Phoenix*. He spoke to Vivian as he came down the companionway. "I was hoping there'd be some other boats here."

Vivian sat at the chart table studying a thick paperback guidebook. She answered without looking up. "Me too."

"What're you reading?"

"The *South Pacific Handbook*. Take a look at this map of Hiva Oa."

Sharon dropped her magazine into her lap. "Will you please sit down."

Victor pulled his face away from the port over the starboard settee. "Mitch just went below. How can you sit there and read fashion magazines?"

"This is how I calm myself. If you're so concerned, go over there and shoot them."

"Don't be ridiculous."

"Then stop it. You don't need to watch their every move. What you should be doing is looking astern every now and then , scanning the beach for Vanzetti."

"Perhaps we should launch the dinghy so we're ready when he arrives. How do you think he'll want to do it?"

Sharon raised her magazine. "The fact that my father was in the business does not make me an expert."

"Sorry, love. I didn't mean to imply anything of the sort."

Mitch studied the map, paying particular attention to one of two horse trails from Hanamenu to Atuona marked by Vivian's finger. "No way. I'm not leaving you here alone."

"But if we both go," Vivian countered, "Jim might take off."

"It's out of the question."

"If he left, we wouldn't have any idea when or which way he went."

"I'm not concerned about him leaving. I'm concerned about him coming over here with you all by yourself."

"Believe me, I'll keep a close watch the whole time you're gone. If he so much as gets in his dinghy and starts rowing in this general direction, I'll jump in ours and zoom over to *Dream Lover*. He can't row as fast as I can motor."

"It's not a bad idea, but I still say we both go."

"Mitch, we've sailed three thousand miles to do this. We can't risk letting him slip away now." Vivian squeezed his arm. "As long as *Dream Lover*'s here I'm safe. Besides, if I go too, I'll miss my sked with Frank. If I can get through to him, I'll have him call Atuona and get the gendarmes to meet you on the trail."

"Why don't I wait and see if you get through to him?"

"Because I may not, and if you don't start for Atuona now, you won't make it back before dark. And I do draw the line at spending the night here alone."

Mitch studied her face. "You've thought this through pretty well, haven't you?"

"It's only ten kilometers according to the map. You should be able to make it over and back in less than four hours, don't you think?"

"Viv, that little map doesn't show the ups and downs. It won't be like running six miles on flat ground. And I wouldn't exactly say I'm rested up."

"You'll make it."

"You're sure you want to do this?"

"I'd rather have a root canal without an anesthetic, but I think it's our best chance of getting this thing over in a hurry."

Mitch massaged his temples. "If I run whenever the terrain allows, I might be able to make it to Atuona in less than two hours. If the gendarme's launch is back from Fatu Hiva, I'll come back in that. If not, I'll try to get one of the other sailboats to bring me around."

Vivian closed the book. "Let's launch the dinghy."

"Oh for God's sake, Victor. What is it now?"

"Something strange is going on."

"What do you mean, 'strange?' "

Victor continued to stare out the port. "Mitch and Vivian launched their dinghy. Then they both went below. A minute later Vivian came back out and now she's headed off in the dinghy by herself."

Sharon got up and moved beside him. Together they watched Vivian come into view from behind *Houdini* and motor directly away, toward the rocky eastern shore two hundred yards farther on. When Vivian neared the rocks, she turned and headed toward the beach. Sharon tossed her magazine on the settee. "What is she up to?"

"I don't like it, whatever it is."

When Vivian reached the boundary where swells formed three-foot breakers, she turned and motored parallel to the beach, as if searching for a place to run the surf and land the dinghy.

Sharon pulled away. "Let's watch from the aft cabin."

———————

Vivian glanced to her right toward *Phoenix* and *Dream Lover*. "Okay, this is it."

Underneath the thwart, Mitch compressed himself like a spring, ready to propel himself over the inflatable's port bow the moment Vivian gave him the word.

Vivian throttled down to an idle. "Wait. Jim just came on deck."

"Shit. Forget it."

"Hold on, he didn't look this way. He's going forward. Litea's following him, I don't think they've seen us. Get ready."

"Viv—"

"Get ready, damn it!"

"Viv, when you get back to *Houdini*, get out the flare gun and load it. And don't go to *Dream Lover* unless you have to."

"Get set."

"Did you hear me?"

"Yes, I heard you!"

"Monitor 16 on the VHF. Once I get on a boat, I'll keep calling you until I make contact." He took one last look at Vivian's resolute face.

"They're both looking forward. GO!"

Mitch slithered alligator fashion over the side and disappeared. Vivian throttled up, motoring straight ahead, now half way along the three hundred yard stretch of steeply banked beach.

Mitch frog-stroked underwater. He kept his eyes open but to little avail in the murky water. He felt a swell overtake him. His head emerged in a breaker's face as it curled and catapulted him toward shore. He pulled hard to keep the wave from somersaulting and driving him headfirst into the black sand. The wave crashed and in its foam he coasted toward the steep beach. He rolled on to his back in the shallows. Jim and Litea lifted their wooden dinghy, preparing to flip it right side up. Jim faced the bow, his back to Mitch. They started to flip it over. Mitch rolled, dug the toes of his running shoes in the wet sand and sprinted up the beach.

Victor stood beside Sharon looking out one of the aft-facing ports. "God damn it, look at that!"

"Don't panic yet." Sharon lunged from the aft port hole to one that looked toward *Phoenix*. Jim paused after attaching a halyard to his dinghy's lifting bridle. It appeared to Sharon as though he glanced in Vivian's direction. "Now you can panic. Get your gun."

"Why? What is it?"

Sharon sat on the bed and slipped on her deck shoes. "Mitch and Vivian pulled their little commando stunt while Jim was standing on deck and we were down below. What does that tell you?"

Victor sank to the berth, staring at himself in the mirror over the vanity. "That's it then. Let's hoist anchor and get the hell out of here."

"Damn you, Victor, don't you give up on me now. It may be they still believe it's Jim. However, we can't risk allowing Mitch to get to Atuona. You've got to stop him."

"Christ, Sharon, if Vivian sees me headed ashore minutes after she's dropped Mitch off, you know she'll do something. She'll go to Jim and Litea—or try to motor to Atuona by herself. She'll radio for help. Face it, love, it's hopeless. We have no choice but to run."

"Nothing is ever hopeless, and you've given me an idea. Maybe Vivian *won't* see you go ashore after Mitch."

"What, you think she's not going to be on the alert?"

"No, she'll be watching, but what if she sees us headed in the opposite direction, out of the harbor, like we're headed out to go snorkeling?"

"In the dinghy?"

"Yes. On the way in you saw the beach in the other valley that's just over this ridge, right?"

"Yes, but—"

"I'll take you ashore there. There must be some kind of trail leading from that bay up to the trail to Atuona. Who knows, it might even be a short cut. You may be able to intercept Mitch rather than having to chase him down. After I've dropped you off I'll come back and make sure Vivian stays put and doesn't use her radio."

Vivian reached the far end of the beach and made a tight U-turn. She allowed herself a quick glance at Jim and Litea, who now had their dinghy upright and were preparing to hoist it over the side. Overcoming the urge to look for Mitch among the palms required every ounce of will power she could muster. She waited until reaching the midpoint of the beach again before casually scanning shoreward. Unlike the vegetation-choked beach at Hana Moe Noa, Hanamenu was open and airy, the brush cleared away and each coconut palm spaced with a farmer's precision. Yet there was no sign of Mitch, no movement of any kind. She strained to catch a glimpse of him darting from palm to palm, but saw nothing.

She quickly scanned the modest house and outbuildings set back from the beach. The former occupants had boarded the windows. A Gauguin painting had more movement. She sighed and turned the inflatable toward *Houdini*.

Mitch peered from behind a palm. Time to go. He glanced at *Phoenix*. Jim and Litea had their hands full winching their dinghy off the deck. He turned and sprinted to a palm farther in; stopped, looked, ran to another one. With the house between him and *Phoenix* he turned and ran inland. Eventually the earthen path became a slightly raised walkway of black stones set flat-side-up in the loamy soil. Though smooth enough for walking, the uneven stones made running treacherous, necessitating his full concentration and an irregular leaping gait to avoid twisting an ankle. The walkway widened into a narrow road and wound in easy curves along the valley's level floor. It crossed a tiny stream in a small stone arch held up by crude but effective keystones. Trees and bushes closed around him.

Numerous pathways lined with small black stones, shaded by overhanging trees, branched off the road every fifty to seventy-five feet. Mitch yielded to his curiosity and slowed for a quick glance. A walkway on his left lead to several large rectangular pads of rocks carefully fitted together. Another side street branching to the right was the same. Each pathway lead to several raised stone foundations. The entire valley resembled a new housing development where paved streets, cul-de-sacs, sidewalks and curbs await the building of new homes. He soon realized that it was a development, but not a new one. The corner posts and frames were gone, the thatched roofs gone, the cooking fires, the pigs and chickens, all gone. The farther he ran, the more foundations he saw. They were everywhere, as far as he could see on either side of the road. Hundreds, perhaps thousands, of people had once lived here. Henry would have spent days going through this place.

Vivian had motored half way to *Houdini* when she heard Litea's high-pitched voice shout her name. Her first impulse was to pretend not to hear her above the outboard's purr. She held the tiller steady. The last thing she wanted to do was visit *Phoenix*. Litea called again. Something told her to turn and wave. Litea returned the greeting but didn't motion for Vivian to come to *Phoenix*. Jim stood behind Litea, not waving, just watching. Vivian shivered, feeling like a mouse running in the shadow of a hawk.

Back aboard *Houdini*, she punched the VHF radio's power button and pulled the flare gun case from its locker. After inserting a 12-gauge meteor shell in the single-shot pistol and closing its action she laid it on the refrigerator beside the companionway steps. Out of the galley port, her eye caught a flash of movement. Sharon and Victor had launched their dinghy and were pulling away from *Dream Lover's* stern. They turned toward *Houdini*. At first Vivian thought they were coming over, but Sharon held the tiller hard over, continuing the turn until they headed out toward Grosse Tour and the entrance to the bay. Vivian had counted on Victor and Sharon being around. Now she was left alone with Jim and Litea. She made a silent wish that Victor and Sharon would not be gone too long.

Sharon rounded the lofty Grosse Tour at full speed, drenching Victor in salt spray as the large inflatable's beam slammed against two-foot wind chop. One hundred yards out from Hanaheku's beach she throttled down and searched for a smooth spot in the surf.

Victor waited to speak until he could be heard over the outboard motor without having to yell. "I've thought of something else you'll need to worry about while I'm gone."

Unconcerned, Sharon continued to scan the beach as she answered. "And that is?"

"Didn't you tell Jim you'd be giving him a call as soon as I went ashore and left you alone?"

She chopped the throttle to idle and looked at him. "You're right. I'd almost forgotten."

"He'll be watching every move you make when he sees you return without me."

Sharon thought for a moment. Whatever was on her mind brought a curve to her lips "I'll put him on ice first and it shouldn't take more than a couple of minutes."

"How do you propose to do that?"

"Handcuffs."

"Ah yes, of course. I should have guessed. What about Litea?"

"I doubt if the little bookworm will even notice he's gone. Even if she should become suspicious, she'll be stranded on *Phoenix* without a dinghy. And I don't think we have to worry about Litea swimming anywhere. Get ready to jump. I'm turning in here."

Victor moved up to where he sat on the bow tube with one foot half over the side. "Provided I intercept Mitch, what should I do?"

"What do you think?" She pushed the tiller over, aiming the bow at the black sand beach.

"I mean, shall I bring him back here to the beach so we can—"

"No! Ye Gods, Victor." She glanced over her shoulder to time the swells coming up from behind. "It's too risky to bring him back. Do him wherever you find him. If possible, make it look like an accident. If not, we'll worry about orchestrating a plausible confrontation between him and Jim afterwards."

Victor stared at her blankly.

"Don't give me that look. We both have blood on our hands." She motored in on the smooth slick behind a small breaking wave. "Now get out and spin me around."

Victor could see further discussion was fruitless. He jumped out in crotch-deep water and pushed the dinghy's bow around.

"Happy hunting," Sharon twisted the throttle and sped away. The inflatable became momentarily airborne as she flew off the crest of a forming breaker.

Vivian occupied her mind and hands with a bottle of spray wax and a dust cloth. Despite yesterday's sponge bath, *Houdini*'s varnished interior had a bad case of water-spots and fingerprints left over from the passage. She turned on the ham radio and listened to the Christian Science Monitor's short-wave news broadcast while she worked, pausing every few minutes to look out a porthole toward *Phoenix* and *Dream Lover*.

"Poor *Houdini*, you're like a horse that's been ridden hard and put away wet." She buffed the main cabin's forward bulkhead. Each stroke brought back a swirl of reddish brown luster. As she caught herself talking to the boat, it occurred to her that at some point during the last few months, *Houdini* had become more than a boat, even more than a home. Irrational as it was, it seemed this cocoon of fiberglass and teak had purposefully sheltered and cared for her and Mitch. More than once Mitch had said 'she takes better care of us than we do of her,' and in many ways that was true. She had certainly protected them during their encounter with Andres.

She finished the bulkhead and peered out the port hole for another check. *Phoenix's* lapstrake dinghy still trailed astern of its mothership. Neither Jim or Litea were on deck. No sign of Victor and Sharon. Satisfied, she turned and sprayed wax on the dining table. It hadn't occurred to her that today was Memorial Day until the newscast said American Desert Storm soldiers in Iraq, waiting to return home, had celebrated the day with a barbecue.

Minutes later, Sharon's voice on the VHF interrupted the newscast. Vivian turned down the ham radio's volume.

"*Phoenix, this is Dream Lover,*" Sharon repeated.

Jim's voice came back. "*Dream Lover , Phoenix here, go ahead, Sharon.*"

"*Oh, hi, Jim. Say, I hate to trouble you but I've got a bit of a problem over here.*"

"*Oh? What's that?*"

"*I've just returned from dropping Victor on the beach and I find that one of the automatic bilge pumps is running dry and won't shut off. Victor's skulking about looking for ruins and I'm not due to pick him up for a couple of hours. Do you think it will be all right until he gets back?*"

"*Ah, well, the motor might burn up.*"

"*Oh dear. I've tried every thing I can think of. Could you possibly pop over and have a look?*"

"*Sure, no problem. Be right over.*"

At the rear of the deserted village, the flat valley floor narrowed to a gorge and the stone road dissolved into a dirt trail barely wide enough for two people to pass each other. From there it began a series of switchbacks zigzagging up the valley's steep west wall. The relatively profuse vegetation of the valley immediately gave way to sparsely scattered low shrubs, peeking from amid jumbled volcanic rocks.

Half way up the slope, Mitch stopped at a sharp turn in the dusty trail to catch his breath and observe the anchored boats. The beginnings of a good sweat ran down his face and neck. The terrain was nearly as barren as the flanks of the precipitous cape that he had nearly run into the morning of their landfall. The variety and suddenness of micro-climates in these islands were beyond anything he'd experienced during his Army stint in Southeast Asia.

He doubted he'd reached five hundred feet above the valley floor and yet the combined effects of lack of sleep and over three weeks at sea were clearly felt. Seeing no activity on any of the three boats, he turned and ran up the next leg.

Upon reaching the plateau, the trail curved away from the direction of Atuona, following the valley's rim-rock toward the sea. He had little choice but to follow it and hope that it soon reversed course. Immediately to the left of the trail, elephant-sized boulders interspersed with scrubby trees appeared like entrance gates to a savanna theme park. Ten feet to the right ran the abrupt edge of rim-rock palisades.

Two hundred yards on, the trail turned left ninety degrees, away from the cliff, and entered a gap in the boulders. Before heading inland, Mitch moved to the cliff edge for a last glance at the anchored boats. He looked down. A vertical drop of one hundred feet ended in a steep talus of jumbled rocks, brown grass and low shrubs. The incline cascaded over two more cliffs, ending finally in the dense green foliage that followed the small stream bed on the near side of the valley.

Beyond the palms and beach, the three boats each trailed their respective dinghies, now barely recognizable dots. A small island to the northeast seemed to traverse the hazy horizon like a giant turtle. A gust of warm updraft buffeted him. He stepped back and followed a winding path through the boulders.

Vivian continued staring at the VHF radio after it had gone silent. "Sharon, I hope you know what you're doing." They should have told her and Victor about Jim last night. She moved to the port hole over the galley stove and watched Jim arrive at *Dream Lover's* transom. Sharon led him below. After watching a few minutes with no sign of either Jim or Sharon on deck, Vivian turned the volume back up on the ham radio and resumed the therapy of buffing. The newscaster wrapped up his summary of world events.

"Ethiopian rebels captured the operational base and headquarters of that country's air force today, destroying the government's main line of defense. An Austrian jet crashed in

Thailand. All 223 persons aboard are presumed dead. In US sports, Rick Mears captured his fourth Indianapolis 500 auto race today, tying A. J. Foyt's record.

"Turning to US business news, a verdict was reached Friday in the David-and-Goliath software copyright infringement suit of tiny QuidProTech, Incorporated, of San Francisco versus industry leader, Seattle-based Xysta Software. In a surprise decision, the court found in favor of QuidProTech, awarding them the full 200 million dollars sought in their suit. In making its findings the court stated, quote, The features of Xysta's software are so nearly identical to those of QuidProTech's product, that it is inconceivable they could be the result of accidental, parallel development, end quote. Speaking on behalf of Xysta, Reynolds Winter, president of Winter, Lewis and Associates, a Vancouver-based advertising and public relations firm told reporters, quote—"

Vivian stopped buffing and put down her dust cloth.

"Xysta has advised its independent distribution channels that release 1.0 of their software has been suspended indefinitely, end quote. In a separate statement, Xysta's President and CEO, Bob Stagg, revealed that Xysta has entered into negotiations with QuidProTech to acquire licensing rights to incorporate QuidProTech's product into Xysta's set of integrated software tools."

"News of the court's decision set off a maelstrom of stock market activity. On the New York Stock exchange, Xysta's stock fell fourteen-and-an-eighth to seventy-two-and-a quarter before trading was suspended. Meanwhile, on the NASDAQ market, QuidProTech's stock soared nearly fifty percent to an all-time high of twenty-nine-and-a-half. The Dow-Jones Industrial Average ended the day at 2913.91 up 27.28.

Vivian turned the ham radio off and sat down at the chart table. 'QuidProTech,' the odd name had sounded familiar in brief mentions on earlier broadcasts but hadn't registered. Jill, that's where she'd heard it before. That was the new client Jill had signed just prior to selling her business. Vivian didn't recall Jill mentioning QuidProTech's being located in San Francisco and yet it was 'San Francisco' or something else in the broadcast that had triggered the sudden association.

A dizzying tornado of thoughts swirled in her mind. She struggled to put the pieces in order.

Xysta, the household name and defendant in the lawsuit, was based in Seattle. That she knew. The president of a Canadian advertising and PR firm had acted as a spokesman for Xysta. The agency was based in Vancouver.

Victor and Sharon were from Vancouver. Victor had been a senior partner in a Vancouver advertising agency. Perhaps this same firm represented Xysta.

Xysta had just lost a multi-million dollar lawsuit to QuidProTech, Jill's former client.

Although it was quite warm in *Houdini's* cabin, a chill ran down Vivian's spine, causing the hair on her arms to ripple from her shoulder to her wrist. Suddenly, like an old tape recorder brought down from the attic, her mind played back the conversation she and Jill were having with Victor that morning at the yacht club when Bill hit Henry in the face. Victor had been telling her and Jill an amusing anecdote about his first ski trip from Vancouver to the US Rockies with his college roommate. Jill had laughed and said it was odd because a client of hers had once told her a nearly identical story. Jill hadn't mentioned the name of the client's company, only that it was based in San Francisco. Vivian recalled the conversation either evaporated at that point or they had been interrupted by the altercation between Bill and Henry.

The roommate Victor mentioned must have also been Jill's San Francisco client, someone at QuidProTech. Two hundred million dollars had changed hands in an expensive lawsuit. If fraud were involved, people could go to jail. "Oh no. Oh my God." *Sharon took Victor ashore.* "Mitch! Victor is after you!" Victor had gone a different way. Perhaps there was time to catch Mitch before they met. Vivian hurried up the companionway.

"*Going* somewhere?"

Startled, Vivian jumped, nearly falling back down the steps.

Sharon stood in her dinghy looking over the gunnel, steadying herself by holding on to *Houdini's* port caprail with her left hand. The short barrel of a palm-sized, gold automatic barely protruded from her right. It pointed directly at Vivian's face. "Very *good*, Vivian. Victor *is* after Mitch, and with any luck, the once-great Olympian will intercept him well before he reaches Atuona."

Vivian put a hand to her pounding heart. "I doubt that. I didn't hear your outboard."

"I rowed. Hold still, I'm coming aboard." Sharon looped her dinghy's painter around *Houdini*'s genoa winch, put a knee on the caprail and grabbed hold of the top lifeline.

Vivian remembered the flare gun. It was out of sight on the refrigerator, inches from her right thigh. Sharon's hands were occupied. Vivian grabbed the pistol and cocked it in one motion. Sharon heard the hammer lock. Vivian aimed at her face.

Sharon freed her gun hand.

Vivian pulled the trigger.

Sharon flinched as the ball of red flame streaked past her cheek. The small comet hissed into the water. Frozen rigid, Sharon felt her cheek and blinked.

Vivian started toward her.

Sharon aimed the automatic at Vivian's face. "You *bitch*! You could have *scarred* me!" Sharon climbed aboard and stood in *Houdini*'s cockpit. Still holding the gun on Vivian, she removed her dinghy's painter from the winch, took two turns around the stern cleat and tossed the excess line into the cockpit well. From the starboard cleat she removed *Houdini*'s dinghy's painter and threw it in the water, letting the red inflatable drift away. Tilting her head, Sharon used her free hand to pull the loose blond hair on the right side of her face forward to where she could see it. A clump of several strands were singed off and welded together. "You filthy, rotten little whore! Look what you've done!"

Sharon extended her arm and took aim at Vivian's face. Vivian cringed and closed her eyes. An eternity went by.

"Not yet," Sharon said. "Hand me that fucking flare pistol."

Vivian handed it to her. Sharon glanced briefly in the direction of *Phoenix* and *Dream Lover* before tossing the gun in the water. "Start the engine. We're taking *Houdini* for a *short* ride."

Sharon's emphasis on 'short' made Vivian feel suddenly weak and very afraid.

Once the trail emerged from the trees and rocks, it curved toward Atuona. Until then, Mitch had worried he'd somehow got himself on the wrong trail, the one that went the long way, following Haava Channel. The dusty path ran almost straight across an arid rolling plain nearly devoid of green vegetation. It made the going easy and he moved at a swift but maintainable jog. Many animal paths intersected the main trail. Some were so well-worn it required his constant attention to keep from getting sidetracked.

He had run for ten minutes when he crested a rise and a dozen wild horses exploded away in a small-scale stampede. The sudden thunder of their hooves and frightened snorts brought him skidding to a halt. The herd disappeared and reappeared as they flowed over low hills and hollows. Mitch trotted after them. An ash gray stallion stood his ground in the center of the trail on a low rise as Mitch approached. The horse suddenly wheeled to face the opposite direction, reared up, then cantered off toward his mares who waited beneath a lone tree to the south.

Mitch was still watching the horses watching him when he reached the summit of the small knoll where the stallion had stood his ground. A tall object below and in front of him entered his peripheral vision. A man's voice shouted, "Hello there!"

Surprised by the nearness of the man, Mitch dodged, stepped on a loose rock, lost his footing and fell sideways off the trail. A spindly bush partially cushioned his fall.

"My heavens! I didn't mean to derail you, sir." The man, clad in crisp khaki pants and matching short-sleeved shirt, hurried to Mitch and offered his hand. "Are you all right?"

"I think so," said Mitch, taking the hand, pulling himself up. The man looked to be in his early thirties, about Mitch's height and weight. A straw fedora tilted back exposed curls that matched his black horn-rimmed glasses.

"I wouldn't have shouted but I was afraid you were going to run me down, too. You jumped like a frightened deer. I'm really sorry. You've got a nasty scrape on your leg."

Mitch brushed off his legs. "It was my fault. I was watching the horses; didn't expect to run into anyone up here."

"Quite a majestic beast, wasn't he? Say, you didn't get that black eye just now, did you?"

"No," said Mitch. Maybe this was a chance to save time. "Are you headed toward Atuona?"

"Just came from there. On my way to a Hanamenu. Why do you ask?"

"I was hoping you could deliver a message to Atuona for me. You're going to Hanamenu?

"Yes. This is the right trail, isn't it?"

Odd, a tourist hiking to such a remote place, alone. "Yeah, this is it." Mitch pointed back up the trail. "The bay is just beyond those trees."

The man turned, looked down the trail and nodded. "Ah, not far to go then." The small, forest green day-pack on his back looked brand new.

"What takes you to Hanamenu?" Mitch asked.

"I'm...an anthropologist; came to study the ruins. Professor Michael Vanzetti at your service." The man stepped forward and extended his hand again.

Mitch shook it. "Mitch Sanford. You planning to stay at Hanamenu overnight?"

"Won't know till I get there. You're on your way to Atuona, I take it."

"Yeah, and I'm afraid I have to get moving."

"What's the hurry? Is there a problem?"

"I...it's a long story." Mitch took a step backwards. "I need to get there and back before sundown."

"I see. Perhaps we'll run into each other when you return." Vanzetti took off his day-pack as he spoke and unzipped it.

"Perhaps." Mitch nodded and turned away. *Anthropologist—studying ruins?* He heard the sound of metal sliding against metal, a sound he'd heard a thousand times in the Army. Instinctively, he sank to his knees, pivoted and sprang.

The action of Vanzetti's automatic slid home, jacking a bullet into the chamber. Mitch's right shoulder slammed into the assassin's stomach. The butt of the pistol came down hard, hitting him in the kidneys as he propelled Vanzetti backward through the air. Vanzetti's back hit the ground. The gun fired, sending a bullet between Mitch's feet.

Mitch seized the gun-hand at the wrist.

Vanzetti thrashed like a beached salmon, struggling to get his breath, fighting Mitch at the same time. His knee caught Mitch in the groin.

Mitch buckled, almost losing his grip. He felt Vanzetti bring the muzzle to his ribcage. He forced the barrel away. Mitch heard a sudden gasp as the killer sucked an energizing breath of air into his lungs. In a deadly form of arm wrestling, the automatic inched its way back. Vanzetti held Mitch like a reluctant dance partner, pulling Mitch's right hand up behind his back.

Mitch squeezed his eyes closed and braced himself for the bullet's shock. His lips touched something soft. He opened his mouth and bit down hard, crushing Vanzetti's ear lobe between his teeth. A piercing scream shattered his ear. Mitch deflected the gun as it fired.

Vanzetti screamed again, this time a more prolonged and guttural scream. His body went rigid, then limp.

Mitch slammed the gun-hand down on hard-packed earth, jarring the weapon loose from Vanzetti's grip. Mitch grabbed it and rolled off. Rising awkwardly to his feet, he looked at the heavy automatic wobbling in his shaking hand, a nine-millimeter Beretta.

Vanzetti clutched his right hip with both hands. Blood soaked his khaki trousers and spread to the tucked-in shirt. A trickle of blood ran down his neck from the mangled ear. He spoke through clenched teeth in hissing groans. "I think my hip's broken."

"Yeah, well, I'm real sorry about that." Mitch looked at the gun again and tested its weight. "Did you come on a *plane*? How do you get a gun like this on a plane?"

Vanzetti tried to roll on to his good side but fell back, groaning. "Trade secret."

Although the man paid no attention, Mitch pointed the Beretta at him anyway. "What's your relationship with Jim?"

Vanzetti's eyes remained closed. "*Jim*?"

"Right."

Vanzetti paused, then groaned: "Never heard of him."

"You don't know anybody named Jim?" Mitch asked sarcastically. Vanzetti didn't respond. "You're not on your way to Hanamenu to meet someone named Jim?" Mitch raised his foot and jammed the sole of his running shoe against Vanzetti's right thigh. Vanzetti's scream echoed back from the mountains farther up the trail.

"Jesus. For God's sake, don't—"

"*Who* hired you?"

Vanzetti's eyes cracked open. "Jim, it was Jim."

"Jim who? What's Jim's last name?"

Vanzetti's eyes closed.

Mitch kicked him again.

"Ow!, god*damn!*"

"I *said*, what is Jim's last name?"

"I really wish you wouldn't do that."

"Then tell me his last name."

"Smith."

"Smith, that's good. You don't know him, do you?"

"Help me get back to that excuse for a town and I'll tell you his life story."

Mitch wiped the dust and sweat from his forehead. "Have you seen the rats on this island?"

Vanzetti's eyes opened and focused on Mitch.

"They're as big as house cats and twice as hungry."

"So?" Vanzetti lifted his head off the dirt.

"If you don't tell me who sent for you—and I mean right now—by tomorrow morning there'll be nothing here but a pile of your shiny white bones."

Vanzetti's head thudded to the dirt. "Kennerly."

"Kennerly? Who in the hell..."

"Philip Kennerly."

Mitch half-turned toward Atuona and started to walk. "Look, pal, if you don't give me a name I recognize, I'm gone."

"Westridge!" Vanzetti shouted.

Mitch stopped and walked back. "*Victor* Westridge?"

Vanzetti sighed. "Right, Victor Westridge."

"Holy shit!" Mitch took off running down the trail toward Hanamenu.

"Hey! Where are you going?" Vanzetti rolled, his gaze following Mitch. "Hey! What about me?"

Mitch turned, trotted backwards and yelled, "If your luck continues, I'll live long enough to make a radio call for help."

Vanzetti slumped to his back.

Mitch turned again and continued running. He prayed Vivian hadn't succumbed to a case of nerves and gone to *Dream Lover* for Victor and Sharon's protection. No longer conserving his strength for the long run to Atuona, he sprinted full speed toward the valley rim. Upon reaching the stunted trees, he dodged through the maze of boulders and emerged on the cliff trail.

Gasping for air, he walked to the edge, his heart pounding in his ears.

He squinted, rubbed the sweat from his eyes and looked again. *Houdini* was underway! "Viv, where're you going?" He looked again. The splotch of color following in *Houdini*'s wake was white, not red. *Houdini* was towing *Dream Lover*'s dinghy. "Oh, no!"

Stepping back, he spun and ran along the cliff trail, concentrating on the ground in front of him to avoid tripping in one of the many crevices that snaked back from the edge. He didn't see Victor crouching between two large boulders, nor did he hear him spring out. Instead, he felt the heels of Victor's outstretched palms catch him on the right shoulder. The impact sent him stumbling sideways toward the edge. He dropped Vanzetti's gun. His legs crossed, tripping him.

At the edge, a split second too late, both feet came under him. With his back to the valley below, his eyes momentarily locked on Victor's. Mitch knew he was beyond the point of no return. His arms waved in a sweeping circle. He dipped slightly at the knees and leaped upward, thrusting his feet outward.

The brief time in mid-air seemed to go by in discrete intervals, like frames of a motion picture film shown one by one. The leap that sent his legs out, brought his upper body vertical, then slightly forward.

He looked down for the edge.

He saw it coming up. He'd have one chance.

He narrowly missed hitting his chin as his arms slammed against the flat rock. His right elbow slipped off; he swung back immediately and threw it on to the hot flat surface. He grimaced, fighting through the pain.

"Incredible." The sound of Victor's voice put him close by. His tone was oddly neutral. "That last move, Mitch, when you jumped into space; that was art. I doubt Nureyev could have done better under similar circumstances. You might have made an excellent diver."

Mitch could not look up, only straight ahead. Merely opening his tightly clenched eyes required an expenditure of strength. Slowly, he bent each arm farther at the elbow, improving his leverage.

Victor's feet and shins came into his limited field of view. A shoe came within reach and kicked the Beretta away. "Based on the shot I heard a few minutes ago, and the fact that you came running back with that item in your possession, I must assume you made the brief acquaintance of our Professor Vanzetti."

Mitch made no attempt to answer, concentrating on conserving his strength. The cliff face pressed flat against his chest; his legs hung free in space.

"Is the Professor still among the living?"

Mitch shifted his weight slowly from elbow to elbow, working them farther on to the smooth rock surface. For the moment, he felt secure. He might be able to support himself with one arm for half a second. He answered Victor using a minimum of air in whispered grunts. "Alive. Not going anywhere." He braced with the left arm and prepared to grab for an ankle with the right.

"What made me think Philip would send someone competent?" Victor backed away to a low rock on the opposite side of the trail.

The rest of Victor from his knees up came into view as he removed a small automatic pistol from his shorts pocket and sat down. He checked his wristwatch and shaded his eyes, looking down toward the bay. It was not the Victor Mitch had known. The eyes were empty, unmoving, lacking their usual good cheer. The lips had no pleasure in them, no curve, no pride. His face seemed flat, devoid of definition. Mitch tried raising himself with his forearms. He hadn't enough strength, not enough leverage.

Victor waggled the gun at him. "Ah, ah, ahh."

"Waiting for me to fall, that it?" Mitch grunted.

"A rather passive approach, I admit. However, it's the one I feel comfortable with at the moment."

"Why not...push me off?"

"And have you pull me over with you? I prefer to let fate deal the next card."

Mitch glanced out the corner of his eye. The cliff edge to his right sloped downward at a shallow angle. Could he kick a foot that high? The choices were unappealing: he could hang until his arms gave out; he could fall attempting to pull himself up; or, he could succeed and have Victor shoot him.

Despite attempts to find the cliff face, his dangling feet touched nothing. He cleared his mind. He tried swinging his legs from side to side, flexing at the waist. He increased their arc with each swing. The motion became evident in his arms and shoulders.

Victor sat upright.

Mitch's arms trembled as they alternated taking the strain. He closed his eyes and clenched his teeth. His splayed hands made sweaty palm prints on the hot basalt.

Victor stood. "Mitch...stop. I will shoot."

Mitch inhaled a long slow breath and locked it in. He swung his right leg up in an all-or-nothing effort. The instep of his running shoe caught the edge. He poured the remainder of his strength into the leg, pulling, straining, holding back nothing. First a knee, then a hip inched over the edge.

He squirmed, wiggled and rolled, hugging the smooth black rock until half his body rested above the lip. Eyes closed, he paused for a breath and waited for the bullet. When it didn't come, he swallowed, pushed and rolled. He lay on his back, his left forearm wrapped over his eyes. He tried to speak, gagged on saliva and tried again. "Where's Sharon going with Vivian?"

"Seeing *Houdini* headed out towing our dinghy is almost as much of a surprise to me, Mitch, as it is to you. However, where Sharon's concerned, I've learned to expect the unexpected, and assume the worst, especially in win-lose contests."

"Sharon wouldn't kill Vivian." Mitch turned his head and looked at Victor.

"Mitch, Sharon's strength isn't her beauty, it's her ability to do *whatever* is necessary. You'd be amazed at what she'll do to get what she wants and keep it."

Mitch rolled his head to the left. *Houdini* approached the mouth of the twin bays.

Vivian steered while Sharon pointed the tiny .25-caliber Browning at her and watched from the port cockpit seat. Sharon seemed particularly interested in the water depth. Every twenty or thirty seconds she glanced away from Vivian to look at the digital depthsounder to her left.

When they passed Grosse Tour and entered open water Vivian asked, "Which way, left or right?"

"Neither," Sharon replied. "Straight ahead."

Vivian observed that Sharon's periodic glances at the depthsounder lingered as the depth increased. It might be possible to leap and grab the gun. The problem was the steering wheel. The large diameter wheel and its spokes formed a picket fence between them. Surprising Sharon would require perfect timing, physical agility and luck. Her chances of success ranged between bleak and dismal. Vivian rotated her ankles to slide her feet apart for better footing. As she did, the toes of her right foot touched the end of the painter to Sharon's dinghy. Another idea occurred to her. "Is it all right if I sit down?" she asked.

Sharon glanced at the depthsounder: 87 feet. *Houdini* began to roll from side to side as they cleared the headlands. Sharon made a courtly gesture with the gun, motioning for Vivian to take a seat.

Vivian sat on the helm-seat. Without staring, she carefully began noting the frequency and duration with which Sharon switched her attention to the depthsounder. Vivian let a minute go by before dropping her right hand to her thigh, continuing to steer with her left. She did this quickly and naturally, but making no attempt to conceal the act from Sharon. But from then on, whenever Sharon glanced at the depthsounder, Vivian slid her hand back until it rested on her hip.

The depthsounder's readings increased rapidly as *Houdini* departed the sunken valley floor and entered open water. After indicating one hundred feet, the numbers climbed upward in a steady progression, adding a foot or more of depth every five seconds. At two hundred feet, the duration of Sharon's glances increased. Yet they still did not last long enough for Vivian to risk a sudden movement. As the readings neared three hundred feet, the digital display held Sharon's gaze longer at each glance. When she looked away at 310, Vivian reached back and located the stern cleat, pulling her hand back to her hip an instant before Sharon turned her head. At 323 Vivian reached back again. This time she quickly removed one turn of the dinghy painter from the cleat. At 357 Sharon not only glanced at the depthsounder, she made a quick scan of the horizon in the direction of Haava Channel. Vivian easily removed a second turn of the bow line from the cleat. Only one round turn of line remained around the cleat, and only the pressure of Vivian's foot on the excess line kept the large heavy dinghy from pulling its painter loose and drifting away. When the next opportunity presented itself she would dive over the stern and swim underwater as far as she could, hoping Sharon would not be able to shoot her or the inflatable from the unstable platform of *Houdini*'s rolling cockpit.

Vivian slid her hand down her thigh, gradually moving it back to the wheel. *Houdini* rolled more than before, now exposed to the three and four foot seas on her starboard beam that bent their way around Hiva Oa's northern shore. Vivian felt the painter line tugging at her foot. Sitting made it difficult for her to apply enough weight on the line to keep it from slipping away. The increased rolling made a reasonable excuse to ask Sharon for permission to stand again.

Before she could ask, Sharon said, "This should be adequate."

Vivian glanced at the depthsounder. It had gone off-soundings.

"Put it in neutral and shut off the engine."

Vivian did as ordered.

"Now get below, but slowly. No sudden moves."

Now might be her only chance to dive overboard. Sharon's tiny weapon looked as though it might not fire a bullet more than a hundred yards. But at four or five feet, it could hardly miss. Lacking the element of surprise, she'd never make it over the stern rail and into the water without being shot. Vivian stood, keeping her weight on the line. With *Houdini* still coasting forward at four knots, she stepped off the painter and quickly moved around the wheel.

"I *said* slowly!" Sharon shouted.

Vivian paused, glaring at Sharon, attempting to freeze the woman's eyes with her own. She then continued on down the companionway. Sharon followed close behind. "Go sit on the settee and keep your hands on your knees where I can see them."

Vivian moved forward and sat down.

"Let's see now," said Sharon, standing at the foot of the companionway steps. "I remember once when we were aboard *Houdini* on the Baja coast and Mitch loaned Victor some odd tool. Now where was that tool box? I don't suppose you'd care to refresh my memory?"

Vivian remained expressionless and silent.

"I thought not. Ah! I'm practically standing on it, aren't I?" Sharon kept a wary eye on Vivian as she bent down and turned slightly. Beneath the bottom step of the companionway she pulled out a drawer. "Yes, here we are." The heavy drawer thunked to the cabin sole. Sharon sat down on the step and began pulling tools at random out of the drawer, stopping briefly to inspect a pair of tin snips and then a linoleum knife.

Vivian had assumed Sharon planned to shoot her and dump her body over the side. When someone eventually found *Houdini* adrift, it would appear as though she, and possibly Mitch, too, had fallen overboard. Whatever Sharon was up to now had her baffled.

Two-thirds of the drawer's tools were lying about on the cabin sole when Sharon pulled out a hacksaw. She held it by the handle bringing the blade close to her face as if examining the size and sharpness of its teeth. "Perfect. Come here." Sharon moved into the recessed area between the navigation station and the starboard quarterberth, motioning for Vivian to pass by and enter the galley.

"Open the doors beneath the sink," Sharon ordered.

Vivian slid past her, knelt down and opened the doors as instructed. She saw the large black hose leading from the sink drain to the through-hull valve three feet below the water line. Seawater filled the hose to within a few inches of the sink drain. Sharon's plan suddenly revealed itself.

Sharon held out the hacksaw. "Close the valve and start sawing through the hose as far down as you can reach."

"Sharon, don't make me do this." Vivian looked up. "Shoot me, but don't make me sink this boat."

"I could kill you first and do it myself. But why should I, when I've got you here to do it for me?"

"Why do you have to sink her?"

"There isn't enough time to conduct a thorough search and make sure you haven't kept a nasty little journal like Jill's. Besides, it's tidier this way and it adds a certain *je ne sais quois* to have you sink your own boat after all the trouble you've given us. I was going to wait until Victor returned and have him do it, but your little flare gun stunt has made me impatient." Sharon pointed her pistol menacingly. "Now close the valve and start sawing."

Vivian reached into the locker and ran her hand down the two-inch diameter hose until she reached the bronze through-hull valve. Grasping its lever-type handle she turned it ninety degrees, closing it. She looked up. "Sharon—"

"Saw!"

Vivian sat on her knees and began to saw into the stiff rubber hose. In a few seconds, water trapped above the valve began to seep out over the thin blade and drip into the bilge. It seemed as though *Houdini* had begun to cry. Vivian fought the emotion but tears of her own soon formed, trickled down her cheeks and fell onto her knees.

Mitch watched *Houdini's* departure until she passed Grosse Tour and entered open waters before turning back to look at Victor. "Even if Sharon is as ruthless as you say, it was *you* who killed Henry and Jill."

"Legally, yes; beyond that I like to think otherwise," Victor replied.

"I *saw* the bodies. Do you expect me to believe Sharon did that?"

Victor did not answer.

Mitch shook his head in disbelief. "Victor...why?"

"As I said, Sharon's not fond of losing."

Mitch peered at Victor from beneath the shade of his arm. "Why don't you shoot me? Or are we waiting for Sharon to do that, too?"

"Yes and no," Victor answered. "I'm curious to see what she's up to. But when you've got your breath and are able to walk we'll go see how Professor Vanzetti is doing."

It took Mitch less than a second to discern Victor's intent. They would go back to Vanzetti and Victor would kill them both with Vanzetti's gun, making it look as if they had struggled and killed each other. Nevertheless, he took Victor at his word, relaxed his muscles and tried to regain his strength. He doubted he could raise his head, let alone stand.

He turned again and looked out toward the horizon. *Houdini* was beyond the headlands, growing smaller every second. He turned back to Victor. "Why did Jill and Henry have to die?"

Victor paused several seconds before answering. "Because of some careless, remarks I made that morning we saw you with them at the yacht club." Victor waved his gun for emphasis. "Christ, I knew Jill had owned her own business. I assumed it was a *gift shop* or a women's *clothing* store; if I'd known she had anything to do with software, I'd have *never* told that story. Even so, I never mentioned Philip or his company. If Jill's reaction—a glimmer of recognition in her eyes—hadn't tipped me off I would never have guessed anything was amiss."

"What story? Philip who? I haven't a clue what you're talking about."

"Jill knew that I had been a partner in what was then the Winter & Associates agency in Vancouver. That was no secret to anyone. What I didn't know, was that due to the nature of *her* business, Jill was also aware that Xysta Software was one of our clients. I only learned that when I read her journal, after it was all over. Jill put it together that I might have been in a unique position to, shall we say, 'borrow' a development copy of a highly valuable new software utility from my client, Xysta, and loan it to her client who, as it happens, was once my roommate at University of British Columbia."

Mitch rolled partially onto his side to face Victor. "You killed two people—your friends—over stolen software?"

"We are talking about a *multi*-million dollar lawsuit and *billions* in potential sales not to mention lengthy jail terms in the event the theft were exposed."

"But on the basis of a look in Jill's eyes?"

"Give me a little credit, Mitch. I phoned Philip the next morning. He verified that he had briefly been Jill's client just prior to her selling her business. They had met face to face only one time."

"I still don't see how you could be sure she knew the whole story."

"We weren't—until that evening when you all went out to dinner at *Los Arbolitos*. Naturally, Sharon and I had decided not to go, but we caught Jill and Henry on their way ashore. Though Jill made a superb attempt to conceal her suspicions, it was clear she had something troubling on her mind. She claimed it was a headache. After you and Vivian met them and left for the restaurant, Sharon and I began debating several unattractive courses of action. The debate quickly evolved into a shouting match and Sharon stormed off for the bar at the top of the lighthouse."

Mitch wiped his face. "This explains why Jill wasn't feeling well that night."

"Yes, I'm sure it does. After cooling off, I followed Sharon up to the *El Faro*. She was in a much better mood. She told me she had a plan. She opened her purse and showed me a crude knife with a name carved in the handle.

"We'd seen the two fishermen in the marina on several occasions. They often tied their dilapidated little rowboat to our dock when they came in to rummage through the refuse bins. On her way to the bar, Sharon saw the knife lying in their boat, instantly recognized its potential, and took it.

"I balked of course, insisting that before going to such an extreme, we had to know Jill not only suspected what I had done, but that she intended to act on those suspicions as well. We also had to know whether she had shared them with anyone other than Henry. It was shortly thereafter that we saw Henry and Jill, returning early and alone."

"So you and Sharon followed them out to *Walden*."

Victor nodded. "It was clear from the moment we arrived that Henry knew the score. Sharon started crying—quite convincingly, I might add. She went on about how I'd been blackmailed into it, not true, unfortunately. She told them I planned to turn myself in if they hadn't done so already. I almost wished they had. Jill volunteered they hadn't told anyone yet, not even you and Vivian."

"Henry and Jill were your friends, Victor! They were giving you the benefit of the doubt."

"Believe me, Mitch, my favored course of action from the outset of this debacle was to throw ourselves on their mercy, but Sharon had made up her mind. She put the fisherman's knife in Henry's heart the instant Jill said the words she wanted to hear. I don't think Henry ever knew what happened; it was certainly the last thing he expected. I held Jill and kept her from screaming. Sharon cut her throat." Victor bowed his head. "I'll never get that sound, that sight, out of my mind."

Mitch rolled onto his back. The haunting images of *Walden*'s main cabin came flooding back. This time they were not static; this time he saw the events that created them.

"I deeply regret you had to be the one to find them, Mitch." Victor looked up again. "Not a day has gone by that I haven't wondered whether they might not have sailed for the Marquesas the following morning without telling a soul. Up to that point, we hadn't really hurt anyone. The terrible irony is that if we hadn't been good friends, Henry and Jill wouldn't have hesitated to inform the police, and they certainly wouldn't have allowed us aboard *Walden* that night."

Mitch shook his head. "*Sharon*. It's still hard to believe."

"Despite her outward appearance, she bears many scars. Her father was a major player in Toronto's crime organization. When Sharon was seventeen, he, her mother and her two older brothers were all brutally executed in the mob's version of an unfriendly takeover. Sharon, luckily, was in her last year at a Vancouver boarding school at the time. She fled the school, fearing they'd kill her, too.

"She somehow survived on the streets of Vancouver for two years. She never talks about that time. Then the head of a modeling agency *discovered* her. The woman had a special fondness for attractive young girls, natural blondes in particular. Sharon moved in with her and—I have to give the woman credit—within a few months, she transformed Sharon into what I believed then, and still do today, to be the most beautiful woman in the world." Victor glanced out to sea. "Ah, *Houdini* seems to have stopped."

Mitch tested the arm hidden from Victor's view. He could barely lift it.

Victor looked at the ground between his feet. "Of course I fell in love the moment I saw her. Unfortunately, it was my love that eventually brought her meteoric career to a sudden end. The agency woman was obsessed with Sharon. When Sharon left her for me, the woman took a drug overdose. The tabloids got hold of a rather lurid and spiteful suicide note. Although it wasn't Sharon's fault, no reputable advertiser would touch her from that point on. She's been understandably bitter ever since, though she hides it well." Victor looked out toward *Houdini* again.

"But you, Victor, you had it made." Mitch lifted his knees slightly, flexing the muscles in his legs.

"Yes and no. Not long before the Xysta Software opportunity presented itself, I learned from our Number One that he had decided Winter & Associates was to become Winter, *Lewis* & Associates instead of Winter, *Westridge* & Associates as I had long been led to believe. A younger man, with an inheritance to buy his way in, took the spot I had worked over twenty years to earn." Victor paused. "There's not much else to tell, really."

Although he lacked the strength to stand, let alone mount a surprise attack with any chance of success, Mitch forced himself to a half-sitting, half reclining position. "You're every bit as guilty of murder as Sharon is, morally *and* legally."

"Steady, Mitch. I'll be following her example soon enough."

Mitch glanced at the small black hole pointed at him. "You won't get away with it, even if you manage to elude the police. Vanzetti said if I killed you and Sharon, at least half his job would get done. Your roomie will send someone to take Vanzetti's place, Victor." It seemed a pointless lie, but saying it felt good. "You'll never be able to relax, never able to enjoy the money."

"Philip, that unmitigated prick! Why is it everyone I trust stabs me in the back? I suspected he might try something like this. I practically accused him of it."

Once Vivian severed the hose beneath the sink, Sharon had her leave the valve closed but forced her to go forward and perform the same operation on a similar hose beneath the wash basin in the head. Without sails or motor to steady her motion, *Houdini* rolled and pitched irregularly. Already sick with grief over what she was being forced to do, Vivian now felt the nausea of seasickness coming on as well. Sharon stood behind her, holding the door frame for support. When the hacksaw blade passed through the second hose, Sharon ordered Vivian to push the severed ends apart as she had with the first.

"That should send her down in a reasonable amount of time," Sharon said. "Now open the val—wait." She looked at the cabin sole beneath her feet. "I've forgotten the easy one, haven't I? Where's your knotmeter thing, the impeller or whatever it's called?"

Vivian wiped perspiration from her forehead with the back of her hand. "I don't know what you're talking about."

"Right." Sharon stepped back two steps. "If it's anything like the one on *Dream Lover*, I'd say it's right about here." Sharon pointed at her feet. "Take out this floorboard."

Vivian didn't move.

"Very well, the hard work is done." Sharon pointed the gun, taking aim at Vivian's face.

Vivian nodded in capitulation and crawled toward her. Sharon backed into the main compartment giving Vivian room to lift the floorboard at the foot of the double berth.

With the floorboard removed Sharon peered down into the bilge. A two-inch round, black plastic tube protruded up through *Houdini*'s hull. An electrical cable emerged from the center of the tube's plug.

"*Voila*," said Sharon, "I do believe that's it. Remove the pin and pull it out, please."

On her knees, looking down into the bilge, Vivian hesitated. Sharon had won. "No. Do it yourself. You're going to kill me anyway."

"True. However, I'd rather have you see the water rushing in to sink your precious boat first, but, if you insist." Sharon aimed again.

Vivian visualized the sea rushing in, *Houdini* going down. Perhaps there was still a chance. She reached down and removed the cotter ring from the plug's retaining pin.

"Isn't it amazing how we'll do anything to stay alive, even if only for a few more seconds?"

With the pin removed Vivian took hold of the plug and looked up at Sharon.

"Go ahead, pull it out."

Vivian pulled the impeller plug out of the through-hull fitting. A geyser of light blue water erupted from the hole, soaking her arms and knees.

"Now the valve in the head," Sharon said, motioning for Vivian to go forward. Vivian did as she was told without hesitation this time, turning the valve's lever until it admitted a second fountain of seawater to breach *Houdini's* hull.

"Two down and one to go," Sharon said, backing up as she spoke. Keeping one eye on Vivian, she paused at the chart table and turned off the main battery switch. "We don't want the bilge pump coming on, slowing things down. Come here now, quickly."

Vivian followed her aft to the galley, hoping Sharon wouldn't shoot before she opened the last valve. For what she was about to say, the more water coming in, the better.

Sharon backed up the companionway until she sat on the top step. Vivian knelt by the galley sink. She hesitated to reach for the valve lever.

"Don't disappoint me now, Vivian."

"How far out would you say we are?" asked Vivian.

"About a mile or so, I suppose. Why?"

Vivian bent down and opened the valve, admitting the third stream of water as she answered. "I was wondering how far you'll have to swim." Vivian straightened up.

"Why would I have to—" Sharon's haughty smile vanished. Her head snapped around.

The shock of seeing her dinghy's painter absent from the stern cleat froze Sharon for the brief opportunity Vivian needed. She rocked back off her knees and lunged for Sharon's gun. Sharon reacted, shrinking back, but not before Vivian clamped both hands on her wrist in mid-dive. Using her weight, Vivian yanked Sharon off the steps. Together, they crashed forward on the cabin sole in a jumble of arms and legs. Vivian rolled, pushing the gun down as they fell. The back of Sharon's hand hit the deck first. The tiny gold gun popped free, skittered forward along the teak sole and fell into the open bilge.

"I can walk," said Mitch. "Let's get on with it,"

"In a moment." Victor stood and looked beyond Mitch at the distant figure of *Houdini* beyond the headlands. "I don't quite understand."

"What?"

"*Houdini* stopped and it looked as though our dinghy had left and was on its way back. But now it doesn't seem to be moving either. I'm not sure anyone's in it."

Mitch sat upright. Without her white sails up it took him several seconds to locate *Houdini* against the vast expanse of sea and sky. "I don't see the dinghy."

"It's back this way quite a ways, hidden in the swells most of the time. There it is! Off to the left. See it?"

Had there been any more than a few white caps, spotting *Dream Lover*'s white tender among them would have been virtually impossible. Mitch caught a glimpse of the white speck moments before it disappeared into a trough. "Got it."

"Can you see anyone?"

Mitch waited for the inflatable to reappear. A couple of seconds passed. He saw it. "No, there's no one in it."

"I'll bet the dinghy got away from them. Sharon will notice. Any minute she'll be turning *Houdini* around and going after it."

Sharon went for Vivian's throat. Vivian grabbed two handfuls of Sharon's hair, pulled her close and let go a short jab, catching Sharon on the left cheek. Though it succeeded in loosening Sharon's choke-hold, the blow provoked her to an even higher level of rage. Shrieking maniacally, she rolled onto Vivian, tightening her grip.

Vivian suddenly felt cool water on her back. The water was already above the floorboards. In an act that was more reflex than reason, she brought both knees up sharply. Like twin catapults, her knees smacked Sharon's buttocks, launching her forward. Sharon's crotch landed in Vivian's face. Instinctively, Vivian bared her teeth and bit down hard on the closest thing to her mouth, the tender web of flesh between Sharon's thigh and mons.

"Ow, ow, OW!" Sharon wailed.

Despite Vivian's attempts to hold her legs, Sharon wriggled forward, kneeing and kicking Vivian about the head and shoulders as she scrambled free.

The water, now better than two inches above the floor boards, sloshed from side-to-side as *Houdini* rolled. Already, the added weight affected her motion, causing her to linger at the limit of each roll.

Both women clambered to their feet and spun to face each other.

Sharon's eyes blazed at Vivian as she massaged the place where Vivian had bit her. "I've had it with you, you cunt," Sharon snarled. "Before you die, I'm going to claw out your eyes and rip your hair out by the roots."

Vivian braced herself against the chart table, her chest rising and falling rapidly as she struggled to catch her breath. "You don't have time," she panted. "We're sinking. Give it up."

"Never."

Vivian backed toward the galley.

"Stay away from that valve, Vivian. I mean it."

Vivian continued to back away.

Sharon charged, growling as she came.

Vivian caught Sharon's outstretched arms with her own. The force of Sharon's charge carried them aft into the quarterberth.

As the two women struggled for advantage, *Houdini*'s rolls continued to increase in both angle and duration. The first wave to break over her caprail slopped gallons of water into the cockpit. Each time *Houdini* rolled to windward, increasing amounts of sea water spilled over the rail. Soon it poured in faster than it drained out through the scuppers and cockpit drains.

One long roll to windward gave Vivian the upper hand. It put her on top of Sharon, pinning her opponent against the hull as *Houdini* lay nearly on her starboard beam. A torrent of water rushed into the cockpit well, cascaded down the open companionway and into the cabin. Vivian pulled Sharon toward her then slammed the back of her head against the inside of the hull. As water surged in around them, Sharon's arms fell away, her eyes closed.

Vivian untangled her legs from Sharon's motionless form. The valves. She had to close them immediately. *Houdini* still lay on her starboard beam, held there by tons of seawater. The galley was above her. Vivian pulled herself part way up then grabbed the corner of the sink.

Houdini began to right herself slowly at first, gaining speed as her liquid cargo shifted from starboard to port. Though the moving water helped Vivian reach the galley, it ultimately slammed her against the stove and submerged her. Dazed and surprised by the water's impact she nevertheless managed to reach the cabinet beneath the sink. Heeled hard to port, the water level covered two-thirds of the locker's opening. She'd have to go under to reach the valve. She took a breath and forced her head underneath the sink. The steady flow of water coming in through the severed hose guided her hand to the valve. Her fingertips touched the handle.

Sharon landed feet first in Vivian's midsection, jerking her hand from the valve, expelling the air from her lungs. Vivian recoiled from the locker, exploded upward gasping for air. Sharon was waiting for her. A roundhouse punch caught Vivian on the forehead above the right eye. The blow surprised Vivian but did little damage. Sharon yowled and grabbed her wrist.

Houdini began to stand again and Vivian with her. She grabbed Sharon by her blouse and slammed her against the companionway steps. Taking careful aim, Vivian cocked her arm. Her fist slammed into Sharon's nose, smashing it flat against her face. Blood flowed instantly. Vivian let fly another blow, and another.

The long roll to starboard carried them into the quarterberth a second time. Vivian forgot the valves, determined to end, once and for all, Sharon's assault. Despite Sharon's attempts to shield her face, Vivian punched continuously, landing blow upon blow to Sharon's most treasured asset, bruising it, bloodying it, but at the same time lacerating the skin of her knuckles on Sharon's broken teeth.

Filled to her waterline, *Houdini* labored on her side, struggling to right herself. The tip of her mast touched the crest of a wave. Most of her designed stability had left her. Water rushed unimpeded over the submersed starboard rail, sending a steady waterfall into the cabin through the open companionway.

"God damn it, Victor!" yelled Mitch. "*Houdini* almost capsized! What the hell is Sharon doing?"

"What I should have guessed the minute I saw them headed out." Victor spoke in a low voice. "I'm afraid she's scuttling your boat." Victor strained his eyes to focus on the heeling vessel. "My God! Sharon must not realize the dinghy's gone!"

Mitch watched as all color drained from Victor's face. Mitch moved to stand. "We've got to get out there."

Victor threatened with the gun. "Sit down! There's nothing we can do."

"If we don't go, they'll *both* drown."

"And just how do you propose we get out there, swim?" Victor waved his hand toward the valley below. "There're no dinghies on the beach."

"Jim! We'll yell our heads off until he hears us."

Victor's chest heaved. "If you'll look closely, you'll see Jim's dinghy tied to *Dream Lover*. Sharon took care of him before she went after Vivian."

"Bullshit!" Mitch looked at *Dream Lover* and saw that Victor wasn't bluffing. "Litea then," Mitch shouted. "She'll swim over and get the dinghy."

"Not likely. Besides, it will be over before we could get to the beach, let alone out to *Dream Lover*."

"I'm not going to sit here while Vivian drowns, Victor. I'll swim out and get *Dream Lover* underway by myself if I have to." Again, Mitch moved to stand.

Victor improved his aim. "Don't move, Mitch. You're of no use to Vivian dead."

Vivian found herself and Sharon submerged as the water inside the cabin rushed to fill the starboard half of the hull. She sensed *Houdini* on the verge of foundering. She pushed herself away from Sharon, knowing she had only a few seconds to close the valves. Sharon grabbed her forearm, forcing Vivian to pull her up. Slowly, gallantly, *Houdini* righted herself at the same time.

"Let me go, Sharon, or we're going down together!"

"So be it," Sharon spluttered through bloodied lips.

Vivian screamed in rage and with the aid of *Houdini*'s roll brought Sharon upright, spun her around, and unloaded a right cross that caught Sharon flush on the jaw, sending her staggering then falling toward the bow, splashing into the water that now rose above the settees, to the level of the dining table.

Vivian wasted no time waiting to see if Sharon wanted more. She dove for the locker beneath the sink. Before she could reach the valve handle, the roll to port and rising water floated her away. She grabbed the locker frame and pulled herself down. It was no use, she hadn't enough air. She came up for a breath. What she inhaled was not air. Salt water had reached the batteries, discharging them instantly and simultaneously creating a poisonous cloud of chlorine gas. Vivian choked and staggered to the companionway, intent on clearing her lungs and returning to the valve.

The sight that greeted her as she climbed the steps stunned her to the depths of her soul. At that moment *Houdini* was perfectly upright. When her eyes rose above the plane of the teak caprails, she saw they were barely inches above the water. *Houdini* would not survive another roll to windward. The cabin would flood completely and *Houdini* would go under. Vivian could not bring herself to leave. She would not let this happen. She had to try for the valves.

Reality came in the form of Sharon grabbing her from behind by the ankles, attempting to drag her back down into the cabin. Vivian pulled one leg free and mule-kicked. Her foot struck something solid. Simultaneously, her other foot was released and she pedaled her legs furiously until she floundered into the flooded cockpit.

Half submerged, *Houdini* rolled hard to port putting her bow completely under. Air whooshed out the starboard ports as water rushed down the companionway. The sound of escaping air was almost a moan, as though the proud sloop knew she was dying. *Houdini* righted herself one last time, her decks and cabin awash. Vivian grabbed the sides of the main hatch, staring into the flooded and eerily lighted cabin that had been her home for more than a year. The water rose up to meet her. She saw Sharon's clawing, swimming disoriented form struggling to reach the light of the deck hatch above her. *Houdini* slipped beneath the agitated surface to the silence below.

Houdini was too far away and too far down on her lines amidst the waves for Mitch to make out whether either of the two women had escaped. One minute *Houdini*'s white decks and cabin roof had been a visible blur on the crest of a wave. When the next wave passed, she was gone. Mitch thought he glimpsed the thread-thin image of her mast. Then nothing. Within seconds he lost track of the place where she had gone down.

His upper lip quivered, angry tears welled up. Turning to Victor, he slammed a weak fist against the rock. "You either *shoot* me, you son-of-a-bitch, or let me go find Vivian."

Victor sat in stunned silence, looking out to sea.

"God damn you!" Mitch growled as he rolled to his knees, preparing to charge.

Victor shifted his attention back to Mitch, altered his aim to the right and fired, sending a .380 slug over Mitch's left shoulder. Instinctively, Mitch hunched as the muzzle blast slammed against his face. Victor returned the gun's aim to Mitch's chest. "Give me a moment, for Christ's sake! My wife was in that boat, too!" It stunned Victor to think Sharon could die. She always seemed so invincible, so impervious to physical or emotional harm. The possibility she would die first had never occurred to him. "Look again, Mitch. Sharon was wearing a white blouse, and with her blond hair, she should stand out against the water."

Mitch scanned the sea. It was hopeless from this distance. "There's no sign of either of them," he admitted.

"I don't understand." Victor repeated the phrase over and over. How would he go on? What chance was there without Sharon? Moreover, what reason? For all her faults, she was his ultimate source of happiness. His mind wandered over the turning points of his life, the bad, the good; meeting Sharon, winning her; the Olympics, winning a medal. He could have faced the humiliation of arrest with Sharon by his side. He would have protected her, shielded her from all blame.

Mitch had kept one foot under him. "I'm going, Victor, I don't care whether you shoot me or not!" He prepared to spring.

"Humor me ten seconds, Mitch, and I may well let you go."

"Humor you?"

"It's quite easy, actually. You may even enjoy it. Simply be still and watch." Victor drew a bead on Mitch's face to make sure he had his complete attention. "I'm counting on you. Not that it makes any difference, Mitch, I realize now that I didn't give it everything I had when I pushed you." Victor looked away, toward the sharp edge of the precipice five feet beyond Mitch's feet. His gaze seemed to trace an imaginary line from the edge back to his feet. A hint of smile curved his lips. He spoke to Mitch without looking at him. "If it's good, tell everyone. If it's not—keep it to yourself." The smile disappeared, replaced by a mask of stone concentration.

Victor lifted his forearm slowly, thumbed the pistol's safety on and flipped the weapon over the edge. His arms dropped to his sides from where they immediately began floating upward as he rose on the balls of his feet. In one fluid motion his arms swung down, forward and curved up in front of him as he took his first step toward the lip. He accelerated into a slow run. His arms returned briefly to his sides and then sliced upward. He vaulted into the air, hands reaching skyward.

Mitch swallowed, though his throat was dry.

Victor's feet came down on the edge. His knees and legs absorbed the landing; they compressed, recoiled and launched him into space. He soared. His legs rigid, toes pointing, arms outstretched, palms flaring up. For an instant, Mitch saw Victor stare across the deep valley of Hanamenu as though he would fly to the peaks on the other side.

The inevitable descent began. He bent sharply at the waist, his arms reaching for his calves, pulling his head almost to his knees. He began to rotate.

Mitch subconsciously counted. *One...two...three...fo*—Victor held the pike. Mitch turned away at the moment of impact. When he looked again, Victor's body lay sprawled face up on the steep slope of loose rock. Sunlight glinted off splashes of red on the rocks above him.

"It was a 10, you pathetic son-of-a-bitch."

––––––––––

Ten feet below the surface Vivian clung to the steering wheel with one hand, her body floating upward.

Thanks Houdini, you took such good care of us. I'm sorry. You don't deserve this.

Vivian released the wheel, letting *Houdini* continue her descent toward the blue darkness below. The sloop looked graceful even as she sank, no longer rolling or pitching, settling proudly on her lines. Streams of tiny bubbles from open ports and hatches rose like chains of pearls.

Vivian popped to the surface, gasped two quick breaths and looked down at the blurred and shrinking outline of *Houdini's* white decks. A burst of large bubbles erupted from the hatch above the dining table. Vivian shuddered, half-expecting to see Sharon wriggle out and swim up after her. She took another breath and looked again. Sharon had not escaped.

Vivian's thoughts turned to Mitch. Treading water and catching her breath, she oriented herself, first toward land, then toward the cleft that had to be the entrance to Hanamenu. *Dream Lover's* dinghy should be somewhere in that direction.

In the troughs, she could see barely twenty feet. But as each wave lifted her, the lowlands along the shore and the tops of the higher waves came into view. For a second or two on every crest that passed, her gaze darted from wave to wave in the direction of Hanamenu, searching for a glimpse of the white inflatable. After rising on a half dozen waves and seeing nothing, she swam toward the bay in the troughs, pausing for a brief scan at each crest.

She felt a stinging sensation in her right hand. Her knuckles were bleeding. The threat of sharks hadn't occurred to her until she saw the stain of blood disappear into the water like a wisp of red smoke.

Something to her right entered her peripheral vision. Was it the dinghy? It was too far to the right. It had to be a whitecap. Wait, the wind. The wind would have blown it that way. She altered course. The timing had to be perfect in order to spot it. She and the dinghy had to be at the top of their respective waves at exactly the same instant.

Several crests lifted her. Nothing. Then something solid, something white and a bright flash, a reflection. That had to be it! The prominent spire of Grosse Tour was just to the left of it, giving her a point to swim for between sightings.

Her mind no longer fixed on locating the dinghy, Vivian felt as if a thousand hungry eyes watched her from below.

Mitch crawled away from the edge and staggered to his feet. Despite Victor's capitulation, he refused to accept what his eyes told him. It was his fault for letting Vivian stay. He could replace *Houdini;* he could replace everything—except Vivian.

The sound of horse hooves running on hard ground grew louder as he turned and took his first stiff steps down the ridge trail.

"MITCH!"

Mitch turned in time to see Teiki emerge from between the boulders on Kehu. Mitch jogged forward as Teiki trotted the stallion after him.

"Mitch, I hear gun. You okay?"

"Yes, but Vivian's in trouble. I can't stop."

Teiki took Mitch's forearm and levered him onto Kehu's back.

Mitch struggled to stay aboard as Teiki trotted Kehu perilously close to the precipice. "What are you doing here? How did you know to come to Hanamenu."

"After I tell gendarmes about explosion I ride trail past Point Teaehoa to see you go Ua Pou. But I watch and you cross Haava channel to Tahuata. I ride back, call cousin Etienne at Vaitahu on Tahuata. Tell him help you. But you no arrive Vaitahu yesterday, so today Etienne walk north, find you at Hana Moe Noa."

"That was your cousin on the beach this morning?" Mitch increased his grip as Teiki reined Kehu around the first steep hairpin turn.

Teiki nodded. "Etienne run back to Vaitahu call me. Say you go other side Hiva Oa. I ride Kehu to Haava again. I don't see you but think maybe you go Hanaheku or Hanamenu. Where Vivian? Who shoot gun?"

When Mitch finished telling Teiki all that had happened, they had reached the valley floor and ridden half way to the beach. Once off the rocky path and onto the hard-packed sandy trail, Teiki coaxed Kehu into a gallop. At the edge of the beach, both men slid off as Teiki brought the small stallion to a skidding stop.

"We swim together," said Teiki. "I go fast, get little boat, come back for you." They both ran for the water, Teiki in the lead. He held up, grabbing Mitch by the arm. "Mitch, someone climbing out of water onto boat."

Mitch's heart leapt up into his throat. Was it possible? Mitch saw a small, dark-skinned form scrambling onto *Dream Lover's* swim platform. "It's Litea." Mitch began yelling her name.

Litea stood and turned. She had heard him.

"LITEA! Come and get us!" Mitch signaled his message with a windmilling arm.

Litea hesitated, looking forward then aft, as if uncertain what to do first."

Mitch cupped his hands around his mouth and was about to shout again when Teiki stopped him and pointed toward Grosse Tour. A white inflatable rounded the base of the volcanic tower and sped toward them at full speed. A shiver started in Mitch's scalp and ran down his back. He held his emotions in check. It could be Vivian. It could be Sharon. The inflatable streaked between *Phoenix* and *Dream Lover*. The driver turned her head for a split second and waved at Litea as she roared by. As she turned, Mitch saw her dark hair. It was Vivian.

Vivian felt as if she'd been holding her breath from the moment she clambered into the dinghy and started the outboard until the instant she saw Mitch standing on the beach.

Overjoyed at seeing him alive and apparently unhurt, she forgot to release the throttle. Shooting through the surf at full speed, she narrowly missed Teiki and rocketed up the beach through the first row of palms before coming to a sudden halt.

Mitch ran up the beach to meet her as she tumbled out and ran back. She leapt into his waiting arms. Still weak from his ordeals on the plateau, Mitch collapsed, sending the two of them sprawling to the sand, kissing as they fell.

Lying beside him on the black sand, Vivian hugged him close for several seconds before she pulled back. "I was afraid Victor caught up with you."

"*You* were afraid? I saw *Houdini* sink! I thought you were on board!"

"I was." Vivian started to cry. "She made me do it, Mitch."

"I know. It's okay, Babe. It's okay."

"But I loved *Houdini*. She was our home. You loved her, too."

"Yes, but it's done, she's gone. We can get another boat." He braced himself over her and brushed her hair aside and looked into her reddened, tear-filled hazel eyes. They were still the most beautiful eyes he'd ever seen. "What I can't get is another you. I love you."

"I love you, too." She sniffed and pulled him to her. She saw Teiki standing a few feet away, smiling. "Teiki. Hi. Has Annette had her baby?"

Teiki came forward and knelt beside them, grinning from ear to ear. "Last night. Baby girl. We name her Vivian."

Saturday, June 8

Vivian sat in a high-backed swivel chair and keyed the mike. "I copy you loud and clear, Frank. How me?" Mitch leaned against the locker beside her.

"The same, Vivian. Been almost a week. You guys must be having a good time."

"We are."

"Where are you?"

"Anaho Bay, on the north side of Nuku Hiva. It's the first truly protected anchorage we've found in the Marquesas. There are steep mountains and high hills all around us, and a long curving beach of white sand. We're anchored in over thirty feet of water and yet we can see our chain lying on the sandy bottom, that's how clear it is. As soon as we got the anchor set we jumped overboard and snorkeled along the coral reef between us and shore."

Glad to hear you're finally having some fun. The police had just given you permission to leave Atuona the last time we talked. Where have you been since then?"

"We spent a few days at Puamau village on the north side of Hiva Oa visiting our Marquesan friends. We sailed overnight to Nuku Hiva two days ago. Yesterday we stopped at a place called Comptroller Bay and hiked up to see the stone tikis in the valley Melville wrote about in *Typee*. Early this morning we moved here to Anaho."

Frank's voice dropped a decibel. *"I take it you're still on those people's boat."*

Vivian glanced up at Mitch. "That's correct, Frank."

"What's its name again?"

"Dream Lover."

"How long they going to let you use it, the authorities, I mean?"

"They want her delivered to Papeete and they've offered us the job. It's about eight-hundred miles, but they've given us a month to get there. We hope to stop in the Tuamotus for a week or two and visit some atolls."

"What then? Are you planning to come home?"

Vivian handed the mike to Mitch. "The jury's still out, Frank."

"Hi, Mitch. Well, listen, Dinah and I talked it over; if you and Vivian want to continue cruising, Walden is yours for the asking."

Images of *Walden's* interior flashed through Mitch's mind. It was sad to leave her behind in Puerto Vallarta, but now it would be painful to see her again, let alone go aboard. He glanced at Vivian. "That's awfully generous, Frank, we'll keep it in mind. *Houdini* was insured, though, so we'll be able to pay for a new boat, if that's the route we decide to take."

"Wouldn't take a dime from you, Mitch. Henry wouldn't have stood for it and neither will we. You two deserve some kind of reward."

"Thanks, Frank. The French authorities tell us they plan to seize this boat and sell her. They've told us that in lieu of payment for delivering her to Papeete they'll give us right of first refusal to purchase her for twenty-five percent of her assessed value."

"How big did you say she is?"

"Fifty-four feet."

"I suppose it's pretty tricked out."

"You name it, she's got it."

"I can understand why you might not want to sail Walden, Mitch. And I suppose if Henry were here, he might take some satisfaction in you winding up with those people's boat. Nevertheless, our offer stands. You keep it in mind."

Vivian took the mike back. "Frank, Have you heard anything from Martinez?"

"Talked to him three days ago. He's received two telexes from Papeete. He said the two fishermen would most likely be released this weekend."

Vivian envisioned Carlos once again casting his *tarraya* in The Pond. "Anything happening with Vanzetti?"

"Yeah, except his name isn't Vanzetti. It's some unpronounceable Eastern European name with no vowels in it. Heard it on CNN. He's being extradited to the U.S. They already have a statement from him, corroborating your story and implicating this Philip Kennerly person. Kennerly was arrested last Monday and charged with everything from conspiracy to commit murder to theft of trade secrets."

"You mentioned CNN, Frank. I take it the story is public knowledge."

"I forgot how long it's been since we talked. The whole story of how you two tracked Henry and Jill's killers all the way from Mexico to the South Pacific has been on all the networks. You're world famous heroes."

Vivian exchanged surprised looks with Mitch. "I think we need some time to absorb that idea, Frank."

"When are you leaving for the Tuamotus?"

"We plan to check out of the Marquesas on Friday."

"Let me know if you want to set up a radio sked again while you're making the passage.

"Yes, by all means. Let's start on Friday if that's okay with you."

"No problem. Whoops. Dinah's signaling that I need to wind it up. Some friends are taking us out to dinner, so I'd better sign off till Friday."

"Take care, Frank. Give our love to Dinah." Vivian signed off and turned to Mitch. "World famous *heroes?*"

"I think Frank may have exaggerated. However, if news about Kennerly's company and Xysta is out, you'd better give Sonja a call so I can talk to your brother-in-law and see if he did what I told him."

Vivian switched the SSB radio from the ham frequency to the long-range radio-telephone frequency for KMI in San Francisco. The high seas operator answered her call and was dialing her sister's phone number in Tacoma when several loud raps sounded on the port side of *Dream Lover's* hull.

Mitch started up the companionway. "Talk to Sonja while I see who this is."

Bill was the last person he expected to see in Anaho. "Bill. Hi...when did you arrive?"

Bill stood in his dinghy hanging on to *Dream Lover's* rail. "Oh, twenty, thirty minutes ago." His expression was neither friendly nor hostile.

Mitch looked over Bill's head and saw *Silver Cloud* beyond the three other boats anchored along the beach-fringing coral reef. "How's it going?"

"Pretty good, pretty good. Marj is back aboard."

Mitch waited for more, nodding. Bill offered nothing. "Great, that's good to hear."

"We're...we're trying to patch things up." Bill looked down. "I forgave her and she's *trying* to forgive me. Anyway, I came over to tell you there's no hard feelings anymore." He looked up and stuck out his hand.

Mitch leaned over the cockpit coaming and shook Bill's hand. "Was this part of the deal?"

Bill flinched, then smiled. "No, no. I'm here of my own free will."

"Thanks, Bill. This takes one large load off my mind."

"As the saying goes, 'all's well that ends well,' and things between me and Marj are lookin' up." An eyebrow flickered up.

Mitch nodded, not comprehending at first. "Oh!...Good!...say, are Jim and Litea still in Atuona?"

"Jim is, Litea isn't."

"Uh-oh."

"Yeah, Litea packed up and moved ashore shortly after you two left for Puamau. She met a young Aussie single-hander at that snack place in Atuona. He's finishing a circumnavigation, on his way home to Brisbane and he invited her to come along. She told Marj she'll sail as far as Fiji with him. They left for Tahiti yesterday."

"What happened with Jim?"

"Litea told Marj she went over to *Dream Lover* and found Jim buck naked and spread-eagled on Sharon's bed, trussed up with two pairs of handcuffs and some rope."

"I gathered something like that must have happened. When we went out to see them, after *Houdini* sank, they were both pretty tight-lipped. What's Jim going to do?"

"Doesn't have much choice. He'll have to single-hand it to Papeete and hope he can pick up crew there or continue on by himself. I know how he's feeling 'bout now. Glad I'm not in his shoes."

"Sharon certainly did a lot of damage."

"Yeah, real sorry about *Houdini*. I guess Sharon won't be causing anymore problems though."

"Not likely," Mitch agreed. "I'll bet Martinez is disappointed about not getting her and Victor back to Mexico."

"*Don't* remind me of that guy. I still wake some nights thinking about him."

"Everything's out in the open now, Bill. He shouldn't bother you anymore."

"True. Well, hey, gotta run. Told Marj I'd be right back." Bill hesitated, and cleared his throat. "I'd say let's get together some evening but I'm not quite ready to go that far."

"I think this is one instance, Bill, where Vivian would undoubtedly share your view."

Bill half-smiled and nodded. "I s'pect we'll be seein' each other here and there anyway." He pushed off, sat down and adjusted his oars.

Mitch waved, turned and went below.

Vivian heard him coming down the steps. "Sonja, Mitch is back, can you put Ted on?" Vivian slipped out of the chair and handed the mike to Mitch.

A man's cheery voice emanated from the radio speaker. "*Mitch, you old sea dog, been hoping you'd call.*"

"Hi, Ted. Frank Fullerton told us the story's been on CNN, so I thought we'd better give you a call. Did you get a good price on the Xysta stock before the word got out?"

"*Got a fantastic price, Mitch, but I didn't exactly buy the stock.*"

Mitch's eyes rolled up as he glanced at Vivian in time to see her shoulders slump. "Ted, what does that mean, 'you didn't exactly buy the stock?'" Mitch's voice rose several decibels.

"*Relax, Mitch, there's nothing—*"

"Ted, all of our retirement money was in that money market account. I asked you to do a very simple thing: put it all in Xysta stock. When we signed those forms before we left, it was with the explicit understanding you would do *exactly* as we said, nothing more, nothing less."

"*I did, I did. More or less.*"

Mitch looked at Vivian before keying the mike. She sat down on the settee. "All right, Ted, we're both sitting down now, what did you do with our money?"

"*Well, I got to thinking: if I put all your money directly into Xysta stock you'd only make twenty percent when it rebounded to the price it was at before they lost the infringement case.*"

"Twenty percent in a matter of a few days sounds pretty damn good, Ted."

"*Yeah, but with the rather meager amount of cash in your money market account—no offense—you couldn't really capitalize on your information. So I bought Xysta call options. That way—*"

"You bought *options* with our retirement money? Ted, are you out of your mind?"

"*Mitch, just a few days ago Xysta July call options were selling for premiums of less than a dollar. When Xysta lost the case, it was a fire sale. People were dumping options for whatever they could get. It was too good to pass up.*"

"Ted, I barely comprehend what you just said. All I remember about options is you can easily lose *all* of your investment, not just a large percentage."

"*True, but the door swings both ways, Mitch. When the news of Philip Kennerly's arrest hit the street, Xysta stock jumped seven points and it's been going up by leaps and bounds ever since. Relax, the options are already in the money again.*"

"Ted, in English, how much money would we have if we sold the options right now?"

"*I couldn't give you an exact figure, but on an average basis, I'd say the value of your options has tripled.*" Ted's voice assumed an air of vindication.

"Are you saying we have *three* times as much money as we had before?"

"*Yeah, but the stock hasn't returned to its pre-trial trading level yet. It could easily reach a fourfold increase by Wednesday. That's when I planned to sell and transfer the proceeds back into your cash account.*"

Mitch sank back in the chair and swiveled toward Vivian. "I guess I owe you an apology, Ted."

"*Forget it. Actually, I'm glad you didn't call sooner. I was a little nervous myself until the news finally broke.*"

"Don't wait too long to sell, Ted, don't get greedy. Three or four hundred percent is an adequate return." Mitch twitched his eyebrows at Vivian.

"*Never fear. By Friday I should be able to tell you the new net figure in your cash account.*"

"I feel as if we owe you something in addition to your commission, Ted."

"Are you kidding? With the information you provided? Rest assured, Mitch, I've been adequately compensated."

"We're planning to start making our way toward Tahiti on Friday. How about if I call you then, just before we raise anchor?"

"You have my office number, right?"

Vivian nodded. "Yeah, got it. Okay, Ted, we'll talk to you then." Mitch passed the mike to Vivian and traded places with her. She said good-bye to Ted and Sonja and signed off with the marine operator.

She looked at Mitch, lying on the settee. "Between the option money and the proceeds from *Houdini*'s insurance, it sounds as if we can do whatever we want. We could fly home from Papeete, buy a waterfront house like Henry and Jill's, get that red Ferrari you always wanted and have enough left over for you to start your own business."

Mitch sensed a tinge of derision in her voice. "Somehow things like that don't seem important anymore. I'm not sure they ever were—if I'd once stopped ten seconds to think about it. Maybe I've finally come to understand Henry's philosophy. To tell the truth, it feels a little uncomfortable to have profited from his and Jill's death."

"Mitch, I still grieve for Jill and Henry every day, and I'd give everything we own to have them back, but you can't say that." Vivian moved to the settee and sat on the edge beside him. "It was a windfall. You didn't even think of it until it was all over. I agree with Frank. If Henry can see us now, I'll bet he's smiling from ear to ear."

"I suppose. Still, I feel like a mercenary. I had no idea we'd make that much. Now that we have it, I don't know what to do with it."

"If money and status symbols aren't important to you anymore, what is?"

"Having a life. Spending time with you."

"Oh, really?" Vivian sprawled on top of him. "So how do you propose we spend our time together? What happens after Papeete?" She rubbed his nose with hers.

"Whatever you want."

"You want to know what I want?"

"Yes."

Vivian lifted herself so she could look directly into his eyes. "Before I die, I want to see this planet and meet its people. I want to take long morning walks on deserted beaches and go for afternoon swims in clear, warm water filled with tiny fish like sparkling jewels. I want to have time to read and think. I want to sleep in late every morning and wake up to find you healthy, relaxed and eager to make slow, passionate love to me. In other words, when our time comes, I want to know that we have lived. That's what I want."

Mitch squirmed under her. "Let me up."

Vivian frowned and moved to secure her position. "Why? What's wrong?"

"I want to see if *Dream Lover* has all the charts we'll need to sail around the world."

ACKNOWLEDGEMENTS

My wife Kay not only read and edited the work-in-progress several times, she also brought home the bacon during the time the book was being written, a debt I fear will never be fully repaid.

Sue Zawadzki, Donna Sassaman, Colleen and Frank Slater, Ora Jonasson, Sherrie Holmes, Jean Chapman Snow, Amy Carlson, Suzanne Hilton, and Roland and Betty Nease all spent many, many hours reading and editing the full manuscript in its early stages, giving me written and verbal feedback that kept me from going off the deep end any more than I did. Any errors that remain are entirely mine.

Nikki Ehrlich DeBoard, Linda Glein, Kathryn Biggs Arnold, Laurel Shultz, Jo Nelson, Jack Eddy, Shirley Tomasi, Dennis Sherwood, Eve Kiehm and Charles Frank read sections of the early manuscript and provided valuable criticism.

Cynthia (CC) Cantwell, Jim Hearing, Heidi and Terry Kotas, Penny McGrew, and Laurie and Dean Singer all read the final draft and gave me the confidence to see the project through to completion.

Author and screen writer Hank Searls, (*Overboard, Sounding, et al.*), took the time to not only read the novel, but also study its structure. He gave me some pretty strong medicine. In fact, he gave me so much I wasn't able to use it all in this book. Hopefully I will get a chance to use the balance of his sound advice in the next one.

Kaye Lofgren, Les Ball, Janet Pedersen, Larry and Judy Burcar, Gary and Becky Crowell, and Roger Rue, all provided assistance in researching the locations in Puerto Vallarta and Atuona.

Steve Essig provided valuable photography and software assistance.

Oregon State University English professor (ca. 1965) Alan Young first made me realize that I could create stories that others might want to read.

My fellow marina, live-aboard neighbor at the time, Mirjam Crago, to whose memory the book is dedicated, was especially encouraging in the early days, always bugging me for another chapter every time I saw her. She was a neat lady.

The book is also dedicated to the memory of John Madell. At the time I met John, he and his wife Harumi were living in Guam where he was working as a consultant with the Guam police force. He had retired from the Los Angeles Police Department, where he had once commanded the LAPD's crime lab. John's critical review of my manuscript was invaluable. He was not only an expert in his field, he was also a heck of a nice guy.

The time gap from when the book was first written to when it was published was unusually long. Consequently, the names of a number of people who deserve to be remembered and recognized have faded from memory. So I humbly apologize and hope they at least know that I'm aware not everyone who deserves to be acknowledged and thanked is included in the foregoing comments.

ABOUT THE AUTHOR

Steve Van Slyke and his wife Kay live aboard their 41-foot cutter sailboat, *Kavenga*, on Puget Sound during the summer months. The rest of the year they live in Puerto Vallarta, Mexico.

Together Steve and Kay have logged over 30,000 miles at sea including a circumnavigation of the Pacific, culminating in a 4600-mile, 38-day passage from Japan to Vancouver Island. The story of their three-year cruising adventure is told in the non-fiction book, *Kavenga's Wake.*

Steve was the Navigation Officer aboard the USS Vesuvius (AE-15), an ammunition ship operating in the South China Sea and combat areas during the Viet Nam war.

Originally hailing from Oregon, Steve is a graduate of both Oregon State University and University of Oregon.

SUGGESTED READING

For readers interested in learning more about the Marquesas Islands and the Marquesan people, I found these three books to be particularly fascinating:

Heyerdahl, Thor, *Fatu-Hiva: back to nature*, Doubleday, 1975

Melville, Herman, *Typee*, Dodd, Mead, 1923

Suggs, Robert C., *Marquesan Sexual Behavior*, Harcourt, Brace & World, Inc, 1966